DATE DUE

Transnational Women's Fiction

Also by Susan Strehle

FICTION IN THE QUANTUM UNIVERSE

DOUBLED PLOTS: Romance and History (*co-edited with Mary Paniccia Carden*)

Transnational Women's Fiction

Unsettling Home and Homeland

Susan Strehle

First published 2008 by
PALGRAVE MACMILLAN
Houndmills, Basingstoke, Hampshire RG21 6XS and
175 Fifth Avenue, New York, N.Y. 10010
Companies and representatives throughout the world

PALGRAVE MACMILLAN is the global academic imprint of the Palgrave Macmillan division of St. Martin's Press, LLC and of Palgrave Macmillan Ltd. Macmillan® is a registered trademark in the United States, United Kingdom and other countries. Palgrave is a registered trademark in the European Union and other countries.

ISBN-13: 978–0–230–53687–6 hardback
ISBN-10: 0–230–53687–5 hardback

This book is printed on paper suitable for recycling and made from fully managed and sustained forest sources. Logging, pulping and manufacturing processes are expected to conform to the environmental regulations of the country of origin.

A catalogue record for this book is available from the British Library.

Library of Congress Cataloging-in-Publication Data
Strehle, Susan.
   Transnational women's fiction;unsettling home and homeland/
   Susan Strehle.
     p.   cm.
Includes bibliographical references and index.
ISBN 0–230–53687–5 (alk. paper)
   1. American fiction—Women authors—History and criticism.
   2. English literature—Women authors—History and criticism.
   3. Home in literature.   4. Feminism and literature—English-speaking countries.   5. Women and literature—English-speaking countries.
   6. Sex role in literature.   I. Title.
PS374.W6S794 2008
823'.914093581—dc22   2007052984

10   9   8   7   6   5   4   3   2   1
17   16   15   14   13   12   11   10   09   08

Printed and bound in Great Britain by
CPI Antony Rowe, Chippenham and Eastbourne

For my son, Adam Spanos
Who may remake the homeland
In the generously scattered, richly thought likeness
Of our unsettled home

Contents

Acknowledgments

This book was begun and finished in Australia, and I owe sunlit debts of gratitude to colleagues and friends in Perth: Brenda Walker, Simone Lazaroo, Delys Bird, Helen Temby, Gareth Griffiths, Sue Lewis, and especially Judy Johnston, who generously provided a perfect home and work space for the book's completion.

I am grateful to many colleagues and friends at Binghamton University: David Bartine, Gisela Brinker-Gabler, Donette Francis, Joseph Keith, Richard Lee, Elizabeth Tucker, and others gave me valuable responses when I presented drafts of this manuscript. Binghamton University Provost Mary Ann Swain provided encouragement and leave time, both of great value. Former colleagues Carole Boyce Davies, Suzette Henke, and Sidonie Smith have contributed important ideas in conversations long ago and in their published work, and R. Radhakrishnan's visit cast a genial light over the project at just the right moment. K. Thomas Chandy provided vital information and a helpful reading of the chapter on Arundhati Roy. I am grateful to Ruth Stanek, Anita Pisani, Priscilla Brunner, and Barb Walling for practical help, unfailing humor, and good will.

Many thanks to Geoffrey Gould, who helped create the cover by making a useable form of a photograph taken in 1940 of my grandparents new home, my fifteen year old mother at the door.

My students at Binghamton have joined me in thinking through this material during several seminars, and I am grateful for their intellectual vitality.

Many thanks to helpful professionals at Palgrave Macmillan, who have been a delight to work with. I appreciate Paula Kennedy's clear communication and belief in the project and Christabel Scaife's quick and intelligent responses. Thanks also to the capable Geetha Narendranath, who oversaw the copyediting and production of the index.

I owe special thanks to William V. Spanos, always my best reader, whose comments and suggestions improved the book and whose conversation enlivened and cheered me through the process. Our son, Adam V. Spanos, emerging scholar and intuitively unsettling thinker, loaned me books, asked unanswerable questions, and inspired deeper reflection.

I gratefully acknowledge permission to quote from the following:

From *The God of Small Things* by Arundhati Roy, copyright © 1997 by Arundhati Roy. Used by permission of Random House, Inc.

From *Paradise* by Toni Morrison, copyright © 1997 by Toni Morrison. Used by permission of Alfred A. Knopf, a division of Random House, Inc.

From *The Australian Fiancé* by Simone Lazaroo, copyright © 2000 by Simone Lazaroo. Used by permission of Simone Lazaroo.

From *The Blind Assassin* by Margaret Atwood, copyright © 2000 by O. W. Toad, Ltd. Used by permission of Doubleday, a division of Random House, Inc.

Excerpted from *The Blind Assassin* by Margaret Atwood, copyright © 2003 by Margaret Atwood. Published by McClelland & Stewart. Used with permission of the publisher.

From *The Blind Assassin* by Margaret Atwood, copyright © 2000 by Margaret Atwood. Published by Bloomsbury Publishing Ltd. Used with permission of the publisher.

From "Morning in the Burned House," in *Morning in the Burned House*, copyright © 1995 by Margaret Atwood. Reprinted by permission of Houghton Mifflin Company. All rights reserved.

From *Morning in the Burned House* by Margaret Atwood, copyright © 1995 by Margaret Atwood. Published by McClelland & Stewart. Used with permission of the publisher.

From "Morning in the Burned House" by Margaret Atwood, copyright © 1995 by Margaret Atwood. Reproduced with permission of Curtis Brown Group Ltd., London.

From *Purple Hibiscus* by Chimamanda Adichie, copyright © 2003 by Chimamanda Adichie. Reprinted by permission of Algonquin Books of Chapel Hill.

From *The House on the Lagoon* by Rosario Ferré, copyright © 1995 by Rosario Ferré. Reprinted by permission of Farrar, Straus and Giroux, LLC.

1
Introduction: Unsettling Home and Homeland

Home has traditionally been thought in the West as a private, secluded space for settlement, separated from the public arena in a dichotomy of separate spheres. Home belongs to women who "settle down" in marriage and then establish residence in a dwelling place; there, they "settle" (order and arrange, stabilize and establish on a permanent basis, subdue and make orderly) domestic affairs. Sometimes they "settle for" home arrangements despite their incomplete satisfaction with those arrangements. Some of them become "settlers" in a new region or colonizers of a new land. On occasion, there are "settlements," small and potentially helpful communities—or property transfers in the event of divorce. Settling homes has been understood for centuries as the most proper occupation for women, shielded as home was thought to be from the aggression, materialism, and competitiveness of the public arena. Home is imagined as a place of domestic order, separate from the outer public world of commerce, government, law, and other social institutions in which men exercise worldly power.

From a perspective conjoining feminist and postcolonial theory, home reveals its deeper affiliation with the public realm, as a patriarchal space where power relations vital to the nation and culture are negotiated. Home reflects and resembles nation: not a retreat from the public and political, home expresses the same ideological pressures that contend within the nation. Home is both target and mirror of marketplace, as central and centering as any institution in the public realm. Indeed, home does the business of nation and carries its agendas forward in time, producing the subjects of nation and empire. It cannot be thought as women's space, but rather the space designed to teach women their own imperial function. Women in homes partner men in brokerages, men behind desks and canons, men with palm pilots and pith helmets.

1

From the perspective of its crucial role in transferring institutions and values down through and into future time, home is a major player in national agendas and the settled heart of the imperial enterprise.

Home is a receiver for public languages and values, a space where national discourse speaks and reproduces itself. Western cultures speak to and construct home's residents through television, newspapers, fashion magazines, comic books, novels, how-to manuals, and Internet chat rooms. More subtly, cultural, national, and imperial values speak through the very practices of domestic settlement: through forms of daily ordering that, as anthropologist Mary Douglas observes, make home a "rigid" regulator of times, tastes, and speech: "home as a virtual community is often absurd, and often cruel," drawing upon "individual strategies of control defended respectively in the name of home as a public good" (279–80). Cultural imperialism appears in the valorization of the efficient "husbanding" of resources, an economics of hoarding one's own sufficiency and keeping others outside locked doors or exclusive gated communities. It emerges in the valorization of accomplished "housewifery," which involves managing resources not your own. Above all, nation and empire speak in the privacy of home through traditions related to their primary function—engendering legitimate, obedient, civilized children. Far from being a "separate sphere" of insulated privacy, home has permeable walls and a vital function in the nation, which explains why it is vigorously defended as a public good.

Like home, homeland connotes a settled, homogeneous place of mythic origins. Homeland is the country-sized space of home, of kin and belonging, and therefore of sentimental unity. Amy Kaplan observes that while references to the American nation as a home are commonplace, "homeland" entered US national discourse only after September 11, 2001, and has since become part of an "official rhetoric" aiming "to tighten and shore up" borders "that had been eroded by the forces of globalization" (2003: 59). She writes, "Homeland thus conveys a sense of native origins, of birthplace and birthright. It appeals to common bloodlines, ancient ancestry, and notions of racial and ethnic homogeneity" (2003: 60). Like home, homeland points nostalgically backward to the origins of settlement as a moment of uncomplicated heroism and, in Kaplan's analysis of contemporary invocations of the homeland, helps wall off foreign spaces, makes immigrants and racialized others suspect, and justifies the expansion of supervisory power: "The notion of 'the homeland' draws on comforting images of a deeply rooted past to legitimate modern forms of imperial power" (2003: 64). Homeland invokes a version of the nation as a sufficient, nurturing home that harkens back to a single cultural origin.

Nations or homelands have often been constructed through narratives of the family, making stories of homeland resemble and reflect stories of home. As Anne McClintock writes in *Imperial Leather*, "Nations are frequently figured through the iconography of familial and domestic space. The term nation derives from *natio*: to be born" (357). The family trope, she continues, "offers a 'natural' figure for sanctioning national *hierarchy* within a putative organic *unity* of interests" (357). The hierarchy subordinates women and children within domestic and national spaces and thus reinforces the gendering of power in public and private arenas. One result, according to McClintock, is that "women are typically constructed as the symbolic bearers of the nation, but are denied any direct relation to national agency" (354). In the settled spaces of home and nation, women are read as representing what they cannot exercise, while the system of representation naturalizes their subordination and renders it invisible. At the same time, the construction of nation as homeland feeds patriotic nationalism and evokes loyalty, even among nationals excluded from the national family. As Edward W. Said writes in "Reflections on Exile," "Nationalism is an assertion of belonging in and to a place, a people, a heritage. It affirms the home created by a community of language, culture, and customs; and, by so doing, it fends off exile, fights to prevent its ravages" (2000: 190). Nationalism envisions the homeland as a special extension of the settled home.

This book interprets recent fiction by women writers from six homelands and finds that the invented homes in these narratives reflect private forms of public exclusions and oppressions. In novels written in English and published in Australia, Canada, India, Nigeria, Puerto Rico, and the United States between 1995 and 2005, the writers use fictional homes to criticize and effectively *un*settle home and homeland. The novels expose the exploitation, arising out of the very myth of settled home and homeland, of people of unprivileged race, class, religion, gender, sexuality, and nationality. The narratives represent home's exclusions and their costs, not only to those denied admission but also to those inside the exclusive home. They detail barbarities committed in the name of the kindred homogeneity of homeland and represent private citizens who assent to and participate in public acts of unsettling brutality. These novels link home and homeland in cruelties perpetrated in the name of protecting settled spaces and national values.

The fiction unsettles, too, not only through its disturbing content— abuse, murder, rape, violence against innocent figures—but also in its disruptive forms. These novels do not take readers home with comforting resolutions. They ground their action in one or more houses that stand for the nation; they invoke the history of a lineage and a dwelling and trace the house's fall or fragmentation to the damaging legacies of imperial domination. While the foundation stories invoke heroism and homogeneity, they appear ironically in narratives that fracture these claims, exposing brutality in the moment of conquest and settlement. Told in often fragmented and multiple perspectives, including those of the victims of exclusion and conquest, these narratives give voice to the homeless and the exiled. They refuse the restorative conclusion, defer the promise of healing, and count the costs of settlement.

In crossing traditional disciplinary boundaries, this book is also designed to unsettle. The time has come to think globally about literature, I believe: the borders separating English and American literature from the literatures of the rest of the world are relics of the imperial age. In the academy, these walls have created privileged territory for the literature of England and America, which formed the canon of works read and taught even in countries like India and Nigeria, just as they gave primacy to writing by men. From a feminist and postcolonial viewpoint, those borders create an incongruous homeland for texts that often speak against the privileging of just such traditions and exclusivities. It is now time to unsettle that territory. As Susan Stanford Friedman writes in *Mappings*, "I remain convinced that a broadly comparative, global/locational feminism can change our analysis of 'home' as well as 'elsewhere,' helping to break repetitive logjams of thought by casting the conditions of home in a new light and by illuminating the structures interlocking home and elsewhere" (6). Global in its range, locational in the way it situates each text, my project suggests that we read local literature best when we approach it transnationally, attending to the overlaps and reverberations among texts from different lands.

Such an approach to literature becomes especially important in what critics have agreed to call "the age of globalization." While Enrique Dussel and others have dated the global age to 1492, with Columbus's arrival in America, Ali Behdad argues that "global flows and world-systems existed well before Spaniards began colonizing the New World, not only in the Americas but also throughout the Mediterranean, South Asia, and East Asia" (63). To suggest the enormous academic currency of thinking about globalization, a keyword search of the MLA Bibliography in July 2006 produced 1510 essays containing discussion of globalization; transnationalism produced 556.[1] In an age that knows itself in terms of globalized cultures and transnational economies and political systems, the study of literary canons enclosed within national boundaries is obsolete—and more, complicit with forms of dangerous and damaging nationalism that are widely repudiated in academic criticism. For many reasons, this is a time for transnational connections and global understandings.

While later chapters will be concerned to speak and read locally, I want to begin by thinking globally about conjunctions between home and homeland and tracing some of their intersecting foundations and functions. As a first principle, both home and nation draw on and perpetuate a fundamentally patriarchal authority, hardly unique to these two institutions. By no accident, the discourse of home and nation points to this authority in allied ways, so that nations—"motherlands" and "fatherlands"—have "founding fathers" and patriarchal homes have "governors." The word "home" points outward—it derives from the Anglo-Saxon *ham* which, as John Hollander observes, "designates a village or town, an estate or possession"; Hollander also notes that "the modern Turkish *yurt* (= tent) contracts down from the wide reaches of the Old Turkic word for 'country' or 'fatherland'" (40). The verb "to domesticate" implies lording it over: it "is akin to dominate, which derives from *dominus*, lord of the *domum*, the home," writes McClintock (35). While home may be linked with women's influence and activity in Western culture, the terms identify a controlling patriarchal power that operates at home as it does in the nation. This power also functions, writes Ketu Katrak, in postcolonial societies inflected by racism: "The domestic, familial arena is the most legitimized space for male domination even when, or particularly when, the male faces racism outside the home" (238).

Both home and homeland are theoretical, virtual, or, in Benedict Anderson's terms, imagined communities, built on the appeal of "a deep, horizontal comradeship," even though patriarchal authority and political power make the real structure far more vertical and hierarchical (16). Home, like homeland, is an ideal that links "fraternity, power and time meaningfully together" in shared sacrifice and triumph (40). While houses, apartments, and other dwelling places are tangible, concrete spaces, "home," in the sense I am invoking, is fully as abstract and invisible, as loaded with emotional and ideological investment, as related to religious imagining and to the hope for immortality, as the concept of nation. Writing about patriotism, Anderson identifies the language of "political love" with "the vocabulary of kinship (motherland, *Vaterland*, *patria*) or that of home," both idioms denoting a natural tie, "something unchosen," a bond carrying "a halo of disinterestedness" (131). As communities offering innate, disinterested solidarity, home and homeland are able to summon the degree of unquestioning loyalty required for the sacrifice of life in their defense. Bonds of attachment to nation and home are reinvigorated by perceptions of threat or loss, as suggested by the resurgence of nationalism in the United States after September 11, 2001.

As implied by the importance of enforceable borders and lockable doors, home and homeland are imagined communities based on the exclusion or assimilation of the foreign. Those who can be admitted to the "fraternity" of "deep, horizontal comradeship" are included; they belong as kin, inside home and nation. Others must be kept outside— those who differ or whose race, caste, religion, gender, or sexuality renders them unfit to be assimilated to the homogeneous collective. Said invokes "the fundamentally static notion of *identity* that has been the core of cultural thought during the era of imperialism": the idea "that there is an 'us' and a 'them,' each quite settled, clear, unassailably self-evident" (1993: xxv). For Kaplan, excluding "them" defines both home and nation. She points out that "domestic" relies on an opposition to "foreign": "*Domestic* has a double meaning that links the space of the familial household to that of the nation, by imagining both in opposition to everything outside the geographic and conceptual border of the home" (2002: 25). Erecting borders and boundaries to enclose the exclusive space of home/land enables the construction of a homogeneous "identity" (one single "us" or "fraternity"). From this perspective, discriminations of race, gender, class, caste, religion, and nationality are basic to home and homeland—put simply, home/land is constitutionally racist, sexist, and chauvinistic.

Another important link between home and homeland is their pledge of an ideal blend of security with personal freedom as the basis for a powerful sentimental appeal. In an essay published in *Subaltern Studies*, Qadri Ismail articulates the "bind between 'home' and 'nation'" as a promise of "absolute" security in communal identity:

> Such security is to be found, ideally at least, only at home: a space that provides not just physical security, but is also without claustrophobia and dysphoria. Metaphorically speaking, nationalism promises to take its nationals home, to end homelessness and homesickness, represents itself as the exclusive and ultimate cure for nostalgia.
>
> (218–19)

Yet these promises are impossible, Ismail argues. For one thing, nationalism constructs women as subordinate to men and thus "women cannot find home in nation"; for another, in keeping the promises, nationalism would have exhausted its obligations and rendered itself obsolete, so "nationalism cannot and does not keep its promises (to its nationals)" (218–19). In fact, Ismail concludes, the logic of nationalism "demands that it conserve, nurture and foster nostalgia, not rebut or terminate it" (281). Ismail's provocative analysis suggests a necessary functional gap between the promises made by nations and homes—a paradisiacal balance between perfect security and perfect freedom—and their imperfect delivery. The promise reminds people of what they feel they have lost, and thus it feeds a nostalgic investment in the home/land by the very impossibility of its achievement. The delivery is considerably worse, as we would expect, for those of unprivileged gender, race, caste, or religion. I would add to Ismail's claims the argument that women, commonly held to be the keepers of home, cannot find home in home either, nor can people whose ethnicity or poverty renders them "foreign" within their culture.

The nostalgia invested in home/land has several important functions, all related to the preservation of power: to protect tradition, maintain the status quo, neutralize dissatisfaction, and silence dissent. As Rosemary Marangoly George puts it, "a nostalgically recycled domesticity" endorsing traditional values "allows for a continued enjoyment of domestic pleasures without questioning or dismantling domesticity's founding assumptions" (1998: 2). Similarly, nostalgic nationalism may be invoked by the nation's leaders to quiet the interrogation of dubious policies by cloaking the issues in a fog of patriotic affirmation: "My country right or wrong," as the cliché has it, or, in the words of President G. H. W. Bush, "I wouldn't apologize for my country. I don't care what the facts are." To protect existing lines of power, home and homeland are mystified in contemporary public discourse and bathed in a golden shower of sentiment. Their veneration obfuscates racism and the exploitations of class and gender on which homes and nations rely. The nostalgia attached to home/land also reinforces the authority vested in both the state and home as institutions, and it generates profit, rousing immaterial desires for the satiation of which transnational corporations market material products. Home and homeland sell; they have been invoked in the United States to endorse candidates, persuade voters to support legislation like the Patriot Act, and promote home improvement products, goods, and services.

Home's appeal rests on the undeniable pleasures it symbolizes and sometimes provides. It stands for the emotional satisfactions of safety, community, and belonging. In *Paradise*, Toni Morrison names the yearning for "speech shared and divided bread smoking from the fire; the unambivalent bliss of going home to be at home—the ease of coming back to love begun" (318). Home promises a continuity of love in which subjects who experience anonymity and indifference in a globalized world can feel cherished and valued for, and perhaps also despite, their unique character and history. With its lockable entrance, it pledges security from the violence of the outer world, though it may conceal and enable domestic violence. It provides a safe space for the preservation of material luxuries, which may comfort, entertain, or confer prestige. Home also creates and signals community, relationship, and bonds of belonging; it can mean acceptance into a family or fraternity, selection as a romantic partner, or the privileges of kinship: "Home is the place where, when you have to go there, / They have to take you in," as Robert Frost's farmer says in "Death of the Hired Man."[2] These pleasures appear in transnational women's fiction; indeed, they attract women protagonists and confer power on homes that mostly fail, in this fiction, to deliver on their promises.

While many of the links between nation and power are evident, home is a less understood conduit of force. Its deep pockets of concealed influence derive from its status as an innocuous, naturalized structure standing for private community and, by the same stroke, standing outside the realms of contested authority. Its relationship to power is invisible; its exercise of power seemingly disinterested and natural. When McClintock observes that "the family itself has been figured as the antithesis of history," "excluded from national power," while paradoxically nations are figured through the trope of the family (357), she identifies the great camouflage of power in both realms—the innocuous family home, outside the historical struggle, and the innocent nation, a homogeneous homeland unified by a family narrative. Carole Boyce Davies observes that home and nation gain power from a distance: "Migration creates the desire for home, which in turn produces the rewriting of home. [...] Home can only have meaning once one experiences a level of displacement from it" (1994: 113).

To understand how a single analysis can make meaningful connections between fictions of home in homelands as widely dispersed and different as Canada, India, Australia, Nigeria, the United States, and Puerto Rico,[3] it helps to remember that colonization focused on reproducing the ideal metropolitan home in the colonies. As Said writes, "Partly because of empire, all cultures are involved in one another" (1993: xxv). Indeed, England exported its own idealized models of home and homeland to all of the nations in this study except Puerto Rico, originally a colony of Spain (which reproduced its allied patriarchal home abroad) and later of the United States. Significant work by postcolonial feminists (including Jenny Sharpe, McClintock, George and others) has explored the painstaking efforts of English women to reproduce English homes in the colonies, while English education inculcated in children of many lands the values associated with English homes. Women writers reflect specific cultural locations, individual positions inside or outside the land about which they write; they are also aware of the shadow cast by the Western imperial home and its associated values. How this spectral home shapes the practices of postcolonial homes is one focus of their narratives.

This project explores women writers' representations of private experience in relation to public and national crises, and in this sense, it commits itself to observing correspondences and homologies. In a famous essay illustrating the overextension of such a methodology, Fredric Jameson argues that "All third-world texts are [...] to be read as what I will call *national allegories* [...] Third-world texts [...] necessarily project a political dimension in the form of national allegory: *the story of the private individual destiny is always an allegory of the embattled situation of the public third-world culture and society*" (69).[4] Instead, I believe that *some* transnational women writers create narratives of private lives that reflect national legacies of postcolonial oppression. This allegorical practice appears in what Jameson called (in 1986) "third-world" texts and also in those he would then have categorized as "first-world." Recognizing the need for carefully historicized readings, I believe these connections between private and public account for a crucial, and often overlooked, dimension of transnational women's fiction.

This book studies the representations of postcolonial subjects' experiences in different cultures while recognizing the uniqueness of each cultural location. The colonial histories of the nations represented in this book vary widely, as do the writers' background and reputation. The evolution of nationalism in a former settler-colony like Canada or Australia differs from that in a land colonized by invasion like India, Puerto Rico, and Nigeria. The history of slavery in the United States gives the mostly black characters in Morrison's *Paradise* a significantly different relation to home and homeland than that of the mostly white, wealthy characters in Atwood's *Blind Assassin* or the black, wealthy characters in Adichie's *Purple Hibiscus*. The Spanish patriarchal traditions influencing homes in Ferré's *House on the Lagoon* resemble but differ from the English patriarchal traditions in Lazaroo's *Australian Fiancé*. The histories of colonialism in the novels branch and bifurcate: Lazaroo's novel exposes the aftereffects of Portuguese and Japanese invasions as well as the British colonization of Singapore and Australia, and Atwood's novel reflects the scars of colonization in Ireland as well as Canada. Among these writers, Morrison has won the Nobel Prize and, like Atwood, she is internationally known. Adichie and Lazaroo are less well known but have growing reputations; *Hibiscus* is Adichie's first novel, and *Fiancé* is Lazaroo's second. Arundhati Roy is widely known, though *God of Small Things* is her only novel; Rosario Ferré is not nearly as famous as she should be, with twenty books in various genres.

My goals in bringing together such a diverse range of books, writers, and nations include expanding the range of knowledge of global literature in English, particularly of women writers representing postcolonial experiences. Powerful novels, written in styles that are both experimental and poetic, these texts dislocate the pledged comforts of home and homeland. In their descriptions of significant houses, the texts identify pretense, falseness, deception, and decay in the edifice that suggest hidden corruption in its founders and inhabitants. Atwood emphasizes the pretentiousness of Avilion, which aspires to confer upper class dignity and antiquity on new button-manufacturing money, and the narrow falseness of Richard Griffen's house, with its "squinty-windowed, ponderous" exterior (295). Ferré reflects the hidden corruption beneath the lavish Mendizabal lifestyle in the progressive rotting of the beams supporting the house on the lagoon. The inevitable discoloration of its white linens reflects the corrupt racism of the Australian house Elsewhere, whose dynastic patriarchs indulge like Ferré's in sexual affairs with raced others. Roy personifies the Ipe house as a rheumy-eyed old man, indifferent to the bothersome children who pursue life in its crumbling and filthy rooms. Adichie's Achike household contains rigorously scheduled black women and children behind high walls, and Morrison's white houses in Ruby contain industrious black women; these homes are clean and tidy, but they wrest their excessive orderings from silenced women. Adichie juxtaposes the Aunt's open, life-filled garden flat, and Morrison the eventual self-disciplined calm of the Convent, against home spaces that oppress, degrade, and subordinate their caretakers.

In connecting these transnational women writers' representations of home and homeland, I explore the territory identified by Gareth Griffiths when he calls for comparative studies of literary texts that address the question, "How are modern post-colonial texts and the societies they seek to represent, despite their many differences, illuminated by their shared experience in colonization and later?" (1996: 176). In doing so, I hold with Susan Stanford Friedman that "comparativist thinking is not [...] inherently eurocentric and bankrupt," but rather capable of crossing cultures in ways that attend to differences and open up what she calls "geopolitical thinking" (2001: 114). Reading Anglo-European models onto the literatures of Asia or Africa differs from tracing the impact of models exported under colonization on the literatures of postcolonial societies, and homogenizing "Third World" or "commonwealth" literatures by articulating their similarities differs from attending to the local issues engaged from divergent perspectives in postcolonial literatures.[5] Conjoining local and transnational, these essays bring a global perspective to local issues and texts, which in turn make transnational issues more specific and meaningful.

The meaning of and relationships among imperialism, colonialism, and postcolonialism have been widely discussed by critics and theorists. While some thoughtful critics have raised problems with "postcolonialism," the term usefully gathers concerns about the aftermath of imperial acts of conquest in the settlement of colonies.[6] I believe that the postcolonial fictions of transnational women writers criticize oppressive historical practices. In writing about postcolonialism, then, I understand it in the terms voiced most clearly by Robert Young: "postcolonial critique [...] is the product of resistance to colonialism and imperialism" (15). Similarly, Henry Schwartz describes postcolonial studies as a "radical philosophy," "not merely a theory of knowledge but a 'theoretical practice,' a transformation of knowledge from static disciplinary competence to activist intervention" (4). Imperialism, the main focus of its critique, is the ideologically driven practice by which one nation imposes its will on others, and colonialism refers to the practice of conquering and settling territories at a distance. Young provides a useful contrast: "Colonialism functioned as an activity on the periphery, economically driven [...] Imperialism, on the other hand, operated from the centre as a policy of state, driven by the grandiose projects of power" (16–17). Ania Loomba suggests a related distinction between the two concepts: we might

think of imperialism or neo-imperialism as the phenomenon that originates in the metropolis, the process which leads to domination and control. Its result, or what happens in the colonies as a consequence of imperial domination, is colonialism or neo-colonialism. [...] Imperialism can function without formal colonies (as in United States imperialism today) but colonialism cannot.

(12)

At the present moment colonialism has been reduced, though not eliminated; imperialism has changed form since the nineteenth century, but it remains a potent force in global interactions.

Forms of imperialism can reside in critical positions that read "home" outward onto the rest of the world. Such a critical imperialism recuperates the logic of center and periphery, approaching global literatures and cultures with distinctions between canonical literature, read for its artistry, and other literature, read for its ethnographic interest. This approach assumes that homeland's standards and values are universal. In writing about global women writers, I am mindful of Gayatri Chakravorty Spivak's warning that "feminist criticism" can approach global literatures with an attitude that "reproduces the axioms of imperialism":

> A basically isolationist admiration for the literature of the female subject in Europe and Anglo-America establishes the high feminist norm. It is supported and operated by an information-retrieval approach to 'Third World' literature which often employs a deliberately 'non-theoretical' methodology with self-conscious rectitude.
>
> (1991: 798)

Producing a certain kind of female subject is, I am suggesting, the goal of home and homeland as well as of some literature. The postcolonial women writers in this study expose that imperative and explore possibilities for resistance. Rather than atheoretical "information-retrieval," the essays in this book bring postcolonial and feminist theories to bear on multiple cultural meanings and after effects of the encounter with colonialism in specific locations.

These writers' use of English raises important issues. As Katrak points out, African, Indian, and Caribbean writing in English is relatively recent, a product of the post-1960s era of national independence; thus "A study that focuses only on English-language post-colonial writers involves some loss, even distortion in terms of the complex reality of linguistic situations in post-colonial areas" (230). Roy, Ferré, and Adichie could have used other languages (Malayalam, Spanish, and Igbo) and, in fact, they incorporate phrases in these languages into the English narrative. Ferré and Roy were strongly criticized for "selling" their work to an international audience by using English. Though all three writers have native fluency in English, some nationalist critics misread disrespect for the local in their decision to use what has become a global language. As Griffiths argues, however,

> The denial of the possibility of using colonial languages to represent post-colonial experiences is a simplistic assertion of authenticity often made alongside dubious claims concerning the ways in which culture is inscribed in language. It assumes that cultures in the contemporary world which continue to function in pre-colonial indigenous languages have not themselves been subject to colonial hybridization and that colonial languages were not available for resistance or opposition.
>
> (1996: 168–69)

The use of English does not preclude access to hybrid cultures, nor would Malayalam or Igbo provide an unmediated and "authentic" recuperation of a static version of the original culture.

Chantal Zabus points out, furthermore, that the English used in post-colonial texts differs in sound, flavor, and grammatical form; she calls it English "with an accent." While Ashcroft, Griffiths, and Tiffin strip it of the capital letter signifying imperial dominance and substitute "the linguistic code, English, which has been transformed and subverted into several distinctive varieties throughout the world" (8), Zabus emphasizes the potential for linguistic hybridity. When the empire writes back, she argues, it does so "by using a language that topples discourse conventions of the so-called 'centre' and inscribing post-colonial language variants from the 'margin' or 'the periphery' in the text" (34). The alterations go beyond recording local dialect, as the writer "uses language variance as an alibi to convey ideological variance" or, in a more radical form she calls "relexification," inscribes local culture and concepts into the modified English language (34–36). Postcolonial writers can use an altered imperial language to expose colonial oppression and resist the practices of empire.

My project requires a large range of reference, including the analysis of six texts set on four continents, drawing on histories of colonial encounters extending into at least nine different nations. Each chapter draws on research in the local history and contexts for the narrative and on the work of postcolonial and feminist theorists appropriate to the region and the text. It is not clear that any reader can know enough of what Sharpe calls "the heterogeneous cultures of the entire non-Western world" (21) to undertake such a project, but I am encouraged by Spivak's observation:

> The position that only the subaltern can know the subaltern, only women can know women, and so on, cannot be held as a theoretical presupposition either, for it predicates the possibility of knowledge on identity. Whatever the political necessity for holding the position, and whatever the advisability of attempting to "identify" (with) the other as subject in order to know her, knowledge is made possible and is sustained by irreducible difference, not identity. What is known is always in excess of knowledge. Knowledge is never adequate to its object.
>
> (1987: 111–12)

In that light, it is possible, valuable, and perhaps even necessary to try to know across the boundaries and barriers of cultural difference crossed in this project.

The chapters in this book focus on representations of home by contemporary women novelists from six homelands bearing the marks of colonialism. The homes in these narratives comment on homeland and make visible six national heritages of oppression—ways in which power is brought to bear on those of devalued race, gender, religion, sexuality, nationality, caste, and/or class. The writers attend to the histories and choices of women in homes and to the cultural pressures that would script and limit their stories. The fictions record pressures on women to accept roles symbolic of home and homeland, together with the passivity and confinement such roles entail. They represent the ways women characters are embodied and the even more various ways in which women's bodies are used, abused, and violated. Beyond feminist narratives of the personal trials of women in private spaces, the global postcolonial awareness of the writers infuses the novels with a political focus on public patterns of conquest and domination. In the history of a house, they recapitulate the history of a nation; in the commercial dealings of a patriarch they figure the competitive ethos, labor practices, and ecological devastations of a homeland. In their analysis of the power dynamics inside the home, these writers explore national contestations of power. The private sphere opens out onto the public and political, as home reveals the other face of homeland.

My reading of home/land in this fiction situates itself at the juncture of feminism and postcolonial theory. Wherever home was mystified, its power relations naturalized and rendered invisible, feminist critics have exposed, quarreled, and questioned. With the deconstruction of the doctrine of separate spheres and the recognition of the cultural work produced in and producing home, feminist theory anticipates the link between home and homeland. Postcolonial theory focuses on homeland, probing the long damaging aftereffects of the hegemonic relationship between imperial nations and the regions they colonize. Each theoretical approach provides lenses that correct for the other's oversights: situating gender in the foreground, feminism can allow national and imperial issues to blur behind it, while postcolonial theory has tended to ignore gender in focusing on national and imperial concerns. Brought together by postcolonial feminists, these approaches enable the exploration of home and homeland and open up the space for this project. Exploring the works of some influential thinkers in the next section, I emphasize continuities rather than separations between women's issues and geopolitical concerns, domesticity and politics, and home and homeland.

Feminist, postcolonial, and postcolonial feminist contexts

Writing about women, home, and domesticity, Western feminists theorize the power relations operating covertly in private spaces. During the last half of the twentieth century, they interrogated previously naturalized assumptions of power and exposed essentializing definitions of women. Feminist analysis provides an important basis for thinking about women's traditional roles—housekeepers and homemakers creating the home, symbol-bearers for the values of nation. A brief history of some important feminist forerunners for this project serves as a vital starting point. The argument for the continuing relevance of feminist thinking has been made best by Susan Stanford Friedman: "Precisely because patriarchal formations have continued material reality, because the historical conditions that led to the rise of gynocriticism and gynesis still exist, these pedagogical and scholarly projects have continued legitimacy and urgency" (1998: 32).

Mid-twentieth century feminists began by contesting the natural relationship between women and home; instead, they argued, women were bored and frustrated in homes and marriages in which they had very little power. In this period, feminist activists worked to liberate women from the settled conditions of domestic life, criticized as oppressive to women's self-actualization and demeaning as a site of tedious, unpaid, repetitive labor. Writing *The Second Sex* in 1949, Simone de Beauvoir characterized married women's lives as tedious and unfulfilling;

while domestic labor is connected with middle-class values, its practice "provides no escape from immanence and little affirmation of individuality" (451). Dependent on her husband and children for meanings, the homemaker creates nothing: "she is subordinate, secondary, parasitic. The heavy curse that weighs upon her consists in this: the very meaning of her life is not in her hands" (456). Adapting de Beauvoir's critique for the American housewife, Betty Friedan argued that women's unhappiness "burst like a boil through the image of the happy American housewife" (22). The social exaltation of women's roles as housewives—what Friedan called "the feminine mystique"—emerged as a cultural countermove: "The glorification of 'woman's role,' then, seems to be in proportion to society's reluctance to treat women as complete human beings" (238–39). Domesticity, for these feminists, means parochial limitation and isolation. "The rejection of domesticity," Rachel Bowlby observes, "has seemed a principal, if not *the* principal, tenet of feminist demands for freedom. The home figures as the place where the woman is confined, and from which she must be emancipated" (78).[7]

To complicate perceptions of domesticity expressed in too simply negative terms, a number of feminist critics set about in the 1980s redeeming domesticity, women who had lived domestic lives, and literary representations of domestic subjects in the genre called "domestic" or "sentimental" fiction. These critics recognized a liberatory potential in domesticity or in women's creative responses to the challenge of domestic lives. Nina Baym's work on the American "sentimental" writers in *Woman's Fiction* (1978) acknowledged the shaping force of the "cult of domesticity" holding that women are fulfilled in marriage and motherhood: "Domesticity is set forth as a value scheme for ordering all of life" (27). According to Baym, women characters in this fiction are empowered by their view of domestic values and come to believe in their own strengths; they hold a "conviction that God's values were domestic" (44). Another important proponent of domestic power, Jane Tompkins argued in *Sensational Designs* (1985) for the importance of women's texts in the American canon. Tompkins read sentimental fiction as a narrative field in which women created forms of authority. She argued that the domestic fiction written for and often by women "is preoccupied, even obsessed, with the nature of power," and advocated reconceiving the home as an arena for women's self-realization: "confinement to the home, which looks to us like deprivation, became a means of personal fulfillment" (160, 165–66). Ann Romines made a similar assessment of the potentially redemptive quality of the ritual repetitions in housework: "A woman who achieved faculty and made effective ritual of her housekeeping was taking on godlike status" (10). These feminist critics emphasized that women can and do transform culturally denigrated structures—the home, the sentimental novel—into creative spaces for their own expression and fulfillment.

Important work on domestic fiction and the ideology of separate spheres appeared in the late 1980s, often in studies of Victorian literature.[8] Mary Poovey's *Uneven Developments* explored the construction of women as domestic and of domestic women as apolitical, emotional, and moral. Poovey described an emphasis in the late eighteenth and early nineteenth century on the apolitical nature of the domestic sphere, effecting its separation from the "so called public sphere of competition, self-interest, and economic aggression. As superintendents of the domestic sphere, (middle-class) women were represented as protecting and, increasingly, incarnating virtue" (10).[9] In *Desire and Domestic Fiction*, Nancy Armstrong explored the role of representation in constructing the "gendering of human identity," which "provided the metaphysical girders of modern culture—its reigning mythology" (14). Armstrong argued that domestic fiction reinforced the gendering of separate spheres and a version of the individual's private domain as "outside and apart from social history" (9–10). Armstrong emphasized the power of language, and especially of fiction, to constitute subjectivity in ways that shape history (25); by implication, representations of home exert a settling force in the realm of homeland.

Feminist critiques of the ideology implicit in the separate spheres have taken several directions. Political theorist Carole Pateman identifies "the dichotomy between the private and the public" as "central to almost two centuries of feminist struggle; it is, ultimately, what the feminist movement is about" (118). Feminists have advocated opening the public to women's full participation, renegotiating the private so that home labor becomes gender-neutral, and privileging the qualities and skills demonstrated by women. They have emphasized the class and race implications of the doctrine of separate spheres, arguing that it "enabled the bourgeoisie to distinguish themselves from other social groups" and constituted "the 19th-century middle class as white" (Blunt and Rose 3–4). Laurie Finke comments on the entwined issues of domesticity and dependency: "To create the male as an autonomous independent agent in the public sphere, bourgeois ideology had to relegate all dependency relations that might undermine that independent selfhood to the domestic realm under the supervision of women" (121). Claudia Tate explores the invocation of bourgeois domesticity in romances by black writers and argues that these versions of an ideal social order were used "to promote the social advancement of African Americans" (5). According to Tate, the popularity of black women's domestic romances in the decades following Reconstruction expressed readers' desire for the stability and authority that accompany bourgeois domesticity.

The gendered assumptions supporting the doctrine of separate spheres have structured the contextual approaches brought to bear on readings of women's fiction. Though women are also historically connected with nature and the outer realm,[10] critics often read women's novels in relation to the inner life and particularly in relation to the psyche. McClintock explains the logic of the connection: "psychoanalysis has been relegated to the (conventionally universal) realm of private, domestic space, while politics and economics are relegated to the (conventionally historical) realm of the public market" (8). Women's lives in homes appear to invite critical interpretations that suppress political, historical, and transnational sites in favor of emotional, spiritual, familial, and universal ones. These forms of analysis reinscribe women as apolitical creatures of feeling, defined by their psychological natures, playing repetitive roles in universal dramas. Homes, by implication, become stages for the acting out of mythic cycles rather than places where worldly power is negotiated on a daily basis.

One recent book that draws on psychology and myth as a basis for reading homes in contemporary fiction illustrates how a feminist approach can ignore national and imperial issues in privileging gender. Roberta Rubenstein's *Home Matters: Longing and Belonging, Nostalgia and Mourning in Women's Fiction* (2001) argues that home "is among the most emotionally complex and resonant concepts in our psychic vocabularies" (1). Home evokes the "yearning for recovery or return to the idea of a nurturing, unconditionally accepting place/space" (4), the nostalgic wish to recover childhood, and the mourning for irretrievable losses (4–5). Homesickness fuses nostalgia and mourning: "characters work through previously unresolved grief as, through them, the authors themselves mourn the loss of historical homelands, communities, and cultural traditions" (8). Morrison's *Paradise*, for example, explores homesickness as "maternal figures with special powers" create "spiritual homecoming for their symbolic daughters" (8). I will have more to say about Rubenstein's reading of *Paradise* in chapter two; here I want to point out some of the elisions of national and transnational issues that necessarily emerge in such an approach.

Rubenstein's introduction announces a focus on the personal feelings of women in and about homes and analyzes these feelings as psychological manifestations. The characters and their authors become clients, "working through" the stages of grief in what self-help psychology books uphold as the model of linear progress toward healthy acceptance. Novels are envisioned as resembling therapy sessions in showing women how to heal. The novel's goal becomes taking the reader home, into what Rubenstein calls a "metaphysical geography" beyond the material realm; thus the critic can emphasize "homecoming." In a reading produced out of this approach, questions come to rest and contradictions are resolved in the closure of home. What is left out, conspicuously, is any analysis of the causes for the women's feelings in relation to power, money, labor, race, class, sexuality, or gender—in short, the material conditions under which women live in homes. In the absence of the worldly weight of these conditions, women's feelings float lightly above the gravity of raced and classed existence. The workings of power erase their own tracks, leaving only the reassuring spectacle of women in homes with feelings that can be "worked through." While ambivalence is expected, there can be no contestation, nor crossings or troublings of meaning in a basic pattern of nostalgic longing and mourning for the lost home.

Such an approach recapitulates the separation of the personal and private from the public, political, and global. It returns home to the status of a private sphere under the sway of the feminine, with emotional issues at the forefront. By implication, it also makes the woman sick and in need of cure or healing. If she gets better, she becomes the good mother or daughter, reinscribed in the language and ideology of home. She may be like a Kingsolver character who "ultimately discovers a deeper knowledge of her true place" or like those in Morrison who accomplish "a passage through nostalgic mourning" (Rubenstein 8). These characters' emotions drive and define them and make them need (psycho) analysis in order to find the passage to their "true place"— which is, without question, a settled home. In the circular logic by which ideology reproduces itself, women and homes become self-confirming mirrors.

Although Rubenstein acknowledges a debt to feminist scholars, her account of the developing nostalgia among contemporary women actually blames "contemporary feminism" for creating a displacement of women from homes. Women have deep emotional attachments to the roles and values of home, but these have been "repressed" under feminism. Feminists like Friedan and de Beauvoir made homes appear like prisons, leaving women split between a public disavowal of home and a private longing to recapture it: "Once domesticity became aligned with confinement and oppression, and once *home* became associated with a politically reactionary backlash against feminism, homesickness went underground" to emerge in fiction as the longing to recuperate "the idea of a nurturing, unconditionally accepting place/space that has been repressed in contemporary feminism" (Rubenstein 3–4). Implicitly, homesickness, nostalgia, and the wish to take one's place in a nurturing home come naturally to women, while the version of home as confinement and oppression was invented by feminists. The operations of political power in homes are not simply erased, but more surprisingly ascribed to the feminists who create an unnatural detachment of women from their "true place."

Alternative approaches that are closer to my own unsettle home by considering its worldly, political circumstances. "Feminist Politics: What's Home Got to Do with It?," by Biddy Martin and Chandra Talpade Mohanty, explores intricate destabilizations of home in Minnie Bruce Pratt's autobiographical narrative, "Identity: Skin Blood Heart."[11] While home exerts a powerful tug on the emotions, Pratt exposes it as an illusion, an exclusionary practice, and a site that disciplines and represses its inhabitants. Pratt's essay, Martin and Mohanty argue, invokes both the pleasures and illusions of home: "'Being home' refers to the place where one lives within familiar, safe, protected boundaries; 'not being home' is a matter of realizing that home was an illusion of coherence and safety based on the exclusion of specific histories of oppression and resistance, the repression of differences even within oneself" (196). Discovering built-in contradictions between "the desire for home" and "the repressions and violence" that operate in and through homes, Pratt questions coherent notions of home and privileged, secure identity (208). As a first step, inner differences (like lesbianism, for Pratt) are policed and repressed; as a second, historical oppressions of race and class (like the multiple victimizations of Pratt's black neighbors) that support the domestic economy of the middle class house are elided. Martin and Mohanty find that Pratt locates the power available to women subjects in refusing the comforts of home.[12] Caren Kaplan makes a similar argument: "We must leave home, as it were, since our homes are often the sites of racism, sexism, and other damaging social practices" (1987: 194).

In addition to a worldly reading of home, approaches that anticipate my own understand women through the poststructuralist demolition of the stable subject. While home contains disputations of power, women in homes can no longer be envisioned as the essentialized figures of nurturance, spirituality, nostalgia, and emotion. As Susan Lurie writes in *Unsettled Subjects*, poststructuralist feminism "stressed not only the multiple referents for the category of 'woman' but also the differences within particular female subjects," producing "the self-different female subject" (1). With a sense that its poststructuralist commitments have led feminist practice to an "impasse," Lurie calls for a return to "the critique of patriarchal power" and to the analysis of gender in representation (2). Feminism, she writes, must "train its attention on the patriarchal policing of female self-difference" and consider "how patriarchal ideology profits from the female subject's negotiation of simultaneous agendas" (22, 4). In other words, a complex awareness of the unsettled and differential subject positions of women needs the counterbalance of focused attention to the worldly operations of patriarchal power. A political poststructuralist feminism can enable the analysis of female subjects whose negotiations of gender are interarticulated with those of race and class or caste.

Among others, Dana Heller and Lynne Pearce write about women and home from just such positions. In "Housebreaking History: Feminism's Troubled Romance with the Domestic Sphere," Heller argues that the motto of second-wave feminism, "the personal is political," poses a challenge to the "ideology of separate spheres" (219). Implicit in the "crossing" or "breaking" of boundaries between private and political arenas is a version of the deconstruction of binaries that would culminate in more sweeping revisions to the practice of reading. Citing Jane Gallop as recommending that feminist critics see themselves as "outlaw agents of a public sphere" rather than holdovers from an enervated domesticity, Heller asks for other choices, including some that question "the usefulness of separate sphere ideology" (220). Pearce articulates a kindred call for other alternatives in her introduction to *Devolving Identities: Feminist Readings in Home and Belonging*. She observes that "women's 'discomfort' and 'marginalization' within our national/neo-national cultures" have "put them in the avant-garde of an alternative way of thinking about our locational homes" (18). Feminists can imagine other "ways of belonging"—including nomadism and the embrace of provisional positions (21).[13] Pearce believes that women's experience with the oppressions of home can make them better citizens, stateswomen, leaders, and visionaries of nation—able to invent flexible and anti-hegemonic homelands. With this possibility, we arrive at the anti-imperialist agenda of postcolonial criticism.

Postcolonial thinking can be brought naturally to critical intervention in the ideology of home since, as I have argued, it is also the ideology of empire. Empire relies on home for its symbolic representation of national values. The "home country" becomes a model for the "outposts," the "metropolis" an ideal for "peripheral" and "marginal" locations. Homeland's domestic order is exported to the colonies in order to suppress and distance qualities constructed as natural to "natives"—above all sexuality, but also all other expressions of unruly physical existence. Empire spreads the ideology of home; home symbolizes imperial values and perpetuates the power structures that fuel empire's advance.

Three major postcolonial critics are what Edward Said calls "exilic intellectuals," having left postcolonial homelands to develop critical positions in and of the West. Interventions in the understanding of homeland by Said, Homi Bhabha, and Spivak are enabling for this project. Said describes himself as "an Arab with a Western education" and *Culture and Imperialism* as "an exile's book"; he writes with great power about the "massive dislocations, waste, misery, and horrors endured in our century's migrations and mutilated lives" (xxvi, 332). Bhabha and Spivak are also bicultural, having left India for positions in Western universities. All three draw on their complex experiences as both colonial and Western subjects to articulate the critique of imperialism. Spivak describes herself in an interview as beyond home and homeland and thus open to the space Said has termed "cosmopolitanism": "I am bicultural, but my biculturality is that I'm not at home in either of the places"; instead, "to an extent, I feel I've earned the right to critique two places" (1990: 83).

All three contest the settled cultural spaces of the national homeland. Said attends closely to the binary divisions erected in the West to assert hegemonic dominance over non-European peoples and cultures. In *Orientalism*, he argues that Europe set "itself off against the Orient as a sort of surrogate and even underground self" (1979: 3); such binary oppositions are, he says, "dear to the nationalist and imperialist enterprise" (1993: xxiv). Bhabha makes a similar point in "DissemiNation," a well-known essay in *The Location of Culture*, when he argues that although the nation is actually "split within itself, articulating the heterogeneity of its population" (148), national narratives aim to produce the illusion of unity and homogeneity and to call patriotic subjects into the fold: "the very act of the narrative performance interpellates a growing circle of national subjects" (145). Disrupting the centrifugal force of these narratives, Bhabha's work theorizes the unsettling of national spaces. Spivak advocates a similar transnational view; the point, she writes, is "to negotiate between the national, the global, and the historical as well as the contemporary diasporic" in order to create "a cosmopolitanism that is global, gendered, and dynamic" (1993: 278). The goal and method of Spivak's analysis is to demolish the cultural supremacy involved in a mystification of "our" home/land.

Reading literary texts, all three theorists reflect at least briefly on fictional representations of home. Said exposes the role of domestic novels like Austen's *Mansfield Park* in supporting the ideology of empire. We are entitled to ask, he writes, why "there was little significant opposition or deterrence to empire at home. Perhaps the custom of distinguishing 'our' home and order from 'theirs' grew into a harsh political rule for accumulating more of 'them' to rule, study, and subordinate" (82). Bhabha engages home in "Locations of Culture," exposing the fissures and estrangements of what he calls the "unhomely."[14] He recognizes that feminism identifies "domestic space as the space of the normalizing, pastoralizing, and individuating techniques of modern power and police: the personal-*is*-the political; the world-*in*-the home" (10–11). Bhabha's concept of the unhomely, drawn from a Lacanian reading of Freud amplified by Benjamin, theorizes in different terms what I mean by unsettling home and homeland, and his thinking about nation, empire, and transnational literature opens up space for my project:

> Where, once, the transmission of national traditions was the major theme of a world literature, perhaps we can now suggest that transnational histories of migrants, the colonized, or political refugees— these border and frontier conditions—may be the terrains of world literature. The centre of such a study would neither be the "sovereignty" of national cultures, nor the universalism of human culture, but a focus on those "freak social and cultural displacements" that Morrison and Gordimer represent in their "unhomely" fictions.
>
> (12)

Spivak has similarly created what she calls "transnational culture studies" in essays that famously read English texts like *Jane Eyre* against Caribbean texts like *Wide Sargasso Sea*, or Indian fictions like Devi's "Stanadayini" (1993: 277). With her sophisticated interlinking of post-structuralist, Marxist, and feminist theory, Spivak has, according to Kaplan and Grewal, "single-handedly cleared the ground for what we now call the field of postcolonial feminist studies" (354).

Among a group of postcolonial feminists whose writings in the 1990s serve as particularly important precursors for my study of home and homeland, Jenny Sharpe reveals in *Allegories of Empire* how British women, seeking more power and freedom during colonial expansion, exploited and supported imperial logic. Sharpe writes that "domestic woman is not the source of female agency nor the passive repository of the domestic ideal but exists at the intersection of the two as a precarious and unstable subjectivity" (11–12). To bolster their claim to power, and in particular to support their claim to the sort of moral superiority that would justify increased emancipation, English women fit their appeal into the very same progressive apologetic on which colonialism rationalized itself:

> They appropriate the moral *value* of womanhood and transform it into a female form of moral *agency*. It is an agency, however, that is contingent upon establishing their racial superiority over Indian women. English women ground their own emancipation in the moral superiority of the British as an enlightened race engaged in raising natives into humanity. [...] the British feminist argument for equality appeals to the idea of social progress on which modern colonialism is founded.
>
> (10–11)

British women thus served as far more active agents of empire than their otherwise disempowered status might suggest. Sharpe's work gives insistent visibility to the racism inherent in the colonial enterprise and to the ways women at home are implicated in imperialism.

McClintock's *Imperial Leather* extends and complicates the relation of home and empire, showing that they shape each other in the interests of wealth. She finds that "the mass-marketing of empire as a global system was intimately wedded to the Western reinvention of domesticity" (17). Home becomes racialized and colonial space domesticated:

> The cult of domesticity, I argue, became central to British imperial identity, contradictory and conflictual as that was, and an intricate dialectic emerged. Imperialism suffused the Victorian cult of domesticity and the historic separation of the private and the public, which took shape around colonialism and the idea of race. At the same time, colonialism took shape around the Victorian invention of domesticity and the idea of the home.
>
> (36)

McClintock's work defines the interlocking ideologies of home and empire, both grounded in racial and cultural superiority that made the domination of colonial spaces and the export of domestic values appear not only justified, but even benevolent. She also observes the gendering of nationalisms—"All nationalisms are gendered, all are invented and all are dangerous" (352)—and of nations, including postcolonial ones. Her analysis leads toward the conclusion articulated by Qadri Ismail, that "women cannot find home in nation" (218).

In *The Politics of Home*, George undertakes a related analysis of the overlapping constructions of home and nation, seen in the context of postcolonial, feminist, and deconstructive theory. George writes, "Homes are not neutral places. Imagining a home is as political an act as is imagining a nation. Establishing either is a display of hegemonic power" (6). While the common rhetoric of home invokes "an ahistoric, metaphoric and often sentimental story line," the feminist critics George analyzes expose the political implications of sentimental narratives of home (11).[15] In readings of English, Indian, and postcolonial texts, George insistently returns to the politics of home places. She concludes with cautious endorsements of "a daily resisting of the safety proffered by safe places": "Perhaps it is time we examined varying notions of home to see what can be recycled in less oppressive, less exclusionary ways" (33).[16]

The works of Caren Kaplan and Inderpal Grewal, writing separately and together, similarly complicate previous thinking about women, home, and empire. In *Home and Harem*, Grewal considers home as a counterpole of imperial travel, a "space of return and of consolidation of the Self enabled by the encounter with the 'Other' " (6). Yet, despite the implication that home enables a return to the imperial Self, she envisions a possible resistance beginning at home: "My project, from a feminist viewpoint, presents home as a place mediated in the colonial discursive space through notions of the harem. I see home not only as the original site of nationalism but also of feminism, since it is here that women can resist nationalist formations by rearticulating them as a site of struggle rather than of resolution" (7). Caren Kaplan considers travel and displacement in *Questions of Travel*, aiming "to historicize the notions of 'home' and 'away' in the production of both critical and literary discourses" (7). She sees historically situated displacements as the condition of postmodern lives: "There is not necessarily a preoriginary space in which to stay after modern imperialist expansion. But identities cling to us, or even produce us, nonetheless. Many of us have locations in the plural" (7). The nostalgic home yields to locations and places, with the recognition that absolute security is a fantasy and displacement always a possibility.

From a kindred feminist postcolonial position, Friedman argues in *Mappings* for the urgency of spatial analysis and geopolitical literacy in the analysis of women, home, and political encounters. Her geopolitical approach focuses on "questions of power as they manifest in relation to space on the planet Earth" and aims to "break down the geopolitical boundaries between home and elsewhere by locating the ways the local and the global are always already interlocking and complicitous" (109–10). Friedman's book places feminism in a contemporary transnational context and establishes the value of spatial reading. She calls for further study of home, highlighting the

> continued need for revisionist feminist work on power relations within the home or the domestic. As ethnographies of dwelling, such work has usefully troubled the concept of home, denaturalizing domestic space and showing that it is anything but 'stable,' and is frequently a site of intense alterity, oppression, marginalization, and resistance for women.
>
> (113)

With its large frame of reference and its invention of a postcolonial feminist geopolitics, *Mappings* is an enabling resource for this project.[17]

Adding an American focus to the study of women, home, and imperialism, Amy Kaplan's work also articulates crucial linkages between domesticity, nation, empire, and racism. Kaplan's work is particularly important for its challenge to "the traditional understanding of imperialism as a one-way imposition of power in distant colonies," exploring instead how imperialism reflects and shapes national culture at home (2002: 1). In *The Anarchy of Empire in the Making of U. S. Culture*, she observes that the domestic is articulated in terms "inextricably intertwined with shifting notions of 'foreign'" (18). Home and nation, interdependent and similarly reliant on "racialized conceptions of the foreign," cannot exclude the foreign; instead, they contain within themselves "those wild or foreign elements that must be tamed" (25–26). Kaplan's analysis enables complex readings of the racism that occurs in both colonial sites and home countries, as the foreign other represents

> the gaping hole upon which the ideology of middle-class domesticity was constructed and reinforced. Under the self-contained orderly home lies the anarchy of imperial conquest. Not a retreat from the masculine sphere of empire building, domesticity both reenacts and conceals its origin in the violent appropriation of foreign land.

[...] "Manifest Domesticity" turns an imperial nation into a home by producing and colonizing specters of the foreign that lurk inside and outside its ever-shifting borders.

(50)

Kaplan's text articulates the function of the racist logic basic to imperialism and makes visible the exclusion of the foreign other that appears throughout contemporary transnational fiction.

Like these other postcolonial feminists whose work I have briefly recalled here, I intend in this project to link domestic practices and imperial projects, women's constructed roles in homes and the conditions for their resistance. My project engages transnational women's fiction that unsettles home, dispels the sentimental narrative of homecoming, and creates displaced, de-nationalized, and sometimes even disembodied women. In the narratives of contemporary women writers from four continents, the stability and value of home come symptomatically undone, and with it woman's status as figurehead for traditional nationalism. Nancy Armstrong reminds us that fiction is "the document" and "the agency of cultural history," both reflecting and normalizing what culture has created and acting as an agent of ideology (23). In this sense, much is at stake in the representation of women and homes in fiction. When contemporary writers move women's bodies out of homes, they interrogate a foundational equation, one on which much else has been built. When they move men's and women's interests— their arts, creativity, and personal energy—out of homes, they begin to unsettle the house. They explore the possibilities for change, dramatize new, more creative and resistant ways in which human subjects may think further afield, and encourage more radical departures than we have yet undertaken from the places we call "home."

2
Homeless in the American Empire: Toni Morrison's *Paradise*

In contrast to Britain, whose visibly imperialist mission led it to colonize much of the world in the nineteenth century, the United States has concealed its imperialism and positioned itself beside the postcolonial "settler colonies" dominated by imperial powers. Public myths of American origins and identity ring with assertions of individual liberty and the rights of the common man, asserted against the oppressions of imperial Britain. Amy Kaplan writes that "Most current studies of imperial and postcolonial culture [...] tend to omit discussions of the United States as an imperial power," in part because nationalist discourse has insistently defined the nation as "inherently anti-imperialist" (1993: 17, 12). Even postcolonial scholars looking at US imperialism can miss it, as do Ashcroft, Griffiths, and Tiffin in their influential book, *The Empire Writes Back*. Listing postcolonial literatures, they include the United States with Canada, Australia, and others as rejecting imperial assumptions: "The literatures of the USA should also be placed in this category. Perhaps because of its current position of power, and the neo-colonizing role it has played, its post-colonial nature has not been generally recognized. But its relationship with the metropolitan centre as it evolved over the last two centuries has been paradigmatic for post-colonial literatures everywhere" (2).[1] In fact, the ideological assumption of a position critical of British imperialism actually camouflages the functioning of the United States as an imperial power.

A distinctive feature of US imperialism, I believe, is an anxiety over race, emerging from the historical enslavement and domination of other races, not abroad and at a distance as in the case of Britain and its colonies, but at home. Edward Said reminds us in *Culture and Imperialism* that "the vocabulary of classic nineteenth-century imperial culture is plentiful with words and concepts like 'inferior' or 'subject races,' 'subordinate peoples,' 'dependency,' 'expansion,' and 'authority' " used by Europe to designate its "others" abroad whose constructed lack justifies white dominion: "certain territories and people *require* and beseech domination" (xxv, 9). Much as Europe defined itself through the construction of an Oriental other—Said notes that "European culture gained in strength and identity by setting itself off against the Orient as a sort of surrogate and even underground self" (1979: 3)—America has in special ways "orientalized" its African American and Native American populations, building a case for Caucasian manifest destiny on its constructed readings of their inferiority. This racial hierarchy becomes more vividly important, more contested, collapsed, and reasserted in post-Civil-War America because descendants of imported slaves and native inhabitants—the victims of American imperialism—remain as citizens, neighbors, and participants in the United States. In the face of claims made by African Americans and Native Americans for civil rights, some apologists for US imperialism publicly asserted that whites must govern, speak for, and represent citizens of color; indeed, as Kaplan observes, the work of writers including Sarah Josepha Hale turns blacks into foreigners and thus strips them of a place inside the national home (2002: 26). The perception of their alien status predates the Declaration of Independence, justifying their importation as slaves by some of the earliest settlers; and it postdates the Civil War, Reconstruction, and the 1898 Spanish–American War,[2] rationalizing an ongoing color line.

Toni Morrison explores these issues of race, empire, and the American home in lectures and essays as well as in justly acclaimed fiction. A passionate reader who insists she is not a critic, she interprets Melville in her 1988 lecture ("Unspeakable Things Unspoken: The Afro-American Presence in American Literature") as a bold critic of the racist premises implicit in American imperialism. The passage bears quoting at length because it reflects her sophisticated understanding of Melville's approach to race and power:

His attitude to slavery alone would not have condemned him to the almost autistic separation visited upon him. And if he felt convinced that blacks were worthy of being treated like whites, or that capitalism was dangerous – he had company or could have found it. But to question the very notion of white progress, the very idea of racial superiority, of whiteness as privileged place in the evolutionary ladder of humankind, and to meditate on the fraudulent, self-destroying philosophy of that superiority, to "pluck it out from under the robes

of Senators and Judges," to drag the "judge himself to the bar," – that was dangerous, solitary, radical work. Especially then. Especially now.
(40–41)

Texts like *Moby Dick* expose the hollowness of Western assumptions (a fraudulent, self-destructive philosophy) of white racial superiority, privilege, and progress, brought to consciousness by the unspoken (and "unspeakable") Afro-American presence in canonical American literature. Melville, Morrison says, exiles himself to an isolated space at the radical fringe where he dares not only to oppose slavery, but also to expose the leaders of his society as participants in an imperial racist deception. "What is being nulled" in the empire and its canonical texts, the "presence-that-is-assumed-not-to-exist" of the Afro-American, reflects deep social anxieties that emerge from the fraudulent assertion of white supremacy and the corresponding repression of blackness (41).

Morrison amplifies her ideas about whiteness, race, and empire in American literature in her best-known nonfiction, *Playing in the Dark: Whiteness and the Literary Imagination.* White and black appear doubled and twinned, "almost always in conjunction," blackness functioning as "the shadow": "a dark and abiding presence that moves the hearts and texts of American literature with fear and longing. This haunting, a darkness from which our early literature seemed unable to extricate itself, suggests the complex and contradictory situation in which American writers found themselves" (33). The slave population provides a powerful occasion for meditations on "problems of human freedom, its lure and its elusiveness" as well as "meditations on terror" (37). A uniquely "American Africanism—a fabricated brew of darkness, otherness, alarm, and desire" comes to serve as "a playground for the imagination" (38); it "informs in compelling and inescapable ways the texture of American literature" (46). Morrison suggests that Africanism serves Americans in the ways Said sees Orientalism serving Europe:[3] it enables America to construct itself, and Americanness more broadly, as white and privileged (47): "Africanism is the vehicle by which the American self knows itself as not enslaved, but free; not repulsive, but desirable; not helpless, but licensed and powerful; not history-less, but historical; not damned, but innocent; not a blind accident of evolution, but a progressive fulfillment of destiny" (52). The presence of the "fabricated" African[4] enables white America to construct itself as the binary opposite to all it fears, an imaginary version of all it longs for and desires (freedom, purpose, agency, innocence, and manifest destiny) wrested out of what it has projected onto the African. An anxious racial hierarchy, asserted at the outset of the colonization of America and then repressed to become the secret, enabling ground of the cultural imaginary, becomes the central and necessary metaphor for American identity. In Morrison's complex assessment, American literature revolves around race because America understands itself through race.

Morrison's fiction imagines characters (black, white, Native American, biracial and multiracial) living in the shadow of the "wholly racialized society that is the United States" (*Playing* xii). I focus on *Paradise* for its ambitious choice to situate a present-day conflict over the shape of home in the context of US history, connecting events in 1976 with origins that antedate the nation's founding. This American bicentennial novel engages home and homeland together, seeing private domestic spaces as shaped by and expressing national policies and ambitions.[5] A novel about the yearning for home, *Paradise* imagines the lives of citizens, including the descendants of slaves whose labor built the nation, left homeless in the American empire. Their efforts to create a separate, safe space inside America have tragic results for the African-American community of Ruby: as if summoned into being by the white cultural imaginary, Ruby's citizens perform the very model of blackness dictated by white culture—separate, silent, invisible, careful guardians of racial purity, practitioners of the very capitalist policies that were used in earlier centuries to justify their ancestors' capture and enslavement. The story of Ruby, explored in the first section of this essay, shows the failure of America as national homeland to open up a space for black citizens to be at home. The stories of the five women gathered at the Convent, analyzed in the second section, dramatize the futile quests of individual "homemakers" to make a home in America. Shaped by an imperialist legacy of racism and violence, America can be neither home nor paradise; it can only exile beings. Said reflects that "Exile [...] is the unhealable rift forced between a human being and a native place, between the self and its true home: its essential sadness can never be surmounted" (2000: 173).

Some critical readings of the novel have suggested that Morrison takes the reader home with the lesson of the women's maturation or their ambiguous afterlife at the novel's end; instead, I see the novel's tentative hope arising from the ways it unsettles common assumptions about the paradise home. Rather than an exclusive place for those who are just the same, Morrison's narrative suggests that paradise might come from an openness to those who are truly other. I believe she holds, with Said, that

No one today is purely *one* thing. [...] Imperialism consolidated the mixture of cultures and identities on a global scale. But its worst and most paradoxical gift was to allow people to believe that they were only, mainly, exclusively, white, or Black, or Western, or Oriental. [...] It is more rewarding—and more difficult—to think concretely and sympathetically, contrapuntally, about others than only about "us."

(1993: 336)

The narrative practices of *Paradise* point in such a direction, allowing Morrison to convey an imagination of better alternatives. The narrator enacts a way of looking, thinking, and understanding that avoids racism, as the third section of this essay argues; readers see the effects of racism on all of the characters' lives, but their skin color is invisible. The first line of the novel identifies one of the five women as white in the eyes of Ruby's men, but the narrator does not use these racial categories. She looks in, conveying motives, histories, and hopes, and she includes characters with flaws and failures in the range of her sympathetic attention. Modeling an understanding of life as process rather than product, the narrator emphasizes changes over time and withholds the closure that would bring the uncertain energies of her narrative to rest. She rejects the imperial aerie—that uplifted perch allowing true omniscience and finality; instead life, art, and understanding remain works-in-progress even as the novel concludes. Morrison's unique narrative perspective, a kind of mosaic insight that resembles omniscience without its totalizing impulse, is a way of thinking "concretely and sympathetically, contrapuntally, about others" and thus a way to re-imagine the paradise home.

Ruby: In and out of the American homeland

The community of Ruby has deep historical roots in the American homeland: these demonstrate the costs to African Americans of a degrading history of slavery, institutional racism, and oppression. While the stories of the women in the Convent reflect the costs to individuals of racism in an atomized modern America that has forgotten history, Ruby's collective story dramatizes the long-term afflictions of a race. That the ancestors of Ruby are a proud, regal, noble people who defend each other and function as a communal society makes their exploitation and abuse all the more bitter. That their descendants turn away from the principles that sustained them through persecution and oppression gives their story a tragic dimension. Under the degrading pressures of a racist and capitalist society, they replicate what has victimized them, reproducing the values of the slave-holding culture that made them homeless. And they do this in the name of settling a home in America.

The ancestors of Ruby came to America as slaves, stolen and exported from their African homes in order to serve a global imperial economy that depended on unpaid labor. Slaves have no right to the privacy, safety, or self-possession that home normally connotes; indeed, they have no time or space in which to be non-economic beings. As Gillian Brown points out, "The distinction between work and family is eradicated in the slave, for whom there is no separation between economic and private status" (15). While they dwell in shelters provided by the owner, they can have only the most ironic relationship to homes—for them, places where they are objectified and abused, places like the plantation in *Beloved* named "Sweet Home." In a double sense, slavery robs them of home: it wrests them away from homelands, family, and ancestral continuities in Africa, and it strips them of the right to be at home or make a home anywhere. Once freed with the end of the Civil War, their primary goal must be to establish homes; separated from Africa by time, space, money, and language, they look for home inside the nation they have helped to build.

Ruby's ancestors take pride in their African heritage and their history of survival through mutual support. Town historian Pat Best calls them "eight-rock, a deep deep level in the coal mines" for their blue-black color, preserved from their arrival around 1770 down through generations of families that intermarried and avoided the taint of Caucasian intermixture (193). Elected to office during Reconstruction, they participate in governing for 5 years; then they are thrown out of office and "reduced to penury and/ or field labor" (193). They walk to Oklahoma in 1890; on the way, a traumatic "Disallowing" occurs, when the travelers are turned away from an all-black town called "Fairly" by its lighter-skinned black inhabitants who see "the sign of racial purity" as "a stain" (194).[6] The Disallowing turns the founding families to the quest for a separate estate—a home detached and insulated from the nation it inhabits, an island-haven where their African heritage and unmixed race will be respected, even prized. The Old Fathers found Haven, which gradually loses population after the depression; the New Fathers return from World War II and found Ruby in 1950, still aspiring to "the one all-black town worth the pain" (5). As Holly Flint points out, however, this very rhetoric mimics white exceptionalism "and gives carte blanche, at least symbolically, to the rest of American society to proceed with its own imperial destiny" (604).

Paradise wonders whether African American people can find or make a home in America, whether its history of racism can ever yield to a nonracist and psychically safe space. As she was completing the novel, Morrison published a meditation on the relation between race and the American home in a short essay titled "Home." Signifying on the metaphorics of house and home, she writes that throughout her career she has engaged questions like "how to convert a racist house into a race-specific yet nonracist home" (5). She wants "to take what is articulated as an elusive race-free paradise and domesticate it;" in other words, "to concretize" a home without racism, a place where difference "is prized but unprivileged" (8, 12). "In my current project," the novel *Paradise*, "I want to see whether or not race-specific, race-free language is both possible and meaningful in narration. And I want to inhabit, walk around, a site clear of racist detritus, a place where race both matters and is rendered impotent" (9). In her essay, Morrison quotes a passage from *Paradise* celebrating women's ability to walk safely at night in Ruby and comments, "That description is meant to evoke not only the safety and freedom outside the race house, but to suggest contemporary searches and yearnings for social space that is psychically and physically safe" (10). In such a paradise home, to use Cornel West's phrase, race matters and racism disappears.

In Morrison's novel, the founders of Haven and Ruby approach their utopian experiment with idealism and commitment. Their enduring pride in a pure African heritage makes race matter; race is rendered impotent to harm in a community comprised of only one race. The founders build outside what Morrison calls "the racial house" by locating Ruby 90 miles from any other town. Lest outsiders accidentally come upon them, Ruby's designers hide all public activity: Ruby has no bus service, no gas station, "no public place to sit down" (67–68), and "no recognizable business district" (45). The drug store has no sign—businesses camouflage their activity so visitors do not find any reason to stop. Ruby detaches itself from the nation in order to create an alternative to the "racist house" African Americans have known.

Conditions "Out There" explain and justify their secession. In the first section, the narrator invokes the powerful dangers in the outer world:

> Ten generations had known what lay Out There: space, once beckoning and free, became unmonitored and seething; became a void where random and organized evil erupted when and where it chose

[...] Out There where your children were sport, your women quarry, and where your very person could be annulled [...] Out There where every cluster of whitemen looked like a posse, being alone was being dead.

(16)

Outside Ruby, there are towns "where Colored were run out of town overnight," left "dead or maimed," or made "victims of spontaneous whippings, murders and depopulation by arson" (112). The decision to enclose and hide the town and to exclude outsiders reflects on the continuing institutional racism in America, expressed not only in violent persecution but also in grinding poverty, substandard education, restricted job opportunities, and the heavy death toll of African Americans in Vietnam.

As a utopian experiment, Ruby aims to be an alternative to what lurks Out There. One important goal of Ruby is safety, especially for the most vulnerable members of the community, the young women. As boys, the twins Steward and Deacon Morgan visited other black towns and saw "nineteen Negro ladies arrange themselves on the steps of the town hall" for a photograph (109). The women wear delicate summer dresses, mostly white, two yellow, and small pale hats. They are slim, scented with verbena, sparkly-eyed, laughing with each other, and elegant in "thin leather shoes," with skin "creamy and luminous in the afternoon sun" (109). These "ladies" leave both twins with a memory "pastel colored and eternal" of beautiful young women who are safe enough to enjoy and display their femininity, prized enough to be recorded on the town hall steps (110). While black women were sexually vulnerable under slavery and, according to Mary Helen Washington, constructed as "automatically immoral," these "ladies" echo in the imagination of the Morgan twins with elegance and safety (38). Light emanates from their eyes and skin, and their apparel signifies ease and protection. Neither preyed upon nor hungry, they are the antithesis of the streetwalker Elder Morgan recalls seeing "sprawled on the pavement" in New Jersey after a white man smashes her in the face with his fist (94). Instead, young ladies who are lovely, chaste, and unafraid symbolize what a black township like Ruby, named for a well-loved woman, can produce and must defend.

Ruby's founders see their town as the longed-for home, and thus they envision an ideal domestic space to contain the "Negro lady." As Deacon surveys his town, it "seemed to him as satisfactory as ever. Quiet white and yellow houses full of industry; and in them were elegant black women at useful tasks; orderly cupboards minus surfeit or miserliness; linen laundered and ironed to perfection; good meat seasoned and ready for roasting" (111). In Ruby, the men admire their wives, "elegant black women," but perceive their value only through the performance of the "useful tasks" of homemaking. Their houses are "white and yellow" like the dresses of the 19 ladies, like genteel womanhood in a warm climate, like the colors of chaste baptism and bridal purity—as well as racial dominance—and "quiet" like the ladies themselves, being focused on industry. Another townsman comments with pride on the "quiet, orderly community" of Ruby and reflects, "Certainly there wasn't a slack or sloven woman anywhere in town" (8). Ruby's domestic space is clean, prosperous, and protected from the ample harm inflicted on black people elsewhere; but it is also a regulated space in which silent women work at narrow tasks.

A third important part of the domestic ideal in Ruby is communal sharing, symbolized in the Oven at the center of town. Regarded as property themselves under imperial capitalism, the enslaved ancestors develop a version of communism. They share goods and help each other through the worst times, acting out the utopian goals that Marianne DeKoven sees crystallized in "Radical Reconstruction, including most notably the Freedman's Bureau (1865–1872)" (111). As Deacon reflects, the history of communal support is basic to the identity of Haven, then Ruby: "families shared everything, made sure no one was short. [...] Having been refused by the world in 1890 on their journey to Oklahoma, Haven residents refused each other nothing" (108–109). When Haven is founded, Zechariah leads a group of men to build a communal oven where families gather to cook and share food. In time, the structure becomes symbolic and takes on a capital letter, and this Oven "both nourished them and monumentalized what they had done" (6–7). The Oven symbolizes the communal values and mutual respect that distinguish the founding families.

The novel shows the tragic failure of the freed slaves' social experiment and the collapse of their dream of a settled home in America. By the 1970s, Ruby has become closed and private, hostile to outsiders, estranged from history. It has become capitalist, with the bank replacing the cold Oven as the central institution. Between Haven and Ruby, sharing has given way to a lust for capitalist profits, shown especially in the Morgan brothers' drive to own, control, and decide. In Haven, Able Flood was the partner of Rector Morgan in founding a bank where "Everybody pitched in" and "bought shares" (115). But in Ruby, the partnership has been dissolved, the shares called in, and the bank becomes the property of the Morgan twins, Deacon and Steward. The brothers foreclose on Menus Jury's house, in which Steward's wife Dovey lives while her sister Soane wonders why Deacon "wasn't worried enough by their friends' money problems to help them out" (107). When Reverend Misner starts a credit union to make emergency loans to church members, in the communal spirit of Haven, Deek and Steward frown: "A man like that, willing to throw money away, could give customers ideas" (56). The bankers patrol the Oven like community police, ironically because they have come to see themselves as owners of this symbol of communal sharing. Symbolic themselves of fraternal mutuality, the twins have previously had intertwined identities like Roy's Estha and Rahel, but significant inner differences drive them apart as the novel ends.

In the struggle to "convert a racist house into a race-specific yet nonracist home," Ruby practices a racial exclusiveness that reproduces the assumptions and ratifies the separations in the surrounding white culture. Excluded by whites, they exclude in return; disallowed by the light-skinned blacks of Fairly, they disallow biracial people. Some of Ruby's leading citizens are overtly hostile to all outsiders, especially to those without "eight-rock" skin. When a white couple with a sick baby drives through town in a snowstorm, they provide only minimal help: distinguishing between "Lost folks or lost whites," they will later discover the bodies in the car (122, 272). They condemn Roger Best's wife as "dung" and prevent Menus Jury from marrying his beloved, both women of "sunlight skin" and thus products of what they consider "racial tampering" (201, 197). In an interview for *The Washington Post* on the publication of *Paradise*, Morrison worries about the book's reception: "'I'm fearful they'll talk about it as a book about racist black people,' says Morrison. 'You think they'll do that to me?' " (Streitfeld B2). In effect, Ruby's leaders reproduce the separatist logic that has driven them, for their own safety, to secede from American society.

The tragedy for Ruby's dream of the race-free paradise home inheres in the way the founders frame the dream home as enclosing the same and excluding the other, generating not only violence against others but also disciplinary control over those at home, who must be kept the same. Thus Ruby's leaders discriminate based on gender as well as race. Though they adore their wives and daughters, women appear to them as the uncontained other, so that, as Morrison says, Ruby's men feel compelled "to manage and govern women" (Streitfeld B2). To invoke the terms in which Morrison characterizes the public response to Anita Hill, "as a black woman, she was contradiction itself, irrationality in the flesh" (*Race-ing Justice* xvi). Instead, Ruby's men need settled (contained, rational, predictable) women: "Women always the key, God bless 'em," says Deek Morgan (61). The patriarchs set up a system of domestic control that objectifies and imprisons the women they love. Wanting orderly houses and believing in industry, they pressure women into occupations that strangle the spirit: "Aunt Soane worked thread like a prisoner" (53). Dreaming of "quiet" houses, they silence women: Dovey and Soane keep secrets from their husbands, Pat Best conceals her views from her father, and Arnette is excluded from a meeting to discuss her future: "I'm her father. I'll arrange her mind," says Fleet (61). Dovey, Soane, and Pat appear alone and silent, reflecting on conditions they will not discuss with their men or with each other.

With a vision of women as beautiful and virginal, the townsmen also police women's sexuality from birth: the Cary girls are named "Hope, Chaste, Lovely and Pure," and Billie Delia endures permanent shaming because, at three, she took off her underwear to ride a horse (208, 151). No wonder, then, that Ruby's men venerate the Oven: powerful symbol of domestic ideals including heart and hearth, it also symbolizes the ideal woman whose sexuality and fertility can be controlled by the man who lights the fire. The cold Oven of the 1970s reflects the domestic losses—infertility, sick babies, miscarriages and abortions, silent and depressed wives, dead sons and estranged daughters—that plague Ruby. As Pat Best comes to realize through her study of the town's history, "everything that worries them must come from women" (217).[7]

Its leading citizens are as conservative as any group in America in their dedication to preserving traditions; their commitment to a change-less status quo makes them stifle their children and close off the outer world. Instead of following the founders in an ongoing quest for a better world, Ruby's men dedicate themselves to protecting what they have. The extended battle over the Oven's inscription shows how text-oriented and static they have become: rather than open the text to new interpretation, they fight with their young people to preserve an old one. They opt out of history, paying little attention to the news of the outside world and seeming to prefer the bunkered safety of Ruby to participation in the events of the day. News of the outer world rolls off and leaves people untouched: few mourn the death of Martin Luther King except the outsider, Reverend Richard Misner; none seem stirred by Black Power or the civil rights movement. Global and national events enter the novel only through outsiders, as when Gigi's grandfather in Alcorn, Mississippi talks about the deaths of King, Kennedy, Evers, and Malcolm X (65) or when Misner weighs his sense of desolation over "the drawn-out abasement of a noxious President" and "the long, unintelligible war" in Vietnam (160).[8] History is mostly mute or absent in a town that appears "still" and "as though no one lived there" (45).

Ironically, then, the town of Ruby comes to perform the very model of African American identity called for by the imperialists who managed the slave trade. Silent by choice on issues of equity and civil rights, invisible in the political movements of their times, Ruby's citizens voluntarily enact the apolitical blackness desired by the most ardent enemies of racial equality. At a time when the de-segregation of schools is occurring all over America, Ruby polices its young to insure that they do not mix with others of different races. Making racial purity the prized element in the community, they recuperate the race-based discriminations of the society that persecuted them; hiding from the violence of white supremacists, they become quiet, invisible blacks whose choice not to intervene enables the continuation of white supremacy. Ruby's leaders spend their energy guarding a status quo that has never yet opened up justice or equal opportunities for them or their children. While the narrator approaches Ruby's patriarchs with a deep sympathy, and while Misner calls them "outrageously beautiful, flawed and proud people" (306), the novel presents them as figures of a tragic blindness, nowhere more pointed than in the violence they direct at the women of the Convent.

As Ruby's men see them, the five women who live at the Convent represent threats to the settled home. All five appear transgressive, and all fail at or opt out of domestic orderings. Each one has in some way run away from home. Their collective life at the Convent defies the conventions that bring women together in "orders." Although they share histories of disastrous relationships, they represent different versions of femininity that threaten Ruby's ideals of virtuous, industrious, chaste women. To be sure, the novel exposes the men's view of the women as incorrect, partial, and deluded; but in their view, the women are "sluts," "one half naked all the time"(Gigi sunbathes nude and dresses provocatively); they were seen "kissing on each other" and may be lesbian (Seneca is not kissing Pallas, but she has had a lesbian encounter with Norma Keene Fox and may be bisexual); they may have crying "Babies hid away," dead (Mavis has inadvertently killed her 3-month-old twins) or alive (Pallas has been raped by strangers and is pregnant, though unmarried); and, "like witches," "they got powers" (Consolata is known to "practice" the gift of "stepping in" or "in-sight") (275–76). From the perspective of Ruby's founding fathers, a racially inclusive group of women living together, headed by a hybrid witch, represents otherness gone wildly sinister.

When they invade the Convent, the men resolutely misread the signs of the women's domestic lives and frame their indignation and outrage in terms of the women's perceived violations of domestic order. Seeking a coven of nasty women, they find signs of domestic sloth; everywhere they look they see dirt and the absence of provident industry. Finding dusty mason jars in the pantry, they assume laziness: "Slack, they think. August just around the corner and these women have not even sorted, let alone washed, the jars" (5). The men misread priorities and miss the industry visible in several rising loaves of bread. Upstairs, they find "soiled things," and "no toilet paper" in the bathroom (9). Seneca's letter from her mother, written in lipstick and carried all her life as a pledge of love, becomes "a letter written in blood so smeary its satanic message cannot be deciphered" (7). In the chapel, remnants of the Catholic nuns strike the protestant witnesses as dangerous idolatry, and "Things look uncleaned" (12). In the basement, whose scrubbed stone floor they do not notice, the men see pictures that confirm the worst: "What they see is the devil's bedroom, bathroom, and his nasty playpen" (17). The men set out to clean the house. They think of the massacre as getting rid of trash, of the women as "detritus: throwaway people" (4). Their guns are "clean, handsome" weapons (3). Their version of domestic order reaches its culmination in the grotesque housecleaning that frames the novel. Where whiteness has not been given priority, they "shoot the white girl first" and thus return to a simple counter-racism that keeps the deadly binaries intact.

The Convent: Making home in a bullet

Early reviews and essays on *Paradise* largely overlooked the stories that bring the four women (Mavis, Grace/Gigi, Seneca and Pallas) to the Convent and gave slight attention even to Consolata's history. Some reviewers found the women to be insufficiently distinguished from each other: Kakutani's negative review objects that almost all the characters are "two-dimensional," and Storace's thoughtful and positive review claims that "The women in the Convent, despite their carefully differentiated biographies, blur together" (Kakutani, Storace 69). As a result, critics often treat the women as a single unit, focusing on the state of accord they reach at the end of the novel and interpreting them as a worthy, saving alternative to the men of Ruby. Versions of this reading can be seen in the titles of reviews like "The War Between Men and Women" and "Worthy Women, Unredeemable Men" (Menand, Kakutani).[9]

More complex essays also read the women as a positive opposite to the men: Magali Michael acknowledges that the individual women "remain quite distinct" but treats them as a unified coalition "that is constructive and inclusive" (652, 650); Justine Tally writes that "In contrast [to Ruby], the Convent is free from the public or dominant narrative" (41); Kristin Hunt believes that "These women have an entirely different relationship with their environment than those living in Ruby" (125); and Roberta Rubenstein argues, "the community of Ruby is based on 'the fathers' law' " while "the Convent might be said to operate on the values of 'the mothers' law' " (146–47). The prevailing view, summed up by J. Brooks Bouson, is that the novel sets up "contradictory value systems embodied in the opposing worlds of Ruby and the Convent" (213).

The women of the Convent and the men of Ruby are actually far more similar than these readings allow, I believe. Morrison herself rejects the view that the novel poses a conflict between opposed genders: "I could be understood to be saying that patriarchy is bad and matriarchy is good. In fact, I don't believe either of those things. I don't deal in these binaries" (Streitfeld B2). To read the novel as a single meditation on the issues that relate the two communities, readers need to register the common preoccupation with home and its failures in both locations; then the novel appears as a single, richly diverse exploration of homelessness in America. The stories of the five women reflect on the failure of childhood homes, where inadequate, addicted, imprisoned, or damaged parents create environments that wound and cripple. In terms the citizens of Ruby would understand, each woman has been disallowed in her original home. Through most of the novel, they escape, lie, wound themselves and others, and grieve in secret for the homes they have lost or left. Their efforts to *go* home to a secure space fail miserably. Their attempts to *make* homes with pathetically inadequate resources fall grotesquely short. The individual stories of the women mirror the collective story of Ruby: both sets of characters yearn for home with a similar intensity.[10] The Convent women have their own flaws and failures, long stages of whining, discord, and drift that make Consolata want "to snap their necks"; the Ruby men have a vital idealism in their quest, which gives them "innocent eyes" and leads Misner to call them "outrageously beautiful" (222, 12, 306). Far from endorsing the women and condemning the men, Morrison asks readers to consider their related yearning for home in America.[11]

Like the citizens of Ruby, the Convent women also bear the wounds of racism, intermixed with those of gender and class. Consolata is bi- or multiracial; the others include one white and three black women, though the race of each one is not revealed. Morrison says, "I wanted the readers to wonder about the race of those girls until those readers understood that their race didn't matter. [...] Race is the least reliable information you can have about someone. It's real information, but it tells you next to nothing" (Gray 67).[12] Because they all remember experiences of racism in America (Gigi's bleeding black boy, Pallas's crazy woman on the escalator, Seneca's neighbors in tenement housing, and Mavis's hitchhiking passengers), traces and afterimages appear in the Convent. Even though the women do not see or speak to each other in racialized terms, race exerts a hovering shadow over their histories.

While Ruby's story reflects on the failed collective home for African American people, the inhabitants of the Convent recall failed homes that comment on the lack of safe domestic harbor for women in America. The five women's stories first appear to be personal and individual; they were not valued, made safe, or given ease in widely separated homes whose gritty feel and spirit-killing lack of hope emerge in detail. They grieve over lost, incapable, or betraying mothers and violent or absent fathers. They remember being dismissed as useless, stupid, and defective, being targets of sexual predation, abuse, and neglect. Their lacks, hungers, and hurts reveal the gendered bias with which they have lived and which has ground their unworthiness deep beneath whatever colored skin they wear. For women, craving the feeling of home leads in one way or another to making home in a bullet: the bullet-shaped Convent where they seek refuge, invaded by men with guns on the first page of the novel, reflects on the state of domestic violence against women in America.

The four women who join Consolata in the Convent have fled from other bullet homes, places where they were abused and neglected. Mavis escapes from a violent, abusive partner whose wrath leads her to the inadvertent murder of her twin babies. Though the deaths are Mavis's fault, the narrative shows a larger picture than what the self-righteous reporter takes from her interview: Frank comes home only sporadically, drinks heavily, and beats her so badly she has been treated eleven times at the local hospital (28). On the day of the deaths, he refused to eat Spam and would not keep the babies, so she took them with her in the Cadillac to the Higgledy Piggledy and left them in the hot car, where they died (22–24). Gigi, named Grace for her mother, has no family: "Her mother was unlocatable; her father on death row" (257). She has spent years on "entertainment and adventure," then worked in the civil rights movement where none of the others take her seriously; of her lost partner Mikey, she reflects, "Nobody could call that love" (257, 256). After she sees a bleeding black boy shot in Oakland, she flees, looking for erotic fulfillment and temporary distraction. Born to a 14-year-old mother, Seneca is abandoned at five in tenement housing and sent to foster care; when a foster-brother rapes her, her foster-mother tends the jagged cut left by a safety pin with pity but refuses to acknowledge the abuse (261). Pallas has been abandoned by her mother at three and raised by a father preoccupied with his work; she takes her first lover to visit her mother and the two become sexually involved. After Pallas flees, she is attacked and raped by strangers (253). For each of these women, home has been a place of betrayal, neglect, and abuse, with varying levels of violence directed against them because they are women.

They gather in a bullet-shaped house, symbolic of the American home-land, with a complex history linked to the abuse of minorities and women. In this house, the novel's meditations on the yearning for home among African Americans and women coalesce, for the place has witnessed, sheltered, and enabled the exploitation and mistreatment of both groups. Originally an embezzler's mansion, the place speaks of "Fright": "Shaped like a live cartridge, it curved to a deadly point" (71). The decorations reduce women to fetish and commodity: there are "female-torso candleholders," "nipple-tipped doorknobs," and "alabaster vagina" ashtrays (72). Though the bullet shape points north toward the "lawmen" who eventually arrive to arrest the embezzler, the bullet-house actually figures the violence against objectified women implied in its decorations and acted out in the murderous invasion that frames the novel. The second inhabitants of the house are teaching Sisters who remove the signs of sexuality as fully as possible and convert the space to a boarding school for Indian girls (224). They hang paintings like the one Gigi sees, of Saint Catherine "On her knees. A knocked-down look, cast-up begging eyes," and an "I-give-up face" as she holds a platter to a lord (74). Favoring obsequious, servile women, and believing that only whites have access to divinity, the nuns discipline their Arapaho charges toward assimilation as subordinate subjects in American culture. They replace the girls' native names, ban their language and their tribal heritage, and even forbid the lullabies of their people (237–38). While they house Consolata, the biracial girl brought from Brazil by Mary Magna, the nuns keep her in a menial servant's position; she does manual labor and is never invited to join the order. The bullet-house has an American history, one recapitulating the oppression of women and minorities.

The bullet-house suggests by contrast what people (women and men of all races) want in homes: they want to be at home, settled at ease in flesh and spirit. They want to be respected, loved, cherished, safe, comfortable and comforted. In the words describing the paradise home at the end of Morrison's novel, they want the "solace" that comes of "reaching age in the company of the other; of speech shared and divided bread smoking from the fire; the unambivalent bliss of going home to be at home—the ease of coming back to love begun" (318). In the absence of such a home, the women are hungry, but as Consolata tells them in the speech that changes everyone, they do not know what they want, so she must "teach you what you are hungry for" (262). Her own life experience leads her to advise the women that they crave mixed blessings of flesh and spirit, warm bread as well as company, shared speech, and love. She invokes the paradise home in which both Eve and Mary can be embraced together: "Never break them in two. Never put one over the other. Eve is Mary's mother. Mary is the daughter of Eve" (263). Eve, the mother of all flesh, is also mother of Mary, mother of redemptive spirit; far from abjuring the body in favor of the soul, Consolata celebrates their unity.

While the balanced and affirming home would satisfy both flesh and spirit, their time in the bullet-house has led each woman to center her energies on flesh alone, leaving her unmet spiritual yearnings to be camouflaged and ignored as best as she can. The women attempt to make the flesh sufficient. Gigi pampers hers, sunbathes naked, wears revealing clothes, and luxuriates in the bath (168). Her inverse reflection, Seneca punishes her flesh to dull the emotional and spiritual pain, "secretly slicing her thighs, her arms. Wishing to be the queen of scars" (222). Mavis, whose lack of acceptable food has led to the death of her babies, turns to feeding the body, while Pallas, who has struggled with excess weight since her early youth and feels like "a butterball" (178), revolts against her own flesh, especially the baby growing inside her after the rape. For 8 years after Mary Magna dies, Consolata seeks amnesia in alcohol.

Linking the novel's interests in race and gender, Consolata's history amplifies the longing for home among the homeless. A child of the streets in Brazil, Consolata is nine, homeless, and already sexually abused when Sister Mary Magna takes her to the United States (223). Her first and last home is the bullet-shaped Convent: an odd, ironic, institutional "home" that is removed from people of "smoky, sundown skin" like her own (223). Though her steady practice of Catholicism and her abiding love for Mary Magna give her comfort, the Convent's pure spirituality does not entirely satisfy her longing for home. Her passionate affair with Deacon Morgan leads Consolata to the flesh. From her first sight of him, he calls out "home" to her. The black founders of Ruby celebrate with a horse race, and it gives Consolata her first glimpses of black skin and "reckless joy" since she left Brazil: "Then a memory of just such skin and just such men, dancing with women in the streets to music beating like an infuriated heart, torsos still, hips making small circles [...] Consolata knew she knew them" (226). She sees Deacon astride a horse, hips rocking in the saddle, and comes alive with desire. For months they make love where two trees grow together, the magical place of erotic fulfillment Gigi has searched for "where fig trees insisted on life" (236). Then Consolata bites Deacon's lip and licks the blood, driving him away and leaving her to reflect that she has made "a simple mindless transfer. From Christ, to whom one gave total surrender and then swallowed the idea of his flesh, to a living man" (240). She explains to God: "Dear Lord, I didn't want to eat him. I just wanted to go home" (240). Similar yearnings to find home in and through passion drives most of the women characters in the novel, who experience erotic desire as a synonym for love and home.

The place where Consolata and Deacon meet for their trysts has all along signaled the impossibility of "going home" through this union. Neither *domus* nor *edificio*, the structure is described as a "fire-ruined house": a non-house that burned 12 years earlier, leaving buckled floorboards, a broken chimney, and an eight-foot-tall ash cowboy warning them away (233–34). Fire, a traditional symbol for the kind of consuming passion acted out in this setting by Deacon and Consolata, ruins the house: "all was lost" (233). The only positive sign amid all the blight in this setting is "a girl with butterfly wings three feet long," an image suggesting the possibility of transformation and flight which has been left by the fire (234). In a novel where the divine presence announces itself to Dovey soon after "A trembling highway of persimmon-colored wings" of butterflies passes over (90–91), the butterfly wings on the girl suggest change and transformation.

Some readers interpret *Paradise* as culminating in the transformation of the Convent women and the recuperation of the paradise home. In Roberta Rubenstein's *Home Matters*, for example, Consolata becomes the "idealized 'good mother' before separation during infancy" and "the idealized, lost love object who is imaginatively constructed through nostalgic longing" (152–53, 148). The Convent signifies home, a place of "unconditional forgiveness and tolerance" (148). Not only are the women restored to home, but they also achieve fulfillment through reunion with the lost mother. The ending takes the women home, to a static, exclusive paradise: "Despite Morrison's expressed intentions to imagine a paradise that is neither exclusive nor static, the paradoxical image with which the novel closes belies these intentions" (158). The novel's final Edenic images exclude men, empower women, and restore an unbroken link between orphaned child and accepting mother: "In the imaginary space where maternal nurturance and filial affection are celebrated/elevated, where racial differences cease to matter, and where earthly and spiritual desires converge, even the most injured and wayward daughters may achieve a state of grace. In that paradoxical Paradise, they find themselves both safe and saved: at home at last in the idyllic but—in more than one sense—exclusive embrace of the Go(o)d Mother" (158).[13]

Such a reading effectually replaces the homes Morrison characterizes through racial, economic, social and political struggle with white, middle class homes where the quest for self-actualization can unfold in privileged psychological terms. That Rubenstein believes the novel ends in a space "where racial differences cease to matter" attests to the inadequacy of such an approach. Indeed, this interpretation recuperates the essentialized (white) maternal woman in the role of maker and keeper of the American home; it understands Morrison as luxuriating in a sentimental nostalgia for a lost past, rather than exploring the dense social currents of a troubled present. It passes over Consolata's demands for discipline, thought, and maturity, as well as her rejection of Western binaries in favor of more complex inclusiveness. It ignores the social and political conditions that make good mothering impossible for women with chronically inadequate resources because of their race, class, and gender—which is to say, virtually every woman in the novel. Such an interpretation assumes that the novel exists to take the reader home to an idyllic embrace, rather than to measure what the last sentence calls "the endless work they were created to do down here in paradise" (318).

To be sure, the novel does chronicle the healthful transformations of Consolata and the other Convent women. After a long period of drinking and willed oblivion, Consolata wakes up sober and becomes a teacher. On a January evening, she prepares a feast, demands the attention of her younger guests, and issues her first commands.[14] As she speaks, the women "do not recognize" her: they have seen her as "sweet, unthreatening" and "safe," a "granny goose who could be confided in or ignored, lied to or suborned" (262). While Consolata said to Mavis,

"Lies not allowed in this place," each woman has told lies and omitted important truths, and Consolata has accepted these falsehoods without complaint while sipping her wine (38). Then, with the table set and the feast prepared, the woman who told Mavis "People call me Connie" (38) announces, "I call myself Consolata Sosa. If you want to be here you do what I say. [...] And I will teach you what you are hungry for" (262). Consolata has known one abiding hunger: "to go home." Her teaching, sketched near the end of the novel, enables the women to heal some of the wounds they have received from being homeless in America. They have "a markedly different look" in their eyes: "sociable and connecting when they spoke to you, otherwise they were still and appraising" (265–66). They have an "adult manner" and they are "calmly themselves," "no longer haunted" (266).

Consolata's work with the women does not furnish a replacement home for them, but rather leads them to accept the nomad's transitional state. She teaches through counter-narratives that replace the American imperial home with inclusive, open, communal spaces. Clearly fantasized as an alternative to all she has known, her imagined race-free homeland has no visible private houses, no exclusiveness or nationalism. In her tales, ownership and possession, with the impulses to control and defend, are strikingly absent:

> she told them of a place where white sidewalks met the sea and fish the color of plums swam alongside children. She spoke of fruit that tasted the way sapphires look and boys using rubies for dice. [...] Then she told them of a woman named Piedade, who sang but never said a word.
>
> (263–64)

This community has public spaces, streets and sidewalks, but no homes with doors that close; ownership gives way to sharing, and difference is prized. Piedade sings of this transformed place with artistry more valued than gold or gems, and her song is given to natives, visitors, and travelers crossing race, class, and gender:

> Piedade had songs that could still a wave, make it pause in its curl listening to language it had not heard since the sea opened. Shepherds with colored birds on their shoulders came down from mountains to remember their lives in her songs. Travelers refused to board homebound ships while she sang.
>
> (285)

Piedade is the bard and maker of the world she sings, as well as the restored ancestor—the "advising, benevolent, protective, wise Black ancestor"—whose recovery, Morrison writes in an essay, allows the descendant to be "regenerated, balanced, and capable of operating on a purely moral axis" (City 39).[15] Piedade replaces the birth-mother in Brazil who abandoned Consolata to the streets and Mary Magna who stole her as a child. Piedade's song reveals the paradise home everywhere and nowhere, a product of art and imagination.[16] She turns her listeners, as Consolata turns the women, from home-bodies to perennial travelers, beings who learn their nomadic condition from her song and refuse the home-bound ship.

The lesson proves useful, for after the women are shot they become homeless. They disappear from the Convent, leaving no bodies to be buried in Ruby's graveyard with stone markers that would name and neutralize—in other words, domesticate—the uncanny energies the women have unleashed. Several of the novel's most perceptive characters imagine them continuing, sensing their energy through a door or window for Anna Flood and Richard Misner, or more simply "out there" for Billie Delia: "she hoped with all her heart that the women were out there, darkly burnished, biding their time, brass-metaling their nails, filing their incisors—but out there" (308). In the last section of narrative, the women appear "out there" to people who think of them: Gigi sees her father in prison, Pallas walks by her mother who is trying to paint her, Mavis eats a meal in a restaurant with her daughter Sally, and Seneca's mother Jean recognizes her in a stadium parking lot. They appear outside, at a lake, coming across the yard, in public spaces or on the street; except for Pallas, they appear in places they have never been, and each of the four ends by leaving a space that was not home. As she reconnects with someone whose absence, betrayal or withheld love has previously driven her to distraction, the traveling woman does not seek "to go home" through a restored bond, but rather moves onward.[17]

The uncertainty of the women's state at the end of the novel reflects Morrison's choice not to let readers go home, either. She leaves mysteries deliberately unresolved: How do the women's bodies and the Cadillac disappear from the Convent? What do their last appearances signify? In these last glimpses, the women are not ethereal spirits but rather embodied: Mavis enjoys grits and eggs and winces when her daughter hugs her, Gigi towels her short hair dry, Pallas collects a pair of sandals, and Seneca works with a friend to heal the cuts on her hands, made this time by accident. Did they die, or do they live? Rather than answer these questions in ways that would close off her narrative and put its wandering energies to rest, Morrison leaves readers uncertain, unhomed.

Unsettling home: Morrison's narrative

One of the most distinctive qualities of *Paradise* is its narrative perspective, which demonstrates throughout the qualities of vision Consolata attains at the end: inclusive, sympathetic, and insightful. The narrator listens with understanding to characters' feelings and repro- duces, in language whose eloquence leads readers to share her pity, the history that explains their most unacceptable emotions. As Jill Matus observes, the narration "belongs to this steady, sympathetic, story- telling voice, whose ability to inhabit many points of view and to pull the past into relation with the present reminds the reader of Morrison's Faulknerian heritage" (156). The narrator sees through the eyes of men and women, through the good and the not-so-good, through characters who could be thought of as "major" in the action and others who are minor and peripheral. Not only does *Paradise* have more characters than most of Morrison's novels, it also looks through more different sets of eyes. It disallows no perspective, excludes no view.

In the central section of the novel, "Divine," for example, the wedding of K. D. Morgan and Arnette Fleetwood appears refracted through at least fourteen different consciousnesses. Lying at the heart of the novel, this section explains why Morrison wanted to title the novel *War* (Mulrine), for both participants and witnesses of this union are furious, disgusted, or despairing. Images of violent breakage and sundering echo through the consciousness of every person the narrator attends: K. D., still smarting from Gigi's rejection and hurt by the loss, feels rage like a gun, as "Anger shot through him like a .32" (148). Arnette feels "a tiny rent" open in her heart and widen "like a run in a stocking," where the loss of her baby occurred (149). While blame could certainly be justified for either K. D., who drove Gigi away with controlling, abusive behavior, or Arnette, who aborted her baby by bashing herself with a broom handle, the narrator does not blame them; she reveals what they feel, how they were wounded, where they continue to hurt. In her approach to these characters (as well as Steward, Deacon, the Reverend Pulliam, and other characters of whom negative judgments are possible), the narrator guides readers, as Michael Wood observes, not "to endorse this view. But we are being asked to understand it" (121–22). By looking *inward*, to thoughts and feelings, rather than outward to skin color or surface, the narrator "destabilizes racial identity," as Linda Krumholz argues (28), and makes motivation primary.

The narrator chooses a pluralist, polyphonic insight, which enables her to present multiple sides and views with understanding. To be sure, the narrative does not endorse the men's act of violence against the Convent women, nor does it look away from the silence in Ruby's homes, the greed in Sargent Person, or the meanness in Steward Morgan. But the narrative includes rather than excludes: for example, during the wedding, Steward recalls instances where the cross marks racism, exploitation, violence, and murder, and he thinks with some justice that "A cross was no better than the bearer" (154). Steward is not only mean; he is also idealistic, thoughtful, and passionately dedicated to the safety of his people. By seeing multiple sides of him, including his memories and dreams and wounds, the narrator creates the complexity and depth that produce sympathy rather than simple judgment.

The narrative perspective in *Paradise* emphasizes thought and reflection over action and event, as the narrator places her focus on mind and memory rather than on plot. Definitive actions occur in the novel: Mary Magna dies; Arnette gives birth; K. D. slaps Gigi and Arnette; Soane miscarries; Scout and Easter die; Consolata loves and loses Deacon; Save Marie dies. All of these events occur "offstage," in the past, and emerge in the narrative later as characters think about their importance. In fact, what "plot" the novel has involves the men's decision to go to the Convent with guns, reflected on by Lone while she tries to avert their action. At the novel's beginning, "They shoot the white girl first" but the sequence hangs suspended—its outcome undefined, its meanings ramifying outward—for 267 pages while the novel backs up to narrate the inner lives of some two dozen characters. The outcome or resolution of the action is far from definitive, as the uncanny energies of these "holy women" resonate beyond their apparent death. The narrator sees plural possibilities, not just single events; she sees in the midst, allowing for change and chance. Thus even the novel's conclusion does not restore stasis, confer certainty, or neutralize anxiety.

While the narrative perspective operative in *Paradise* resembles omniscience, the narrator refuses the totalizing imperative that goes with the godly view. She chooses to know each, but does not claim to know all. She does not add up a series of judgments to produce a single coherent version of truth, as some nineteenth-century omniscient narrators did in their creation of an imperial aerie. She does not sum up her assessment of the wounds of racism in a meta-narrative that transcends the cultural location of each specific incident of racism. Instead, she "steps in"—to invoke Lone's term for the way an outside intelligence can reach the spirit of another being—and amplifies each consciousness with the power of a poetic prose that Margaret Atwood describes as "rich, graceful, eccentric, rough, lyrical, sinuous, colloquial, and very much to the point" (146). She approaches each character with what Richard Misner calls "unmotivated respect," which "was what love was" (146). Morrison comments in an interview that Misner is, among the male characters in the novel, "the one that is closest to my own sensibility about moral problems," and his ideas in this passage echo the forceful sermon of Baby Suggs in the clearing in *Beloved* (Jaffrey; *Beloved* 88). Ironically, none of the characters hears these reflections, for Misner is so angry that he cannot speak; the narrator listens to him *think* some of the most powerful prose in the novel. The narrator does not overtly endorse his vision, but she shares it as a method for listening to the inner lives of the characters. In a novel where so many characters are either silent or silenced, the narrator's ability to perceive and express their inner feelings constitutes a gift. She approaches the most limited, smug, and destructive characters in the novel with sympathetic respect.

A narrative constructed on this set of principles unsettles expectations and changes the reading experience. It frustrates the desire for closure, slows the pace, and requires patience and memory. It forces the withholding of judgments; while the novel does not endorse moral relativism, it requires attention to the reasons of the most flawed and judgmental characters and to the failures and lapses of the most generous of the characters. By looking in, the narrator manages to bypass racial markers and truly, in this way, to clear the racist debris, while exposing the scars and wounds of racism that have shaped her characters' history. By using powerful, elegant language to express their most anguished and inexpressible feelings, she teaches pity for the losses and hurts that make her characters both uniquely individual and part of an undeniable human family. In fact, pity resonates through the novel, appearing not only in Piedade's name and in Consolata's reflections (249, 250), but even in the thoughts of the men who stalk through the Convent: one man "is startled by the whip of pity flicking in his chest" (8) and another man reflects, "Pity" (10).

At the novel's end, the narrator's imagination, language, and art take readers to paradise, which is not an all-black town and above all not a settled home. It is an open place, not nearly as clean as the men of Ruby might prefer—there is "sea trash" around. It is not American and not exclusive, for they let anyone in, "crew and passengers, lost and saved" (318). This paradise is neither so hierarchical nor so complete as

Dante's: "Now they will rest before shouldering the endless work they were created to do down here in paradise" (318).[18] This evolving paradise is a work in progress, a work created by the workers. In the paradise "down here" all will work as well as rest; no slaves, servants, or underclass will do the work while others preen their wings. And this open paradise is approached through art and language rather than through imperial conquest: no land is claimed or taken from others; none are enslaved to build it. Instead, the paradise-home is re-invented in Piedade's song, an art that creates the satisfaction of the nomad at rest in an interstitial space. This amounts to the "becoming minor" of home: an unsettled space that does not exclude, it gives up the illusion of coherence and safety. It is a temporary shelter, made by story, language, and art into Morrison's *Paradise*.

3
The Incandescent Home: Margaret Atwood's *The Blind Assassin*

In Margaret Atwood's fiction, homes are places of coercion, danger, and dread: Rennie's apartment in *Bodily Harm* (1981), invaded by a stranger who leaves a threatening rope; the Commander's house in *The Handmaid's Tale* (1985), where women are categorized and used according to their function; Elaine's childhood home in Toronto in *Cat's Eye* (1988), suffused with anxiety over the endless imperfections her friends detect in her; the apartment in *The Robber Bride* (1993) where Karen's mother beats her and the basement room where her Uncle Vern sexually abuses her; the apartments of Jane and Vincent in "Age of Iron" from *Wilderness Tips* (1991), full of "purposeless objects adrift in the physical world" (162); the Kinnear house in *Alias Grace* (1996), scene of two brutal murders; or the deserted houses of *Oryx and Crake* (2003), containers for the unburied dead. While Atwood's own childhood homes were by all accounts happy, though impermanent places,[1] the homes in her fiction threaten or stifle their inhabitants, especially women.

Homes in Atwood's fiction are also places where women learn their function in the imperial scheme.[2] In deceptively bland and seemingly apolitical ways, homes' mundane practices recapitulate the foundational customs and values on which the Empire rests and which it uses to justify itself. As Said writes in *Culture and Imperialism*, these foundational values include assumptions of identity, privilege, and necessary domination: "Throughout the exchange between Europeans and their 'others' that began systematically half a millennium ago, the one idea that has scarcely varied is that there is an 'us' and a 'them,' each quite settled, clear, unassailably self-evident" (xxv). Imperial homes exclude "them," except as servants: those of races defined as "dark" and those of classes defined as "low" or "working." Imperial homes subordinate women, for women are constructed as inferior; Said reminds us that imperialism includes "notions that certain territories and people *require* and beseech domination" (9). Irrational and intuitive, women require the shaping hand of reasonable men. Imperial homes, then, define "us" as white, wealthy, reasonable, stable, and male, supported by "them" in various serving roles.

Women's subordinate but privileged status makes them apt figurations of Canada's position as a marginalized but privileged settler-colony and Commonwealth member. The white wife or daughter in the imperial house has a position similar to Canada's: secondary, affiliated with but detached from the seat of power, participating in the wealth and privilege of the house but not in control of it. As Diana Brydon observes in her postcolonial reading of Atwood's *Bodily Harm*, "All of Atwood's work" can be explored "from this kind of postcolonial perspective, interrogating its representation of the fractured Canadian subject and the peculiar anxieties of a people simultaneously marginalized and privileged" (93). Brydon does not in this essay consider the resemblance of Canada's position in the imperial house to woman's position in the Canadian house, but Sandra Djwa identifies the connection between women protagonists and Canada in Atwood's early work: "Female artist narrators, such as Susanna Moodie and the 'I' of *Surfacing*, frequently represent Canada in Atwood's early work" (173).[3] Graham Huggan underscores Atwood's play with all such figural representations, and he emphasizes the danger involved in bringing an "allegorical fallacy" to bear in reading fiction: "Such attempts to make canonical works constitutive, however ironically, of national cultural identities is [sic] always likely to lead to oversimplified interpretations that mythologise the history on which they presume to draw and comment" (220). Without overdetermining such connections, however, critics may find evidence of Atwood's complex views of Canadian national identity in her women protagonists.

Their figurations of nation move the experiences of women protagonists in Atwood's fiction beyond the exploration of women's personal or psychological trauma and place the personal as political, in feminist terms. In current critical readings of women writers, women characters' experience is often interpreted as a personal and private encounter with the ills of patriarchy. Women's suffering takes the form of domestic trauma, an outcome of the tradition of gender inequities whose public implications are obscure. But thinking of Atwood's women as Canadians makes visible her additional commentary on Canada's political role on the world stage. Seeing the Canadian dimension of her interests invites postcolonial readings, open to issues of nation and globe as well as person, and aware of Canada's status as both conquered territory on what Atwood terms "the bottom rung on the status ladder of ex-British colonies" (*Strange Things* 2) and simultaneously a conquering nation with its own history of domination and exclusion based on race, class, and ethnicity.[4]

I will argue that in *The Blind Assassin* (2000), protagonist-narrator Iris Chase Griffen reflects both Canada and the woman in the imperial house, equally anxious divided subjects with privilege but no overt power. With its historical range, this novel invites consideration as a national and epochal summary: as several reviews observe, it extends its historical reference from the "colonial heyday through fully-fledged industrialization [...] with an exposition of Canada's women in this same history" (Rebecca Davies 1138).[5] Reviewing the novel in *Canadian Literature*, Coral Ann Howells calls the novel "a social history of English Canada in the twentieth century" and an exposure of guilty secrets within "the old English Canadian Establishment" (Howells 2002). But the novel does not simply situate events in Canadian history: it *reads* Canadian history through the corruption in Canada's imperial homes.

The novel is an ambitious postmodern and postcolonial *Bildungsroman*, in which the young Canadian protagonist learns her place in a home, home-country, and world given over to conquest, deceit, and abuse. The first section of this essay explores Atwood's multiple characterizations of the imperial home through Iris's family, her teachers, and her marriage to Richard Griffen. Seeking with Alex Thomas ways to rebel against the imperial home, Iris makes a bid for escape to a series of temporary rooms. Also during the affair, Alex takes Iris on imaginary flights to other planets through science-fiction narratives. But neither escape manages to leave home, as the second section of this essay shows: free to invent himself, Alex creates only a mimic version of the "sanctioned violence" Iris has already learned at home, and his imagined worlds only repeat the imprisoning planet she already knows. After his death and Laura's, for which she bears responsibility, Iris creates an altered relation to home and homeland. In her narrative, Iris becomes the blind assassin herself—initiate of the inner recesses of the home temple who accomplishes a just revenge.[6] Where the imperial home emphasizes conquest and possession, Iris chooses to dispossess herself, as the third section of this essay demonstrates; she gives the affair with Alex to Laura in a fiction ("The Blind Assassin") whose fame also she gives away. Living in a house she erases by not noticing it, she sells relics of houses like her family home, and her legacy to her granddaughter is not a home but a story. In these ways, Iris liberates herself through her narrative from the enclosing walls and imprisoning ideology of the settled imperial home.

Iris eventually imagines a transient, incandescent home, an airy space outside the walls of empire, which Atwood presents as a preferable alternative. Like other contemporary women writers, Atwood needs to invent an open form of home, one that frees inhabitants from the imperial urge to possess and conquer. In Atwood's recent texts, and particularly in *The Blind Assassin*, this porous and equalizing home takes the form of a home on fire, a burning house. While fire can be a destructive element, as Karen Stein observes, Atwood also uses it to unsettle and liberate the closed space of home.[7] The title poem of her collection, *Morning in the Burned House* (1995), considers the potential in such a burned house; it merits a lengthy quotation:

> In the burned house I am eating breakfast.
> You understand: there is no house, there is no breakfast,
> yet here I am.
> The spoon which was melted scrapes against
> the bowl which was melted also.
> No one else is around.[...]
> I can't see my own arms and legs
> or know if this is a trap or blessing,
> finding myself back here, where everything
> in this house has long been over,
> kettle and mirror, spoon and bowl,
> including my own body,
> including the body I had then,
> including the body I have now
> as I sit at this morning table, alone and happy,
> bare child's feet on the scorched floorboards
> (I can almost see)
> in my burning clothes, the thin green shorts
> and grubby yellow T-shirt
> holding my cindery, non-existent,
> radiant flesh. Incandescent.
>
> (126–27)

In this poem, the burned house (a small cabin used by Atwood's family when she was young) evokes for the poet the memory of all she has lost: her father, whose decline and death form the powerful subject of several poems in the book; her childhood happiness, of a simplicity impossible to an adult consciousness; her own child-body, innocently barefoot and clothed in whatever comes handy. All of the *things* in the poem are now gone, melted and turned "cindery, non-existent" like the "burned house" and "burning clothes." The poem's last noun, flesh, is gone—figuratively cremated in time's fire, long "over" and invisible to the narrating poet, a burned house herself. Yet the non-existent flesh of body and home is also "radiant," emitting an "incandescent" light that allows insight. In the glow of the poem's last word, the house burns endlessly; house, body, and past itself hang suspended between the "bright" but "songless" morning and the threatening "bank of cloud" rising in the east "like dark bread" whose warning of time and change—those forces that level illusions of dynastic permanence—will leaven the child's silence into song. Burning but unburned, radiant with loss and mortality, this house stands opposed to the imperial palace, with its exclusive dominion. Its walls are translucent, gone. The body within it takes a simultaneous stance as both home and absence, an incandescent home.

Learning the imperial home

Iris's education begins at Avilion, the home built by her grandparents and inherited by her parents. Named by her grandmother Adelia for Tennyson's valley where King Arthur went to die, Avilion indicates "how hopelessly in exile she considered herself" from England and European culture (61). Like Lazaroo's Australian home named "Elsewhere," Avilion bespeaks a nostalgic longing for the imperial center. Pretentious and imitation Gothic in design, Avilion seems to the 82-year-old narrating Iris like "Ambition's mausoleum," a monument to the grand dynastic plans of her grandparents (58). According to these plans, the Chase button factory will expand abroad and become "Chase and Sons," echoing Dickens's *Dombey and Son* ("The earth was made for Dombey and Son to trade in, and the sun and moon were made to give them light. Rivers and seas were formed to float their ships").[8] Women bring culture to this enterprise, acquiring European art on improving trips abroad, enforcing European table manners, and wearing European styles. A model European wife, Adelia lends grace to her husband's money, sends her sons off to school where the button business "couldn't coarsen them," and maintains rigid control over the elegance of her appearance even in her dying days (63–64). The imperial wife makes the

Canadian hinterlands seem identical to England and thus recreates the feel of home.

By the time Iris's father Norval inherits Avilion, he has lost an eye, his brothers, his faith, and his ability to be at home anywhere. He returns from World War I broken, full of rage, isolated from the wife he loves, given to drinking and "tomcatting" (79). Iris remembers him looking out the window as if he were outside, looking in, "An orphan, forever excluded—a night wanderer" (81). He has a fractured relationship to Avilion: "This is his home, this besieged castle; he is its werewolf" (82). He no longer looks the part of the courtly gentleman who reigns inside the castle, but rather resembles the monster werewolf such castles as Avilion are built to exclude. Both inside and outside the legacy of his parents' imperial project, he is torn in the depression years between wanting to protect his workers by keeping the factory open and wanting to preserve his wealth by burning the factory for the insurance (167, 221). After his wife dies, he courts sculptress Callista Fitzsimmons, an outspoken socialist (147); but he also spends time with arch-capitalist Richard Griffen, owner of a rival company and a "sweatshop tycoon" (177). Norval, who dies in the turret at Avilion, vacillates between the postcolonial recognition of home's impossibility and increasingly ironic and desperate efforts to recuperate the nostalgic imperial space.

After their mother dies, Iris and Laura are ignored and left to themselves by their father; though they share the same experiences, they take different positions relative to home. Good Canadian youths, they grow up free, but neglected and powerless; they are left alone to explore the spacious dwelling that is their home. Laura does not inherit the yearning for home: "I'm not going to have a husband anyway [...] I'm going to live by myself in the garage," she proclaims at age six (87). Iris, however, grows up divided between longing for home and homeland and a recurrent dream-vision of her house, freighted with expectations, burning to the ground (217). She recognizes the legacy of fractured dispossession that reflects Canada's status as foreign colonial outpost aspiring to Arthurian centrality; yet she is also conditioned by her family heritage to yearn for a secure place inside that fabled home. "I'd wanted to leave home," she realizes, "but have it stay in place, waiting for me, unchanged, so I could step back into it at will" (217).

For Iris and Laura, growing up in their father's house involves learning imperial values and the corruptions that follow imperial power. They are taught by a series of "mimic men," diasporic migrants who reflect ironically on postcolonial subjectivity. Products of conquest and famine, these teachers resemble the Jamaicans whom Edward Kamau Brathwaite calls "mimic men":

> 'Invisible,' anxious to be 'seen' by their masters, the élite blacks and the mass of the free coloureds [...] conceived of visibility through the lenses of their masters' already uncertain vision as a form of 'greyness'—an imitation of an imitation. Whenever the opportunity made it possible, they and their descendants rejected or disowned their own culture, becoming, like their masters, 'mimic men.'
>
> (204)

In Canada, they find work in Avilion, the most British of households, where they impart the most British of lessons and values. In Homi Bhabha's terms, they serve as the hybrid "sign of the productivity of colonial power, its shifting forces and fixities; it is the name for the strategic reversal of the process of domination through disavowal (that is, the production of discriminatory identities that secure the 'pure' and original identity of authority)" (112). Speaking ironically for the "purity" of cultural values, these teachers measure the potency of the colonial power that has produced them as "grey" imitations.

Among their tutors, two stand out for their dedication to empire: Miss Violence and Mr. Erskine. Miss Violence leaves them free to browse in the library that grandmother Adelia chose for her husband, where Iris reads imperial classics depicting the conquest of distant lands. Miss Violence favors British Romantic poetry and fiction, full of love and melancholy (156). She epitomizes the decadent sentimentality that comes with the decline of the British empire and, thus, seems to belong at Avilion, with "its obsolete Victorian splendours" (157). Their next tutor, Mr. Erskine, more actively (and sadistically) beats the values of empire into the girls:

> His idea of Geography was the capital cities of Europe. His idea of Latin was Caesar subduing the Gauls [...] or from Ovid's *Metamorphoses* [...] The rape of Europa by a large white bull, of Leda by a swan, of Danae by a shower of gold [...] "*Rapio, rapere, rapui, raptum,*" said Mr. Erskine. "To seize and carry off. [...]Decline." *Smack* went the ruler.
>
> (163)

Resentful product of English class domination, Mr. Erskine imitates upper-class learning and culture, producing a version of "greyness" that reconfirms the authority of the class structure. He anticipates Iris's husband Richard in several ways, including his preference for brute conquest, his pedophilia, his groping of Laura, and his effective teaching of Iris how to cheat, feign, and forge. Mr. Erskine is the novel's only English citizen and one of its clearest representatives of imperial corruption.

Reenie, however, is Iris's most important teacher of women's role in the imperial home: she teaches that girls must repress and deny sexuality, observe and preserve lines of race and class, and beware the omnipresent gaze of empire.[9] Poor, working class, and one of eleven children in a family of Irish immigrants, Reenie lives in a row house amid factory workers (91). Like Brathwaite's Jamaicans, she turns her back on Irish culture and imitates the colonial power that allowed the potato famine and thereby flung her family across the ocean. Grey ventriloquist, Reenie speaks for the purity of Victorian English womanhood from which she is excluded and by which she is devalued. She wields an endless supply of maxims and clichés, many of them warnings against men (they can't "leave well enough alone," 88) and women who show too much flesh ("*She's asking for it, she'll get what's coming to her*," 178) or women who fall ("*Why buy a cow when milk's free*," 317). About Iris's wedding night, Reenie advises her to "*Grin and bear it*" (241). Reenie's racism emerges in her comments about Alex Thomas, as does her commitment to the class boundaries that measure the long oppression of her family: "He's most likely some half-breed Indian, or else a gypsy. He's certainly not from the same pea patch as the rest of us," she says on first seeing Alex, and later calls him a "young thug who looked like an Indian—or, worse, a Jew—and [...] a Communist into the bargain" (182, 192). Orphans like Alex appear dangerous to Reenie because they can cross class and race barriers, and they may be the product of transgressive sex: "*Born in a ditch, left on a doorstep*" (179). Being visible and identifiable, always under the imperial gaze, women must exercise caution: "People could see you," Reenie warns (178); "We'd made a sorry spectacle of ourselves," she avers (192), and "People are talking," she admonishes (200).

Iris's final and most coercive teacher is her husband Richard Griffen, *the* twentieth century echo of an imperialist who "preferred conquest to cooperation" in all of his dealings (371). Griffen's name identifies him as a monster, like Norval, and a hybrid mix of fierce predators, with a body like the British lion but the head and wings of the American eagle. He proposes to Iris in the Imperial Room, an appropriate setting for his goals in founding a home with her: the largest restaurant in Toronto, it has square pillars and a look of "congealed opulence. It felt leathery, ponderous, paunchy—veined somehow" (227). The grand décor of the room suggests age and decay in Iris's metaphors, a sort of stodgy decadence that Richard does not see.[10] Several references link Richard with empire: he repeatedly speaks at the Empire Club, giving speeches that are covered in the conservative *Mail and Empire*. Richard takes Iris to Europe on their honeymoon, but leaves her to tour alone while he pursues international profits; she sees representations of empire, including a statue of Prince Albert, surrounded by the continents in the form of "exotic women roiling and wallowing around his feet, spewing out fruit and wheat" (301). After the war, Richard takes Iris and Laura on the maiden voyage of the *Queen Mary*. When the King and Queen visit Ottawa in 1939, Richard and Iris attend the royal birthday party (456). In various ways, Richard defines himself as an upwardly-aspiring, backward-looking mimic man.

Having married an 18-year-old girl, Richard takes control, establishes the home he envisions and, with help from his sister Winifred, teaches Iris the decorative role of the imperial wife. Richard chooses their dwelling, to which Iris never refers as "home," and keeps Iris like a child with no say in the affairs of the house. Like Richard, it is pretentious, self-enclosed, and small of soul and vision: "angular and graceless, squinty-windowed, ponderous, a dense brown like stewed tea," with "fake-chalet half-timbering" (295). Winifred decorates the house, filling the bedroom with an "endless cream-coloured bed" with a muslin canopy, "as if on safari" (307). The adventure-safari of Richard's erotic fantasies can only involve the forced conquest of natives ("*Rapio, rapere*"), with the cream color staging the youth and innocence of both the fantasy-conquest and Richard's young bride.

It takes Iris a long time to articulate the nature of her marriage, and some of her pointed judgments are those of the 82-year-old narrator with clear hindsight. On her honeymoon, she perceives Richard's desire to educate and shape her (303). By 6 months later, she understands that "My job was to open my legs and shut my mouth" (332). By a year into her marriage, Richard is writing on her body in a code of bruises: "It was remarkable how easily I bruised, said Richard, smiling. A mere touch would do it.[...] I was sand, I was snow—written on, rewritten" (371). From this exchange, she understands that he has known other women to bruise, that he enjoys hurting her, and that he particularly enjoys making his mark of possession and domination on her delicate flesh. She comes to see the bruising not as an exceptional misfortune to befall her as an individual, but rather as part of the system of imperial culture: "Placidity and order and everything in its place, with a decorous and sanctioned violence going on underneath everything, like a heavy, brutal shoe tapping out the rhythm on a carpeted floor" (371). Who, or what, sanctions the violence? The culture of the brutal shoe with its regular, and regulating, beat.

That shoe beats on the carpeted floor of home: home comes to represent for Iris the source of order and decorum that enables violence to go on behind closed doors and curtained windows. Home functions to hide sexuality, to give the appearance of placidity and measure: home is the carpet that muffles the beat with its softening fabrics and pretense of detached and superior civilization. Homes are family spaces where sexuality can be cloaked and denied, as Norval insists that "Sexuality, although it was never spoken of, was to be nipped in the bud" (159), yet indulged in privacy with Callie and even, perhaps, with Reenie (388). In homes' concealed spaces, sexuality can be practiced against the desires of one partner, as Iris describes herself as "repelled" by Richard's activities (371). Containers of social spaces and private bedrooms, homes can enable and represent colossal hypocrisies. Richard, for example, tries to convince both sisters that he worries about Laura's safety and feels she must live with them for protection; as it turns out, he uses the camouflage of home to blackmail and seduce 15-year-old Laura.

By "sanctioned violence," Iris's statement reflects a belief that Western imperial culture condones and even honors the qualities that lead men to conquer, possess, and inscribe their own names on virgin land and women. This culture approves of men's sexual exploits as an allowable expression of their adventurous and dominating spirit, as Iris indicates when she describes Norval's brothers' affairs with "loose girls"; as long as they are from elsewhere, the townspeople approve (63). Her father goes "tomcatting" in Toronto before her mother's death, and people know: "Oddly enough, both my mother and my father were more respected in town because of it. Who could blame him, considering?" (79). After Liliana dies, Norval's affairs are even more acceptable: "tomcatting" is held to be a male prerogative and need, an expression of every man's right. Richard's affairs with other young women, or his leaving carefully placed, concealable bruises on his wife, are not different in kind or degree from what all men are permitted. His pedophilia only shades toward the impermissible: Iris's mother married at 18, her father endorses her marriage to Richard when she is 18, and Richard's efforts to emphasize Iris's youth are not exceptional in a culture that values youth in women. Iris does not complain about the bruises, or leave Richard for his violence and control, because these behaviors are normal in the Canadian culture she inhabits.

It remains true, as some reviewers observed, that Richard is simply villainous;[11] even Iris recognizes that "I've failed to convey Richard, in any rounded sense. He remains a cardboard cutout" (479). Beyond a plausible illustration of the distances between them that keep Richard mysterious to his wife, Richard's lack of a *personal* story with unique individual explanations for his behavior places the emphasis, by default, on the *social* and *typical* qualities of his story. Richard violates moral and social rules in his abusive conquest of Laura, accomplished through lies, manipulations, and deceptions. He intends to hide these actions under the privacy of home while he rises to public prominence, and he almost succeeds. Indeed, he manages to keep his actions concealed from Iris; and Iris fittingly keeps them as her story's great, illicit secret, almost to the end of the novel. The secrecy that enables a man like Richard to commit what could be called child abuse and statutory rape emerges, I contend, from the unwritten codes of the imperial home: Laura protects his secret out of shame (sexuality is not to be spoken of), guilt (she was persuaded by blackmail and lies but not raped), and reluctance to cause pain to her sister. Laura might not be believed (as Iris did not believe that Mr. Erskine groped Laura); very likely, Laura would be blamed (as Richard, Winifred, and the clinic director do later blame her). As an institution, home extends its protection to Richard, while withdrawing it from Laura.

Moreover, as Anne McClintock writes, larger—national and global—structures rest on the naturalization of these family hierarchies: "The metaphoric depiction of social hierarchy as natural and familial," she claims, depends "on the prior naturalizing of the social subordination of women and children within the domestic sphere"(358). Richard's power over Iris and Laura, subordinated to his control and conquest, extends its logic to Prince Albert's rule over the feminized continents. Even more pointedly, the subordination of her grandmother and her mother provide models for Iris's submissiveness and Laura's, and these in turn ratify the national model as a family ruled from the top by inherited (white, male) power. However they resist it, this lesson drives the education of Iris and Laura. It sends both women away from home and unsettles home and homeland.

The body's home: Alex Thomas and "The Blind Assassin"

Women's exile from home extends even to the body, home or dwelling place for beings in the world, with meanings that are also shaped by imperial culture. In *The Blind Assassin*, women's bodies are disciplined into forms and behaviors that estrange—or more simply, most of Atwood's central women characters are rendered unable to be at home in their bodies. As a young wife, Adelia designs 12-course dinners for Benjamin's guests but must not be seen eating in company; "chewing and swallowing were such blatantly carnal activities" (60). Pain is no more permitted to the body than pleasure: dying of cancer, Adelia dresses formally each day and walks with perfect posture around her garden. As Iris describes her own relationship with Richard, he seems to require her to be *all* body, while concealing the earthliness of embodiment. She is to spend most of her time perfecting her body by diminishing its natural character, removing hair, skin, and odors and shopping endlessly for clothes and accessories. He wishes her to be sexually available for his desires but to have none herself; if she does not take pleasure in sex, "then she would not be liable to wander off seeking it elsewhere" (241). She is to be a beautiful but empty body, one carefully controlled by Richard's tastes and desires. His most habitual gesture, suggesting the reins or the leash, is to put his hand on the back of her neck (297).

Iris responds by escaping from home in order to find pleasure; her meetings with Alex Thomas in a series of loaned and rented rooms that are neither his home nor hers liberate her from the home place that forbids women's pleasure. She chooses Alex because, from the beginning, he opposes all that homes like Avilion stand for; his Marxist sympathies have led him to the labor camps for the unemployed, and he objects to the class system that makes "exclusive" homes exclude the poor. In his own personal history, he reveals a striking identity with the homeless: an orphan found in an unknown east European country as a young child, "I was found sitting on a mound of charred rubble, in a burned-out house. Everyone else there was dead" (189). With a background like that, "At least you're never homesick," Alex says (190). Throughout the narrative, Alex never has a "home" and never seems wistful about founding one. He is a creature of nature and the outdoors: he first appears on the grass at a picnic (176); Iris re-encounters him on the street and reaches out "like a drowning person beseeching rescue" (321). Their first, uncertain meetings occur in parks; he stands outside Iris's window at night; they make love under a bridge. "Is this where you're living?" she asks him in one place; "This is where I'm staying," he replies. "It's a different thing" (109).

The relationship with Alex Thomas holds the potential to link Alex and Iris in the sort of house, improvised and without walls, burning but unconsumed, that Atwood invokes in the poem, "Morning in the Burned House." Alex traces his roots to the burned house that is both the past and the body. He appears to understand the body's impermanence and to celebrate its capacity for pleasure. Alex attracts and holds Iris in part because he allows the body its due: he speaks of bodies without euphemism and accepts their hungers and functions. Where Richard conquers and overpowers Iris, Alex "puts his arms carefully around her, brushes his lips over the side of her neck, her throat" (110). Alex accepts the impermanence of the relationship, telling Iris she will "get over it [...] You'll live" after it ends (30) and, on another occasion, memorizing her so he will have the image "Once I've gone" (124). Iris chooses Alex for his body, flesh which "is so condensed, so dense. Fine-grained, charred" (252). She chooses him for the promise, implied in their first kiss which turns her bones "to melting wax," of a passion that will fire her own body and free her to inhabit it (218). The affair itself is liberatory and transgressive because of Iris's active agency: she seeks Alex out, goes to him when she chooses, and deliberately indulges the body's pleasure. Because she feels a complex lack of freedom in her addiction to the pleasure, she controls the frequency of their meetings: "she stretches out the time between, rationing him. She stands him up, fibs about why she couldn't make it" (261). The relationship gives her "amnesia" and "oblivion," even "immolation": it extinguishes the "higher" self constructed along imperial lines, the part carefully taught to repress the body. In their passionate unions, Iris becomes the incandescent house: "She renders herself up, is blotted out; enters the darkness of her own body, forgets her name. Immolation is what she wants, however briefly. To exist without boundaries" (261).

Alex enables Iris's escape from the imperial home because he stands as empire's other. His most damaging sign of otherness is dark skin, which Fanon remarks on as bringing "Consciousness of the body [as] solely a negating activity" for a black man who "does not know at what moment his inferiority comes into being through the other" (323). As Reenie puts it, Alex is "not from the same pea patch" as the northern Europeans: he is "darkish" in Iris's first look, Indian, gypsy, or Jew in Reenie's view, and "darkly tanned" in the photograph; his daughter is "a dark little thing" (182, 176, 4, 446). From the perspective of English Canada Alex is an invader: an immigrant, exiled by war from a nameless east-European country, a stranger with unknown heritage. He also functions as the other man, much as Zenia functions as the other woman in *The Robber Bride*;[12] in this role he stands as alternative and opposite to the heavily imperial Richard. Alex wears clothing that resists class placement, preferring blue work shirts without ties: Iris calls his style "indeterminate" and observes that university students affect this "proletarian mode" (176).

His speech and accent give no clue, either, to his class and wealth, and his very refusal to be "placed" in the social hierarchy is an affront to the system that assumes everyone should aspire to be "one of us." His otherness extends even to the movement, where his allies appear to be suspicious of him and to distrust his education; he doesn't trust them either, but suspects they may turn him in (272, 275). Eventually he goes to Spain, where he is shot at from both sides (460).

Otherness, difference, and a lack of known roots could provide a source of freedom in a corrupt closed system; Alex might define himself as some form of nomadic and hybrid subject, a postcolonial migrant. He could reinvent himself as what Shannon Hengen calls a "postimperial" Canadian: recalling "the old oppressions of a Eurocentric view (or the oppressions of racist and sexist views) by undercutting those oppressions through other, New World characterizations" (1995, 272). Alex himself suggests such an open position with his politics, certainly liberal, possibly socialist or Communist, definitely on the side of the people and against the consolidated power of empire. He appears to recognize his own freedom from inherited definitions of identity and value when he says he "doesn't need to know who he really is, in the usual sense" (190). Much later, Iris will translate this freedom into an invitation when she tells her granddaughter Sabrina, "the sky's the limit. Your legacy from [your grandfather Alex] is the realm of infinite speculation. You're free to reinvent yourself at will" (513).

Alex passes up the chance to transform himself into a postimperial Canadian, however, primarily from a failure of imagination. The sections of the book devoted to Alex's stories ("The Blind Assassin," "Alien on Ice," "Lizard Men of Xenor," and "The Peach Women of A'a") reveal that he recycles tired formulas, making minor shifts in the workings of class but maintaining traditional stereotypes and oppressions of gender. The virgins of Sakiel-Norn are not only silenced but also tongueless and mute; those of A'a are made of peach-juice and feel no pain when men hit them; the women of both planets exist to satisfy men's sexual fantasies. The woman in "Alien on Ice" is called "B": "The woman is always B, which stands for Beyond Belief, Bird Brain, or Big Boobs, depending on his mood" (277). Alex calls his work "junk" and "tripe," admitting that he writes it to sell "thrills" to working class readers whose intellects he clearly disdains as fully as those of beautiful blondes (280, 460). Four of Alex's stories are briefly narrated in the novel; even the title narrative is intentionally thin, a schematic idea about class exploitation and passion between an Alex-like blind assassin and an Iris-like mute beauty. When Rebecca Davies complains in a review that the "dubious sci-fi novella" is "unwieldy and obscure," "the one section of the novel that strains to convince," she responds to an intended weakness in these plots, part of Atwood's characterization of Alex. While Atwood has used the science or speculative fiction genre for trenchant critiques of the status quo, including the abuse of women in patriarchy and the misuse of the planet in capitalism (in *The Handmaid's Tale* and *Oryx and Crake*), Alex writes what will sell, and therefore he recapitulates and endorses in his fiction some of the most damaging and offensive assumptions of the system he opposes. He is one of the novel's many blind and self-deluded characters: he advocates the overthrow of the wealthy, but engages in a long affair with a wealthy woman, whose fur coat and expensive silk stockings he finds a turn-on. He stands for the empowerment of the people, but writes stories that validate white men's conquest of women, children, and alien others. He wants meaningful change in the ways humans are valued, but thinks and writes about women as non- or sub-human. He says "He's tired of them, these women.[...] tired of bashing their heads" (250), but he repeats the same misogynist characterizations and the same violence against women.

Alex's behavior with Iris, chronicled in the narrative entitled "The Blind Assassin," reflects the same misogyny.[13] He repeatedly reduces Iris to her sexuality, thinking of her as a *"Cunt on stilts"* and as a prostitute who "screw[s] for a living" (276, 23). He urges her not to worry, because "You'll get thin, and then your lovely tits and ass will waste away to nothing. You'll be no good to anybody then" (107). He accuses her of wanting only sex from him and of inventing feelings to save face (111). At another point, he compares her to an animal, a begging dog. He wounds her on several occasions, jealous of her marriage and angry when she stays away; yet he is no different from Richard when he sees a bruise on her thigh, product of the "sanctioned violence" of home, and "wished he'd made it himself" (276). Attracted to Iris for her blonde beauty, Alex silences, ignores, and misreads her as fully as Richard does. When she comments on the story he has been constructing, he responds, only partly in jest, "Oh? You've got your own ideas?" (341). He rejects the ending she invents, and he doesn't understand when she tells him he has imagined the Peach Women wrong (356). Unable to imagine women, he cannot open up an alternative space in which Iris could live, rent a room, make friends with a Greek woman downstairs, and wait for him (465). The relationship gives Iris entry to her own body, but it limits her so narrowly *to* the body that it provides no alternative to her home.

The sections of the novel narrating their relationship extend far beyond its relative time and thus keep Alex—whom Iris meets in autumn 1934, and who dies in Holland in winter 1944—present throughout her memoir of a life of 82 years. While the memoir is mostly narrated in the preterit, the sections describing the lovers' meetings are narrated in the present tense: the affair takes on a timeless, reiterative and endless quality, while the remainder of Iris's life occurs in the finite time of single events. Characters are not named in the sections presenting the affair, only designated by "he" and "she," unlike the memoir that attaches specific names to actors. This strategy makes the man and the woman larger than life and typical of all lovers; it helps expand the relationship to near-mythic proportions. The affair appears as a separate text, entitled "The Blind Assassin, by Laura Chase" within the novel, and chapter titles designate selections from this text.

While these narrative techniques work to enlarge the relationship and separate it off from the other events of Iris's life, the novel's structure simultaneously undermines the special status of the affair and reconnects it to the same imperial culture that infuses every other aspect of the text. The novel is divided into fifteen parts; "The Blind Assassin" appears together with Iris's memoir in parts one (prologue) and fifteen (epilogue); it also appears in parts two, four, six, eight, ten and twelve, where Iris receives the telegram informing her that Alex has died. Iris's memoir comprises the whole of parts three, five, seven, nine, eleven, thirteen, and fourteen. The parts of the novel containing sections of "The Blind Assassin" also contain other texts: articles from five different newspapers or journals, a section of an alumni association bulletin, and a letter from the director of the Bella Vista Sanctuary regarding Laura. Clipped or saved, mostly public and impersonal, these texts represent the imperial gaze and voice, and they keep that cultural perspective in the foreground during the chronicle of the affair.

The news articles always take the side of empire, proclaiming civic values and virtues; among them, the most obvious are those by fictitious Elwood Murray, editor-in-chief of the *Port Ticonderoga Herald and Banner* (whose ambitious name reflects Elwood's sense of imperial weight, as the herald makes royal proclamations and the banner is the monarch's flag or standard). With greater complexity or less, the articles retrieve from daily events simple lessons and conclusions, all aimed to praise the perfection of the existing state. Elwood writes, for example, that Norval Chase donated factory "seconds" to poor people in the Depression, helping to keep "Port Ticonderoga a law-abiding town" free of "Communist-inspired bloodshed" (108). An editorial in the guise of a news brief, this article congratulates Port Ticonderoga on having a businessman of honor who can uphold property and avoid the challenges of unions and Communism. The *Toronto Star* reports Laura's death and concludes with a warning to the city: neglected streetcar tracks are to blame, so "City Council should take note" (3). The *Globe and Mail* reports Richard's death in terms of its importance to the state. In an obituary noting Richard's memberships in the Empire Club and the Royal Canadian Yacht Club, this paper calls on the Prime Minister for a statement. These texts from the news media serve to voice and shape public understandings of events in ways that reconfirm an imperial perspective.

Among the clipped articles, five are society and gossip notes from *Mayfair*, a magazine published in Montreal for the Canadian elite. These record Iris's engagement party (127–28), a costume ball organized by Winifred (273), the voyage of the Queen Mary (347–48), a party celebrating the birth of Aimee (403–404), and a royal garden party in honor of a visit by the King and Queen (456–57). In each of these, the columnist describes the clothing worn by various guests, including Iris and often Laura. Intended to record and celebrate the wealthy world of high fashion, these pieces also reflect the emphasis placed on clothing in judging the success of the society wife. They mark significant differences between the world of Richard's wife, full of attention to the surfaces of things and to worldly status, and the world of Alex's mistress, where lavish clothing can only be dangerously conspicuous in surroundings full of poverty and want. These society page articles capture the hollowness of the role allowed to a society wife: Iris's participation in the events recorded on the society pages is as superficial and empty as the events themselves. She tries to "get out of it, her life" through Alex (409); yet the articles show that, in the eyes of the imperial scribe, she never ceases to play her role successfully; she always appears beautiful, well-dressed, and worthy of notice.

The news articles and other documents do not intrude on Iris's memoir; they only appear in the parts of the novel with "The Blind Assassin." Indeed, the novel includes almost as many clippings and documents (19) as chapters of "The Blind Assassin" (26), creating the effect of a regular alternation between escapes (the lovers' flight to romance, with the secondary diversion of the science fiction tales narrated by Alex) and returns to public reality through the news. The premise beneath these inclusions is that Iris's large steamer trunk, part of the matched luggage from her honeymoon (285), contains the typescript of "The Blind Assassin," a series of clippings and documents, and at the end, the hand-written chapters of Iris's memoir. The trunk is left to Sabrina, her granddaughter and Alex's, who must be imagined putting the manuscript into a final order that includes Myra's epitaph written after Iris's death (519). Whether we imagine Sabrina or Atwood as the arranger of the text, the news pieces provide a deliberately ironic counterpoint that deflates the romance.

Choosing the incandescent home

Iris has been a victim of imperial corruption and conquest, to be sure; her father virtually sells her into marriage with a wealthy elitist, and both men use her for their own purposes. In her role as Canada, Iris is a partner in name only, chosen and used for her assets, and denied a voice in any decision. Just as Prince Albert, in the statue Iris sees on her honeymoon, pays no attention to the "exotic women" whose riches he commands (301), Richard ignores Iris in pursuing his ambition to gain power and respect. As Atwood observed in *Survival*, however, victims have choices, including the choice to transform their position into creative non-victimhood (38–40). Iris cannot accomplish this transformation until she recognizes the extent of her complicity with the imperial system that has shaped her. Like Canada or any other colonized culture, she has internalized some values and habits of the oppressive ruler and adopted some assumptions of the elitist capitalism that reduces her to an exchange value.

Her first complicity occurs in her use of Alex: with similar motives as her father, Iris is "tomcatting" in this relationship, in which she takes the role of the colonizing power and Alex becomes the exotic dark native who can be visited for her pleasure. The rooms where she finds him resemble overseas territories, remarkable for their stains and tatters, their signals of a poverty she finds foreign and oddly glamorous, being "real." She thinks of the absent inhabitants of these rooms as "other people," and passers by outside speak "unknown languages" (253, 341). Iris uses Alex as a way to escape her life temporarily, but she does not intend to leave the marriage any more than Richard does. On one occasion, she tells Alex that she will leave home when he returns from Spain; but though he begs her to leave "now," she won't: "Where would I live? In some rented room, all by myself? Like you, she thinks. What would I live on?" (361). Alex accuses Iris of visiting him for sex, of "loving it"; when she replies, "I don't love *it*, I love you," he observes, "Or so you think. It saves face" (111). He understands her emotional attachment to him as both limited (she won't leave Richard) and invented to excuse and legitimate her desire. Alex's most subtle and profound insights into Iris occur in a passage where he asks himself why she keeps coming back:

> Is he some private game she's playing, is that it?[...] She wants a love story out of him because girls do [...] But there must be another angle. The wish for revenge, or for punishment. Women have curious ways of hurting someone else. They hurt themselves instead; or else they do it so the guy doesn't even know he's been hurt until much later. Then he finds out. Then his dick falls off. Despite those eyes, the pure line of her throat, he catches a glimpse in her at times of something complex and smirched.
>
> (276)

Alex suspects that Iris uses him as a pawn in "some private game" she plays to exact revenge against her husband. The love story she would like to invent with Alex is camouflage for something deeper and more abusive, just as the innocent eyes and pure line of her throat mask "smirched" (dirty, dishonored, defamed, soiled) qualities in her.

Of course, the recognition of that moral stain does not occur to Alex at all, or not certainly: it *does* occur to Iris herself, who writes this self-evaluation later and places it in Alex's mind. It reveals her guilt for having used Alex, for having failed to love him enough, and for having treated him as she herself was treated, as an object—a "human sacrifice," in Atwood's terms (Gussow). As a self-assessment of her motives, it explains the central impulse to punish Richard when he finds out "much later" and then "his dick falls off." Cleverly using language appropriate to Alex's consciousness, Iris expresses rage at the phallus, plausible given the sexual battery to which Richard has subjected her. But her revenge involves a double castration: she appropriates Alex's penis in order to remove Richard's, even though this leaves Alex unmanned. Elsewhere in the narrative she asks if he is ever "unfaithful" and he replies, "I couldn't stand to lay a finger on any other woman. I'd sick up" (345). Whether this is literally true or not, Iris has taken Alex to use as a tool for her own purposes, and thus she judges herself to be "smirched."

The second, and worse, complicity—the heart of her guilt and grief—occurs in Iris's behavior to Laura. Because it is the crucial event in her narrative, Iris begins with Laura's death in May 1945. Laura "had her reasons," Iris writes (1), though these do not emerge until page 500. Laura is crushed by two acts of imperial conquest, invasions by sovereign others who treat her as an object. The first is Richard, who persuades

Laura to have sex with him during the summer of 1936 in order to "save Alex" (487). The inventive and determined Richard, realizing how important Alex is to Laura, tells her that Alex will be captured and shot unless she gives in. Afterwards, Richard tells her (as he has one year earlier told Iris) that he is "Besotted" with her (500). Within a few months Laura is pregnant and locked up in a "Sanctuary" for an abortion, followed by electro-shock therapy under the false claim that she has imagined the whole episode. Eight years later, Iris not only fails to understand and believe her sister's story, but she delivers two cruel blows herself on hearing it: she tells Laura that Alex died in the war 6 months earlier, so her sacrifice has been for nothing; then that Alex has been her own secret lover, and thus that he would not return and was not worthy of Laura's devotion. Richard's abuse of Laura is heinous enough: he lies, preys on Laura's vulnerability, destroys her innocence, and uses her. But Iris's abuse of Laura, not Richard's, drives Laura to suicide. Competitive, jealous, vindictive, full of the spite of a resentful older sister, Iris tells Laura that Alex was her own possession, not Laura's. "Who else did he have?" Iris asks rhetorically, mocking Laura's fantasy of Alex returning to her (488).

In her response to Laura, Iris not only fails her sister, but she also recapitulates the same imperial dynamic that underlies most of the pain in her own life. Iris "trumps" Laura's claim on Alex and thus attempts to squash her sister's confidence that Alex would return to her, that he ever cared for her, that they had an important relationship. While Laura "had only the haziest notions of ownership" (83), Iris asserts exclusive possession of Alex, even suggesting that Laura was beneath consideration as his friend: "who else did he have?" Ironically, at the moment she says these things Iris believes the father of Laura's baby must have been Alex (486), and throughout the novel Iris wonders who else Alex *does* in fact have. Iris's jealousy of her sister has several grounds: Laura meets Alex first and invites him to dinner; she has serious conversations with him first; she likes him first; and she first saves him, hiding him in Avilion. Iris knows from beginning to end that "Alex was the only man Laura had ever shown any interest in" (486). Her decision to tell Laura in one breath that Alex has died and that he was her lover is neither casual nor accidental: it is "a knife in the back" (488).

Iris's resentment also has a basis in personal history, as she reveals when, at this juncture in the text, she recalls the day after their mother's funeral: "Laura was sitting on the ledge beside me, humming to herself complacently, secure in the conviction that everything was all right [...] because she'd made some secret, dotty pact with God" (487).

Seeming to have an inner line to God and the lost mother, Laura possesses what Iris desperately lacks: a sense of comfort and hope instead of desolation. Iris is mindful and sometimes jealous over possessions, while Laura doesn't pay attention to technicalities of ownership; she both takes and gives freely. Laura simply takes and uses any of Iris's belongings that she wants: powder, pens, photographs, clothes, or perfume. She gives Iris a copy of the photograph of the two of them with Alex at the picnic, with herself cropped out—because, she rightly believes, "that's what you want to remember" (220). Although Laura seems to love Alex, she shares this precious image because she is not possessive.

Iris's confession of the affair to Laura is an act of imperial aggression. Alex's death would have been survivable, though Laura "went very white. It was like watching wax cool" (488). What Iris then says plants a flag in the territory, claims retrospective possession of all of Alex's attention and love, and proclaims a conquest over her sister: "I got the telegram [...] He shouldn't have done that, considering Richard. But he didn't have any family, and we'd been lovers, you see—in secret, for quite a long time—and who else did he have?" (488). Not only does Iris claim ownership over what was loaned but never really earned or possessed, she also takes him away from her sister. In this act, Iris echoes Richard, who only threatened to take Alex away; and she smashes Laura's sense of Alex's identity as well. In an exercise of power, she takes away both the future Laura has fantasized and the past on which Laura built the fantasy.

Iris atones for this destructive claim with other acts of dispossession. First, she "gives" Alex to Laura in the narrative, "The Blind Assassin," written as Laura's confession of an intense love affair of her own. Second, she gives the book, and the considerable fame, glory, and adulation it generates, to Laura; Laura is venerated as an important author when the book is published as her posthumous writing, while Iris lives virtually unnoticed in "the long shadow cast by Laura" (41). Third, she gives Laura a voice in the book, allowing Laura to be her collaborator by a kind of focused memory that keeps Laura present in the text. In the way she writes, including Laura's voice as well as her own in scenes with Alex, she attempts to share where she had earlier excluded. For example, when "He" lights a cigarette in "The Blind Assassin" by "striking the match on his thumbnail," "She" says "You'll set fire to yourself" (10). This incident recasts one at the picnic where all three characters meet for the first time; Alex "lit a match with his thumb" and Laura says, "You shouldn't do that [...] You could set yourself on fire" (177). Though "she" is primarily Iris, "she" includes her sister, the necessary and beloved other, twin, opposite, *semblable* and *soeur*: "I can't say Laura didn't write a word" because in "what Laura would have called the spiritual sense— you could say she was my collaborator. The real author was neither one of us: a fist is more than the sum of its fingers" (512–13).

Another important act of dispossession occurs when, after learning of Richard's abuse of Laura, Iris does what she could not contemplate before: she leaves Richard's house. Taking only her daughter and a few things, she leaves financial demands backed up by the threat of revealing publicly what Richard did to Laura. She returns to Port Ticonderoga, where she buys with Richard's money a house more modest than any she has lived in before. The house is close to the "small limestone row-house cottages originally built for the factory workmen" where Reenie lived (387). A long way from Avilion and from Richard's lavish Toronto house, Iris's final house takes its identity from the working-class neighborhood that surrounds it. While Iris takes enough money from Richard to buy the house, she does not get much more; she comments on how the bankers look down on her: "I feel despised there, for having so little money" (144). While she was unwilling to leave Richard earlier because she feared being without money and job skills, she turns out to run a successful business selling antiques, starting with some of her own possessions. Not only does the business appeal to her for the chance it offers for further dispossession, but it also enables her to recycle objects from wealthy families to the use of a wider range of people. As Karen Stein points out, Iris's "disposing of the family heirlooms" also "indicates her rejection of a tradition that kept women subservient, passive 'angels in the house"' (151).

Her vengeance on Richard is deftly accomplished; as Atwood says in an interview, "Of course, you know who the blind assassin really is. Ultimately it's Iris" (Gussow). First she publishes "The Blind Assassin," which stirs up public talk about the family; then "Someone" makes "an anonymous phone call" and reveals Richard's connection to the Bella Vista Clinic: "There was some correspondence between Richard and the director that was particularly damaging" (509–10). Seemingly, Iris made the phone call, and she must have released the damaging letter from the director to Richard that appears in her collected documents; anonymously and quietly, she has ended Richard's political career by revealing his behavior with Laura. He accuses Iris, in their last conversation, of having "done this on purpose, he said, to ruin him" (510). To get the blade to his heart, she sends him a copy of the novel in order to show him first-hand what she tells him in the last conversation: "all the time you were having your squalid little fling with her, she must have been in and out of bed with another man—one she loved, unlike you" (510). Fittingly, Iris highlights the insult to Richard's sense of possession of Laura, insisting that not only did he never win Laura's love, he did not even have sole use of her body. Richard goes to Avilion, to the boat called the *Water Nixie* where he first had sex with Laura, and dies with the book at his elbow, evidently a suicide over the failure of his romantic and political dreams.[14]

Iris makes the crucial discovery late in the novel that she can abandon the imperial home and relocate herself in the self-consuming, incandescent home. She lives in a house she virtually does not notice and never thinks about. She spends most of the last year of her life outside, revisiting places in her story; she writes outside on the back porch, and she dies "while sitting in her back garden" (519). Inside the house, she feels as though "I am trespassing," and her possessions appear estranged and worthless, "The scattered bones of *home*, the rags, the relics" (56–57). This home, and the very idea of it, died long ago, and what remains has no value, except to mark its passage. Iris has founded no dynasty, and when she visits her lawyer to discuss what she will leave, it is not her home but rather her story that matters—this too is a set of scattered pieces. Her narrative turns out to be written for her granddaughter Sabrina, the "Dear Reader" or "ideal reader" for whom, Atwood says in *Negotiating with the Dead*, every writer writes (151). Although Sabrina remains in India, perhaps trying "to atone for the sins of her money-ridden, wrecked, deplorable family" (433), Iris's story gives her the generous gift of dispossession from this family: "You're free to reinvent yourself at will" (513).

As a figure for Canada, Iris implies that nations may be able to re-invent their relationship with the centering home of empire through acts of dispossession. Her lifelong experience suggests that leaving home is not so liberating, but rather leaving home behind or giving home away is. The conservative pull of the very notions of home and family, the sentimental axes of stability and order, can only reinforce the former colony's need to affiliate with its parent, the seat of empire. For Canada, by implication, true reinvention requires giving up the last traces of nostalgia for Britain as the symbolic home, and coming to see it much as Iris sees Avilion, as "ambition's mausoleum" (58).

In the process of writing the narrative, Iris recognizes that the imperial home, with all of its exclusive divisions of "us" from "them," carries its own inevitable corruption implicit in the categorization of a "them" who are, by definition, available for use. Whether the working poor, driven out of town when they lose their jobs in the Depression, or servants like Reenie who become ventriloquists of their masters, or waitresses like Agnes, or socially conscious "dark" young men like Alex, or girl children like Iris and Laura, all those who are not "us" can be exploited as conveniences. The solidity, respectability, and seeming permanence of home, with its hidden spaces and conditioned silences, enable corruption and abuse. In response, marking the culmination of the fire imagery that unifies the novel, Iris sets fire to the imperial home. She recalls an old saying from the war years, *"Keep the home fires burning,"* which made her "picture a horde of women with flowing hair and glittering eyes, making their way furtively, in ones or twos, by moonlight, setting fire to their own homes" (478). Iris herself becomes one of these furtive, avenging women. Her narrative could be read, in the terms from Said with which I began, as the narrative of one of "us" who discovers that she is one of "them." Having married empire—or its imitation—she intends merely to flirt with its other, imagining at first that she can remain "inside" the imperial home while meeting Alex in a series of rooms. The novel records crucial changes in her perceptions of home as her memoir, Atwood's novel *The Blind Assassin*, burns down that old, exclusive dwelling.

4
House of Paper: Rosario Ferré's *The House on the Lagoon*

The Caribbean has an unusual status as "home" to migrants, settled, after the extinction of its native dwellers, by people who left other homes and homelands. Most of the migration, forced and free, occurred because of empire; the migrants and their descendants thus bear the marks of colonial and postcolonial identities. After emerging from colonization and slavery to become hybrid and multicultural, Caribbean societies struggle with questions of identity: how to understand and represent their own cultural position, in the absence of origins, at/as crossroads of cultures? Stuart Hall calls the Caribbean "the first, the original, and the purest diaspora [...] we are the break with those originating cultural sources as passed through the traumas of violent rupture" (6). In ways as various as the number of island cultures, the resulting societies became diasporic, Hall continues, by which he means open to "integration, assimilation and cross-influence," involved in "complicated processes of negotiation and transculturation which characterize Caribbean culture" (7). Thinking of the scars and diminishments in Caribbean lives, M. NourbeSe Philip writes, "Colonialism shapes the lives of all who bear its brunt, warping and stunting the natural growth of individuals" (20). Caribbean narratives wrestle with cultural identity, finding both hope and shame in individual answers to these questions.

Puerto Rico is my chosen focus here for its double colonial history, first as a colony of Spain for 400 years and then as a territorial possession of the United States. In Amy Kaplan's trenchant analysis, the US Supreme Court ruling in 1901 that Puerto Rico was "a possession of the United States and therefore not immediately included within the jurisdiction of the Constitution without a specific act of Congress" provided grounds for US imperialism "at a pivotal juncture in its history, when the United States shifted from continental expansion to overseas empire, from absorbing new territories into the domestic space of the nation to acquiring foreign colonies and protectorates abroad" (2002: 2).[1] A hybrid postcolonial homeland, Puerto Rico retains cultural and linguistic connections to Spain while it has added layers of US culture. With a history of colonization, slavery, poverty, and diasporic crossings, Puerto Ricans wrestle with questions of identity.[2]

Home and homeland are framed as double aspects of the battle for identity in *The House on the Lagoon*, a National Book Award finalist, published in 1995 by Rosario Ferré. Ferré may not be as familiar to an international audience as she should be: Puerto Rico's most highly respected contemporary woman writer, she has since 1970 published nine books of fiction, two of poetry, and six of critical essays—some of each in several editions—and a memoir about her father. She has also published dozens of short stories, poems, and critical articles in magazines and anthologies, translations of books, stories, and poems, her own and others, into both English and Spanish, and several children's books. In 1970 she founded an important journal, *Zona carga y descarga*, to publish the works of young Puerto Ricans and to give voice to women's perspectives. Prolific, widely read, educated in the United States (she received a PhD in Latin American literature from the University of Maryland in 1987), Ferré would have the renown of figures like Atwood and Morrison but for the fact that most of her writing has appeared in Spanish. Perhaps to claim a larger public readership, Ferré published *The House on the Lagoon* in English; it was her first text to appear in English before being translated into Spanish in 1996, by herself.

Ferré writes about the problems of Caribbean identity in a postcolonial context. In an Op-Ed piece for *The New York Times*, she writes: "As a Puerto Rican writer, I constantly face the problem of identity. When I travel to the States I feel as Latina as Chita Riviera. But in Latin America, I feel more American than John Wayne. To be Puerto Rican is to be a hybrid. Our two halves are inseparable; we cannot give up either without feeling maimed" (1998). She goes on to call Puerto Rico's historical situation "a paradox" and to emphasize the positive aspects of being "hybrid": "We are mulatto-mestizo, bilingual and proud of it" (1998). Much of her writing explores the negative face of hybridity, tracing schisms and hierarchies of class, race, gender, and national origin that arose from a history of colonialism; as Mariela Gutierrez writes, "she thinks of herself, above all, as chronicler of her own country's socio-political history" (12). Her recent fiction, in particular, explores the divisions, contradictions, and disagreements between Puerto Ricans over their complex national heritage and perennially undefined political status as a commonwealth of the United States. Ferré articulates the tensions implicit in claiming nationality for a hybrid people, ambivalent because they are

> two things at the same time. Nationalism is a much more accessible attitude: you are one thing only and defend yourself against the invasion of 'the other.' [...] Nationalism as an ideal inspired most Latin American countries during the nineteenth and twentieth centuries.[...] But in Puerto Rico the formula doesn't work anymore.
>
> (Kevane and Heredia 66)

In Ferré's fiction, the impulse to simplify complex hybridities into a unitary nationalism results in civil war within families. Indeed, one image in *The House on the Lagoon* sums up the conflict in Puerto Rico: the Afro-Caribbean Petra "swore she had seen a two-headed chick break out of an egg, the heads furiously pecking at each other" (320).

Her fiction, Ferré explains, always engages Puerto Rico's history and politics. Writing about love, about women's lives and Puerto Rican families, she inevitably writes about politics: "I tried to show the connection between the political conflicts of our country and the types of emotional relationships that evolve between husband and wife, father and son, brother and sister, lover and lover, as a result of this conflict. For the past 90 years our country has been torn by an undeclared civil war" (1987, 9). In every family and organization, she explains, half the members support statehood, while the other half oppose it with "fanatical" intensity; "All our citizens are, in short, potential enemies, latently at war" (1987, 9). Her own history reflects the schism, as she rebelled against her father, governor of the island in 1970 and a pro-statehood figure, and against a family whose considerable wealth came from contracts with the US government (Hintz 12–14). Like many of her feminine (and feminist) characters, she has staunchly favored independence, insisting on the need to respect and preserve Puerto Rico's Caribbean-Hispanic language and culture. By 1998, however, in the Op-Ed piece I have cited, Ferré writes that because the United States is now increasingly Hispanic, and Puerto Rico could therefore maintain its cultural identity while accepting a legal place in the country to which it has belonged since 1898, she will support statehood in the next plebiscite.[3]

To understand the political form and focus of Ferré's novel, the early reviews are particularly instructive: *House* was reviewed more widely in English than any of Ferré's previous books, partly because it was a National Book Award finalist. Of five early reviews in English, three fault the novel as "derivative" of Gabriel García Márquez (Grossman, Stavans 691) or as an inferior imitation of Isabel Allende (Stavans 691, Ellen Friedman).[4] A generational chronicle that includes characters who believe in magic, *House* is compared to the magical realism made internationally popular by García Márquez and Allende; but it differs, and reviewers complain that it isn't quite magical enough and doesn't either follow or expand the formula. One reviewer feels that the Puerto Rican political issues are not important; "Not much is at stake [...] The conflict between Puerto Rican statehood and independence does not approach the dimension of the conflict Allende depicts between fascism and democracy" (Ellen Friedman). Such a reading betrays a cultural bias in favor of conflicts that have mattered in Europe and the United States and indifference to the conflict that has for 90 years, as Ferré writes, been "anguishing for the Puerto Rican community" (1987, 9).

While *The House on the Lagoon* invokes some elements of magic, I will argue that it takes a position nearly opposite to magic realism. There are in the novel no inexplicable intrusions from other worlds and no fantastic events: what occurs is entirely explicable in social, political, and worldly terms. Nothing in the novel occurs by magic, like Clara's prophecies fulfilled in Allende or the rain of flowers in García Márquez; characters who believe in magic in Ferré, including Petra Avilés, do not accomplish anything through it. The text does not occur in a mythic "Macondo" or an unnamed Chile or Colombia but rather in Puerto Rico, within specifically named towns and suburbs. Donald Shaw has argued that like other "Post-Boom authors," Ferré returns "to the here and now of Spanish America" and to "confidence in the referential function of language" (11). One reviewer points out that Ferré becomes deliberately more accessible in *House*, "mimicking early forms of realism à la Balzac and Zola" (Stavans 691); indeed, this novel grounds itself in social, political, and cultural history. The narrator, Isabel, educates readers by providing detailed information about her country: "The greater part of our island's bourgeoisie consisted of seafaring immigrants, people from the Canary Islands, the Balearics, and Corsica, as well as from mainland Spain and France," she writes (15), and "By the middle of the nineteenth century, the black slave population in Puerto Rico totaled almost one-fourth of the inhabitants" (59). Throughout the novel, similar details emerge about the economy, political parties, agricultural industries, literature, social habits, and marriage patterns of Puerto Rico.

Ferré's novel also differs philosophically from magic realism: while magic realism aims to weave an imaginary net that suspends the laws of quotidian reality, this text works instead to show how reality shapes what can be imagined. Isabel, a former ballet student, an aspiring writer, and a student of literature (185), criticizes forms of art that aim to provide a comforting alternative to historical reality. Her mother in law, Rebecca Mendizabal, provides the most striking example of decadent art: she gathers a salon of wealthy people who aspire to live beautiful lives, "wear beautiful clothes, visit beautiful places, and occupy their minds with beautiful thoughts" (45). Unlearned, they produce simple compositions that "were never very good" (45). While the rest of the world critiques traditional art forms and explores contemporary conflicts, "in Rebecca's literary salon poets still sang of gardens full of roses, ponds skimmed by snow-white swans, and foam-crested waves spilling over the beach like lace-hemmed gowns" (45). Unlike these poets, Isabel and Ferré practice a contemporary version of social realism. Their art sheds light on the erratic historical evolution of cultural and familial patterns, home and homeland. *House* reflects a commitment to art immersed in the actual national history that makes magic unlikely, misinterpretation common, and artistry necessarily self-reflexive.

The House on the Lagoon uses the title house to reflect, in a complex allegorical way, the Puerto Rican homeland, set on Caribbean waters.[5] The narrator attends closely to the house—to its qualities as a building and to its status as a symbol for the Mendizabal family—as well as to the evolution of both over time. Like Atwood's *Blind Assassin*, Ferré's novel chronicles much of the twentieth century; it begins on July 4, 1917, on the day young Spaniard Buenaventura Mendizabal arrives in Puerto Rico just as the island celebrates the Jones Act granting residents American citizenship. It concludes with social upheaval during the plebiscite of 1982, when residents vote to maintain commonwealth status. The novel narrates the founding of a personal and national house, the struggle to resolve conflicts over race, class, and gender, and the eventual destruction of this house as a result of these tragic conflicts. Throughout, Ferré highlights the catastrophic consequences of life under colonialism, here through the eyes of the pro-Independence group called (after the assault rifle) AK 47:

the island's soaring rate of drug abuse, twenty percent unemployment rate, thriving black market, illicit minimum wage, and the shameful condition of public schools and municipal hospitals. In the AK 47's opinion, these ills were the result of the island's colonial status, which led to a confused sense of identity and a lack of self-respect.

(359)

While the wealthy Mendizabals are insulated from many of these social ills (for example, they fly to the United States for medical services), they do not survive their internal disagreements over Puerto Rico's identity. Their house falls, like other literary houses inhabited by corrupt families: like Poe's "House of Usher," Ferré's house collapses in on itself in the book's last line, and like "Sutpen's Hundred" in Faulkner's *Absalom, Absalom!*, it burns to the ground as the disinherited last son watches.

In and out of the exclusive house

The house on the lagoon begins with an imported, purloined Western design, reflecting Puerto Rico's "stolen," imported, and imposed identities as a Caribbean culture colonized by Spain and by the United States. A Czech migrant, Milan Pavel steals a portfolio of Frank Lloyd Wright's designs and reproduces them in Puerto Rico (40–42). Conjoining references to the nation's colonial histories, Pavel bases the Mendizabal house on a Wright masterpiece, but adds Spanish touches (a "Gaudiesque design," after the great Barcelona architect Antoni Gaudí i Cornet, on a door in the cellar, 236). He adds a mosaic rainbow at the front entrance to suggest peace and racial inclusiveness, a place where all "colors" come together harmoniously; a golden terrace behind the house floats over the lagoon, suggesting prosperity and openness (48).

Life in the house on the lagoon belies these symbolic promises, however: black and biracial Puerto Ricans are not allowed to enter by the front door, but are housed in the cellar and exploited as under-paid servants. Petra and Brambon, followed by their kin, live in small earthen "cells" meant for storage (236); meanwhile Buenaventura's imported hams, intended for the cellar, hang in his wife Rebecca's closets because he obsesses over profits and theft. The spring enclosed in a basement room properly belongs to all: "I had no right to build my house over a public fountain," Buenaventura says as he dies (258). Intended to symbolize the island's natural beauty, the terrace instead signifies commercial affluence and a version of gilded escapism. Properly mated despite their divergent tastes, his for commerce and hers for art, both founding Mendizabals share racist values and a willed indifference to the plight of the poor. While Buenaventura makes money, in part through camouflaged alliances with fascist European groups, Rebecca mistreats her black servants and, with her wealthy young friends, celebrates "the beauties of the bejeweled Art Nouveau world" (45).

The house on the lagoon has a second incarnation as a Spanish Revival mansion. When he comes home to find his wife, nearly naked, performing Salomé's dance of the veils on the golden terrace, Buenaventura calls a halt to the Art Nouveau era of decadence, sensuality, and art for art's sake. He flogs Rebecca, tears down the house, and has an austere mansion built in its place with "granite turrets, bare brick floors, and a forbidding granite stairway with a banister made of iron spears" (67). Suspended above the entryway, and commemorating Buenaventura's pride in his Spanish Conquistador ancestors, is "a spiked wooden wheel that had been used to torture the Moors during the Spanish Conquest, which he ordered made into a lamp" (67). Only the cellar and terrace remain from the original house, because they are structurally necessary; otherwise, the second house recalls the austere and spartan décor of the Spanish monastery from which Buenaventura's ancestors set out to bring white European civilization to the New World. Replacing the rainbow mosaic at the entrance, the torture wheel recalls Spain's long racist history. Isabel hints that Buenaventura may exploit Petra sexually (as he does financially); he certainly uses her relatives, the black women of Lucumí, "where he made love to them on the sand for a few dollars" (213). Isabel notices black children with gray-blue eyes (213), and even Quintín "had to admit" that her account of his father's behavior is true (247). During this second phase when Buenaventura rules the house, Isabel notices that the "huge steel beams" supporting the terrace from underneath are "all rusted and half eaten by the salt air" (235). The house is weakened by corruption and decay, reflected in the patriarch's cloaked sexual exploitation, racism, and class oppression.

The house enters its third phase after Buenaventura and Rebecca die, when Quintín restores it to its original state. He finds Pavel's copy of Wright's plans and effectively reproduces the copy, restoring the mosaic rainbow, "Tiffany-glass windows, the alabaster skylights, and the burl-wood floors" (299).[6] But though he recreates his mother's house in tribute to her, Quintín also recapitulates his father's sins. Like his father he cares more for public opinion than for honesty and pursues wealth at the expense of values; like him he dominates, silences, and even beats his wife. He exploits the workers at his company, forbids his brother and then his son to marry biracial women, and exerts rigid control over his family. While Buenaventura paid his black mistresses for sex, Quintín rapes Petra's young black granddaughter and then denies that the biracial child born 9 months later is his. Under Isabel's threats, he adopts Willie and raises him; but near the novel's end he denies again that Willie is his son and disinherits him. Over the 65-year span of the novel's events, the Mendizabal family does not resolve its own fractures or improve its relations to women, minorities, or the poor; instead, the hierarchies, exclusions, and oppressions grow worse, more personal and invidious. Fittingly, by the end the house, copied from a stolen copy, is rotten at the core. Mangroves and crabs infiltrate the cellar to weaken its foundations, already corrupted by rust. Petra's dying curse on Quintín is fulfilled: in denying Willie, he loses everything, and the Mendizabal house burns down.

The novel's critique of colonial legacies appears in the fate of the wealthy Mendizabal family, but Puerto Rico's doubly colonized status weighs even more heavily on those who are poor. When Buenaventura first disembarks in San Juan and observes people on the streets, he sees two classes—well dressed and prosperous inhabitants who look like "foreigners" ("blond, tall, and well-built"), and the poor, whom he calls "natives," who "were of sallow complexion, medium height, and a delicate frame" (18). Standing barefoot on the sidewalk, these poor people "looked thin and pale, as if they rarely had three meals a day" (18); he also sees "a mob of barefoot children" from the local school (17).[7] While Buenaventura notices the poor, Isabel imagines him finding in their plight an opportunity for profit; he founds a food import business because he reasons that "people always have to eat" but devotes most of his inventory to imported Spanish delicacies for the wealthy (33). Most of the novel's wealthy characters ignore the poor, avoid the slums, and rationalize the vast disparity between classes as simply the way things are.

Narrating most of *The House on the Lagoon*, Isabel observes the poor at every turn; her watchful concern keeps this forgotten class present throughout the narrative. She names the slums that surround every city and town on the island: Los Caracoles in the mountains near Adjuntas (102); Machuelo Abajo and the Silver Spoon near Ponce (168, 180); Las Minas beside the elegant houses in the elegant Alamares district of San Juan (10). Isabel records the stories of people who live in each of these places, making the novel both broadly inclusive and attentive to the neglect of the poor. In the first pages, she notices an arthritic old man who cares for the spring before Buenaventura takes it over; the old caretaker is killed with a blow to the head, "but nobody paid much attention" (11). Buenaventura gets away with murder, Isabel implies, because the law does not protect the poor in Puerto Rico. Social services like sanitation, education, electricity, and police protection are slow to arrive in the slums, and poor children suffer first and worst. During the war, "Children went barefoot, their heads full of lice and their bellies swollen with parasites. When they ran down the street, their souls barely clung to their bones, like fragile kites made of tissue paper" (31). In 1954, she notices a "group of street urchins in rags" (198–99). In 1982, she sees pitiable children who have been abandoned by addicts, like the "black baby who was so thin he looked as if he had the bones of a sparrow" (393). By noticing these poor children, and by recording glimpses of their precarious lives beside the Mendizabals' opulent ones, Isabel remembers the costs paid by those outside the imperial frame.

Many of the poor are black or biracial: these disenfranchised and exploited people have a special history and legacy of oppression. In telling the story of Puerto Rico's twentieth century history, Ferré emphasizes the ongoing racism in the culture.[8] Racism is passed along through generations by both colonizing cultures: the Spanish Conquistadors saw the native populations of all of the New World lands they invaded as barbaric savages and the black slaves they imported from Africa as reminders of the Moors they had fought to extinguish. Spanish priests kept "Bloodline Books" to track marriages free of Jewish, Islamic, and black or biracial ancestry, Isabel points out (22). But as wealthy Puerto Ricans begin to travel in the United States, they discover the same privileging of whiteness in the self-proclaimed land of the free; they witness segregation and suspicion of their olive skin despite American lip-service to equality under the law (25). While Puerto Rican institutions like the university are de-segregated, and while businesses serve all races, the wealthy continue to believe that a "pure white" pedigree—called "a clean lineage"—is "worth a family's weight in gold" (22). Though integration appears to have created progress in Puerto Rico, racism remains active; as Isabel writes, "San Juan's bourgeoisie were among the most prejudiced in the world; they concealed their racism with polished good manners" (338).

Counter-balancing the primacy of whiteness as a desirable quality in marriage, Isabel describes its opposite face in the construction of black and biracial women as exotic and desirable for sex. Through the lens of her mother-in-law Rebecca, Isabel hears a highly charged version of the ways wealthy white men gaze on the other:

> the sons of the well-to-do began to eye the bare arms and shoulders of the beautiful mulatto girls, who, following the American custom, went everywhere unaccompanied and worked where they pleased. The beauty of the quadroons, which until then was a

hidden treasure, was suddenly discovered by the young men of 'good families,' and there was a veritable epidemic of racially mixed liaisons on the islands.

(23)

While wealthy girls follow Spanish customs, the "mulatto girls" or "quadroons" behave provocatively: they bare their skin, move and work freely, go about without chaperones, and make their beauty visible to young men. As Rebecca construes it, the very exposure of these girls to boys of good families creates disease, "a veritable epidemic"—not of marriages, naturally—but of "liaisons" with the potential for more biracial children on the island.

Black and biracial people are reduced by the racists among San Juan's bourgeoisie to consumable bodies: whether they work as maids, cooks, or chauffeurs, or cater to other bodily appetites, they are appraised, hired, and used as bodies. Thus Quintín, picnicking on his favorite foods at Lucumí Beach, approaches young Carmelina as yet another treat for his consumption in a chapter titled "The Forbidden Banquet." Excusing his rape of the girl, he later blames it on his consumption of crab, "an aphrodisiac" that accounted for his irresistible hunger (356). In a similar way, his grandfather Arístides compares the "beautiful mulatto girl" Tosca to a delicious, edible bird: "Her dark skin was like quail's flesh; it was tender and at the same time tasted of wilderness, of tangled bushes and acid earth" (134, 136). Just as quail are hunted for their gamy but tender flesh, so Tosca seems to him exotic in her earthy wildness and yet ready to be tasted and consumed. Another "very beautiful" "light-skinned mulatto," Ermelinda, has at 16 similar edible attractions: "Her eyes were the color of molasses and her skin was a light cinnamon" (218–19). Combining sugar and spice, she attracts a wealthy lawyer, Don Bolívar, with "sensuous lips" and a "lustful gleam" in his eye, who takes her as his mistress. While Isabel shows that all women are assessed for their abilities to satisfy men's desires in this intensely patriarchal society, she emphasizes ways in which wealthy men reduce black and biracial women to exotic sexual bodies.

The most extreme story of objectification and use, however, is that of Tony Torres, an openly gay young man who is poor and biracial. Tony is recruited from the slum of Machuelo Abajo on a lie and a pretense: ballet master André Kerenski wants to dance the Firebird with a young student, Estefanía, for whom he lusts. He cannot dance openly with a student, his wife points out, or the fathers will take their daughters out of his school (168). Unable to recruit wealthy boys, Kerenski finds and trains Tony

Torres, "a fifteen-year-old mulatto with finely chiseled features" with "curly hair, and skin as smooth as bronze" (168–69). Tony is feminized by his curls, his smoothness, and his fineness; he is sexualized and further feminized by Kerenski's emphasis on his homosexuality as the crucial basis for his selection. Like the biracial women in the novel, Tony is objectified and used, his honor and his future stolen by his benefactor: concealed under an elaborate mask, Kerenski substitutes for Tony in the performance, stripping him of the starring role. Kerenski, the master and teacher, thus uses his power to erase Tony. While Kerenski is exposed and forced to leave the island, Tony's fate is worse: he "vanished from sight. He never went back to Machuelo Abajo, and no one ever heard of him again" (179). Publicly used, Tony does not survive the metaphoric rape.

Puerto Rico's black population takes on an important role in the novel through Petra Avilés, explicitly named by Isabel as "the rock on which the house on the lagoon had stood" (384). Petra, her partner Brambon, and other kin take care of the house and the various Mendizabals who live there. They are poorly paid, criticized and rebuked by Rebecca; yet Petra has the pride and dignity of a monarch. Far from characterizing her as a passive, edible morsel, Isabel describes Petra as a warrior with rock-like skin and power in every gesture: "She was six feet tall and her skin wasn't a watered-down chocolate but a deep onyx black; when she smiled it was as if a white scar slashed the darkness of the night" (58). Buenaventura chooses her as his personal servant not for her beauty but for her competence: he respects her for her knowledge and skill with medicinal plants. The granddaughter of an Angolan chieftain, Petra holds her own family together for over 90 years.

Despite her nobility and strength, Petra's place in the Puerto Rican house is in the dirt-floored basement. In the version of "upstairs, down-stairs" played out in the novel, the Afro Caribbeans, whose labor fills the bankrolls of the wealthy and keeps their houses functioning, come in through the back door, sit on cast-off furniture, and sleep in small "cells" in the basement. The government ignores their medical needs (Petra's granddaughter Alwilda is lame for life), fails to provide telephone service or sanitation, and neglects basic police protection in areas like Las Minas (Petra's daughter Carmelina is killed by a lover and Alwilda is raped by a stranger in Las Minas, 240–41). The novel implies that, despite being the rock on which the nation was founded, these citizens continue to be targets for prejudice, abuse, and neglect.

Perhaps the most insidious aspect of prejudice is the unconscious privilege accorded to whiteness in the cultural imagination. Unques-tionable because unseen, it spreads an invisible poison through the whole society. While Ferré exposes racism throughout the narrative, the painting of baby Carmelina shows most innocently this most guilty assumption of white superiority. Raped at 14, Alwilda brings her baby daughter, named Carmelina after Alwilda's dead mother, for Petra to raise. Rebecca's friends call the baby "a black Kewpie doll," and Rebecca passes Carmelina along to her own daughters Patria and Libertad, telling them "It's a new doll" (244). The girls enjoy playing with "their new toy" until one of them says, "I'm tired of playing with a black doll. Let's paint Carmelina white, to see how she looks" (244–45). In unquestioned ways, these wealthy daughters internalize their parents' objectification of all black people and their faith in white superiority. When they spread white paint all over the baby, they poison her with lead—apt symbol for the racist sickness spread throughout Puerto Rican society.

The fall of the house on the lagoon emerges from the same racist plague: the drive to keep his bloodline "pure" or "clean" or "white" leads Quintín Mendizabal to actions that poison his relationships with his brother, his sons, his servants, and his wife. In Ferré's complex characterization, each of these relationships is already under siege, compromised by jealousy, greed, arrogance, and the heritage of patri- archal control. Nonetheless, the catastrophes that bring down the house are all about wanting the baby to be white—and sacrificing lives and loves to make it so. Quintín and Rebecca collaborate in preventing his younger brother Ignacio from marrying Ermelinda's beautiful daughter, Esmeralda, because she is part black. Quintín later forbids his son Manuel to marry Esmeralda's daughter Coral for the same reason. Having raped Carmelina, the same white-painted baby raised in his house, Quintín agrees under threat from Isabel to accept her son Willie as his own; but years later he disinherits Willie, denies his paternity, and proclaims, "I'd rather be dead than have mulatto grandchildren" (347). In a land of hybridity and olive skins, in a place where the settlers look more "sallow" than white (18, 139), the obsessive focus on whiteness destroys the house of Mendizabal. Ironically, Quintín gets his wish and ends up dead.

The battle to maintain white power through "pure" breeding is also a war to control the narratives of culture, history, and values that constitute national identity. White control of the official stories of Puerto Rican culture has involved the silencing of black and biracial voices, the marginalization of slave narratives, and the suppression of Afro-Caribbean family chronicles and genealogies. Alongside the Mendizabals' generational saga, then, Ferré writes some parts of the Avilés' story. The earliest known Avilés ancestor is Petra's grandfather,

Bernabé, "whose African name was Ndongo Kumbundu" (58). Born in Angola, he "had been chieftain of his tribe" before Portuguese traders capture and enslave him and sell him to a sugarcane hacienda owner in Guayama, Puerto Rico (58–59). The storytellers, Petra's mother— then Petra, then Isabel—carefully preserve his African name in order to remember what Puerto Rican history has erased. Bernabé's religion and politics are also respectfully recorded: "Slaves from Angola, Kongo, and Ndongo shared fundamental beliefs and language, part of a rich culture. They had their own religion, and their chieftains were spiritual leaders whose duty was to look out for their people" (59). In Puerto Rico, the slaves are baptized as Christians and forbidden to speak Bantu: "Bernabé had a terrible time accepting this. One's tongue was so deeply ingrained, more so even than one's religion or tribal pride" because "It was attached to one's throat, to one's neck, to one's stomach, even to one's heart" (60). Bernabé leads the plans for a secret slave uprising, which is foiled by accident. To punish him, the white community gathers with the slaves at the town square; the barber slices Bernabé's tongue off and cauterizes the wound with a red-hot iron (62). While the outcome is not recorded, Bernabé is in a meaningful way extinguished with the double loss of his language and the tongue attached to his heart.

Petra Avilés honors her silenced ancestor, keeps his legacy alive, and restores his tongue through her own speech. She preserves the African practice of herbal medicine; she worships the same spirits and keeps the symbolic effigy of Elegguá her mother hands down to her; she speaks at least some Bantu, and she sings a lullaby to baby Carmelina "in a strange language that Alwilda had never heard before" (243). She maintains the self-respecting pride of a chieftain's descendant: "Don't sit her on the floor. She's an Avilés and should be conscious of her rank," Petra says to Alwilda (242). Though she is born in Puerto Rico and lives her whole life there, Petra looks back through Bernabé to the African homeland. When she dies, she asks her relatives to cremate her body on Lucumí Beach, "so the mistral would blow her ashes toward Africa" (383). In Petra's life, her grandfather's vision persists.

Petra also gets a unique revenge on those who perpetuate the racist logic that enslaved and silenced her grandfather, and she does so through language. She tells Quintín that Willie, his biracial son, is "also an Avilés," and if Quintín disowns him, she will tell Willie the secret of his parentage (372). She does: on her deathbed, Willie calls her "Grandmother," and later he tells Isabel that he knows the family story (383). Petra also curses Quintín for disinheriting Willie, swearing "by Elegguá—he who is more than God—that one day you'll be sorry!"

(372). Quintín dies, not through the direct action of any supernatural force; rather, he beats Isabel savagely in their boat, and she steers the boat under the terrace to hit him in the head with an iron beam (407). By his own brutality, Quintín fulfills the curse Petra has spoken. He loses both sons: Manuel by his own acts and words, and Willie by the truths Petra reveals. He not only loses his wife, as he has feared throughout the novel, but dies at her hand as she acts in self-defense. He is killed by his own decaying house.

Petra is also characterized as the enabling force behind the narrative of *House*, and thus her story and Bernabé's survive to take their place in the Puerto Rican national chronicle. The manuscript itself is under threat: Quintín has found and read sections as Isabel writes, and he finally decides that he will burn it to prevent publication: "and if you publish it, I'll kill you," he says to Isabel (375). Isabel gives the manuscript to Petra, who preserves it by giving it to Willie; thus she enables the novel's eventual publication. Petra is also a supportive force behind the novel's composition, providing information and perspectives on the family story to Isabel, as well as a model of woman's strength. Though nothing in Isabel's manuscript suggests that Petra has any role in motivating or shaping the writing, Quentín says three times that he believes Petra is somehow its source. The first time he speculates, "Something, someone, was pressing Isabel to write these awful things about his family. A mysterious force seemed to be driving her. Could Petra be behind all this?" (249). The second time he seems sure: "Petra was going to keep on driving Isabel until she finished the novel" (293); he adds that "behind Isabel's lens he felt Petra's malevolent eye following his every step" (294). As Quintín becomes more fearful and guilty, he thinks "Isabel wasn't under Petra's spell at all" but rather, "She was Petra's ally, and they were writing the manuscript together in order to destroy him" (374). In these paranoid but perhaps insightful suspicions, Quintín conflates the two women, crediting Isabel's completion of the written story to Petra's strength and determination. In this way he also suggests that the manuscript should be envisioned as a Puerto Rican hybrid, a creation of black and white together.

Isabel's paper *House*

House tells Isabel Monfort Mendizabal's story, set in a larger context where home opens out on homeland. Isabel is the current inheritor of the dilemma of national identity: from the outset, the novel focuses on her choice of a house and a partner and connects those personal decisions to public cultural dilemmas. Rather than placing her decision at the end, as a nineteenth century novel might do, this text opens with an ominous scene from the time of her engagement to Quintín: cruelly and savagely, he beats a young man who sings a love song to Isabel outside the hedge around her house. She is betrothed, this incident warns, to a latter-day conquistador, a literal descendant of the Spanish colonizers, and one who uses gratuitous violence to mark his territory and protect his empire. Given Isabel's race (she has a "clean" lineage, 22) and class (middle), her decision to marry into the imperial house appears inevitable; once she has done so, however, the entire attention of the narrative turns to the question, what will she make of a bad marriage? How can she create a space for herself inside that home and homeland?

Like Isabel Archer, who has similar intellectual ambitions and a kindred innocence, Isabel Mendizabal illustrates the plight of women who marry controlling men; the novel reflects a feminist sense of the oppression of women in patriarchal homes, especially traditional Hispanic ones. Strongly influenced by early feminists, Ferré writes women's stories in all of her poetry and fiction.[9] In some of her most famous stories ("The Youngest Doll," "When Women Love Men," "Amalia," and "Sleeping Beauty," for example), marriage is figured as an imprisonment of the woman, who loses her right to express herself and becomes a doll—a decorative plaything under her husband's control.[10] Women's oppression figures centrally in *House* as well: the house of Mendizabal is patriarchal, dynastic, and coercive to women; and other figures from the same social class exploit wives and mistresses. But this novel broadens its critique and connects gender, race, class, and cultural tradition, so the problems confronting Isabel and other women reveal their inextricable links to a whole social system. The novel's first sentence begins to make these connections explicit: "My grandmother always insisted that when people fall in love they should look closely at what the family of the betrothed is like, because one never marries the bridegroom alone but also his parents, grandparents, great-grandparents, and the whole damned tangle of the ancestral line" (3). Damned in the sense of blasted, cursed, hopeless, and ill-fated, the tangle into which Isabel marries is the Puerto Rican family. The novel's structure underscores the breadth of Isabel's tangled family connection, telling in its first half the stories of grandparents, parents, acquaintances, shopkeepers, and members of various social classes. Isabel connects the story of her marriage and family to narratives concerning Esmeralda Márquez, Petra, Mauricio Boleslaus, and others. Throughout her account, Isabel focuses on relationships between the family and the Puerto Rican community.

The novel ultimately resolves Isabel's relationship to that family and community in violence and exile. Isabel kills Quintín in self-defense, in the midst of a brutal beating he inflicts on her as she flees the house. Her biological son, Manuel, stands at the very end "watching the house on the lagoon burn to the ground" (407).[11] Isabel and Willie flee to Florida, and in an epilogue placed out of order before the last events, Isabel reveals that they live "in a small hotel on Anastasia, a narrow island on the peninsula's western coast" (379). She ends, then, outside the imperial house that has defined her Puerto Rican years, in the transient rented space of a hotel; she leaves her homeland for a narrow perch on an island across the water. Her sons are separated but similarly stripped of any role in the Mendizabal legacy—one radicalized in Puerto Rico and made unsuitable for Quintín's dynastic ends, the other a painter in Florida who inherits only the knowledge of his father's virulent racism. But the exile she chooses leads Isabel to what Susan Stanford Friedman calls "A poetics of dislocation" recognizing home as "a place that must be left, as a place whose leaving is the source of speech and writing"(2004: 205).

Isabel has spent most of her married life, the 27 years between 1955 and 1982, passively acquiescing to her husband's domination and control. While her values differ significantly from her husband's, her efforts to create an alternate Puerto Rican family—one racially inclusive, respectful of women's intellectual and cultural contributions, charitable to the poor—appear weak, ineffectual, and doomed. She is helpless to intervene in the dramas of the Mendizabals: Ignacio's frustrated love and suicide, the Spanish viscounts' decadent spending and Rebecca's partying, Quintín's theft of the company business and refusal to loan Ignacio money. When Quintín rapes Carmelina and Willie is born, she makes one of her few strong stands, insisting that Willie be adopted and raised as their child. But after Quintín agrees, Isabel falls into the same pattern of living as that of her mother-in-law Rebecca:

> I was content to be Quintín Mendizabal's wife and willingly took over the role of mistress of the house on the lagoon. I kept myself looking as young as possible, was concerned that our children perform well at school, saw that the cooking and the laundering were impeccably done.
>
> (329)

Isabel settles for home's pleasures, enjoys the Mendizabal wealth, and abandons both her writing (she notes that "I wrote very little, if at all," 329) and her concern to make a better world. Her passive acceptance of her husband's control becomes especially problematic in the novel's present, 1982, when he pressures her to sign a revised will disinheriting her sons and commands that Petra be sent away: she "agreed with Petra in everything but was so afraid of Quintín I didn't dare open my mouth" (373).

Isabel eventually renounces the house on the lagoon along with the privilege she has enjoyed there, through the writing of *The House on the Lagoon*: she writes her way from house to *House*. Creating a family chronicle and national history, she sees imbricated patterns that call her to create new relationships. She encounters what Stuart Hall terms the "traumas of violent rupture" that make the Caribbean a diasporic space and, by narrating the stories of the "damned tangle" of her extended family, she comes to prefer a hotel in exile over the racist, sexist, and classist edifice that perpetuates imperial values. The importance of her narrative becomes clear when she reveals that "It was only three months ago—on June 15, 1982, to be exact—that I began to write *The House on the Lagoon*" and that her writing occurs "at Willie's prompting": "He was always telling me how important art was. It was the one thing that helped make the world into a better place, he insisted" (330). Between June and November, when the plebiscite takes place, Isabel recounts the story of the national family, writing her manuscript in sections as she gives up her previous investments in the physical care of the house. While she does not challenge Quintín verbally during the process, her writing disputes the forms of privilege for which he stands.

The novel, then, is the story of a woman writing her own life story; all the magic that occurs, in the sense of transformation, happens through Isabel's pursuit of what Suzette Henke calls "scriptotherapy": "autobiography is, or at least has the potential to be, a powerful form of scriptotherapy" (xv). To show how challenging Isabel's narrative becomes, Ferré includes ten sections purportedly written by Quintín as he finds and reads hidden chapters of the manuscript and three sections in which Isabel comments on her writing and Quintín's reading. These self-reflexive sections highlight the text's construction of differing accounts of familial and national history. While one reviewer complains that Quintín's "critiques are not given much space or [...] intelligence" and "offer neither an alternate view nor reveal a facet of Quintín that is not available from Isabel" (Ellen Friedman), these sections effectively emphasize the writing process and its transformative impact on Isabel, Quintín, and their relationship. They show how Isabel's writing takes positions threatening to her husband's values and versions of events and help establish her account as an anti-imperial narrative. They loosen her authority as narrator and foreground the constructed and contested nature of all historical accounts.

Quintín's attitude toward Isabel's writing includes some moments of condescension and others of grudging respect, but even when he admires her achievement he simultaneously fears her power and determines to destroy her work. In reading the first section, Quintín reflects a patronizing investment in Isabel's project. She has always wanted to write, and he encouraged her because "He didn't want Isabel to be just another bourgeois housewife; he wanted her to amount to something, so he could be proud of her" (70). He expects her work to rely on his background as an historian and to confirm his version of events: "he thought they could embark on the project together" (71). Even in the first section, however, Quintín feels indignant over Isabel's use of information he has given her, her distortions of historical fact, and her creation of versions of his parents that contradict his own memories. By the second section, he is "worried" (105), then "embarrassed as well as betrayed" (107). In the third and fourth sections, he finds strengths in her writing and admits to great interest in the story: "He was amazed by his wife's perseverance. She had written the new material entirely without his help; indeed, she rarely asked him questions anymore"; he adds, "She was becoming a better writer as the novel progressed; she was blossoming before his very eyes" (186–87). His admiration breeds resentment of her success and anger over her willingness to expose family secrets. He focuses on persuading her not to publish by convincing her that her work is worthless. He thinks about errors and misinterpretations in Isabel's versions of events and characters, narrates different versions of some stories, and writes critical, condescending notes in her margins. By the fifth section he begins yearning to destroy the manuscript (249). In the tenth section he decides to destroy it and confronts Isabel, "his face white with anger," when he cannot find it: "How *dare* you write it!" (375). He threatens her with death if she publishes the manuscript: "I'll kill you" (375). Near the end, he tells her the novel is "not a work of art" and that "it distorts history" (386).

Through his value-laden comments on the stories she has told, Quentín reveals how far Isabel's version strays from his own invested understandings, which are those of the dominant culture in Puerto Rico.[12] He is repeatedly dismayed at her revelation of "private" or "secret" information about his family, principally their flaws and failings, but never at the failings themselves. He is "shocked by her revelation" of his father's black mistresses but reasons that "most men had mistresses" and "independence was part of a man's nature" (247–48). His greatest distress occurs over her politics: he finds her manuscript "tainted with feminist prejudices" and exclaims, "Feminism was the curse of the twentieth century!" (108). Staunchly in favor of statehood, he hates her commitment to independence and regards nationalists as "fanatical" terrorists (149); therefore his grandfather, who ordered the murder of unarmed young cadets, was actually a hero (151). He observes that her ancestors were far lower on the social scale than his: some people called "the Monforts little more than white trash" (247). Desperate to imagine Isabel as an innocent victim of outside manipulation in the writing of her novel, Quintín posits the malign influence of Petra behind her manuscript: he sees Petra as "a spider" weaving the "web of lies" in Isabel's account (249, 75). While Isabel's narrative describes biases of race, class, and gender in the ruling families of Puerto Rico, these prejudices come vividly alive in Quentín's sections. His careless assumption of the superiority of his conquistador ancestors and of the malice of the black woman who is his other dramatizes the reasons why Quintín must find Isabel's narrative profoundly threatening.

The changes in Isabel as she writes appear in the trajectory of her hiding places for the manuscript, revealed in Quintín's sections. Quintín finds the first chapters behind a "two-volume" Latin dictionary "bound in red leather" (70): this hiding place reflects the western origins of Puerto Rico's Spanish colonial era and Isabel's affiliation with the power, suggested by the red leather, vested in Eurocentric discourses. The second set of chapters turns up in the kitchen, hidden in the *Fannie Merritt Farmer's Boston Cooking School Cook Book*, written in English and imported from the United States (106). This hiding place suggests Isabel's invocation of the modern imperial power of the United States, supported by her use of the English language in her manuscript. The next set of chapters eludes Quintín for a long time; then he finds them in his mother's elaborate desk, hidden in a secret compartment where Rebecca kept her own poems. He locates six more installments in the desk, though Isabel knows that he is reading the manuscript and thus leaves it there deliberately (197). Her use of Rebecca's own hiding place suggests that Isabel has begun to understand some parallels between them, the two writing mistresses of the house on the lagoon.

Rebecca accepted a place inside the imperial house and, in the process, paid with her voice and values. As Isabel describes Rebecca's youthful desires, Rebecca wanted an imperial lord, imagined as a conquering figure; but she wanted to be a partner in the enterprise, with regiments of her own: "She wanted a true monarch, one who could subdue her with a single glance. A sovereign with shoulders spread like infantry battalions, strong cavalry thighs" whom she might respect as "A real commander in chief, who would raise her slumbering regiments at a command" (27–28). She marries instead a man who beats her unconscious, razes the house she has designed, pays other women for sexual services and begets children with them, impregnates her four times despite her reluctance, gives away her library, and names his daughters and his ships after his nationalistic aspirations: Patria and Libertad. Once he has conquered her will, Buenaventura reduces Rebecca to "a broken doll" (66) and a silent, obedient implement of his imperial will. The writing process helps Isabel see her own position more clearly: while Quentín has come to resemble Buenaventura, she has followed Rebecca. When she finally takes her manuscript out of Rebecca's desk, she acknowledges the need to struggle for a different ending to her own narrative.

The final hiding place Isabel chooses for her fictive "house" is in the care of the African saint Elegguá, who is "more than God," conduit to Petra's ancestors and thus to the Puerto Rican family's African past (64). She carries the papers to the cellar and gives them to Petra, moving the manuscript into the protective care of the African saint and the Afro-Caribbean woman who has been "the rock on which the house on the lagoon had stood" (384). This final protective power actually saves the manuscript: Elegguá turns out to be an effective guardian of Isabel's anti-imperial—and by extension, anti-western—narrative. Before her death, Petra stores the manuscript in a cardboard box holding Elegguá's "toys" and gives the box to Willie, who is the biological link between Mendizabal and Avilés families (383). Although Quintín fights with him for possession of the manuscript as all three family members leave the house, this hybrid offspring of two Puerto Rican lines manages to hold on to the story of his roots. It will be the only heritage he takes out of Puerto Rico.[13]

Isabel's writing struggles against the legacies of empire in both its content and its form. Not only does she identify the abuses of power that accompany the conquistadors, old and new, and their brutal oppression of those they construct as other, she also makes feminist forms of resistance central to her way of telling the Puerto Rican story. As Ben Heller writes about Ferré, for Isabel "writing Puerto Rican culture does not imply a masculine relation to the soil of the homeland (dominating it, erecting upon it a spiritual architecture) but rather a feminist embrace of a fluid non-place, the vulnerable location of the inbetween" (414). Writing in the first person, she refuses to become what Augustus Puleo describes as "the individual masculine voice that appears allied with political and economic interests that define history" (232).[14] She includes her own other in several ways, without presuming to appropriate its voice or subsume its story under her own. Her repeated observations of the poor, the marginalized, the black and the biracial keep their struggles in the foreground. More dramatically, she includes the voice of Quintín, allowing space for his complaints, criticisms, and corrections in the final version of her story. Beyond the more common strategy of including plural narrators to create relative perspectives, the narrative device in *House on the Lagoon* creates conflicting versions, with sections by her husband actually contesting and undermining Isabel's accounts. She chooses not to conquer and eliminate his voice. Though she wishes for a reader with "an understanding heart," she refuses to coerce her reader's sympathy, agreement, or support by the simple deletion of her husband's negative opinions (380). There is obvious merit to some of his observations: she makes errors of fact in putting German submarines off Puerto Rico in 1918, for example, or a hot dog vendor on the island the year before (73–74). His observation that she portrays men as villains, women as victims, while "there were good men and bad men in the world, and the same was true of women," exposes a feminist bias in her narrative (108–109). Her inclusion of Quintín's criticism of her manuscript highlights her own investments in the story. Its most significant effect, though, is to identify her as an anti-imperialist narrator.

The implications of her narrative stance include, but go beyond, a move to dismantle authority and create undecidable contradictions. For example, Quintín writes twice that Isabel has red hair (111, 246); Isabel describes herself as "raven-haired and olive-skinned" (173). Does Quintín's account gain credibility because he makes the observation twice, or is it suspect because he wants to create a fiery-tempered Isabel? Does Isabel report her coloring in a neutral way, or is she exchanging appearances with Estefanía, who was preferred by ballet-master Kerenski? These questions lead to a suspension of authority for both narrators. As Julie Barak writes, "through the interweaving of Isabel and Quintín's narratives," Ferré deconstructs "the authority of the authorial voice" (33). In Barak's view, the whole text is Isabel's, including Quintín's sections, yet the narrative aims to show that both the historical view represented by Quintín and the literary view represented by Isabel come unraveled, with the meaning of events lost in doubled inauthenticity (33–38). While I agree that some details are deliberately made undecidable by the contradictory narratives, I see Quintín's narration as crucial to Ferré's purposes: he needs to be imagined as Isabel's opponent, wrestling for the supremacy of his version of the familial and national story, while Isabel demonstrates a different relation to authorial power by allowing his voice to remain. Ferré's desire to convey Puerto Rico's story to an English-speaking audience invalidates Barak's conclusion, that readers "can no longer tell the difference between, nor really care about the significance of, the 'real' story," so the novel becomes "a widening gyre in which the reader forever spins" (38). Instead, the doubled narrative undermines the power of the single account and creates an anti-imperial mode of authorship.

Isabel's narrative, contested by Quintín, foregrounds the battle waged over the construction of history: it shows high stakes for those involved, who become invested in their own accounts and desperately committed to silencing other versions. Isabel understands the influence of historical accounts and the weight of all they repress; she writes about the nuns who taught history to Quintín's grandfather Arístides: "The history of the United States was taught thoroughly at their school, yet Puerto Rican history was never mentioned. In the nuns' view, the island *had* no history. In this they were not exceptional; it was forbidden to teach Puerto Rican history at the time" (91). Indeed, even US President Woodrow Wilson implied that Puerto Rico was too primitive to occupy the civilized time of history:

> The nuns of the Annunciation taught Arístides that the island had begun to exist politically when the American troops landed at Guánica. President Wilson had said so himself in a speech in 1913. "The countries the United States have taken in trust, Puerto Rico and the Philippines, must first accept the discipline of law. They are children and we are men in these deep matters of government and justice."
>
> (91–92)

In the name of what Benedict Anderson calls "imagined community," the nuns teach Puerto Rican children to affiliate with the United States, source of their identity as a nation. Before Guánica, the land was simply an ahistorical island, the people a childish set of natives incapable of managing the basic acts of a civilization. For the nuns, there *is no* Puerto Rican history; for the makers of the policy forbidding its teaching, traces of this history must be repressed in order to induce the Puerto Rican "children" to "accept the discipline of law" imposed from outside by a paternal colonizing power.

The history to be repressed includes all traces of other national influences and of the damaging costs of imperial conquest. Since the United States has replaced Spain, history starts anew, and no invidious connections should be made between Spanish exploitation of the island's natural and human resources and the new era inaugurated by US troops. Historical and ongoing practices of racial and economic oppression must not be mentioned; slavery cannot appear in the nuns' curriculum. The goal of permissible historical narratives is to create "a true civic spirit" based on the ideals of liberty and justice for all, and stories of how Puerto Rico or the United States have fallen short of those ideals, or subverted them, must be repressed. As Ania Loomba writes, "nations are communities created not simply by forging certain bonds but by fracturing or disallowing others; not merely by invoking and remembering certain versions of the past, but making sure that others are forgotten or repressed" (202).

In this context, Isabel's narrative remembers what has been forgotten; more, it deliberately returns what has been repressed. Quintín's opposition to her narrative, refutation of her facts, and deadly struggle to find and destroy her manuscript show the degree of threat he finds in her anti-imperial version of Puerto Rican history. She includes those who should have no place, like Petra, Esmeralda, and Tony Torres; she portrays the upper class as corrupt, decadent, and guilty; she traces racism, rape, and exploitation into the very house of privilege. As Irma López writes, "Isabel's writing gives voice to personal and collective histories which imperial ideology did not recognize" (138, my translation).[15] Where she touches on actual historical events and figures, she interprets them in ways outside the boundaries of authorized history. The American governors appointed to rule Puerto Rico, for example, live pampered lives inside the Governor's Palace, isolated by their inability to speak Spanish and indifferent to the lives of the people (122). President Harding removes the one governor, Emmet Montgomery Riley, who "got involved in risky island affairs": shocked by the workers' poverty, he tries to pressure the island's sugar planters and American sugar mills to pay higher wages (122, 124). His successor, Governor Blanton Winship, chooses instead a relationship of exchange; he brings the beauties of the island to the United States and the authority of the United States to the island. He commissions a coffee-table book of photographs of the island's natural beauty, with "angel-hair waterfalls, cotton-candy clouds, sugar-white beaches, cows pasturing up and down velvet-green hills— and not a single starving peasant to mar the beauty of the landscape," to be sold on the mainland (125). Winship appoints Quintín's grandfather Arístides as the first Puerto Rican chief of police, orders him to attack a group of unarmed teenaged nationalist cadets, and then denies responsibility for the decision, blaming Arístides for the massacre (126–31).

This event, the "Ponce Massacre," appears in histories of Puerto Rico;[16] Isabel's account focuses on the role played by a Puerto Rican who has become so ardent a supporter of statehood that he willingly obeys the order to attack. By exposing abuses of imperial power and the damage these inflict on the national and personal family, Isabel constructs a counter-history, even as she admits the fictional nature of her writing and allows Quintín to voice objections to the accuracy of her facts.

The novel represents Isabel's battle to wrest history from Quintín's control, to create an anti-imperialist account of past events. Adopting a Western view of history, authorship, and authority, Quintín believes that writing should convey historical truth through a detached and objective perspective; for this reason, all of his sections appear in the third person. They also claim omniscience, reporting Isabel's feelings and motives as if he could reliably know them. In his sections, Quintín claims authority over history and truth, which he sees as equivalents; he proclaims in the first section that he is "a historian himself—he had a master's degree in history from Columbia University" (71). He objects to Isabel's novel because of its "blatant disregard of history" (151); he tells her, "history is unalterable. A novelist may write lies, but a historian never can" (311). Isabel, on the other hand, struggles to de-colonize writing from the claims to authoritative truth and to create a kind of historical narrative in which both form and content refuse imperialist domination. She believes that "Nothing is true, nothing is false, everything is the color of the glass you're looking through" (106). Unlike Quintín, she freely claims her own subjectivity; she performs in the first person and thus, as Sidonie Smith writes, her "narrative performativity constitutes interiority. That is, the interiority or self that is said to be prior to the autobiographical expression or reflection is an *effect* of auto-biographical storytelling" (109). She makes autobiographical fiction into a way of narrating history; as Begoña Toral Alemañ writes, "The dividing line between fiction and History dissolves and fiction assumes, then, the role of an *other* History, questioning the naturalization as irrefutable truth of historical imperialist discourse" (93, my translation).[17]

From Quintín's perspective, the novel describes the tragic destruction of a house and family that made significant contributions to Puerto Rico's evolving politics and economy. But from the perspective Isabel and Ferré adopt, the text explores assumptions about class, race, and gender that enable the Mendizabal family to become wealthy and powerful at others' expense; then, as Puerto Rico evolves toward a post-colonial consciousness, the imperial home based on a purloined Western design is brought down by its latest inheritor. The home reflecting the white, upper class legacy of control over the Puerto Rican homeland does not survive as a monument to permanence, either through the dynasty or through the art museum Quintín hoped to found. Instead, Isabel's invented house is all that remains. Within its paper walls, it gives Puerto Rico a new historical counter-memory that includes and remembers.

5

The Decolonized Home: Chimamanda Ngozi Adichie's *Purple Hibiscus*

Writing about the early steps toward revolution in colonial societies, Partha Chatterjee argues that "anticolonial nationalism creates its own domain of sovereignty within colonial society well before it begins its political battle with the imperial power. It does this by dividing the world of social institutions and practices into two domains—the material and the spiritual" (6). It grants the West dominion in the material realm of economy, statecraft, science and technology, even emulating Western practices. But an emerging anti-colonial nationalism declares sovereignty over the private domain of the spiritual, including language, education, and the family, for this realm bears "the 'essential' marks of cultural identity [...] This formula is, I think, a fundamental feature of anticolonial nationalisms in Asia and Africa" (6). An outer, public realm might express a surface resemblance, even allegiance, to the West, but the domestic realm remains a sovereign space for national culture and thus the space where the culture's movement toward independence can first be imagined.

While Chatterjee's formula describes the process leading toward independence in South Asia, it is notably inadequate for Nigeria. Colonized by Christian missionaries from the mid-nineteenth century, long before it became a British colony and protectorate in 1914, Nigeria first encountered Western domination in the spiritual realm. Catholic and protestant organizations from Europe and North America sent missionaries to Nigeria between 1842 and 1892, recruiting Africans who helped to spread the faith throughout the south (Falola 40–42). The use of European languages throughout Africa followed 1884; Kenyan writer Ngũgĩ wa Thiong'o argues in *Decolonizing the Mind* that the capitalist powers of Europe sat in Berlin and carved an entire continent with a multiplicity of peoples, cultures, and languages into different colonies.[...] African countries, as colonies and even today as neo-colonies, came to be defined and to define themselves in terms of the languages of Europe: English-speaking, French-speaking or Portuguese-speaking African countries.

(4–5)

Nigerians, of course, speak English, and their education follows Western models, often in church schools: "In many places, the church and the school went together. This aided conversion, as parents sent their children to the mission if only to secure education" (Falola 42–43). Culture and family life, the other areas Chatterjee identifies with the spiritual domain, were also Westernized among the new elite that emerged: "Many members of this elite imbibed aspects of Western culture and began to think of transforming Nigeria according to the Western model" (Falola 43). The spiritual domain was colonized first in Nigeria, as suggested by the large-scale southern conversion to versions of Christianity that were controlled from abroad and led by imported European clergy; these condemned "most aspects of traditional religion and society as the work of the devil" (Isichei 326).

Above those on any other continent, African colonies, like Nigeria, had to be subjugated at the spiritual level first in order to convert and humanize the African. As the racial other of the West, the African was not Orientalized, in Said's sense, as a figure representing "romance, exotic beings, haunting memories and landscapes, remarkable experiences" (1979: 1); though the African, like the Oriental, *did* reflect "the idea of European identity as a superior one in comparison with all the non-European peoples and cultures," the African was seen without the fascination and romance associated with the Oriental—and with added racism as well as guilt emerging from Western ownership of African slaves. As Frantz Fanon writes, the African was imagined by the West as soulless, subhuman, devoid of spirit:

For colonialism, this vast continent was a den of savages, infested with superstitions and fanaticism, destined to be despised, cursed by God, a land of cannibals, a land of 'niggers.' Colonialism's condemnation is continental in scale. Colonialism's claim that the precolonial period was akin to a darkness of the human soul refers to the entire continent of Africa.

(1961: 150)

Therefore, the Western colonial enterprise strove above all to transmit spiritual values, as if to confer or even create humanity in the process. V. Y. Mudimbe explains in *The Invention of Africa* that colonization

> also broke the culturally unified and religiously integrated schema of most African traditions. From that moment on the forms and formulations of the colonial culture and its aims were somehow the means of trivializing the whole traditional mode of life and its spiritual framework. The potential and necessary transformations meant that the mere presence of this new culture was a reason for the rejection of unadapted persons and confused minds.
>
> (4)

Colonization acted to trivialize traditional culture and spirituality, leading Africans to believe that their very humanity depended on a wholesale rejection of the African past.

Implicit in Africa's acquisition of a Western spiritual orientation are forms of cultural alienation, an internalized sense of inferiority, and a colonized mind or soul. When Africans abjure their own history and traditions, especially at the level of religious belief, their ancestors and their unconverted kinspeople become "unadapted persons and confused minds." Indigenous culture takes on the unenlightened and barely human aspect in which it appears to a racist Western view. As Fanon writes in *The Wretched of the Earth*, colonialism works to "demean history" for oppressed peoples; it "turns its attention to the past of the colonized people and distorts it, disfigures it, and destroys it" and convinces them that "if the colonist were to leave they would regress into barbarism, degradation, and bestiality" (149). African people, by implication, buy into what Said calls the "flexible *positional* superiority" of Europeans (1979: 7) and thus their own inferior human status. In *Black Skin, White Masks*, Fanon explores the operation of an inferiority complex of the soul in Africa and its diaspora:

> Every colonized people—in other words, every people in whose soul an inferiority complex has been created by the death and burial of its local cultural originality—finds itself face to face with the language of the civilizing nation; that is, with the culture of the mother country. The colonized is elevated above his jungle status in proportion to his adoption of the mother country's cultural standards. He becomes whiter as he renounces his blackness, his jungle.
>
> (18)

The spiritual colonization that appears to have been inextricably tied to Western imperialism in Africa leaves indelible, brutalizing and neutralizing traces. It makes revolution—especially the sort of home-grown, quiet pre-revolt inside private domestic spaces that Chatterjee finds elsewhere—impossible at worst, delayed at best. It leads to an African literature "produced in the crucible of colonialism," as Simon Gikandi observes (2004: 379); as he writes elsewhere, it makes African postcolonialism "a code for the state of undecidability in which the culture of colonialism continues to resonate in what was supposed to be its negation" (1996: 14).

In Nigeria, Africa's most populous nation and one of the poorest countries in the world,[1] British colonization ended in 1960 with independence and Commonwealth status. But the four decades following independence have been disastrous, in part because of the attenuation of traditional cultural values. As a legacy of Western teachings about African barbarity, Nigeria appears to be plagued by barbarous forms of oppression, sectarian violence, and massive corruption. Government is precarious, just as the West predicted: "Between 1960 and 1996 there were no less than ten officially known coups" (Osaghae 14). Between 1985 and 1998, under the consecutive dictatorships of Generals Babangida and Abacha, conditions grew intolerable for Nigerians, with rising unemployment, fuel shortages, school closures, "increased religiosity and the cultivation of fatalistic complexes which served to reduce the spirit of protest," and a "brain drain" as educated Nigerians fled the country: "The best and brightest of Nigeria are gone," says Chimamanda Ngozi Adichie (Osaghae 205, Spencer). The Ghanaian writer Ama Ata Aidoo has the protagonist of her novel, *Our Sister Killjoy*, comment that "Nigeria not only has all the characteristics which nearly every African country has, but also presents these characteristics in bolder outlines" (52). In a poetic meditation on Nigeria's combined beauty and tragedy, she writes:

> Household quarrels of
> Africa become a
> WAR in
> Nigeria:
>
> (52–53)

A house divided between the Islamic, Hausa-speaking north and the Christian south, itself divided between a Yoruba-speaking West and

Igbo-speaking East, with cultural tensions reflected in the civil war attempting unsuccessfully to found a Republic of Biafra (1967–70),[2] the Nigerian nation was artificially created out of colonial occupation and British commercial interests: "Nigeria was a British colonial creation" (Osaghae 4). It has paid a high price for its colonial history.

Nigerians, then, are twice colonized and doubly unhomed, for both public and private spheres are given over to the Western voices that condemn the African. For African women, the yoke of patriarchal oppression added to the legacy of imperial domination creates especially heavy burdens. Patriarchal beliefs and customs, raging from polygamy and circumcision (or female genital cutting) to the privileging of men in marital systems and the favoring of sons, survive in various African countries from traditional cultures. The underlying assumptions of male priority and power met reinforcement from Western patriarchy in and after colonialism, leaving African women doubly oppressed. As Carole Boyce Davies observes, "The liberation of Africa is directly connected to the liberation of women" (1986: 4). An emerging African feminism has begun to appear in literature, traditionally "the preserve of male writers and critics," she writes, contesting the practice of "turning a blind eye to women in African literature" (1, 2). Davies argues that "Theoretical African feminism understands the interconnectedness of race, class, and sex oppression" and thus calls for critical exploration of the representation of these issues by African writers (11).

To explore the fictional representation of contemporary Nigeria, I have chosen Chimamanda Ngozi Adichie's first novel, *Purple Hibiscus* (2003), because like other transnational women's novels it links the private troubles of home with the public crises of nation. Adichie narrates the stories of a Catholic family, the Achikes, and their connection to the worlds of township, professional life, economics, news, religion, and culture in Nigeria. The novel contrasts two homes, one owned by Eugene and enclosed by high walls, the other rented by his sister Ifeoma and open to a wide range of Nigerian life. Educated and converted in the first generation of missionary schools, both of these central characters practice Catholicism and raise their children in the church, though their father, Papa-Nnukwu, practices traditional African worship. Religious differences, crucial in Nigerian politics between Islamic north and Christian south, explode in a public coup that brings violence, corruption, and fear—all reflected in private homes where the impulse to revolt in the name of self-worth, survival, and independence comes into a contradictory and complex relationship with the self-abnegation, repression, and African self-hatred ingested together with Western religion.

Their struggle to end spiritual and political colonization and achieve independence spins some characters out of Africa, into exile, imprisonment, or death. For other characters, including the narrator Kambili, decolonizing the soul can only occur in a decolonized home—these become necessary first steps toward independence in Nigeria.

At home behind walls

Eugene Achike lives in a spacious house in a walled compound; his daughter Kambili reports from her second floor bedroom, "The compound walls, topped by coiled electric wires, were so high I could not see the cars driving by on our street" (9). He chooses the Daughters of the Immaculate Heart Secondary School for his daughter because of its walls; these are also "very high" and "topped by jagged pieces of green glass with sharp edges jutting out. Papa said the walls had swayed his decision when I finished elementary school" (45). In Abba town, his ancestral home, Eugene has a four-story white house with high compound walls (59). These walls have a practical function; they protect the wealthy inhabitants from the political instability and desperate poverty of Nigeria. They also serve a symbolic function, identifying the disciplinary boundaries that separate, repress, and police, keeping order and marking divisions between those who belong "at home" and those outside—as Amy Kaplan reminds us, those excluded from the domestic are "foreign."[3] Indeed, Eugene interprets walls as forms of social and moral discipline designed to tame and domesticate: "You could not have youngsters scaling walls to go into town and go wild" (45). For a Nigerian subject like Eugene, whose internalized Western perspective renders his own race foreign and condemns his innate nature for its tendency to "go wild," the walls of home symbolize the need to subdue the ever-present barbaric impulse within and to keep out the barbarians at the gate.

Eugene walls off segments of time for his children, Jaja and Kambili, creating daily schedules that structure their activities and prevent idleness, frivolity, and wasted time. The schedules represent time in a grid: "Papa liked order. It showed even in the schedules themselves, the way his meticulously drawn lines, in black ink, cut across each day [...] He revised them often" (23–24). The rigid black lines on the schedules serve the same function as the high walls around the house: they police the boundaries of the permissible. To this end, Eugene punishes his children for small infractions of lateness: once Kambili is "a few minutes" late running to the chauffeured car after school, and Papa slaps her face hard enough to leave marks on her skin and ringing in her ears (51). Both children are criticized for staying ten minutes longer than Eugene has allotted with their "heathen" grandfather, Papa-Nnukwu (69). The object of Eugene's rigid control over the children's time is discipline, or keeping them inside the walls, unable to "go wild" in barbaric ways. The schedule polices their young black bodies, keeping them from the sins to which flesh is liable; it restricts their minds within the limits of academic work, Catholic devotion, and interpretation of current events under Papa's watchful guidance.

Eugene's disciplinary control transfers his own self-hatred to his children. Conditioned in the Catholic missionary school to deny and renounce the body, Eugene beats his wife and his children. He trains them to expect punishment and pain and to live in fear of his fierce disapproval when they transgress any of the elaborate household rules governing proper behavior. Even his love expresses itself with the infliction of pain: he alternates between impregnating his submissive wife Beatrice and beating her so brutally that she miscarries. He shares "a love sip" of his tea with Jaja and Kambili, but the tea is always too hot and burns their tongues. Kambili associates her father's love with a painful branding: "I knew that when the tea burned my tongue, it burned Papa's love into me" (8). Pleased with Jaja, "Papa had hugged him so tight that Jaja thought his back had snapped" (22). Love, hatred for the body, and the punishing infliction of pain in the name of righteousness intertwine in Eugene's complex negotiation of his position as a hopelessly sinful black Nigerian Catholic.

Eugene is what Althusser has called an "interpellated" subject, one hailed or called by the *Logos* and, with his obedient response, one who inscribes that Western Word in every aspect of his being—and then interpellates his family as well. Sent by his father to the mission school, he served as a houseboy for the parish priest for 2 years and as a gardener for the priests while in secondary school; he was rewarded with university study in England (24). Eugene condemns his father's empty worship of "gods of wood and stone" and believes that he was redeemed from emptiness only by his conversion: "I would be nothing today but for the priests and sisters at the mission" (47). As a teenager, he says, he sinned once against his own body; when the priest saw him, he poured boiling water over the sinning hands (196). Eugene learns the lesson well—black flesh must be disciplined and mortified for its own good, or it will slide back into sinful self-indulgence. His brutal punishments of his wife and children are dedicated to righteousness, which he understands through the simple rules he learned at the mission school.

The God who has hailed Eugene is white, English, and angry, particularly with the sins of black Africans. Therefore Eugene tells his children not to speak Igbo: "We had to sound civilized in public, he told us; we had to speak English" (13). Eugene renounces and erases the African names he and his wife Beatrice must have been given at birth; they are known only by their English (presumably Catholic confirmation) names. Emulating the God whose Word he follows, Eugene "changed his accent when he spoke, sounding British, just as he did when he spoke to Father Benedict. He was gracious, in the eager-to-please way that he always assumed with the religious, especially with the white religious" (46). Eugene prefers the British Father Benedict above any of the Nigerian priests who visit the church, and he teaches Kambili to imagine a "blond Christ" and a God with "wide white hands" and a "rumbling voice British-accented" (178, 131, 179). An imported God who commands British restraint and Victorian repression, the deity who has called Eugene forbids nakedness, spontaneity, laughter, song, and joy. Like the British God, Eugene does not approve of Nigerians: "These people cannot drive," Papa says of his countrymen (45), and of his wife's albino father: "He did things the right way, the way the white people did, not what our people do now!" (68). Eugene has learned self-hatred together with his Western religion, and it spills over into contempt for Nigerians, for blacks, and for his own Nigerian family.

Ironically, however, Eugene is also one of the most upstanding citizens of Igboland. He follows the rules of Christian charity, giving copiously to the church, to social projects like hospitals and schools, and to the poor and needy. Called *omelora*, "The One Who Does for the Community," he provides food for the whole village of his birth at Christmas (56). He makes some of his donations public, but he also gives several anonymous gifts of large sums to the suffering people of his country (297). Eugene refuses to hand over the bribes demanded by the police; he shows his papers and lets the police search the car: "anything but bribe them to let him pass. We cannot be part of what we fight, he often told us" (111). Even more honorably, he publishes a newspaper that tells truth to power, reporting on the military dictatorship's corruption and brutality. Father Benedict pays Eugene public respect because "he used the *Standard* to speak the truth even though it meant the paper lost advertising. Brother Eugene spoke out for freedom" (5). After a military coup takes power, "Only the *Standard* had a critical editorial" calling for a return to democracy (25). When the military regime abducts and kills an activist named Nwankiti Ogechi, Eugene defies the corrupt leadership and prints a story about the events; government agents arrive with "a truckful of dollars" to bribe him, but Eugene tells them "to get out of our house" (200). He supports the critical honesty of Ade Coker, his editor, and accepts the personal risk of assassination by the government. A man of principle, Eugene serves the public with his newspaper and his money and, in his public life, follows the ethics of his church.

Adichie understands Eugene as a product of spiritual colonization, one sickened from the conquest of his soul by an alien, hostile perspective. She does not dismiss or blame him, but thinks of him as "complicated," a self-conflicted outgrowth of his religious education (Vawter). In an interview, she says that his public and private behaviors both "stem from the same thing—this need to do right" that leads to a demand for justice in the public realm and to punishment of his family in private (Vawter). She notes that in Eugene's generation, the missionaries ran the only schools, and "They taught him a faith that came with self-hate" (Vawter). In a similar tone, Eugene's sister Ifeoma points out that her brother "was too much of a colonial product" but says this "in a mild, forgiving way, as if it were not Papa's fault, as one would talk about a person who was shouting gibberish from a severe case of malaria" (13). Making literal his metaphoric sickness, Eugene is physically ill through much of the novel, bloated and covered with a rash that comes from being poisoned by what should feed and sustain him. Fittingly, the poison is administered in his quintessential British passion, his cup of tea.

For those who live with Eugene in the home behind walls, Foucault's insights into the modern technology of discipline certainly apply: though punishments are still visited on the body, the more effective restraints come from an internalized voice monitoring every speech and gesture. Jaja and Kambili, inheritors and makers of Nigeria's future, are produced as perfect subjects of despotic prison rule: perennially watchful of their own potential sins, they live in constant, chronic fear. They cannot lock their doors but must be visible to the father/judge at any moment. They follow carefully scripted rules for when to speak and what to say; their speech is as formulaic and empty as that of Atwood's handmaids. They are also silent, unnaturally self-restrained for children, as Ade Coker notices when he visits. "They are always so quiet," Ade observes; "So quiet.[...] Imagine what the *Standard* would be if we were all quiet" (57–58). Ade, modeled on a beloved Nigerian newsman named Dele Giwa who was killed by a letter bomb, sees the vital link between private silence and public submission to dictatorial rule that persists among terrified Nigerians (Adebanwi).[4]

Eugene controls every aspect of the lives of his wife and children, paying special attention to what goes into and comes out of their mouths; in this way, he takes possession of both bodies and minds. Suggesting the sacred and ritual nature of food in Eugene's mind, communion is the most important thing to enter; he watches the whole congregation closely to identify those who do not partake, and Jaja's refusal on Palm Sunday triggers the crisis that opens the novel. After the children pay their brief annual visit to his father, Eugene demands, "Did you eat food sacrificed to idols? Did you desecrate your Christian tongue?" (69). He beats Jaja, Kambili, and Beatrice with a belt when Kambili, needing Panadol for cramps, eats corn flakes before Mass and thus breaks the Eucharist fast (100–102). Saying a lengthy grace before each meal and a lengthy prayer of thanks afterwards, Eugene transforms family meals into ritual occasions over which he presides as priest and intermediary, bringing his fallen and sinful kinfolk toward salvation. Ironically, new food and drink products made at his factory are treated with eucharistic solemnity at these meals, with ritual praise directed at Papa's wisdom in marketing.

Eugene polices the words that come out of their mouths with an equally fierce attention, muting his wife and children and leaving an almost paralyzed Kambili yearning to say the approved thing. She and Jaja ask each other "questions whose answers we already knew" in order to avoid "the ones whose answers we did not want to know" (23). They speak with their eyes, avoiding speech about troubling topics like their father's beatings. Their mother Beatrice rarely says much: "She spoke the way a bird eats, in small amounts" (20). "Awkward and tongue-tied" at school, Kambili is unable to make friends with her classmates, and at crucial moments she finds that "my words would not come" (49, 139). She stutters, afraid of the judgment that always finds her words inadequate. She yearns to say the thing her father will approve, but almost never does; "God will deliver us," she says once, and his endorsement is sweet: "I felt as though my mouth were full of melting sugar" (26). Colonized and interpellated themselves by their father, his priestly Father, and the white British patriarchal God, these young Nigerians cannot approve their own speech unless it declares their utter subjugation. They live in the self-canceling shadow of their father's own unworthiness.

Beatrice, the mother who seems to Adichie to resemble "the rather familiar Battered Woman," is too meek and conquered to help her children (Adebanwi). Grateful to Eugene that he did not take a second wife, especially after she fails to produce more children, she stands by helplessly while her husband beats Jaja and Kambili. She has "a limping gait," "vacant" eyes, "sagging breasts," and a tired, defeated look (62, 34, 7); she is frequently beaten for failures and sins. The novel begins, after a prologue, with Beatrice's announcement to Kambili that she is pregnant and eager to have another child. She loses the baby when Eugene beats her because, sick and nauseated, she asks to wait in the car rather than visit the priest (29). She loses a second child months later when he batters her for some unnamed sin (247). Whenever she is beaten, she polishes the glass étagère with its "beige, finger-size ceramic figurines of ballet dancers in various contorted postures" (7). These fragile dancers are markers of Western art as well as miniaturized women, suggesting that she is as alienated from her culture as Eugene; but the loving care with which Beatrice washes and dries them in a soft towel suggests that she finds solace in them as symbols of power, artistry, and bodily self-control. They represent strength in fragility and thus some hope for the vulnerable members of the Achike household.

The prosperous home hiding violence and oppression reflects the Nigerian homeland as well: the wealth that attracted Britain—oil deposits; minerals including tin, gold, and coal; fertile land—has also been a magnet for corrupt leaders hungry for personal gain. In telling the story of the colonized home behind high walls, Adichie represents the social conditions that surround, reflect, and illuminate Eugene's fierce desire for social justice and democracy, tragically admixed with personal brutality. Thus the head of state during the events of the novel—a combination of military dictators Babangida and Abacha, according to Adichie[5]—claims to intend improvements for Nigeria's economy, but in private he participates in the heroin drug-trade for personal gain (38). The state does not invest in hospitals, schools, roads, or technological improvements; shortages of fuel and food affect even the middle class, and electricity goes off frequently in the power-rich nation. The state does not pay workers, including teachers and university professors: "They tell us the Federal Government has no money," Ifeoma says (76). The police set up roadblocks to extort money from travelers and, in the process, they shoot people (103). In the market, soldiers with whips demolish vegetable stalls and beat the poor women who try to sell produce (44). Whatever their professed commitments to the people of Nigeria, these rulers simply ignore the helpless despair of the poor. They retreat to compounds with high walls of their own.

The garden flat

A sharp contrast to the wealthy, walled compound in Enugu, Aunty Ifeoma rents a flat on the ground floor of a "tall, bland building with peeling blue paint" in Nsukka, where Adichie herself grew up (112). In front, "a circular burst of bright colors" emerges from Ifeoma's garden, an undisciplined mix of roses, hibiscus, lilies, ixora, and croton that announces her sense, with Voltaire's Candide, that one must cultivate one's garden. This garden flat is open to the street, to the neighbors and to many visitors, to the news, and to the unexpected. At dawn, the door to the verandah "was half open," letting in the light (167); at night, Aunty Ifeoma sits on a stool on the verandah talking with a friend (242). From the kitchen, one can see the road and the people passing (147). An uncontrolled space where visitors, friends, students, and university colleagues come and go, the flat does not hide the lives of its inhabitants but rather immerses them in their culture. These lives are far less wealthy and protected: frayed and mismatched furniture, small rooms, worn and chipped tile, and meals with more vegetable and less meat show that Ifeoma's family struggles financially. They have a large, rich library, however, and good places to read and study. While nature is kept at bay outside the house in Enugu, flowers bring the garden inside in Nsukka (114).

As reflected by her creation of the garden home, Aunty Ifeoma herself is an empowering force in the lives of her children, her students, and her kin. Where her brother's controlling practices re-colonize his children, Ifeoma encourages independence and self-respect. As Kambili realizes when she watches Father Amadi coaching boys for the high jump, Ifeoma lives by a positive faith in people:

> It was what Aunty Ifeoma did to my cousins, I realized then, setting higher and higher jumps for them in the way she talked to them, in what she expected of them. She did it all the time believing they would scale the rod. And they did. It was different for Jaja and me. We did not scale the rod because we believed we could, we scaled it because we were terrified that we couldn't.
>
> (226)

With his colonized perception of the sinful, fallen state of Nigerians, Eugene cannot help policing his children: since he himself has failed, he can only raise them to fear their own failure. Ifeoma wears her Catholic faith differently, finding a dimension of respect for all life and thus divine love for African people and traditions. While Kambili has been told that flesh must be covered and that it is sinful to look on nakedness, Ifeoma accepts the body as part of the natural world. When Kambili calls her grandfather a "pagan," her aunt replies that he is not a pagan but "a traditionalist" (81) and later wakes her at dawn to witness the dignity of Papa-Nnukwu's worship (167). Renouncing the radical sinfulness that plagues her brother, Ifeoma raises her children to think critically, speak freely, and believe they can achieve what they set out to do.

Ifeoma stands for fearless pride, joy, and freedom, and while she advocates as her brother does for a democratic Nigeria, she also lives these principles in private. She is associated with laughter, from the first announcement of her presence in the compound at Abba town ("Her laughter floated upstairs," 71) to her prayers ("Aunty Ifeoma and her family prayed for, of all things, *laughter*," 127). Her family celebrates at the dinner table: "Laughter floated over my head. Words spurted from everyone [. . .] you could say anything at any time to anyone, where the air was free for you to breathe as you wished" (120). Kambili describes Aunty Ifeoma as "tall, exuberant, fearless, loud, larger than life" (95). Ifeoma refuses Eugene's offer to buy her a car in exchange for her submission to his sense of religious standards, and she refuses to keep quiet at the university when the dictator appoints an administrator to control academic freedom (95, 222–23). When local police come to the flat to ransack and threaten, Ifeoma demands, "Who sent you here?[. . .] Do you have any papers to show me? You cannot just walk into my house" (230–31). Ifeoma *does* discipline her children when they are disrespectful to others, but her reprimands and physical punishments, accompanied by long verbal explanations, come without the brutality and flesh-hating violence of Eugene's beatings (245).

For Jaja and Kambili, Ifeoma de-colonizes the home, the African body, mind, and soul. She shows them how to throw off the colonizers' assumptions imposed by their father and take pride in African flesh and spirit. She wears shorts and slacks and encourages Kambili to borrow some of Amaka's; she wears bright lipstick to call attention to her fearless free mouth. A builder of bridges between Western and African religion, Ifeoma worships as a Catholic but respects her father's animist faith and refuses to impose Catholicism on him as he dies. Her family's worship at home includes Igbo songs, bringing the Latin rosary into the Nigerian context. She takes Kambili and Amaka to Aokpe, where the Virgin Mary is supposed to appear; she also takes a group including Jaja and Kambili to see the native *mmuo* or walking spirits (274, 85). While Eugene has forbidden Jaja the initiation into the spirit world, which was traditionally considered the first step toward manhood, Ifeoma's son Obiora did participate with her encouragement (87). Even in the seemingly minor venue of popular entertainment, Ifeoma advocates for Africa finding itself rather than importing the West: "I don't understand why they fill our television with second-rate Mexican shows and ignore all the potential our people have," she says (123). Ifeoma re-constitutes and celebrates the repressed Nigerian spirit. Without sacrificing her background in Western religion and thought, including the education that has earned her a lectureship at the university in Nsukka, she throws off the colonized soul and makes herself at ease in an African body. In the process, she demonstrates the precarious possibility of creating a decolonized home.

Precarious, of course, because the police do invade it, the soldiers close the university, and the Nigerian state makes it impossible for Ifeoma and her children to stay in the country. Ironically, this most partisan Nigerian finds that she cannot work, feed her children, or live in safety in her own country, and she therefore emigrates to America. There, her home adapts still further to Western customs, leaving Nigerian ones behind—Amaka comments that, with her mother's two jobs and the family's busy schedule, they do not spend enough time together (301). More important, the anti-colonial thinking Ifeoma tried to introduce within Nigeria has lost a powerful advocate. But the potential remains, firmly planted in Kambili: when she visits the garden flat after Ifeoma's family departs, she finds that "Nsukka could free something deep inside your belly that would rise up to your throat and come out as a freedom song. As laughter" (299).

The other liberating force in the novel is Father Amadi, the young Nigerian Catholic priest who is a friend of Ifeoma's in Nsukka. Like Ifeoma, he incorporates song and Igbo language into the worship services he leads. Like her, he has faith in the young people of Nigeria— in their strength and beauty, mental and physical. His Catholicism does not repress, deny, or condemn the flesh; he wears shorts, goes running, and hugs his parishioners. He coaches young boys at sports, and he describes his faith in them as something he needs for himself: "I need to believe in something that I never question" (226). In a similar way, he supports Kambili and gives her a kind of respectful attention that helps to heal and liberate her. Because her religion and her father have constrained her imagination and repressed her natural desire for love, Father Amadi is uniquely positioned to assist in her transformation. He is the Father who approves of young Nigerians, who accepts his own and others' embodiment, who practices a Catholicism that does not dwell on sin but on charity. He evokes Kambili's laughter for the first time; he brings her to an artist to dress her hair; he teaches her to sing; he compliments her beauty and encourages her to try out for a part in a play. "You can do anything you want, Kambili," he tells her (239). He is a decolonizing force, and Kambili's unreserved love for the young priest leads her away from the system of self-hatred that has interpellated her father.

Father Amadi, too, has to leave Nigeria before the novel ends; he is sent to Germany as a missionary because it, like other Western countries, has lost priests. His gift of a transformed, decolonized religion to young Nigerians is put on hold, at least for some time, as is their gift to him of a future in which he can believe. Kambili's cousin Amaka suggests that, in taking the Western god back to the West, Father Amadi should take an African version: "The white missionaries brought us their god [...] Which was the same color as them, worshiped in their language and packaged in the boxes they made. Now that we take their god back to them, shouldn't we at least repackage it?" (267). Father Amadi has, in effect, repackaged the Catholic religion with liberating effect inside Nigeria; but once he leaves for Germany, he is not clearly able to shift Western ideas of god or of Africans. His letters describe experiences of racism—the German lady who "does not think a black man should be her priest"—and of an equally racist exoticization of the African: "the wealthy widow who insists he have dinner with her every night" (303). Father Amadi's transfer to Germany is another loss for the movement to decolonize the home in Nigeria, though it may open greater understanding in Europe.

"Things started to fall apart at home"

Adichie's novel opens with a reference to Chinua Achebe's *Things Fall Apart* (1958) and, behind Achebe, William Butler Yeats's famous poem, "The Second Coming":

> Things fall apart; the centre cannot hold;
> Mere anarchy is loosed upon the world,
> The blood-dimmed tide is loosed.
>
> (184)

Yeats's poem must have seemed to Achebe relevant to the situation in Nigeria during the early 1900s, when white missionaries appeared among the Igbo to bring the story of Christian advent, together with the condemnation of African animist faith. Achebe's title refers to the suggestion in Yeats's poem that the Christian era has dominated one historical cycle, about to end, in which "the blood-dimmed tide" of imperial conversions and the resulting destruction of innocence have unleashed "mere anarchy"—not divine purpose or justified sacrifice, but a scattering that reduces to mere "things." After the Christian era, some new "rough beast" "Slouches towards Bethlehem to be born," leaving the prophecy of a second coming ironically undermined in its fulfillment: hardly Christ returned, the next era will be ushered in by a barely human "shape" with "A gaze blank and pitiless as the sun." A pointed critique of the Christian era for sanctioning murder, conquest, and racism in the name of imperialist expansion, this poem provides an apt reference for both Achebe and Adichie as they write about the Christian legacy in Nigeria.[6]

In several interviews Adichie acknowledges indebtedness to Achebe, the most prominent Nigerian novelist and one of the most widely read African writers.[7] The opening line of *Purple Hibiscus* is a deliberate allusion: "Things started to fall apart at home when my brother, Jaja, did not go to communion and Papa flung his heavy missal across the room and broke the figurines on the étagère" (3). Although Achebe was born in 1930 and Adichie in 1977, Adichie lived for some years in a university house in Nsukka where Achebe and his family had lived previously. Both Igbo writers began their careers studying medicine, which Adichie explains by saying that good students in colonized countries are expected to pursue practical and lucrative fields like medicine (Spencer). She says that Achebe's work "has inspired me more than any other writer's," in part because he "swiped at the disgusting stereotypes of Africa" and told other African writers "that our stories were worthy" (Randomhouse, Anya). Having grown up reading English fiction, Adichie found that Achebe "gave me permission to write about my world.[...] what he did for me at the time was validate my history, make it seem worthy in some way" (Garner). She finds similarities between her fiction and Achebe's:

> We are both aware of how the legacy of colonialism has insidiously trickled down into ordinary Nigerian lives. We both celebrate Igbo culture in its magnificent ordinariness. We both portray the complexities of Christianity in Nigeria. We are both impatient with the inept leadership in Nigeria and with the way we Nigerians excuse corruption and never demand the best of ourselves and our leaders.
>
> (Randomhouse)

When Achebe's son sent her an email saying, "Dad has read *Purple Hibiscus* and liked it very much," Adichie was thrilled: "My idol was telling me I was doing a good job. I was so ecstatic. I went slightly crazy" (Garner).

In both Achebe's and Adichie's novels, the "falling apart," takes place on levels that connect the family home and the larger community, although as Joseph Obi points out, the community in Achebe's Umuofia is dynamic and evolving rather than crumbling in any simple sense (78). Like Achebe's Okonkwo, Adichie's Eugene regards himself as a leader, one who takes care of (inspires, gives to, feeds, monitors, judges, criticizes, punishes) the community from which he stands apart. In both novels, things begin to fall apart for these fathers at what they take to be the point of achieved success: they have children, material wealth, loyal wives, social standing, and titles. The falling apart occurs over a span of time in which their sons become consciously resistant to what they perceive as the father's brutal and dictatorial practices. Both fathers do not survive their losses: Okonkwo hangs himself and Eugene dies of poison, which his wife Beatrice puts in his tea over a period of a few weeks. Both novels record the fathers' tragedy—for them and for their communities, things fall apart.

In *Purple Hibiscus*, the focus on Jaja and Kambili reflects a more positive outcome as well; the children liberate themselves from the deeply inscribed self-censorship and repression of the colonized home. As the older child and the male in a patriarchal society, Jaja takes the first bold steps; indeed, the novel opens with his dramatic refusal to take communion on Palm Sunday. Jaja's earliest rebellion comes when, breaking a long conspiracy of silence, he reveals to Aunty Ifeoma that his father deliberately broke his finger (154). In Nsukka he becomes a capable and dedicated gardener, working on his knees in the soil, and he learns to kill and pluck a chicken (225, 235). He thrives on the liberty and on Aunty Ifeoma's belief in him: "If Aunty Ifeoma leaves, then I want to leave with them, too," he tells Kambili (235). When the children return to their father's house, Jaja asks for the key to his room, symbol of his father's control over his private space—the gesture suggests Jaja's refusal to remain in the colonized home (191). On Palm Sunday, he reasserts control over his bodily home; not only does he decline communion, but he also refuses to participate in the ritual sampling of a new product from his father's factory, and he leaves the table "before Papa had said the prayer after meals" (14). Five days later, Jaja forcefully asserts his demand to leave Papa's house, insisting that he and Kambili will go to Nsukka for Easter Sunday, leaving "today, not tomorrow. If Kevin will not take us, we will still go. We will walk if we have to" (261). In defying his father, Jaja gains courage and self-respect, just the qualities the father has inadvertently prohibited for his son, and Kambili sees that "fear" "had left Jaja's eyes and entered Papa's" (13).

Though her transformation is quieter, it is Kambili who fulfills the promise of the title and achieves a rare flowering. At the outset, she is more fearful than her brother, more silenced by her father's (and her culture's) misogyny, and more traumatized by the punishments. Kambili's first act of resistance comes, not against her father directly, but against Jaja, and it occurs before Jaja has taken his first steps. When he tries to pull her away from the annual fifteen-minute visit with their "heathen" grandfather, Papa-Nnukwu, she resists. Drawn to her African grandfather with a special tenderness, Kambili respects Papa-Nnukwu's age, his wisdom, and his animist faith that she has been trained to abhor; she appreciates "the easy way he threw the molded morsel out toward the garden [...] asking Ani, the god of the land, to eat with him" (65). Aware of her grandfather's frailty, she refuses Jaja's hints and delays their departure out of concern that he has no drink with his food: "Jaja nudged me. But I did not want to leave; I wanted to stay so that if the fufu clung to Papa-Nnukwu's throat and choked him, I could run and get him water.[...] Jaja nudged me again and I still could not get up" (66). In this first act of silent rebellion against her father, she refuses to condemn the aged ancestor for his traditional faith, even before Aunty Ifeoma helps her understand its difference from her father's rigorous Catholicism.

Spending time with Aunty Ifeoma and her family outside her father's colonized home changes Kambili as much as it changes Jaja. Like her brother, Kambili becomes competent: she learns to cook, to run, and to laugh, and she develops the physical strength to help carry water into the flat. Ifeoma and her daughter Amaka are especially important models of women's independence and outspoken courage for Kambili, who has learned only passivity from her downtrodden mother. They teach her to stand up for herself, to talk back—lessons that directly contradict the submissive silence her father has required. When she does speak, they cheer her on: "So your voice can be this loud, Kambili," says Amaka (170). They encourage her to accept and enjoy her body, to wear shorts and lipstick. They teach her African traditions: Ifeoma wakes her early to witness Papa-Nnukwu's morning prayer and takes her to see the tribal spirits or *mmuo*. They encourage freedom, laughter, song, confidence in herself as a young black woman, and faith in Nigerian people—all things prohibited in her father's house.

Father Amadi provides crucial support for Kambili's transformation because he combines the authority of the Catholic Church, uniquely important in her understanding of the world, with respect for young Nigerians. Safely impossible to consummate, her crush on him liberates her to discard her father's repressive teachings and to subscribe to a far more liberal interpretation of her religion, her people, and her life. Where Eugene's Catholicism involves the condemnation of black Africa and especially of its flesh, of the Igbo language, of song, and of joyful noise, Amadi celebrates all of these things both in private and in his church services. Where Eugene's punishments reflect a sustained condemnation of his children, Amadi's gentle and loving attention to her affirms Kambili's dignity and value. With him, she learns to smile, to ask questions, and to laugh; she will eventually sing Igbo songs with him and tell him she loves him (177, 179, 276). She finds in her association with Father Amadi a bridge between the religion she accepted as a child and the new faiths she needs: in herself, her voice, her body, her race, her gender, her nation, and her future. He shows her the way to the decolonized soul in a version of the Western religion that embraces and honors Africa.

Kambili's definitive moment of rebellion against her father consists of a passive resistance to his colonized Western view that conveys her implicit respect for Africa. When Eugene discovers the painting of Papa-Nnukwu that Amaka has given to Kambili, he is enraged; he tears it to pieces. Kambili chooses her grandfather's version of Africa over her father's:

> I suddenly and maniacally imagined Papa-Nnukwu's body being cut in pieces that small and stored in a fridge.
> "No!" I shrieked. I dashed to the pieces on the floor as if to save them, as if saving them would mean saving Papa-Nnukwu. I sank to the floor, lay on the pieces of paper.
> "What has gotten into you?" Papa asked. "What is wrong with you?"
> I lay on the floor, curled tight like the picture of a child in the uterus in my *Integrated Science for Junior Secondary Schools*.
> "Get up! Get away from that painting!"
> I lay there, did nothing.
> "Get up!" Papa said again. I still did not move. He started to kick me. The metal buckles on his slippers stung like bites from giant mosquitoes. He talked nonstop, out of control, in a mix of Igbo and English, like soft meat and thorny bones. Godlessness. Heathen worship. Hellfire. The kicking increased in tempo, and I thought of Amaka's music, her culturally conscious music that sometimes started

off with a calm saxophone and then whirled into lusty singing. I curled around myself tighter, around the pieces of the painting.
(210–11)

Although she understands from the outset that the painting is destroyed, and that it "represented something lost, something I had never had," she defends the African familial heritage it symbolizes with her life—indeed, she nearly dies from the long and savage beating (210). Amaka's representation of her grandfather—condemned and destroyed by her father—evokes Kambili's own emerging subject position as an African, and thus she puts her own body on the floor in silent defense of her grandfather. For the first time, she refuses to obey her father's commands; indeed, she minimizes the brutal beating and tunes out his words, reducing his speech to garbled formulas. She leaves the scene of the beating to recall Amaka's music—a pro-African music with "lusty singing" that she heard in Nsukka, the place of her decolonization and symbolic rebirth—and finds in those associations the courage to ignore her father. No longer dependent on his approval for her sense of worth, she claims a separate position honoring the fragments of an African past: "I curled around myself tighter, around the pieces of the painting" (211).

As well as a position from which she must defy her father, Kambili also finds an independent voice. When she recovers from the beating, she goes back to Nsukka, and for the first time she breaks the family's code of silence and admits that her father put her in the hospital (220). Later, when Jaja insists that they return to Nsukka for Easter, it is Kambili who tells the reluctant driver Kevin that Eugene "said you should take us to Nsukka" (262). She says something funny that makes Amaka laugh, she tells Father Amadi which flower is sweet to suck, and she expresses the religious sense she feels in Aokpe (266, 269, 275). As Adichie says in an interview, "I think really *Purple Hibiscus* is about Kambili finding her voice" (Vawter). The voice, muted and dominated by her father's colonized perspective at the outset, becomes Kambili's own by the end and thus capable of telling a story of decolonization.

Purple Hibiscus is consistently told through Kambili's voice and perspective, but she does not give a single, linear account of chronologically ordered events in the fashion of a naïve child narrator like, for example, Huck Finn. Sidonie Smith writes that in the absence of a coherent, unified subject, autobiography emerges from estrangement and performance: "Autobiographical narration begins with amnesia, and once begun, the fragmentary nature of subjectivity intrudes" (109). Kambili's life story narrates just such fragmentation and invented coherence. She provides glimpses of a later knowledge, of a perspective shaped by the events: "Things started to fall apart at home" suggests, for example, her awareness of the crisis on Palm Sunday as part of a process that begins earlier ("Nsukka started it all," 16) and culminates later. The narrative is divided in three sections, dated "Palm Sunday," "Before Palm Sunday," and "After Palm Sunday," as well as an epilogue placed in "The Present"—a time almost 3 years later when Beatrice and Kambili visit Jaja in prison and tell him that he is soon to be released. The "Palm Sunday" section provides brief glimpses of events and knowledge from a prior time, together with hints of a perspective on the meaning of Palm Sunday that Kambili creates much later. "Before Palm Sunday" anticipates perspectives that emerge only after Easter.

Because it reveals glimpses of Kambili's later knowledge, her telling voice takes on the double-consciousness that Du Bois identifies in African Americans as a "sense of always looking at one's self through the eyes of others, of measuring one's soul by the tape of a world that looks on in amused contempt and pity" (11). R. Radhakrishnan identifies a version of double-consciousness in diasporic migrants who have become permanently divided: "If the diasporic self is forever marked by a double consciousness, then its entry as legitimate citizen into the adopted home is also necessarily double" (1996: 174). Kambili's narrative situates itself in such a doubled, self-consciously alien space; it combines an innocent account of her bewildered experience of her family's disaster and dispersion with a knowing, ironic backward look that shapes the representation. She emphasizes the rash on her father's face, for example, long before she reveals its source in the poison administered by her mother. She tells of her father offering a "love sip" of his tea, an offer made ironic by the tea's symbolic status as the quintessence of his British aspirations and the source of his death (8). She locates the beginning of the family's disasters, its earliest chronological event, in her mother's proud and happy announcement that she is pregnant (20); after she loses this baby and the next one, Beatrice will kill her husband. While Kambili often underscores the things she did not know ("I did not know she had been trying to have a baby," 21) or could not understand ("I did not even think to think, what Mama needed to be forgiven for," 36), the narrative itself selects knowingly as it enacts Kambili's doubled position combining innocence and experience. Her voice comes from a place in between, a no-person's-land, not at home.

The narrative structure follows a liturgical calendar that increases the ironic displacement of its young narrator. Following the family's orientation toward the Christian church calendar, the narrative places events around Christmas, Palm Sunday, and Easter. While it makes occasional mention of months, it does not place events by date or year; instead, the liturgical calendar forms the novel's primary chronological framework. But given its focus on the liberation of Jaja and Kambili from an oppressively constructed, exclusionary version of the Christian faith, the novel's invocation of the church calendar can only be ironic: the Christmas nativity, for example, marks Kambili's first recognition that she loves her "heathen" grandfather and her outspoken, feminist aunt. Palm Sunday culminates in Jaja's refusal to take communion and Beatrice's decision, after a rash-infected Eugene breaks her figurines, that she will not replace them. He dies soon after Easter Sunday, another ironic inversion. Easter marks another act of resistance against the church: Jaja and Kambili spend Easter in Nsukka, where their cousin Amaka refuses to be confirmed. She takes a principled stance against the requirement that she must choose an English name: "When the missionaries first came, they didn't think Igbo names were good enough.[...] only an English name will make your confirmation valid. 'Chiamaka' says God is beautiful. 'Chima' says God knows best [...] Don't they all glorify God as much as 'Paul' and 'Peter' and 'Simon'?" (272). Though Ifeoma and Father Amadi try to persuade her to compromise, Amaka holds firm and refuses to join the other young Nigerians being confirmed on Easter. Each of these ironic invocations of the church calendar measures a need to stretch the Western church's understanding to include respect for African traditions and people.

Like Chinua Achebe, Adichie writes her novel in English but incorporates Igbo words and phrases, often without translation.[8] She weaves Igbo words and phrases into conversations as she represents bilingual Nigerians who speak publicly in English because of the wish to "sound civilized," but often think and feel in Igbo (13). Adichie's choice of language, like that of any African writer, takes place in a complicated context: does an African's use of a European language reinforce colonial structures of power, or can it call them into question? Writing in 1984, Ngũgĩ wa Thiong'o made a powerful case for writing in African languages as the best strategy for "decolonizing the mind." The imposition of European languages on colonized African peoples was, he argued, a crucial means of "spiritual subjugation": "The domination of a people's language by the languages of the colonising nations was crucial to the domination of the mental universe of the colonised" (9, 16). Expressing his support for African nationalism in the 1970s, Ngũgĩ began to write in Gĩkũyũ, seeing the use of his own Kenyan language as "part and parcel of the anti-imperialist struggles of Kenyan and African peoples" (28).

Yet other African writers have seen the freight carried by the language, or *what* they write, as more important to the anti-colonial project than the vehicle. In his exploration of Chinua Achebe's fiction, for example, Isidore Okpewho identifies a radical rejection of imperial domination in Achebe's use of English containing Igbo. He believes that Achebe follows "an antihegemonist urge to deconstruct the dominance of the empire in the linguistic landscape of his work" (28).

Adichie follows a similar path, creating an Igbo-inflected English that reflects her critical view of the colonial heritage and her faith in Nigerians' ability to surmount and recast that heritage. Some 20 years later than Ngũgĩ, Adichie writes in an emergent global context, one where nationalism shares space with the recognition that transnational commercial interests exert a shaping force on the internal politics of all nations and, indeed, dictate which artistic voices can be heard. In the formulation of Hardt and Negri, transnational capital

> operates on the plane of *immanence*, through relays and networks of relationships of domination, without reliance on a transcendent center of power.[...] capital sweeps clear the fixed barriers of precap-italist society—and even the boundaries of the nation-state tend to fade into the background as capital realizes itself in the world market.
>
> (326–27)

Where Ngũgĩ believed that decolonization could be achieved through the reaffirmation of African languages, it appears after 2000 that addressing the new global empire in a language available to the widest audience, both within and beyond the African continent, now carries more anti-imperial force. One Nigerian reviewer noted that "Books by Nigerian women writers are a rarity" (Atta), and Adichie herself told an interviewer, "I couldn't have published my novel in Nigeria without the money to pay the publisher" (Garner).[9] Like Arundhati Roy, Rosario Ferré, and other contemporary writers, Adichie remakes English as she imagines a pathway to the decolonized homeland.

Like other contemporary women writers, Adichie does not conclude her novel by taking her characters or her readers home or by suggesting any easy resolution for the ongoing problems of race, gender, and reli-gious heritage that emerge from Nigeria's colonial past. Indeed, *Purple Hibiscus* ends in prison, the ultimate enclosed disciplinary space. Jaja has confessed to his mother's crime and served 31 months in a brutal jail, deprived of food and sunlight, covered with scabs and the scars of many beatings; but with the death of the latest dictator,[10] Jaja will be released in the near future. He has paid the price for the murder committed by his mother—indeed, he seems to have known before she confesses to the children that she poisoned Eugene. "I should have taken care of Mama," he says twice (289), reflecting a complex understanding that Eugene's beatings, leading to repeated miscarriages, have pushed Beatrice to her own desperate rebellion. Hardly a defiant political act, the murder reflects private despair—she cannot divorce or change her husband, she cannot take responsibility or face him as he dies, and she cannot even convince people of her guilt when she tries to confess after Jaja is imprisoned. Her children continue to pay the price for her passivity and fear, as she turns into an unkempt, hollow figure incapable of creating a nurturing home (295). With Ifeoma and her children in exile, Father Amadi sent off to Europe, Beatrice mentally unfocused and Jaja in prison, the home and homeland have been hollowed out even in their liberation. True, the corrupt head of state and the father interpellated by the West are gone, and Kambili plans to plant purple hibiscus after Jaja is released. But the flowering of Nigeria is deferred to another day.

6
Exiles and Orphans: Arundhati Roy's *The God of Small Things*

Among the "small things" invoked by the title of Arundhati Roy's novel are Indian people, who become things when they are objectified for use, small when they are regarded as insignificant. In addition to spiders, ants, birds, inanimate objects including a child's plastic watch, and concepts like trivial utterances and brief attention spans, small things include beings regarded as expendable. The novel's trenchant critique of India emerges in its portraits of the subaltern—those who are invisible, powerless, swallowed by history. These include especially members of the outcaste Untouchables, called *harijan* or "children of God" by Gandhi and by themselves *Dalit*, meaning broken, trampled upon, and oppressed.[1] They include poor workers, the crippled, the maimed, and the mad. They include those racially darker, closer to the Dravidian roots of South India. Although women have special status by virtue of matrilineal traditions among the largest group of Hindus in the state of Kerala, where Roy was born and the novel occurs, women become small things in the novel's patriarchal households. Poignantly, children are the novel's prime example of small things: they are abandoned, neglected, orphaned, and lost.

As for the "God" of small things, Roy's title is ironic: this god, identified throughout the novel with the Untouchable carpenter Velutha, proves mortal. He is murdered, brutally kicked to death by "Touchable Policemen" acting as agents of the government, who claim divine sanction: "It was human history, masquerading as God's Purpose, revealing herself" (288, 293). After the graphic murder, there is no salvation for either the large or the small things Velutha has cherished; the sparrow falls unseen,[2] Ammu dies, and the children are separately exiled into grief and emptiness. The novel's title reflects with some bitterness the *absence* of any divine mercy, overarching purpose, or providence for the most vulnerable segment of Indian society.

Indeed, Roy's novel portrays India as a confused, chaotic land riven with prejudice, violence, and cruelty. Roy comments on the condition of her homeland in the first evocation of the title, juxtaposing Big God and Small:

> something happened when personal turmoil dropped by at the wayside shrine of the vast, violent [...] public turmoil of a nation. That Big God howled like a hot wind, and demanded obeisance. Then Small God (cozy and contained, private and limited) came away cauterized, laughing numbly at his own temerity.[...] Small God laughed a hollow laugh, and skipped away cheerfully. Like a rich boy in shorts. He whistled, kicked stones. The source of his brittle elation was the relative smallness of his misfortune.
>
> (20)

Big God is the public force of national history, howling its demands that violent, damaging traditions be endlessly recirculated. Small God is the private despair of domestic life in such a country, wryly consoled in its hopelessness.

In the title of her novel, Roy provides a metaphor for the intricate relatedness of home and homeland, personal and national arenas of turmoil: the god of small things is cauterized in the hot winds of the Big God. Like other contemporary women novelists, Roy writes about private events in a family home, but places them in a public context that conveys a pointed political critique. The domestic site of the novel is full of self-absorbed carelessness, indifference, and overt cruelty. The nation sacrifices its human potential, preserving traditional discriminations of caste, gender, race, and religion. Written in English and published in 1997 to praise and criticism, the Booker Prize, lawsuits, and worldwide sales,[3] Roy's novel takes place in the village of Ayemenem during 2 weeks in December 1969, when the family tragedies occur, and several days in May and June 1992, when the long-separated twins return at 31 to the decaying family home.

In addition to her only novel, Roy has also published several books of political essays and one of interviews. Her non-fiction comments pungently on the same conditions as her novel, focusing on the Indian homeland. Roy voices an abiding concern for what she calls "the ordinary person," in ways ranging from the 2004 book title, *An Ordinary Person's Guide to Empire*, to a multitude of references in the essays: "how can ordinary people counter the assault of an increasingly violent state?" she asks in the *Guide* (111). She refers to the plight of the poor ("As for the Indian poor, once they've provided the votes, they are expected to bugger off home," *Power*, 16), to those displaced by dams in India (who "are the non-people, the *Adivasis* [original tribal inhabitants, outside the caste system] and the *Dalits*") (*Checkbook*, 24), and to the "oppressed and vanquished people" who are victimized by the state (*Guide*, 107). Roy criticizes the power structure in India, but sees her homeland in a global context; she also criticizes the United States, Britain, South Africa, and other nations. Most of all, she indicts governments that wage war, imprison, and starve citizens; she accuses the United States in particular of conducting a "New Imperialism" waged through economic sanctions, creating "mass death without actually going out and killing people" (*Guide*, 87–88). She criticizes abuses of state and corporate power and the victimization of ordinary people.

In India, vast numbers of citizens become small things as a result of their birth in a nation that upholds an oppressive caste system. Caste hierarchy justifies abuses of power, particularly the victimization of *Dalit* and *Adivasi* peoples, to which Roy refers in her essays and in *God of Small Things*. Caste, a distinguishing feature of Indian society, is termed by Ethnohistorian Nicholas Dirks "a specter that continues to haunt the body politic of postcolonial India," predating the Raj but nonetheless in subtle ways "the product of an historical encounter between India and Western colonial rule" (17, 5).[4] It is roundly condemned as "graded inequality" by *Dalit* leader Dr. B. R. Ambedkar (60) and as "sanctified racism" by *Dalit* activist V. T. Rajshekar (54). A product of Hindu faith in cycles of reincarnation, the structure of caste identity[5] justifies systemic inequality by blaming the victims; as Rajshekar writes:

> the Hindu religion provides an effective ideology for the suppression of resistance to injustice, having as a central tenet of its propaganda the idea that those in the lower castes are poor and suffering because of their misdeeds in the previous birth.[...] as their sufferings are of their own making, and in fact reflect the working out of some inexorable justice, the higher castes are absolved of any responsibility for their condition.
>
> (60–61).

For a passionate defender of human rights like Roy, caste violence against India's millions of poor people, including the Untouchables— variously called Scheduled Castes and Scheduled Tribes,[6] Depressed

Classes, Other Backward Castes, *Dalits* and *Adivasis*—evokes outrage and protest.

In one of the interviews with David Barsamian in *The Checkbook and the Cruise Missile*, Roy reflects on her early life in Kerala in ways particularly helpful to an understanding of home/land in *GOST*. She says that her novel is about the village in which she grew up, "their society and its intrinsic, callous brutality" (8–9). Kerala, she says, is "progressive and parochial simultaneously. Even among the Syrian Christians [including the central characters in *GOST* and Roy's family][...] you have caste issues" (2).[7] Kerala is "riven with internecine politics" with many factions and no resolution: "eventually everything remains frozen in a sort of political rigor mortis" (3).[8] After Roy's mother, Mary, won a ruling in the Supreme Court giving women equal inheritance, "They taught fathers how to disinherit their daughters" (4). Growing up in Ayemenem, Roy says, "was a nightmare for me. All I wanted to do was to escape, to get out, to never have to marry somebody there" (5). Her mother had married a Bengali Hindu and then divorced him to return to town (as Ammu does in the novel), and Roy refers with distaste to "the way we were treated by that town, the way things were when I was a child, compared to now" after the success of her novel (8). Roy's representation of homeland emerges from a critical alienation—"I'm not a patriot," she says (95); yet she also calls India "my place" and says, "I cannot see myself living away from India" (95–96). While Roy lives in India, her writing reflects the detached, exilic consciousness of the diaspora.

This is an alienation from the India that evolved *after* independence as well as *out of* the experience of colonization that preceded 1947. The novel's critique extends to British colonialism, through the crippling Anglophilia that haunts many of the characters and renders Chacko servile and self-defeated, and to American imperialism, through Rahel's experiences in the United States as a racialized minority.[9] It extends also to globalization, visited on the village in 1992 through television, corporate advertising and World Bank loans. But Roy focuses on what independent India has made of its own rich and multiple heritages: in the name of order, it perpetuates a low-level bureaucratic thuggery in imitation of its colonial oppressors, and in the name of social stability, it enforces traditions of gender oppression, caste hierarchy, and state-sanctioned violence against "expendable" citizens. As Susan Stanford Friedman explains, "Roy's integration of gender and caste into the story of the nation [...] demonstrates how feminist geopolitics engages locationally—that is to say, *spatially*—with power relations as they operate both *on* the nation and *within* the nation" (2001: 117). Friedman's analysis highlights connections in the novel between specific acts of power in the village and Indian and transnational forces.

My own approach emphasizes the estrangement from home and homeland that arises for Roy's characters, male and female, under these conditions. Not only do Indians abroad become diasporic, novelist Amitav Ghosh writes, and not only does India maintain a close relationship with its diaspora, having "no vocabulary for separating the migrant from India," but also "the culture seems to be constructed around the proliferation of differences [...] To be different in a world of differences is irrevocably to belong" (78), but, argues postcolonial theorist R. Radhakrishnan, to belong in a diasporic sense. The nation form, and particularly India, is "internally heterogenized, 'diasporized' from within," and thus location replaces "home":

> the very idea of a proper and non-contingent home in the diaspora is fundamentally contradictory. For after all, what is the diaspora if not the denaturalization of "home" by the concept of "location"? Caught up in a constitutive "between-ness," the diaspora imagines home in opposition to discourses of ontological authenticity and domestic propriety. It is precisely to the extent that home is not natural that the diaspora is able to perform and inaugurate its representations of home as radical and incorrigible "lack."
>
> (2000: 3–4)

An amplification of his argument in *Diasporic Mediations* that diasporic subjectivity involves a necessary "double-consciousness" (with a nod to W. E. B. Du Bois), while home "becomes a mode of interpretive in-betweenness," Radhakrishnan's analysis provides a fertile ground for understanding Arundhati Roy's novel (1996: xxii, xiii).

Roy's India is internally diasporic, I will argue, problematizing the whole notion of "homeland"; Roy calls it her "place" but not her "home." The nation is heterogeneous and hybrid, mixing cultures, religions, languages, and ethnicities. Its history of plural colonialisms, Mughal and British, left marks of rupture and discontinuity; independence and partition led to massive and violent migrations. As Roy tells one strand of the national story, the characters in the Ayemenem family experience the doubled forms of identification typical of diasporic subjects, ironically looking to English models, more than to India, for their sense of custom. The word "diaspora" comes from Greek words for "across" and "to sow or scatter seeds," and it normally refers to "people who have been dislocated from their native homeland through the movements of migration, immigration, or exile" (Braziel and Mannur 2003: 1). Such dislocations do occur in the novel: Chacko migrates to England and then Canada; Ammu leaves her community for marriage to a Hindu tea-planter in Assam; the tea-planter migrates to Australia; Rahel leaves India for the United States. At the larger level, India emerges as a land of internal dislocations, a space where belonging itself is troubled.

GOST represents the discovery of such a diasporic consciousness by two children who learn what it means to be homeless, growing into the split and doubled consciousness of exile. The first section of this essay explores how the important houses in the novel reproduce alienation and reflect a public history of social inequality. The second section traces the development of a doubled, diasporic consciousness in Estha and Rahel as they undergo the traumatic collapse of family life in 1969. The third section considers the unthinkable desire between Ammu and Velutha as it brings the house down and reduces both characters to political bodies. The fourth section examines the twins' return to Ayemenem in 1992, in a homecoming that refuses comfort or resolution. The fifth and final section argues that the telling of *The God of Small Things* is as exilic and errant as its content, articulating a version of diasporic double consciousness in the narrative perspective.

Houses and homelands

Like other novels of home and homeland, *God of Small Things* attends closely to houses, rooms, hotels, and other dwelling spaces. The novel's most significant house is personified as a decrepit and indifferent old man:

> It was a grand old house, the Ayemenem House, but aloof-looking. As though it had little to do with the people who lived in it. Like an old man with rheumy eyes watching children play, seeing only transience in their shrill elation and their wholehearted commitment to life.
>
> (157)

Distant and detached, indifferent to the inhabitants' passions, this aloof, unseeing old man figures both the Ipe family in its relationship to Rahel and Estha and, on a larger scale, India in its relationship to citizens. Far from maternal and nurturing, the aloof old man calls attention to the necessary hunger and loneliness of children who struggle for life in such a house. The old man/house/nation takes the long view from a great age, overlooking the transient children immersed in time: they are small things to a family priding itself on its grandness and antiquity. The house is closed, windows and doors locked tightly by Baby Kochamma in 1992; indeed, in the novel's first reference the house suggests a deliberate self-enclosure: "The old house on the hill wore its steep, gabled roof pulled over its ears like a low hat" (4). The personified house can scarcely see or hear, and neither can the residents: Rahel and Baby Kochamma sit together in a silence described as "Swollen. Noxious," as 40-watt bulbs dim their vision (22).

As in other transnational women's fiction, the house reflects the family that has lived in it for over a century, and the family story, which emerges in fragments as the novel unfolds, comments on the poisons at work in the nation at large. I reconstitute the genealogy so dispersed in Roy's text in order to make visible the legacies of patriarchal arrogance, caste racism, and gender oppression that run through several generations of Ipes and reveal a politics linking home and homeland. The family traces its honor back to an event in 1876, when 7-year-old E. John Ipe is blessed by the head of the Syrian Christian Church. This event gives him a life-long nickname, *"Punnyan Kunju—Little Blessed One"* (23), invoked over a hundred years later by Comrade Pillai to enable another villager to trace Rahel's lineage and thus identify her: "Punnyan Kunju's son?[. . .] His daughter's daughter is this" (123). An oil portrait of this venerated ancestor hangs on the front verandah, commemorating his supervisory gaze and his pride in the Patriarch's blessing.

Much of the poison in the family comes from the Blessed One's offsprings, Benaan John (Pappachi) and Navomi, called Baby Kochamma. Of their childhood in the Ayemenem House, the narrator says little; however, both become obsessed, bitter, vengeful adults. John, always "a jealous man," resents any attention given to his wife; he beats her every night with a brass vase until one night when his son objects, and then he never speaks to her again (46–47). An entomologist, he discovers a moth but loses the chance to give it his name, after which his "maleficent" expression reveals self-hate and a competitive, vengeful streak. Formally dressed, "charming and urbane with visitors," Pappachi in private becomes "a monstrous, suspicious bully, with a streak of vicious cunning" (171–72). Baby is similarly two-faced, competitive, quick to lie and deceive, and always mindful of the public eye. Jealous of women who have married, she competes with Ammu, delights in her misfortunes, and dislikes the twins (44). During the events of 1969, she lies and manipulates (the twins, Mammachi, the police, Chacko) in an attempt to preserve her own position in the house.

Beyond the private meagerness of their individual lives, this brother and sister take willing places in a system perpetuating cultural discrimination on the basis of gender, caste, and race. They measure everything by the standards of the metropolitan center and express contempt for India. Chacko calls them "a *family* of Anglophiles" who are "trapped outside their own history and unable to retrace their steps because their footprints had been swept away," a reference to the racist practice requiring Untouchables to crawl backwards with a broom, erasing their own polluting footprints (51). Family members become split between pride and self-hatred—for their near-British but not-British status—in their love for the nation that conquered and colonized them. They adopt the "double-consciousness" Du Bois describes as a "sense of always looking at one's self through the eyes of others, of measuring one's soul by the tape of a world that looks on in amused contempt and pity" (5). Chacko refers to a war that "has made us adore our conquerors and despise ourselves," neatly excusing his family's complicity with the colonizer (52).

Brown people themselves, Pappachi's family members prize whiteness, and they measure value by standards of British style, custom, and respect. Pappachi dresses in wool suits and fawns over white visitors, while Baby falls in love with a green-eyed Irish priest. Baby distinguishes herself from the "sweeper class" by referring to Shakespeare and adopting a British accent; she teaches the twins English poetry and makes clear her preference for their light-skinned half-English cousin Sophie. Both Pappachi and Baby treat the Untouchables as polluted and display race and caste prejudice against their dark-skinned Paravan neighbors. Baby claims that "They have a particular smell, these Paravans" (243). More of an opportunist, Mammachi despises Untouchables but exploits their labor. She hires Velutha as the pickle factory carpenter and underpays him, but thinks "he ought to be grateful" (74). The irony in their Christian adherence to Hindu caste discrimination resonates: Velutha is a Christian, since his grandfather converted to avoid starvation. The "Rice Christians" have separate churches and fewer benefits than other Untouchables "because officially, on paper, they were Christians, and therefore casteless" (71).

As each generation becomes increasingly damaged by their experience in the Ayemenem House, Chacko and Ammu spend their early lives trying to escape it and their later lives in exile. Sent to England to study at Oxford, Chacko escapes with barely a backward glance, while

Ammu is refused further education. Chacko marries without telling his family and settles in England, returning to India only after Margaret asks him for a divorce. Ammu accepts the first marriage proposal she receives, but when her Hindu husband turns out to be alcoholic and abusive, she can only return to Ayemenem. By 1992, the house is full of decay and rot, with "filth" clotting every interior space, including the "rotting upholstery" of the furniture; the study is "rank with fungus and disuse" (84, 148). Baby Kochamma has abandoned her ornamental garden, the pond "stagnant" and "scummy," the cherub repaired by Velutha "forsaken" (178).[10] The Ayemenem House has fulfilled the un-homing promise implicit in the image of the aloof old man.

On the opposite shore of the Meenachal River, the History House appears to be the Ayemenem House's opposite but in fact turns out to be the same. It, too, is a grand old house on a large rubber plantation, surrounded by a deep verandah (291). It, too, is a decaying imperial house of wealth and pride, with a colonial heritage and portraits of old ancestors supervising the life below. Like the Ayemenem house it has witnessed the breaking of the Love Laws and the inevitable punishment of its owner, Kari Saipu:

> The Englishman who had 'gone native.'[...] Ayemenem's own Kurtz. Ayemenem his private Heart of Darkness. He had shot himself through the head ten years ago, when his young lover's parents had taken the boy away from him and sent him to school.
>
> (51)

For a family of Anglophiles, the lesson taught by this story would not involve the abusive decadence of English colonial power, but rather the degrading results of going native. The close links between the History House and the Ayemenem House suggest kindred schizophrenias about loving and abhorring the native.

Ironically, this empty dwelling with its tragic past is where the central characters go precisely to escape history. Ammu and Velutha cross the river at night seeking private moments of purely personal time. History is their enemy, imposing the barriers of caste and class that make their union impossible; they can only begin to think of each other when "History was wrong-footed, caught off guard" (167–68). To find a space outside this scarring history, away from the Big God, they seek shelter on the verandah and stick to the small things. The children use the house as well to escape history: Estha first decides to prepare a hiding place there because the Orangedrink Lemondrink Man knows where he lives. After their damaging encounter with the Big God, the children attempt to create a private safe space, with a few personal treasures, on the verandah.

History House takes on historical status when the Kottayam Police convert the private domestic space of the verandah to a public stage, performing a rite of exorcism designed to rid the community of a scapegoat. To reaffirm the historical caste distinctions that prevent alliances between Untouchables and women like Ammu, a group of policemen acting as "history's henchmen" brutally beat Velutha (292). They methodically cripple him, and then they destroy all traces of the children's hideaway to erase evidence that the twins were there on their own and Velutha did not kidnap them. In this way, they remake history, creating the version that justifies the murder they have just committed, while converting the space from an innocent private retreat to the History House. Symbolizing this transformation, Rahel's watch, with the timeless time of childhood painted on it, falls and disappears in the back yard. Meanwhile Roy, following Foucault, gives a history back to those whom "History" has attempted to erase.

In a homeland where all of the homes are scarred by history, Velutha's hut shows the same Big God at work on a poor, Untouchable family. The house is low and earthen: "The low walls of the hut were the same color as the earth they stood on, and seemed to have germinated from a houseseed planted in the ground" (195–96).[11] Within the one-room house, one corner is for dying without medical care; Velutha's mother Chella died where her son Kuttappen now lies, paralyzed from the chest down (197). Almost bare of possessions, the room contains two pictures cast off from the Ayemenem House: "a benign, mouse-haired calendar-Jesus" and a small poster picturing a blond girl, tears on her cheeks, writing a letter, with the caption, *"I'm writing to say I Miss You"* (199). These discarded hangings reflect the sham generosity of the Ayemenem House and suggest some of the gaping absences in the hut: the absence of blond whiteness and the power that accompanies it, the absence of education and literacy, the missing luxury of sentimental tears over the lost mother, the failure of Christian love for this family or their kind.

Every other space in the novel shows at least some of the scars of a public history of social inequality, poverty, and caste bias, emerging in a chain of images of waste, dirt, and excrement. In an interview with Reena Jana, Roy refers to "the horror of the settings—a crazy, chaotic, emotional house, the sinister movie theater" (4). The Abhilash Talkies, another space for escaping from history into mass-produced Western fantasies, is defined by filth, from the toilets to the spit-stained steps to the "dirtcolored rag" with which the nasty Orangedrink Lemondrink Man wipes the counter (91–93, 97). The Hotel Sea Queen exudes an "oldfood smell" and has an elderly bellboy with "dim eyes" and tattered, dirty clothing (35, 108). Ammu dies "in a grimy room" in the Bharat Lodge (154). The Cochin airport has "birdshit on the building" and "spitstains on the kangaroos" (134), while the train station, the Cochin Harbor Terminus, has "Gaunt children, blond with malnutrition" and air "thick with flies" (284–85). Worst of all, the Kottayam Police Station smells of excrement—Baby Kochamma's upstairs, Velutha's in the cell below (303). In these sad, damaging places, the oppression of poor and outcaste Indians emerges as their humanity is reified and sullied.

The novel observes a great many homeless people. Like Rosario Ferré, Arundhati Roy notices the poor, the maimed, and the mad—those Thomas Pynchon has called the "preterite." Murlidharan, for example, sits cross-legged and entirely naked on a milestone outside of Cochin, having lost both of his arms and his mind in a bitter week in World War II (61). Murlidharan is homeless, but doesn't know it; he has retreated into the rooms inside himself, counting keys (61). A black busker in the United States sings in the subways; an old coolie with bowed legs works at the railway station; a homeless, cold puppy follows Estha (85, 86, 16). A taxi driver lives in his car, with no other place to stay (107). A blind man and a leper chat about the Cochin Harbor Terminus "as though they had *picked* this for their home" (285). These are, writes the narrator, "Hollow people. Homeless. Hungry" (285). Glimpsed in public spaces throughout the novel, they serve as reminders that some must pay the costs of a society organized by strict hierarchies. Emblems of an internally diasporic India, they bear the private burden of public indifference.

Belonging to the imperial house

Like children in other contemporary postcolonial fictions, Rahel and Estha are raised to take places in the imperial house. The adults who live with them—Mammachi, Baby Kochamma, Chacko, and especially Ammu—teach them to be well mannered and proper, in imitation of upper class citizens of empire. In particular, they are taught to obey their elders and to follow rules; to avoid dirt and rudeness; and to be self-restrained, decorous, and quiet. Having seen hypocrisy and brutality inside the mask of the well-behaved citizen, Ammu knows the failures obedience can produce as she knows their personal cost. Nonetheless, she raises her children to win prizes for comportment and docility "in the Indo-British Behavior Competition" (139). She warns the twins not to be like their father, who had the class manners of a clerk, but rather to behave like "aristocrats" (80). In this Ayemenem House version of the rules, good form is paramount in all things—kindness, generosity, and decent treatment of others matter less than spit bubbles. Even in questions of language, form precedes meaning: Baby Kochamma corrects the twins' English pronunciation and Ammu ignores the content of their journals while correcting their spelling mistakes and fussing over their penmanship.

At the same time as the twins are produced as docile citizens with the manners of empire, they are also given a second, conflicting message: they don't belong and aren't wanted. Their deeper education, as they harmonize the two sets of instruction they receive, plunges them into diasporic double-consciousness. They are the latest branch of an aristocratic house, but not proper heirs or full members: in a family of Syrian Christians, they are "Half-Hindu Hybrids," thus not acceptable in either community (44). Their mother is blamed for her marriage and divorce, and the twins are offered only meager acceptance. Baby Kochamma resents their presence and begrudges their moments of happiness: "She was keen for them to realize that they (like herself) lived on sufferance in the Ayemenem House [...] where they really had no right to be" (44). When Estha falls on the bed in an undecorous performance of Caesar, Kochu Maria tells him bluntly, "These aren't your beds. This isn't *your* house" (80). And Sophie Mol, bringing her mother's version of family gossip from England, explains to the twins "how there was a pretty good chance that they were bastards, and what bastard really meant" (129). During the course of the novel, the twins are rejected by Chacko and, more catastrophically, by Ammu (82, 276). These insistent messages send Estha and Rahel into exile long before they leave home.

As children, Estha and Rahel develop what Radhakrishnan calls diasporic double-consciousness. They are not at home; not only are "they" all wrong, but "home" itself is unstable. They are asked to perform as Ambassadors of India, but dressed in Western clothing and told not to speak Malayalam (133). In an American version of British India, Estha wears Elvis Presley clothes and combs his hair in an Elvis "puff" while Rahel has a Western sequined "airport frock." In fact, the twins are required to perform a version of India imitating Britain under colonization, a servile role at best. Making their performance more complicated, they are performing Britain to the British, the newly arrived Margaret and Sophie Mol.

Though the narration is anything but chronological, the novel's events begin with the main characters' trip to Cochin to meet Sophie Mol and Margaret at the airport; this trip exposes deep fault lines in the Ayemenem House and initiates crises that will destroy the family. Asked how she started writing the novel, Roy responds, "I actually started writing with a single image in my head: the sky blue Plymouth with two twins inside it, a Marxist procession surrounding it. And it just developed from there" (Jana, 5). The dialogue among family members in the car, amplified by background information provided by the omniscient narrator, establishes despair and self-absorbed detachment in Chacko, anger and self-absorbed longing in Ammu, fear and self-absorbed pettiness in Baby Kochamma. Young and innocent, the twins have not understood their essentially orphaned situation in this toxic home: the novel tells the story of their struggling to understand their position through the next 2 weeks. The dialogue in the car begins their education by establishing that while Sophie Mol is prized and welcomed, they are not. Their mother has no future and no standing in the house, and her frustration erupts in anger at the children. Their uncle Chacko, whose love they crave as a substitute for the father who abandoned them, denies responsibility for them and calls them "millstones around his neck" (82).

The Marxist rally establishes a public dimension to the private crisis in the car. The same social system that enforces gender inequalities—giving Ammu no legal standing, education, or property, leaving her dependent on her brother—also maintains inequalities of caste and class. The marchers demand better wages and conditions for poor workers and an end to the use of caste names to address Untouchables (67). Protesting the long-standing injustices that have kept *Dalits* poor, landless, and oppressed, assorted men in the march carry "a keg of ancient anger, lit with a recent fuse" and an edge "that was Naxalite, and new" (67). As observed by the Human Rights Watch study, *Broken People: Caste Violence Against India's "Untouchables,"* the Naxalites both initiated and aroused violence; they assassinated landlords, some of whom organized private militias that murdered *Dalit* villagers believed to be sympathetic to the Naxalites (4). The Naxalite movement was stifled by "a brutal police crackdown"; the government continues to persecute suspected sympathizers outside the law, using "extrajudicial executions, torture, and forced disappearances" (36–37).[12] In the novel, the march establishes the conflict between the poor and the government that will erupt in sanctioned violence against Velutha at the end, and it places the

Ipe family on the side of the landlords and the government, despite Chacko's theoretical Marxists sympathies.

The Ipes' car exposes their status as wealthy landlords, members of the privileged class whose living comes through the exploitation of the poor. Pappachi had bought the large imported Plymouth from an Englishman in order to flaunt his own importance; in its grandeur, it looks "absurdly opulent" (63). The marchers see it as a symbol of the wealthy, oppressive class in India. They christen Baby Kochamma "Modalali Mariakutty," or little Maria the Landlord, an appropriate title given the pickle factory and land owned by the Ipes (76). They make her into a "mimic man" in reverse: Baby, who prefers English, is forced to say "Long Live the Revolution!" in Malayalam and to wave the red flag, in what she experiences as a humiliating imitation of their protest (77). For the children, this is another estranging moment: their family stands accused of participating in oppression, and one of the accusers, glimpsed in the crowd of angry men, is their beloved friend Velutha.

Their experience in the seedy and threatening "Abhilash Talkies" theater confronts the twins with the unbridgeable distance between the dream of a loving, recovered family, as that dream is sentimentally artic- ulated in the film, *The Sound of Music*, and the reality of their sundered and conflict-ridden family. In the film, the widowed Baron loves his "clean white children," whose family becomes whole again with the love of Julie Andrews; in the theater, the twins are not "clean white children" and the imaginary Baron "cannot love them. I cannot be their Baba. Oh no" (102). The Orangedrink Lemondrink Man pollutes Estha, handing him a penis to hold while he masturbates; Estha concludes that he could not deserve a father's love. Linked by his "gummy eyes" to the aloof Ayemenem House, the Orangedrink Lemondrink Man succeeds in abusing the well-trained, obedient Estha, yet identifies the strange- ness of the home whose teaching has made Estha so non-Indian: "First English songs, and now *Porketmunny!* Where d'you live? On the moon?" (98). Estha is caught in what Radhakrishnan calls "constitutive 'between- ness,' " neither English nor Indian, not of this planet. Similarly, Rahel is split between Austria, India, and her sense of the absences in her family home. Upset by her mother's praise for the sinister and grimy Orangedrink Lemondrink Man, she says "petulantly," "So why don't you marry him then?" (106). Her petulance reflects her awareness of how far this man is from the Baron, and thus how far she and Estha remain from the loved Von Trapp children. Ammu's response, the warning that she loves her daughter less, underscores the lack in a family where mother love is variable and finite.[13]

Sophie Mol's visit, with her mother Margaret, makes the twins aware of their own devaluation. Sophie's skin color, much lighter than the twins', matters in the Ipe household. Margaret is called "white" with freckles, and Sophie has "bluegrayblue" eyes and "pale skin [...] the color of beach sand" (137). The first thing Kochu Maria says to the almost-blind Mammachi when Sophie arrives is, "She has her mother's color [...] she's very beautiful [...] a little angel" (137, 170).[14] Close to Rahel's consciousness in this scene, the narrator draws the implicit comparisons: "Littleangels were beach-colored and wore bell-bottoms. Littledemons were mudbrown in Airport-Fairy frocks" (170). Sophie Mol is described as "Loved from the Beginning," while the twins are not (129). Mammachi and Baby Kochamma court Sophie Mol throughout her visit, making visible their preference for her. Even Ammu shows irritation with her children when they fail to perform properly at the airport. Precariously undervalued before the visit, the children become newly conscious of their outsider status.

The crisis 2 weeks later, during which Sophie Mol and Velutha die, leaves them orphaned in a far broader sense. They run away from home in the middle of the night, responding to Ammu's "careless" and damaging explanation for why she has been locked in her room: "Because of you! [...] I should have dumped you in an orphanage the day you were born! *You're* the millstones round my neck!" (239–40). This speech transforms the twins from "Ambassadors of India," knowing where they stand, to "Bewildered Twin Ambassadors of God-knows-what" (240); in a sense, it ends their family life and does, effectively, dump them in the orphanage.

Bringing the house down: Ammu and Velutha

Ammu is bitterly angry with her home and homeland: the promises made by the social structure to women in her class have been, in her case, betrayed. Her parents make clear their indifference to her; they do not arrange a match within their own community that would allow her to escape. Her father flogs her, and the alcoholic man she marries beats her too. When her husband begins to pressure her to have sex with the British overseer of the tea-plantation and then turns his violence on the twins, Ammu returns "unwelcomed" to Ayemenem (42). She works in the factory, but has no claim to inherit property or her parents' wealth. Because she is female, Ammu has no *locus standi* or legal place to stand; the twins hear this as no "locusts stand I" and Ammu comments, "Thanks to our wonderful male chauvinist society" (56).[15] While the twins discover their outsider status during the course of the events in 1969, Ammu knows from the beginning. She returns to the Ayemenem House knowing "there would be no more chances" (42).

If she has no hope, Ammu has developed a fierce anger and a sharp tongue. She has the reckless courage that comes of having little to lose; though technically a child of wealth and privilege, she identifies with the poor and downtrodden because she has, from her earliest years, been treated as unwanted and undeserving. One of her earliest memories is her father's deliberate destruction of a pair of boots that was, at the time, her prize possession. Under her father's cold, calculating cruelty, she "developed a lofty sense of injustice" (172). She ridicules Chacko to his face for his oppressive sexual exploitation of the poor working women in the pickle factory, calling it "Just a case of a spoiled princeling playing *Comrade! Comrade!* [...] forcing his attentions on women who depended on him for their livelihood" (63). Her experience of being disinherited in the house of wealth leaves Ammu with an "Unsafe Edge" and instigates "the reckless rage of a suicide bomber" (44). Like the suicide bomber, she sometimes hurts the innocent as well as those who deserve her criticism. Her rage at Baby and Mammachi, for example, spills over in the caustic words she flings at her children.

What leads Ammu to the affair with Velutha—a catastrophic and unimaginable coupling—is first of all the perception of him as fired by a kindred rage. The Marxist march surrounding the Plymouth is thus an important beginning for Ammu as well, for she is attracted to the powerful, masculine anger of the protesters. As the men chant, "the arms that held the flags and banners were knotted and hard" (67). When hands slam against the car window and fists bang on the bonnet, the men's fury directs itself like Ammu's against her father's ostentation and pride. At that point, Velutha appears: "in a white shirt and mundu with angry veins in his neck. He never usually wore a shirt" (68).[16] For Ammu, this moment marks the beginning of interest, as Velutha brings his masculine anger to public and political action. He is recostumed for the march, in which differences of caste and class among party workers, students, and laborers are made invisible, thus suggesting altered conditions in which their union might be possible.

When Rahel identifies Velutha and calls out to him, Ammu responds with a quick anger that puzzles Rahel for years (69). This anger makes sense only when Ammu reflects on her attraction the next day: her daughter's call has endangered Velutha, both among the marchers who could misinterpret his connection to the wealthy family and, as subsequent events make powerfully clear, among the adult Ipes in the car, who *do* condemn him for his presence among the marchers. Ammu, on the other hand, hopes "it had been him [...] She hoped that under his careful cloak of cheerfulness he housed a living, breathing anger against the smug, ordered world that she so raged against" (167). Indeed, it is precisely this possibility of finding an ally in her rage against the stifling order of her home/land that makes Ammu look twice at Velutha. When she does, she sees "a man's body. Contoured and hard. A swimmer's body" holding her daughter in dappled sunlight, and suddenly "*she* had gifts to give him, too" (167–68).

Ammu chooses Velutha's body as the focus for her rebellion against the order of her social world because, like her own body, his is heavily policed by Hindu caste proscriptions. In a brilliant analysis, Partha Chatterjee argues that caste aims at the control and reproduction of laboring bodies:

> Caste attaches to the body, not the soul. It is the biological reproduction of the human species through procreation within endogamous caste groups that ensures the permanence of ascribed marks of caste purity or pollution. [...] the necessity to protect the purity of his body is what forbids the Brahman from engaging in acts of labor that involve contact with polluting material and, reciprocally, requires the unclean castes to perform those services for the Brahman. The essence of caste, we may then say, requires that the laboring bodies of the impure castes be reproduced in order that they can be subordinated to the need to maintain the bodies of the pure castes in their state of purity.
>
> (194)

The lavish attention paid by Ammu to Velutha's body removes it from the world of labor, so definitive of caste rank, and places it in the realm of pleasure and desire. His stomach has "ridges of muscle" that rise "like the divisions on a slab of chocolate" (167). He has "a white, sudden smile," leading one reviewer to dub him "the subaltern with perfect teeth" (167, Kumar 87). On his back, a leaf-shaped birthmark suggests his closeness to nature. Velutha's identity exceeds his role as laborer, and that excess of muscle, of beauty, and of "physical ease" with her children attracts Ammu (167), leading her to touch the Untouchable and thus to revolt against caste and class.

Shortly after she looks at him for the first time, however, two simultaneous events reveal Velutha's helplessness beneath the appearance of muscular power that has attracted her. Told in widely separated chapters, they anticipate and explain the ease with which Velutha will be crushed in punishment for the affair. In the first, Ammu herself recognizes his powerlessness in a dream: "a cheerful man with one arm held her close by the light of an oil lamp" (205). In this dream, Ammu sees the symbolic castration of one who "raised his flag and knotted arm in anger" by a powerful social order; her dream links Velutha with the homeless, armless madman Murlidharan. While Ammu dreams, Chacko, still wearing the tight Western suit he wore to the airport, goes to Comrade Pillai to inquire about Velutha's relation to the Communist Party. Pillai reveals that Velutha is a party member and "Highly intelligent"; yet he urges Chacko to send him away, because other workers in the factory resent the benefits and caste-work being given to a Paravan (262–64). In this scene, Marxist principles vanish as the opportunistic Pillai colludes with the landlord and betrays Velutha, both by revealing his party membership and by urging Chacko to fire him.

Velutha is the authentic subaltern in the text, the victim of Indian culture and of the Ipes. His name, meaning "white," points to the very dark skin that keeps him securely locked in an Untouchable body. Despite his presence in the march, he never articulates the kind of anger at the social system that Ammu voices. Indeed, he is largely silent, as Spivak leads us to expect when she identifies "one of the assumptions of subalternist work: that the subaltern's own idiom did not allow him to *know* his struggle so that he could articulate himself as its subject" (1987: 111). Even when Mammachi spits on him and screams, he responds with restraint: " 'I'll have you castrated like the pariah dog that you are! I'll have you killed!' 'We'll see about that,' Velutha said quietly. That was all he said" (269). The narrator implies that Velutha *does* know his struggle and his position as a subject; she writes that Velutha had known "that one day History's twisted chickens would come home to roost" and that he brings "a lucidity that lies beyond rage" to the confrontation (268). Yet the representation of Velutha's mind directly following the crisis focuses on his lack of language and his inability to make decisions. His disembodied mind "jabbered useless warnings" (270). With Pillai, Velutha hears himself "slipping into incoherence," saying things which do not matter (271). Pillai's words fragment into empty slogans: "Sentences disaggregated into phrases. Words. *Progress of the Revolution. Annihilation of the Class Enemy*" (272).[17] Velutha becomes stripped of language and reduced to a political body, what Spivak calls "a signifier for subalternity" (1987: 117).

At that point his body is used by the posse of "Touchable Policemen" as a blank slate on which to write the lessons of Indian caste history.

The narrator describes in excruciating detail the damage they do in the name of preserving the status quo. As a political body in the grasp of the state, Velutha is stripped of masculinity and strength; he is unmanned and even overtly feminized by the police, in fulfillment of Ammu's dream. Three days before the catastrophe he had allowed Estha and Rahel to paint his nails red. When they discover the sign of his kindness to the children, the police mock him as a bisexual or transsexual, playing at exaggerated femininity themselves as they mock Velutha's bleeding, broken body: "they noticed his painted nails. One of them held them up and waved the fingers coquettishly at the others. They laughed. 'What's this?' in a high falsetto. 'AC-DC?' " (294). Inevitably, to punish Velutha for the crime of sexual transgression (and reassert their own masculinity), another one "flicked at his penis with his stick" and then "lifted his boot [. . .] and brought it down with a soft thud" (294).[18] Velutha commits a crime of the body, touching what has been forbidden from early recorded history in India. The police reduce him to a broken body, then make their final statement on keeping his body in its proper place: when he dies they dump his body in "the pauper's pit" (304). Not a carpenter, not an innocent man, certainly not a Christian, Velutha becomes a body buried with the other unredeemed subaltern bodies that have been brutalized by the Indian state. As Homi Bhabha writes, "It is precisely in these banalities that the unhomely stirs, as the violence of a racialized society falls most enduringly on the details of life: where you can sit, or not; how you can live, or not; what you can learn, or not; who you can love, or not" (15). In transgressing long-established prohibitions, Ammu and Velutha encounter what Bhabha calls "the unhomely."

Their 2-week passion is both homeless and unhoming, spinning them into exile and death. Consummated on the banks of the river and later moved to the deep verandahs outside the History House, the affair never has a place indoors; it is betrayed by Velutha's father, scorned by Ammu's mother, given a home nowhere. While Velutha is beaten and locked in the jail, Ammu is locked into her room. After Velutha dies, Chacko breaks down the door to tell Ammu that she must send Estha away and leave the house herself. Her expulsion comes, not because of the affair itself, but because she goes to the police to vindicate Velutha—not simply because she breaks the love laws but because she acknowledges her affair in public. In Baby Kochamma's eyes, this act brings dishonor on the house and requires Ammu's exile. Poverty and disease, migrations from one cheap transient lodge to the next, do the rest; Ammu dies 4 years later and is refused burial in church land. The lovers' deaths leave the Ayemenem House to decay along with its aloof and indifferent inhabitants.

In a place with no foundation

The events of December 1969 leave the twins mired in grief and guilt, orphaned, exiled from the very possibility of home. Velutha disappears into "a Hole in the Universe," Ammu follows, and the twins are left behind, "spinning in the dark, with no moorings, in a place with no foundation" (182). The twins return to Ayemenem in 1992, in a home-coming that refuses comfort. In the intervening years, each of them has been profoundly exiled and unhomed, their losses compounded by their separation from each other; both are rootless, unanchored, chronic wanderers. Estha is "Returned" like a package to his father in Calcutta, while Rahel is allowed to remain in Ayemenem, mostly ignored by her kin (17). Estha withdraws into silence and begins walking. His silence reflects irresolvable guilt for having said "Yes" over Velutha's dying body and being soiled after singing out loud in a theater. Estha is lost to the world of story because, not only does he not speak, he no longer puts together narratives of cause and effect. He becomes the pure diasporic consciousness, almost estranged from the planet he inhabits, without volition or language.

Her exilic consciousness makes Rahel a wanderer like her brother. After being expelled from three schools, Rahel studies in Delhi without finishing a degree, then marries an American "like a passenger drifts towards an unoccupied chair in an airport lounge," an image revealing the casual and temporary nature of her intentions (19). She migrates to Boston, divorces, works in New York and Washington. Transient in all of these places and never tempted to return to Ayemenem, Rahel evades the past by staying in motion. Memories of India come to her during this period in fragmented glimpses that leave "huge tracts of darkness veiled. Unremembered" (69–70). Rahel chooses not to look back; she never settles in a job or house, and she never goes home.

Rahel's return unleashes the memories that comprise her inheritance from her family and her nation; like the manuscripts of Atwood's *Blind Assassin* and Ferré's *House on the Lagoon*, the narrative itself constitutes a legacy. In *God of Small Things*, Rahel is both the heir and the primary consciousness reflecting on the scrambled past, with an omniscient narrator revealing things she could not know. She returns to Ayemenem only because Estha, more than ever a reified object, is "re-Returned" (21). Because she remains in language, it falls to Rahel to grapple with the meaning of the events that blighted both siblings' lives. The text, then, evokes the conventions of what Spivak calls the narrative "of the development of a feminine subjectivity, a female *Bildungsroman*, which is the ideal of liberal feminist literary criticism" (1987: 116). Roy's novel undermines these conventions, leaving Rahel stranded in exile rather than produced as a finally liberated subject.

The return after long absence highlights several changes in the house and the surrounding area: the small village of Ayemenem and the river have come under the influence of globalization. The river now smells "of shit and pesticides bought with World Bank loans"; it has been reduced to a "swollen drain" by a barrier created to allow increased rice production (14, 118). It is polluted by factories and by expanded shanties along the banks, made toxic to fish and swimmers (119). The village is full of "Gulf-money houses" built by people who make their money working outside India (14). The History House has been bought by a tourist hotel chain, surrounded by transplanted ancestral homes now used to house rich tourists. These elements provide clear continuity between Roy's fiction and her political speeches, interviews and essays. In a Reuters interview in 2005, she says, "When the only logic is the market, when there is no respect for ecosystems, for the amount of water available [...] then we are in for a lot of trouble" (Denyer). While the rich tourists have a swimming pool and the Gulf workers their new houses, the poor, living in a slum screened off from the hotel, have only low mud hutments for shelter and the river for a privy (119).

Rahel and Estha do recover fragments of the past; indeed, their reunion gives each of them a vital reconnection with the entity they had been as twins. Early in life, they "thought of themselves together as Me [...] As though they were a rare breed of Siamese twins, phys- ically separate, but with joint identities" (4–5). They share dreams and memories; so intense is the continuing mental bond that Estha knows when Rahel has returned to Ayemenem, and Rahel knows when Estha appears at the Kathakali performance. Together they re-find objects like the notebooks in which they wrote essays to be read by Ammu. As young adults, they understand the meaning of some events that baffled them as children, including Ammu's grief over the death of Velutha and her responsibility for the events. But the real significance of their return is that it plunges them back into the memories that each has tried, in the 23 intervening years, to repress and erase.

The twins commit incest in the room that had been Ammu's. In this same room in 1969, just after Ammu dreams of Velutha as the one- armed "God of Small Things," the children recall being inside their mother's womb, kicking her to produce the silver stretch marks on her stomach (210–11). Their sexual union years later amounts to a tragic, doomed effort to recapture that uncomplicated connection, including the bond with their lost mother, and to return to a simple time before death, loss, and betrayal. As the scene begins, Estha reflects that Rahel has Ammu's mouth and the two recall the length of their intertwined identities (310). Similarly, Consolata Sosa describes her passionate desire for Deacon in *Paradise* as an effort to recapture her own lost place: "I just wanted to go home" (Toni Morrison 1998: 240). The twins find some version of the lost past, briefly, as they share physical intimacy and hold each other. However, the incest does not disperse the clouds of guilt and grief or take them home. Indeed, it shows them that home is utterly lost, for "what they shared that night was not happiness, but hideous grief" (311).

To underscore the point, the narrative makes clear that Rahel is as unwelcome as her mother had been; she and Estha are not permitted to remain in the house. In her callous way, Baby Kochamma suggests this at the beginning of the visit, when she does not welcome Rahel home, but rather asks, "How long will you be staying?" (29). Later, Baby demands again to know "how much longer she planned to stay. And what she planned to do about Estha" (179). Refusing even the lightest gesture of hope that would transform the novel to a female *Bildungsroman*, Rahel has neither plans nor prospects. Echoing her mother, she has "No Locusts Stand I" (179). The text does not resolve the question of the twins' future, providing no glimpse of the aftermath of their incestuous union. Constituted as a diasporic consciousness, Rahel carries with her the lesson she has learned: not to make herself at home.

Narrating exile

The telling of *The God of Small Things* is as exilic and errant as its content, with only the narrator's wry, ironic omniscience and her intense concern for the small things to substitute for a narrative home-base. That sense of a reliable narrative foundation arises in traditional novels from steady, chronological time, linear progression, mythic cycling, or clear causal unity; instead, Roy creates a scrambled, fragmented, and nonlinear narrative surface. While one critic finds "mythic ambience" and images "of circularity, unity and wholeness" in the novel, and another calls the novel "a secular myth" and alleges that "Roy's purpose is recuperation, although her tone of bitterness and despair often masks the conviction that secular myths [...] have a redemptive power," the narrative resists unity, rejects wholeness, and finds momentary joy but not redemption in intense perception (Nair, 49, 55; Kanaganayakam, 141). It is far more radical as a narrative than most novels that sell millions of copies worldwide; its disjunctive narrative form suitably represents and extends the novel's commentary on exile.

Many of Roy's critics want the novel to provide consolation and resolution and, especially, to heal the wounds left by the events of 1969 with the twins' return home in 1992. They wish, that is, for a healing repair of the fractured bond and a true homecoming that would close the circle and position the incest, second rupture of the Love Laws, as a restorative response to the first. One critical reading thus constructs eroticism as "home": "Rahel, after a youth gone awry, returns to her childhood home and her soul-twin Estha to rediscover his pain and to offer him her body as an unnameable balm" (Bose, 59). Another critic poses the recovered memory of the re-united twins as a source of renewal: "Thus Estha will be able to travel 23 years back to disentangle his role as an unknowing victim [...] and perhaps move on with his life"; the incest "serves to set free Estha's and Rahel's 'hideous grief' and long-stifled pain as Estha can finally admit 'the reason for his silence'" (Balvannanadhan, 100–101). But in the text, there is no freeing from grief and pain, no balm for Estha, no bedside chat in which the twins resolve the past and plan a future. In fact, Estha remains silent, Rahel has no plans, and the Ayemenem House is more toxic and inhospitable than ever. As Roy says in an interview, "The book is a very sad book and somehow the sadness is what stays with me" (Simmons). Its commitment to giving that sadness scope, together with moments of joy in the small things and luminous rage at a culture of injustice, accounts for the unusual juxtapositions of mood in the novel.

The form, style, and language of *God of Small Things* are distinctive; they raise questions about why Roy adopts such a markedly fragmented, repetitious, idiosyncratic approach to narration. Not everyone has approved; a reviewer in *The Guardian* dislikes "the extent to which style dominates, to the point where the story itself is in a stranglehold," the novel at times "desperately overwritten" (Clark). For Marta Dvorak, Roy panders to Western tastes, exoticizing and commodifying India, but does so with a clumsy, exaggerated style; her discourse is "oppositional in a comfortingly predictable manner" and her writing flawed by "structural overkill" and "stylistic tics" (43, 55). Among several essays in the French formalist collection on Roy's novel, Dvorak's study argues that style should be governed, as grammar books dictate, by moderation: "Used moderately, these rhetorical devices can be aesthetically pleasing"

(58). Roy's rule-breaking immoderation, her repetition and excess, seem to Dvorak indulgent, both "postmodern tricks of the trade" and a "marketing" strategy (61). An essay on "excess" in the same collection shies away from the meaning of what exceeds boundaries in Roy's novel, concluding unhelpfully that "the whole tale is made of analepses and prolepses" (Cingal 99).

Roy's style forms an integral and appropriate part of her portrait of children who fall, through traumatic losses, into exilic consciousness. At the simplest level, the narrative is a jumble of fragments, a fallen Humpty Dumpty whose irresolvable pieces mark the loss of wholeness in the children's lives. It includes snippets from many cultures, pieces of an emerging global world. Bilingual like the twins, it uses some Malayalam words and phrases as well as English. As a narrative committed to small things, it reproduces songs, recipes, signs, slogans, poems, journal entries and spelling lists, nursery rhymes, part of the burial service, and even wrestlers' sub-verbal grunts. The very multiplicity of pieces—from the cultures of Kerala, England, the United States, the Communist Party, India, and beyond—makes summation impossible. The pieces are not "fragments shored" against ruin but, from the very land of Eliot's resolution (*"Datta. Dayadhvam. Damyata."*), they are part of the ruin itself. The twins cannot form a coherent whole out of these fragments; the narrative doesn't try.

While it multiplies shards of texts and cultural citations, the narrative also jumbles and fragments time, breaking chronology into multiple repeating pieces.[19] The opening chapter reveals all of the major events: Sophie Mol's death, Velutha "lying broken" on the floor, Ammu's despair, the separation of the twins, Estha's silence, Rahel's rootlessness. Roy has said that "for me the book is not about what happened but about how what happened affected people" and that "the structure of the book ambushes the story" (Simmons 4). By revealing outcomes at the beginning, she de-emphasizes plot and, with the scrambled fragmentation of the structure, she reveals how these events affected the twins: they are caught in unresolved repetitions, thrown about in time, limited to distorted and partial glimpses. The narrative alternates between 1969 and 1992, but not predictably; Chapters 3, 5, 7, and 9 begin in 1992, but then the regularity disperses and 12 and 17 begin in 1992. Within the story of 1969, several sections back up to tell previous events, but the history does not emerge in chronological order. Chacko's marriage and divorce, for example, are told in Chapter 13; but his grief on leaving his baby daughter Sophie appears in Chapter 4. Many of the sections beginning in 1992 return to segments of the past: to a visit to the doctor before 1969 in Chapter 5, to Ammu's death and cremation in 1973 in Chapter 7, to a visit to Velutha's hut in 1969 in Chapter 9. The disruption of sequential time reflects the twins' disorientation: they are left with scrambled memories experienced in tumbled and varying (dis)order.

The style itself is fragmented, repetitious, and excessive. One of the novel's ways of representing the consciousness of children is to reflect their fascination with the malleability of language: the ways words can be broken apart to suggest menace (Lay Ter), put together in fresh ways to create new things (Bar Nowl), or conjoined to surprise (suddenshudder). Sentences too are broken and fragmented, paragraphs sometimes made of a single shard: "A small forgotten thing" (121). These experiments point to the consciousness of bright, verbal children who know the rules (in two languages) and enjoy breaking them; at the same time, they point to the stunning broken-ness of the children's world and the absence of predictable ground, the "Locusts Stand I" on which to build. Some phrases circulate like repeated refrains through the text. Roy says, "Repetition I love, and used because it made me feel safe. Repeated words and phrases have a rocking feeling, like a lullaby" (Jana 4). These refrain-phrases touch the emotional nerve-centers of the novel: the smell of Velutha's blood ("sicksweet like old roses on a breeze"), the speed of loss ("things can change in a day"), or the finality of death ("a hole in the universe"). The repetitions may provide the comfort of recurrence, but every one of them announces the impossibility of return, recuperation, or redemption. Their very excess makes the novel overtly styled, emphatically written—though in a colloquial way suited to children rather than the formal, ornamented way of adults.

Its combination of two kinds of narrative perspectives enables the novel to have it both ways, combining limited viewpoints with broader, ironic knowledge. The novel uses a perspective that is attached and involved, a version of third-person-limited point of view that moves freely from the children to various adult actors; it also uses an omniscient narrator, ironic in its superior knowledge and later understanding. The attached and involved perspectives have different fragments of limited knowledge, and many are clouded by bias. The omniscient voice can be imagined as that of the adult Rahel, looking back with a novelist's imagination of things she didn't see, or as that of Arundhati Roy, bringing a viewpoint from outside the world of the characters. In the conjunction of these two kinds of observation, the narrative finds a corollary for diasporic double-consciousness, both vested in events and watching from outside with a larger understanding that enables the critique of nation. The combination enables the narrator to accomplish two contradictory goals: to represent the events of 1969 as they appear to the baffled, emotionally vulnerable twins, whose frame of reference is the home; and to reflect on underlying motives, social and cultural forces like racism and caste prejudice, seen in the context of the national homeland.

Like the narrator of Morrison's *Paradise*, Roy's narrator adopts an inclusive position in her third-person-limited visions, conjoining multiple perspectives while resisting totalizing conclusions. Committed to seeing the small things, the narrator finds a consciousness to look through in almost every scene; for example, one of the Kottayam policemen on the way to brutalize Velutha notices that "Crimson dragonflies mated in the air" and "wondered briefly about the dynamics of dragonfly sex" (289). While the narrator often looks through the eyes of the young Rahel and Estha, seeing with the imaginative vividness of a child-consciousness, she also enters the interior lives of Baby Kochamma (who "realized with a pang how quickly she had reverted to thinking of them as though they were a single unit once again," 29), of Chacko (who "was puzzled at the turn the conversation had taken," 263), and of Ammu (who "laughed out loud at the idea of walking naked down Ayemenem," 212). The narrative sees into Comrade Pillai (who "knew that his straitened circumstances [...] gave him power over Chacko," 261), Velutha's brother Kuttappen (who "thought with envy of madmen who could walk," 198), and Inspector Thomas Mathew (who "congratulated himself for the way it had all turned out," 246). These multiple vantage points give the narrative breadth and inclusiveness, prevent any sentimentalizing of the twins, and create an ironic, omniscient patchwork.

The omniscient voice lifts the narrative into knowledge and reflection beyond that available to any of the characters and links the novel with the kathakali performance it describes. Kathakali, the omniscient narrator explains, links performer and audience in unfolding stories whose ending is known: "kathakali discovered long ago that the secret of the Great Stories is that they *have* no secrets.[...] You know how they end, yet you listen as though you don't" (218). The kathakali performer re-creates the stories anew each time, selecting which small things to dramatize and how to reveal intersecting moods: "He can fly you across whole worlds in minutes, he can stop for hours to examine a wilting leaf" (219). The stories are his home: "They are the house he was raised in, the meadows he played in. They are his windows and his way of seeing" (219). Like the Kathakali Man performing the Great Stories, Roy reveals her end at the beginning, leaps stretches of time, pays vivid attention to the seemingly small, and makes the stories of human desires, losses, and loves into a capacious house with wide open windows.

And yet, I would argue, readers do *not* know how the novel will end, for it chooses to focus its final chapter on events well outside what can be thought in India. With the lovemaking between Ammu and Velutha, the text violates the very core of caste prohibitions, which erect rigid separations between polluting and upper caste bodies. Such customs aim to protect a certain version of home: above all, they prohibit the sexual union of a woman like Ammu and a man like Velutha. In the last chapter, Roy does violence to these proscriptions and, by implication, to this version of home. In Velutha's kindness to the children, the novel has seen a warm humanity not imaginable within the codes of caste; in Ammu's fiery determination, it has represented strength not imaginable under the conventions of gender. But the novel's most transgressive moments are these, by no accident the focus of the lawsuit filed against Roy for obscenity; critic Pumla Gqola aptly calls this conclusion "a moment of insurgency" (119). If reciprocal passionate desire can be fulfilled between a woman of good family and an outcaste Paravan, the version of home/land protected in India for centuries crashes into dust. This hope speaks in the novel's last word, "Tomorrow."

7
The Home Elsewhere: Simone Lazaroo's *The Australian Fiancé*

The fiction of contemporary Australian writers reflects uneasy, even anxious national relationships with other homelands; indeed, one study of the Australian national character is titled *Anxious Nation*.[1] An original member of the Commonwealth established as a federal state in 1901, Australia has an uneasy affiliation to the United Kingdom; it also has ambivalent relations with Asia, its heavily populated northern neighbor whose migrants it has rigorously restricted; and it has guilt-ridden relations with the aboriginal descendants of the peoples who inhabited the land before British settlement. All three of these relations appear in fictive texts about the Australian homeland, a space continuing to negotiate its national identity. As if to reflect Australia's origins as a penal colony, Australian novels explore the foundation of homes that model empire itself as corruption or crime. Australia's location as a Western outpost in the heart of the East leads some Australian novelists to focus their fiction on the Orientalism implicit in national relations to Asian peoples, especially the fetishization of Asian women. In the novels of contemporary Australian women writers, national anxieties about these cultural relations appear reflected in homes suffused with tension and conflict.

Aboriginal peoples and their descendants form an important source of cultural anxiety and a haunting presence in contemporary Australian fiction. Writing about ethnicity in settler societies in a book subtitled *States of Unease*, David Pearson argues that structurally, just as "relations between settlers and metropole represent external relations of colonialism in a world of states, relations between settlers and aboriginal peoples can be depicted as internally colonized. The indigenes become captives within their own territories" (13). In Australia, the period of settlement from the late eighteenth through the nineteenth century was characterized by confrontations that were "often bloody" and sometimes "premeditated genocide" (31). The descendants of aboriginal peoples have lived in poverty, on reservations, on sheep stations owned by Europeans, in city slums. Under the guise of "Aborigines Protection Acts," state governments took thousands of mixed-blood children, products of white settlers' contact with (and often rape of) aboriginal women, away from their parents and their home territories in the twentieth century (Pearson, 33). The fracturing of family units—memorably represented in Nugi Garimara/Doris Pilkington's memoir *Rabbit-Proof Fence*, made into a film in 2002—recapitulates the disruption of earlier collectivities and the blurring of their differences in the general term "aboriginal."[2]

The closeness to Asia and distance from the British model culture have led to other anxieties about population and identity. Australia maintained an official immigration policy, called "White Australia," from its independence in 1901 ("with explicitly anti-Asiatic sentiments formalized in the 1901 Immigration Restriction Act," Pearson, 85) until 1973.[3] The goal was to recruit ten British immigrants for every one "foreign" migrant, though in practice migration was opened to refugees and migrants from homelands throughout postwar Europe. Asian migration, however, remains restricted even after 2000, with an evaluation of "personal suitability" and financial stability, including that of relatives already working in Australia (Pearson, 86). Nations that emerged from the former British Empire remain the primary source of migrants to Australia, although a gradual increase in Asian migrants—highly select, and "held to strict financial and skill-based entry standards"—has occurred ("Australia," 51). Lisa Lowe's observations about Asian immigrants in the United States (which had its own policies restricting Asian immigration)[4] are relevant to Australia as well. Asian immigrants, she writes,

> have played absolutely crucial roles in the building and the sustaining of America; and at certain times, these immigrants have been fundamental to the construction of the nation as a simulacrum of inclusiveness. Yet the project of imagining the nation as homogeneous requires the orientalist construction of cultures and geographies from which Asian immigrants come as fundamentally 'foreign' origins antipathetic to the modern American society that 'discovers,' 'welcomes,' and 'domesticates' them. A national memory haunts the

conception of the Asian American [...] in which the Asian is always seen as an immigrant, as the 'foreigner- within,' even when born in the United States.

(5–6)

The nationalist conception of homeland entails the narrative of one homogeneous family of citizens, and thus, as Amy Kaplan writes, the designation of those who don't fit into home as "foreign"—whether inside the borders or outside (2002: 50). Lowe's work reminds us that Asian peoples, like those of African and Dravidian descent, have been identified in many societies as "the contradictory, confusing, unintelligible elements to be marginalized and returned to their alien origins" (Lowe, 4). Contemporary Australia can be understood as living with the persistent aftermath of colonialism, including policies designed to preserve and protect the whiteness that came from its British settlers, even while recognizing the pernicious effects of racism on all of the nation's peoples.

   Reflecting this unease over Australia's status and history, postcolonial theory has had a significant impact, with powerful advocates for both the theory and the literary texts of the postcolonial world, in Australia. Bill Ashcroft, Gareth Griffiths, and Helen Tiffin published *The Empire Writes Back* in 1989 and the large *Post-colonial Studies Reader* in 1995; both texts popularized postcolonial thought and made it more readily teachable. These three Australian scholars argue forcefully for expanding the canon of English literature beyond the United Kingdom and especially for the importance and value of literary perspectives from the former settler colonies. Tiffin protests the continuing centrality of British literature:

> While 'post-colonial' and generally counter-canonical courses of various kinds have multiplied within English departments, this increasing pluralism has not displaced the emphasis on British literature; in many cases the effect of apparently radical challenges to the canon has been, paradoxically, a reinforcing of the status and fetishization of the Anglo-canonical.
>
> (155)

Griffiths objects that the effect of privileging European theory, applied to European texts, has been "once again to marginalize or ignore the creative and critical writing which has emerged from the post-colonial world itself" (1996: 167). He advocates the study of literary texts from postcolonial sites, including settler colonies, because of the valuable "contribution made by the literary texts of the post-colonial world themselves to the theorization of the issues of post-colonialism," understanding theory as "the articulate response of people to their cultural and political situation" (1996: 173). Advocating the importance of postcolonial literatures and theories, Ashcroft, Griffiths and Tiffin have brought attention to the merits of Australian writing.[5]

Ashcroft, Griffiths and Tiffin assume that postcolonial theory has a fundamentally political motive in resistance to imperialism; this assumption underlies the notion that the colonial outposts of empire *can* "write back" to the center. They observe that its political goals make postcolonial theory a natural ally of feminism:

> Feminist and post-colonial discourses both seek to reinstate the marginalized in the face of the dominant, and early feminist theory, like early nationalist post-colonial criticism, sought to invert the structures of domination, substituting, for instance, a female tradition or traditions in place of a male-dominated canon. But like postcolonial criticism, feminist criticism has now turned away from such simple inversions towards a questioning of forms and modes, to unmasking the assumptions upon which such canonical constructions are founded.
>
> (1989: 175–76)[6]

Ashcroft, Griffiths and Tiffin see postcolonial literature as taking the language of English empire and writing back in what they call "english" (1989: 8). Their approach to postcolonial theory as a mode of resistance from the margins leads logically to their advocacy of the literatures of Australia and other former settler colonies, understood as "writing back" to the traditional British canon.

In contemporary Australian literature, writing from the margins contests power in the Australian home and homeland. In a nation whose only Nobel laureate in literature to date is Patrick White, several women writers reflect on gender inequalities in patriarchal homes.[7] Among the works of the most sophisticated of these writers, explorations of women's subordination to oppressive fathers intertwine with interrogations of the Anglo-American literary canon, so the fiction claims a space for women in home, nation, and literary canon simultaneously. Mardi McConnochie's novel *Coldwater* (2001), for example, tells of Charlotte, Emily and Anne Wolf who live with their brutal father, Governor Wolf, on the prison-island named Coldwater off the coast of New

South Wales. The penal settlement and the year, 1847, evoke Australia's foundation; references to the Bronte sisters and their characters in the text point to the British origins of the Australian literary tradition. In this literary tour-de-force, the sisters convert the British elements with which they begin into uniquely Australian stories as they struggle to escape from the oppressive legacy of patriarchal control. They manage to achieve varied forms of liberation from the prison home, and Anne arrives at a symbol for Australian independence: "A more impermanent dwelling could not be imagined, but the little tent was clean, fresh, and new"—and it takes on the qualities of a place where she can write: "It was the clean slate she had been looking for" (304).[8] Like other contemporary transnational women writers, McConnochie imagines the story of nation in terms of home, and she prefers the impermanent freshness of the postcolonial space because it allows her to clear away, even as she acknowledges, the writers who have influenced her.

Sally Morgan's autobiography, *My Place* (1987), invokes the racism of empire and its legacies in postcolonial Australia. *My Place* traces Morgan's quest for her aboriginal ancestors, their homeland within Australia, and their stories. She is 15 before she understands that her grandmother is not Indian but rather the biracial child produced from a white farm-owner's rape of an aboriginal woman enslaved on his sheep-station. Morgan's mother appears to be the product of another white man's rape of her grandmother when she was young; Morgan's mother marries a white man who later expresses contempt for aboriginal people, and Sally and her siblings "could pass for anything" (139). Her discovery of her "place" in Australia coincides with her discovery of racism: "Up until now, if we thought about it at all, we'd both thought Australia was the least racist country in the world, now we knew better" (139). She tells her mother that Australia "should feel ashamed": Aborigines were in fact enslaved—"we had slavery here, too" (151). The policy of removing biracial children from aboriginal parents led several family members to spend parts of their childhood in institutions, and Sally's mother was terrified that she would lose her children. Granduncle Arthur says, "You see, the trouble is that colonialism isn't over yet. We still have a White Australia policy against the Aborigines" (212). As for finding "my place," the text does not lead any of Morgan's family members to their homeland, to secure knowledge of their roots, to reconnection with lost kin, or to any physical or mental space like "home." Though her mother calls Australia "our land," the Morgans have no "homeland" (306).

Regarded as one of "the three leading prose stylists working today in Australia" (Birns, 232), Brenda Walker invokes in her fourth novel,

The Wing of Night (2005), the settling—and traumatic unsettling—of home and homeland. One of five novels shortlisted for the prestigious Miles Franklin award for 2006, *The Wing of Night* re-imagines the Australian experience in Gallipoli, where over 35,000 Australian and New Zealand men—almost a third of the ANZAC troops in Turkey—were killed or wounded in 1915. Only 14 years after independence and nationhood, Australians volunteered to fight in Britain's defense; yet, as both Walker's novel and Peter Weir's film, "Gallipoli" (1981), reveal, Australians came to believe that Britain exploited them, deliberately sacrificing soldiers who were sent with bayonets against Turkish guns. The battles at Gallipoli crystalized an Australian identity, one replacing a tradition of loyal affiliation to England. In foregrounding the set of events that lead Louis Zettler, a wealthy West Australian farmer, and Joe Tully, a doctor's son fallen in class after his father dies, to the disastrous battle in August 1915, Walker focuses on a definitive moment in the emergence of Australian national identity.

Although Walker's Australian men are brave in the face of death, this unusual novel emphasizes the costs of war—the stunning speed and finality of death, the endless damage to survivors both male and female, who remain haunted by grief and guilt—and imagines traumatic losses at the core of home and homeland. Louis Zettler is shot and "buried quickly" (76). Joe Tully is blown out of a sniper's hole, "flung high in the air above Anzac Cove and he shattered when he landed" (179). Though Joe survives and returns to Australia, he suffers recurrent hallucinations and crippling guilt, in part because he has shot and killed a young Turkish soldier. At home, Elizabeth Zettler manages the farm after her husband's death but feels "that she had dropped like a stone to some internal floor of her self" (118). Bonnie Fairclough, already marked by the terrible violence of her young husband's suicide, mourns her new lover Joe's disappearance after Gallipoli. This novel finds unhealable traumatic wounds in home as well as homeland, focusing much of its attention on Australian women's struggles to make sense of the homes they are left to inhabit in the "bright emptiness that lasts for a long, long time after a war" (248).

In writing about the irrecoverable losses that emerge from war, Walker effectively unsettles the Australian home and homeland. The novel does not draw nationalist pride from its wartime setting, but rather suggests that nations at war sacrifice their young quite pointlessly and with reverberating costs. Indeed, Gallipoli demolishes the distant homeland where no bullets were fired: Australian homes are both emptied and haunted by ghosts of the dead, widows like Annie Crane scramble for food as they raise children alone, and maddened and grief-stricken soldiers take to the roads as swagmen. Five years after the war Elizabeth employs Joe Tully and eventually becomes his lover, but continues to yearn for her husband, to save his place in the bed, and to ask everyone, including Joe, for details about his death. Although no external impediment prevents their union, it never finds or makes a home—no safe indoor space of their own, nor any future for them despite her pregnancy with his child. Recovery is impossible, leaving only the need to patch together sufficient spaces and approximate relationships.

For a text that combines attention to all of these Australian issues— women's issues in patriarchal homes, women's claim to an artistic space and voice, and the politics of racial issues in the nation—I turn to Simone Lazaroo's second novel, *The Australian Fiancé* (2000).[9] A poetic and deceptively simple fiction by a Malaccan-Australian, this novel explores the Australian home and nation from a minority perspective, as both author and protagonist migrate to Australia from Singapore. Describing the "often-uneasy reception of minority writing by mainstream critics," Shirley Tucker observes that " 'migrant literature' may be perceived as unwelcome, discomforting and illegitimate: straying into Australian spaces without proper credentials" (2003: 179). Pam Allen notes that while Australian writers have explored the relationships between Australia and Asia, "it is rare for Australian readers to get a perspective on them from an Asian-born writer" (28). Lazaroo uniquely explores Australia from both outside and inside; a doctorally educated writer, she takes a postcolonial feminist approach to her story of Australia that makes her novel especially suited for this study.

Both domestic and national betrayals cast long shadows in this text. From its title onward, it addresses the choices men and women make of domestic partners, their proposals, desires, and intentions as they settle a home. Much of the action occurs inside the fiancé's family home in Broome, Western Australia, as the young woman protagonist he brings there with the promise of marriage learns the objects, values, and customs of home. She has much to learn about Australian homes: like Lazaroo she identifies herself as Eurasian ("The Christao [Eurasians] are descended from those Malaccans with both Portuguese and Malay blood," notes a character in Lazaroo's first novel, 19).[10] While Lazaroo emigrated to Australia at 3, the young protagonist of her novel grows up in a shophouse in Singapore, where poverty and trauma following the Japanese invasion of the island in World War II leave her unprepared for the role of woman of the house in Broome. Inevitably, the engagement is broken; the fiancé's parents object to her race, expose her traumatic past, and arrange to deport her. The fiancé accepts their decision, leaving the protagonist stripped of home and recognizing, as she counts her losses, that homelessness is her inheritance from her British father and his imperial homeland.

While creating a home with a chosen mate and learning the customs of home in a new land form the ostensibly conventional subjects of the novel, it more radically unsettles home by exposing its affiliation to a corrupt empire. In *The Australian Fiancé*, the hunger for home, imagined as a place of acceptance, safety, love, and belonging, drives the protagonist's hopes; but hope evaporates as the Australian home shows a hollow skull and an inner structure based on classist exclusivity and racist exclusion, deception, hypocrisy, and a fundamental hostility to difference. Home acts as the agent of empire, reproducing its customs, enforcing its values, and rendering alien and homeless all those who cannot be subjected to its codes. Australia's anxieties come together in the expulsion of the young Eurasian woman near the end of this novel, for as Shirley Tucker observes, "the portrayal of relationships between Australian men and Asian women has been invariably seen as metaphor for cross-cultural tensions on a range of political, economic and national levels" (2000: 153). In Lazaroo's novel, the tension is resolved by the fiancé's decision to break the engagement and marry a suitable Australian instead.

Hybridity and homelessness

The novel chronicles the protagonist's discovery of herself as alien, an outcast without family, a resident without home. She is not named, except as "the young Eurasian woman," 20 years old as the novel begins, whose status enlarges as she comes to represent every-woman of mixed race in the aftermath of war.[11] Her understandings begin at the level of nation, as she comes to see Australia's commitment to an exclusionary whiteness. She confronts a uniquely Australian form of racism at the border, where the "White Australia Policy" restricts immigration to those of European ancestry. From a document stamped *"Secret,"* a customs officer reads, "The Minister holds the view that persons who are not of pure European descent are not suitable as settlers in Australia"; he goes on to explain that an immigrant's blood should be "at least fifty-one per cent European" and their appearance sufficiently white to guarantee that they can pass for Europeans (80). The Eurasian woman is admitted to the country, not because she can explain that she meets the criteria (she does: her father is English and her mother a mix of

European and Asian), but rather because the customs officer regards her as an object possessed and guaranteed by the fiancé: "Just being yours makes her ...well ...at least eighty per cent" (81, ellipses Lazaroo's). But her hybridity remains an issue, indeed becomes an increasing issue, once they enter the country. Her understanding of her situation as a postcolonial subject grows by the day once she arrives in Broome. It will grow global and philosophical as she perceives the deeper implications of the British empire's lingering hold over the Australian nation.

Almost all of the characters in the novel are, like the young Eurasian woman, designated not by personal names but by race, role, or relationship. The Australian fiancé functions as a nameless representative of his nation and class, and of men of privilege who propose lightly to women they perceive as desirably exotic but find, down the road, they cannot marry. Like Faulkner's Thomas Sutpen, the fiancé is a "nothusband,"[12] as anticipated by the fact that his young partner is never called the fiancée (Faulkner, 7). At 31, he is called young by the narrator (24), and he is also identified as "the handsome Australian" (26). In the first section of Lazaroo's novel, "Singapore," the protagonist's family members are introduced: the Eurasian mother, the English father, who photographed things that fly before he returned to England with his camera and died, the Aunty, and the 4-year-old child who was born just after the war. In the third section, "Broome, Western Australia," the fiancé's servants and later his parents appear: the housemaid, the gardener, the cook, and his mother and father. While their designations make these characters general and representative, they also level categories of "major" and "minor" by rendering all of them equally nameless, as if their individuality was forgotten. The housemaid says of an "Asian woman" who took photos of the people in Broome, "What her name lah? Carn' think" (111).

Curiously, the principal home of the novel has, unlike most of the characters, a name: the palatial house of the fiancé's parents in Broome bears "the name *Elsewhere* on a shiny brass plate by the front door" (86). Elsewhere refers to the great undifferentiated set of places that are not *Here*; elsewhere might be anywhere, but in particular "else" points to something *other* or *different*, not the selfsame or identical. In the context of the fiancé's family-life in Broome, *Elsewhere* invokes *Here* as the seat of empire, its home in England. A home named *Elsewhere* promises to reproduce that seat, to regulate its cultural practices according to the same imperial logic so that the great mass of global territory lumped together in the concept of elsewhere can erase its difference and become the same. Indeed, novelist and art critic Drusilla Modjeska comments ironically on the Australian sense of distance from the cultural center; she writes, "One of the paradoxes of working as an artist (or writer) in Australia is that we have to know about elsewhere, while elsewhere rarely knows about us" (1999: 180). By invoking a yearning for the cultural center, the home to which the fiancé brings the young Eurasian woman signals her impossibility and eventual exile, and more broadly empire's foundational exclusion of the foreign other, on its door. Late in the novel she realizes, "*I will always be homeless in this house*" (185).

The young Eurasian woman epitomizes a form of otherness that is both sufficiently similar to attract the fiancé and yet alien enough to require exclusion. The Australian's attraction to her rests on her exotic difference; in an early conversation he reveals that

> he'd always been fascinated by Asia, how he'd always hoped for a greater [...] *intimacy* with Asia.
> 'What kind of Asian *are* you, by the way?'
> She manages, coolly, 'I am *Eurasian.*' This is how she sees herself. This is how she would like to be seen.
> 'Ah. Eurasian. East meets west. Like in the Noel Coward song.'
>
> (28)

The Australian's perception of Asia as the sexualized other appears in the language of "fascination" and "intimacy," and his question to the protagonist requires her to place herself, not in terms of an individual family history, but rather within the racial category he has exoticized. In choosing to define herself as Eurasian, she gives priority to her Eurasian mother, who comes from Malacca, over her father, the English man who found his own Asian exotic in the mother. As the fiancé's comment suggests, her "Eurasian" status signals the hope that East can meet West and thereby makes their union thinkable—at least in a formulaic musical-comedy world. More to the point, her origins suggest an explanation for his attraction: she is only a little other, but mostly and reassuringly the same. In her facial features, of all the young women he might see in Singapore in 1949, he could find a recognizable European beauty commingled with traces of the Asian exoticism he clearly seeks.

Others see the Eurasian woman as a disturbing sign of racial hybridity. The mixture of races visible in her face threatens the conception of race as an immutable boundary, like species, across which breeding could not occur; racial purity would then be a biological imperative. A Malay taxi driver in Singapore looks on her with contempt because "she's *chap cheng*, mixed up blood" (26). A Chinese man paddling a sampan misses her Asian roots altogether, calling her and the fiancé "Eengliss tourists" (39). But for the Australian immigration officer, committed to enforcing the White Australia policy excluding immigrants who are not at least 51 percent European, "She looks to be somewhere around fifty per cent European ...which is nowhere, really" (81, ellipsis Lazaroo's). The fiancé's mother sees her as "greenish skin" and "slanting eyes, untrustworthy" (106); the father as "Tasty. Exotic" but "Cheap as chips" and "dangerous. Disease everywhere" (108).[13] Both regard the union as unthinkable, the grandchildren that would emerge from it as non-white and therefore unacceptable. The housemaid, herself a biracial mix of Nyul Nyul aboriginal, Indonesian, and Japanese, identifies the Eurasian woman not by her race but by her function, as "the boss boy's flank," and by the power it confers; she always addresses her respectfully as "miss" (95).

While her hybridity threatens and confuses others, she is more deeply troubled by the wartime experiences that have rendered her what Suzette Henke calls a "shattered subject" with a fragmented self-perception and a sense of alienation from her own body.[14] Her body is not her home but an alien object, not her own, and not continuous but fragmented. In the war, though she represses this history until late in the novel, her 14-year-old body was captured and used by the Japanese in a brothel full of children: "hers became a body of war, invaded" as the soldiers rape her: "the blind heedless hack hack hack at her membranes and senses" (120–21). Like the soldiers, she objectifies herself, turning the experience from one she suffered to an event for a body not clearly related to her. She escapes in imagination, finds pictures of exotic places that she shares with the other girls to help them survive, and afterward builds a wall around that body. When the war ends, the protagonist becomes "the body of hunger" (17). When she learns to desire the Australian, she becomes "A body of my own pleasure" (89) and even, at least briefly, "my body of love" (122). As if each body belonged to a different person, none of them her own except the last, she fragments her history and dissociates herself from the object-bodies that experience stages in her life. She observes herself detaching her body but stops short of commenting on the implications of this habit: "The way I wore my body then: as if it had nothing to do with me" (122). Her body—"it"—is worn rather than inhabited, a thing rather than a home. In the same way she has no dwelling-place that she can think of as home, she has a detached, abstracted relation to her own body and cannot feel at home in her own flesh.

In the same way, she denies the child conceived of rape on her "body of war." She pretends before the Australian, the child herself, and the reader that the child is her sister, not her daughter. Even when she describes the birth late in the novel, she is careful to preserve the ambiguity of the child's parentage:

> In the street outside our shophouse window I heard the midwife refuse, even after my mother offered her extra money. We did our best with help from no one.
> The waves of pain dumped us over and over again.[...]
> Long trembling stretch of birth.
> Long trembling stretch of the baby's first breath.[...] Afterwards the baby grew into the child.
>
> (165–66)

The plural pronouns mask who is giving birth, who helping. "The baby," later "the child," detaches and distances the protagonist from this offspring of a hated Japanese soldier, one among many brutal invaders. Sixteen when the baby is born, she does not want to care for the child; she notes that "I find it difficult to show her affection" and the child is four before "For the first time I see her face clearly" (163). Her denial of the child, her daughter, is the crucial lie on which her affair with the Australian founders and, more crippling still, her alienation and self-objectification thrive. The revelation of the mother–daughter relationship between them, hinted at but concealed throughout much of the novel, forms the crisis point; her acknowledgment of her daughter occurs only after the fiancé has ended the engagement and the child has drowned on the beach.

Narrating estrangement

The fragmentations of the protagonist's history and identity have their correlative in an appropriate stylistic device: the narrative perspective of *The Australian Fiancé* alternates between first- and third-person-limited, as the protagonist wrestles with an "I" she wants to escape and a "she" she needs to own. The alternations are irregular, as are the lengths of the fragmented sections of narrative divided sometimes by empty space between paragraphs, sometimes by a looping line. The relation between the content of any section and the perspective in which it appears cannot be predicted; some of the traumatic moments in the protagonist's life are narrated in third person (her account of her rape in the Japanese brothel and her discovery of her mother's death), but others are narrated in first person (the scenes when the fiancé breaks the engagement, when he meets the woman he will later marry, and when the child dies). The alternations continue from the beginning of the novel to its end, even though the narrator changes after the child dies: she tells the fiancé the child was hers before she returns to Singapore (196). While that admission ends the lie, it does not heal the rifts in the protagonist's spirit, and the first–third alternations continue in the epilog spanning 30 years in Singapore.

Whether first or third person, the protagonist's narrative has the quality of self-detachment, a tendency to abstract what might be personal (like the experience of childbirth), and a habit of de-personalizing the most private and individual moments with language that theorizes, conceptualizes, and strips the moment of body and imme-diacy. When she meets the Australian, for example, she is riven with hunger:

> It is as if she has left her senses, has become blatant appetite, a naked salivator. She's being waved around on the end of a stick for everyone to see. She wants to weep with the shame of being reduced, despite her attempt at the New Look, to this. A hunger.[...] for being made anew. For being made whole. Or, for wanting to forget.
>
> (24)

The protagonist feels a desire so focused and ferocious it expresses itself as a bodily imperative or hunger; yet the move toward specificity breaks and fragments into the abstract naming of the hunger (to be "made anew" or "made whole" or "to forget"). Her hunger exposes her, moving toward the body with the images of appetite, nakedness, and saliva-tion. But as if the invocation of the body's hungers makes her too vulnerable to those who prey on bodies and appetites, "she" is suddenly skewered, waved around on public display by an unseen hand, and the body becomes marshmallow or kabob in the face of an even larger— but abstract and invisible—hunger. This passage evokes and erases her body by turns, culminating in the naming of her desire to be made anew (soldiers have made her old at 14) or whole (she has been rent: "She'd torn and torn and torn" 121). Or to forget: the language of her narrative enacts a repeated re-membering of the body, "for everyone to see," followed by a turning away and forgetting. Neither position stills the restless energies of the narrative.

In every context, the twin poles of the narrative pull it back and forth between embodiment and leaving, denying, or forgetting the body, between metaphors that draw their vividness from the body and abstractions that renounce it. The protagonist learns to experience sexual pleasure in the following terms:

> she feels the long trembling stretch of beginning go on, and on; wider and deeper, until it's almost complete. Astounding. A bead of perspiration drips off his face into her eyes. There is a moment of blindness before an impression of him comes to her complete and she calls his name.[. . .] Always, these moments of blindness before beauty.
>
> (117)

Her experience of pleasure occurs in abstract terms, with the specific and concrete bead of perspiration dripping from him to her as she loses sight, becomes air and sky. Time and events stop, verbs drop away, and the experience of bodily pleasure takes her away from her body altogether.

At the other extreme, when she wakes from a brief nap on the beach and finds the child's dead body at the "hem" of the tide, she narrates a mixed recognition of the import of this body and a denial of what she holds:

> the child looks fast asleep when I find her. A slight frown across her brow, like a venerable scholar's; turning to deep knowledge, retreating into herself. But as I draw closer I notice the child's open mouth is blue, as if bruised. I kneel to get a closer look.[. . .] quite suddenly, not all of me is there, because I don't want to address the evidence I hold in my arms.
>
> (186–87)

In this passage the specific, detailed examination of the child's bodily appearance evaporates into stunned denial of her reduction to bodily matter in death. The child becomes "the evidence," more than her mother can bear. The protagonist's own body drops away again, in pain as in pleasure: her mind disconnects from her senses and part of her goes elsewhere.

Inheriting home(land)lessness

The protagonist's suffering and fragmentation are personal and individual, reflecting on young women's psychological trauma amid experiences of vast upheaval like war. But other elements in Lazaroo's novel link the personal with the political. The novel's meaning and importance ramify outward because the protagonist is the Singaporean daughter of an English father who has abandoned mother and child to return to London. "The Empire had come to reign well before I was born" (5), the protagonist begins, identifying herself as a postcolonial subject. As a fatherless child she yearns for acceptance and even assimilation by the imperial center into which her father disappeared, and therefore she tries to master the father's language. Her mother speaks "swooping Singaporean English" as well as a Malay dialect and Cantonese; "I spoke pieces of all these languages, but at school I learned the English the Irish nuns told us was *proper*.[. . .] I believed proper English would make me complete, re-unite me with my father, give me entry into the nation that had been closed to me when he died" (12). She writes proper, even eloquent English, speaking always in the voice of authority and power, though she reproduces colloquial variations in the speech of her mother, her aunt, and various servants in Australia. Her father's absence leaves her open to the invasion of the soldiers, just as the insufficiency of English protection leaves Singapore open to Japanese invasion.

Her father owns the authoritative gaze of the camera, his way of looking at Singapore through "the hard edges of the Empire's machinery" (5). His hobby was photographing "things that fly" through the technological eye of a "quick new 1929 Rolleiflex twin-lens camera" (13). The purpose of his photography is to prove to his lover that "the spirits she feared did not exist": only material objects that can be captured on film are real, while the rich mythic culture of Singaporean ghosts and spirits can be dismissed (13). Ironically, the photographs he leaves behind are under-exposed and unfocused, looking more like immaterial motion than material proof for his mechanistic theories. The father's possession of the technological lore of the camera sets up his daughter's attraction to the young Australian, who walks off the ship wearing a camera that takes her back to her father's images of flight: "Her ears are dinning with the flurry of wings as she notices the camera around his neck" (19). Like her father, the Australian overdetermines the mechanics of photography, fussing with light meters and virtually ignoring the subject he shoots.

Her father is empire, indifferent to the fates of his colonial children, distant and then dead. She is the illegitimate daughter of empire, left to survive as she can amid poverty, war, and hunger. How inevitable that she should accept the Australian, who functions as the favored son of empire, when he offers: "if you would come with me . . . If you like my country, you can stay, we will marry" (55, ellipsis Lazaroo's). The move to Australia takes her closer to that central fatherland and in other ways re-unites her with her father. But while she undertakes the move in hopes of finding the home she has yearned for, experience teaches her that empire's bastard children are homeless from their birth, homeless in their heritage, and more than homeless if they dare to look homeward to empire. The lack of personal names invites readers to consider broader connections, transforming the protagonist's alienation and fragmentation from a private, psychological experience, the affair of an individual, to the postcolonial subject's drive for voice, authority and home.

The protagonist's experience of homelessness extends backward to her earliest memories in Singapore. Late in the novel, when the fiancé tells her that he cannot marry her without losing his home, she thinks "Home. I can almost see the back walls of the Emporium, he does not know how bare and damp; I can almost see I inherited homelessness from my mother and father" (181). Her inheritance is the shophouse or Emporium, bought by her father, willed to her mother and then to the protagonist, to which she almost never refers as home: a place of tin and plywood on the edge of the kampong, it has two small rooms, a leaking tap, a table, a bucket, and sleeping mats for furniture. She thinks of the makeshift architecture of the Chinatown in Broome as a similar "empire of impermanency" (86). Beyond its flimsiness and poverty, the lack of belonging and security it provides, the protagonist's first dwelling is an induction in homelessness: it is *not* the home her mother wanted, *not* the sentimental story of love-marriage-home she dreamed of for herself and yearns to see fulfilled in her daughter's narrative. The Emporium is all she received from the Englishman who never married her, a "nothome" from a "nothusband."

Experiencing deprivation, loss, and hunger, the mother passes along to her daughter the narrative of an unattainable, sentimentalized home. The protagonist's abiding memories of childhood and adolescence involve the mother's warnings against flesh and sexuality, as the mother who loved an Englishman out of wedlock urges her daughter to wait "for the right Eurasian boy from the same church as ours" (9). This fantasized boy would build a home "in one of the Eurasian enclaves"; after a traditional wedding, the pair would enter this "home with taps and a porcelain toilet bowl, a home with a proper altar in its own alcove and a grandmother in her own armchair in the sitting room. A home where a child might learn what a family really was" (10). In this daydream, the daughter will marry a boy from the same race and church, live in an "enclave" of her own people with the "proper" relation to divinity and to her mother and daughter. The allure of this version of home crosses nations, races, and classes. If the details differ (rather than a white picket fence, plumbing and an altar), the underlying sentiment remains the same: the home radiates security and belonging, family unity and acceptance. The protagonist's mother has not been able to achieve such a home in her own life, but she passes the dream and the "heart-shaped hopes" unquestioned to her daughter (10).

The novel implies, though, that the mother's nostalgia for the unattainable home, fueled by her own legacy of homelessness, opens her daughter to the fragmentation, self-repression, and loss she experiences in her own fruitless pursuit of the home. It conditions her desire for the Australian: from the first, visibly a man of property and an owner of homes. It mandates her denial of the child, whose birth marks her story's fatal divergence from the fairy-tale legend leading to the newlyweds' home. The nostalgic longing for home impels her in the direction of empire, her father's homeland and the place of his absence, therefore the locus of the home elsewhere that never materialized for her mother and herself. It foreordains the protagonist's vulnerability to an Australian who gazes at the world through his camera and "takes photos to help him remember what is his" (125).[15] The mother's unsatiated yearning for a home with an armchair determines her daughter's departure with the fiancé for Elsewhere, a home that will teach and then expel her.

Learning the imperial home

The novel's central section and thematic heart narrates the protagonist's education in the ways of home as empire. She learns from the servants, especially the housemaid with whom she identifies; from neighbors and acquaintances, both those who ignore her and those who welcome her; from the fiancé's parents; and from the woman who begs at the door. Her education unfolds in quick glimpses and slowly understood details that reveal imperialist power, domination, and control operating inside the home in the same ways and for the same ends as in the nation at large. Empire, revealed as racist exclusivity and oppressive use of the other, makes the beds of *Elsewhere*. It dictates who may lie with whom, who will lie to whom, and what will issue from the lying.

Indeed, beds explain empire's need for authority and control while they also symbolize the drive toward private safe spaces in the home. While imperial expansion involves the conquest of native populations, including the sexual subjugation of those natives deemed (in the father's words) "tasty" and "exotic," empire requires dynastic restrictions on who may inherit wealth and power. The beds of home are meant, not for sexual pleasure, but for reproductive duty: for the production of legitimate heirs. Beds are meant to contain sexuality, to neutralize its potential for difference—for a decentering encounter with the uncanny energies of radical otherness—and in that way to authorize the (re)production of the same. On arriving at *Elsewhere*, the protagonist recognizes these qualities in the bed at the core of the house:

> The fiancé ushers me to the centre of it all, to our bed. It is a four-poster bed, each post carved like a liana climbing a slender trunk, a crowned lion in the centre of the headboard.[...] the sheets and pillowslips are the yellow of old linen washed in pale orange dust, like a blush. His monogram is encircled by fine embroidered vines in the centre of each plump pillow.
>
> The yellow bed is high, creaky, irrefutable. It is the bed of the Empire.
>
> I lie on it.

(88)

Images of concentric circles place the British imperial lion in the center of the headboard in the center of the house, marking the connection between home and nation as expressions of the same "irrefutable" authority. The family monogram, also centered and encircled, declares its affiliation with empire and its power to impress the heads on the pillows; the protagonist wakes up one morning with the mark of this monogram "incompletely branded" on her forehead (182). The tight stitching on the quilt bespeaks the tidy regularity of empire, and the vines climbing the posts and finely embroidered on the pillowslips signify the capitulation of nature, the wild luxuriant feminine elements of vegetal fecundity, before the imperial and disciplinary order of the slender phallic trunk or its representative, the circular monogram.

The only errant detail in the picture is the color of the sheets, a falling away from the whiteness of empire through the infusion of colored native dirt, the orange dust. The "yellow" sheets define the "yellow bed" which comes to define the protagonist, seen as insufficiently white herself or as part of Asia's "yellow peril" (106). She tells the fiancé that the yellowing of the sheets, which he says are monogrammed in Singapore by "little Chinese ladies," comes from "the sweat of the underpaid needle women" (93). When the fiancé's parents arrive, the mother brings "new linen to fortify Elsewhere" (105), strengthening it against the native, the soiled, and the colored, and the fiancé praises the new sheets as "Nice and white" (106). Aware that she falls, like the sheets, away from pure whiteness, the protagonist tries to wash the sheets herself that afternoon, a sign of her yearning for imperial approval. The fiancé, oblivious to the yellow sheets puckering "like skin" in the white wash, tells her not to do such work (109). He does not acknowledge his own preference for whiteness, either, until his parents insist.

Among the lessons of empire the protagonist learns at Elsewhere, the primacy of whiteness is the most important. Empire wears, favors, and thinks white: the "immaculately pressed whites of the pre-war pearling masters" worn by the Australian when she first meets him (18–19), the "shimmering white frock" with matched sandals and handbag he chooses for her to wear to a New Year's party (138). The White Australia policy regulates the skin and blood of immigrants, but the fiancé gets her a certificate of exemption, which is "dazzlingly white" (81). Her skin is not described as white, but neither is the Australian's: when she meets him he is called "dust-coloured" and "the colour of new unvarnished rattan, pale gold" (18–19). Later, when they live on a boat in the harbor where he teaches her to swim, she refers to "our brown bodies" (118). His mother's whiteness comes in part from makeup (133). Relative in nature, a question of shades, whiteness is made absolute in empire—in the paper that exempts her, in the valuation of lineage, in the reins of power. Empire expresses its racism in degrading the other, excluding people of color, and guarding the purity of lineage.

The protagonist also learns the hierarchical system of class undergirding the roles, duties, and disguises proper to women who inhabit homes like Elsewhere. Imperial women *do* virtually nothing and produce nothing but themselves as graceful, decorative objects. A neighbor across the road demonstrates the daily routine of a woman of class:

> a pale woman in a robe shows her face behind a pane of glass every early afternoon, just long enough to reveal her face haloed by curling papers, her eyes by white cream.[. . .] only re-emerging just before evening, dressed in cream, coiffed in gold, as delicately tinted as a cold-climate Christmas-tree angel for her husband's daily return. Yawning.
>
> (97)

The neighbor spends her days in beauty routines designed to defy nature, halt aging, and produce the right colors and textures to evoke the center of empire in this tropical province. Like the fiancé's mother, the neighbor is probably dyed and permed, covered in a mask of powder and foundation, bejeweled and corseted. Her yawning reflects the boredom of one who has no purpose, the exhaustion of one who works hard at empty tasks. Her labor at the mirror is made possible by the labor of a corps of servants who cook, clean, garden, and meet the needs of the household in Broome, and by the labor in Singapore of the "little Chinese ladies" who monogram sheets, and by the labor of the Chinese launderers who clean and press the clothes shipped abroad. The fiancé's mother explains, " 'It's very easy for your standards to drop in a town like this.' She wrinkles her nose. 'To go native' " (133). Empire expresses its commitment to standards through the women of class, who hold nature at bay in the civilized "disguises" they labor to maintain. The more unnatural the appearance, the more false and glossy and out of place, the more it is valued as "civilized."

The fissures in empire's story of itself appear to the protagonist at Elsewhere. Within the sentimental story of home, she comes to see rigid exclusionary principles at work; she gathers mounting evidence of the lies, hypocrisies, disguises, and pretenses that mask abuses of race, class, and gender. Late in the novel she learns that the aboriginal woman who begs at the kitchen door, a thin, proud woman with a child, has had an affair with the fiancé's father: "I know how invisible this family make you feel, miss. I bin his father's flank long time ago" (195). In this family, which is so determined to exclude and exile her, she sees the way empire operates, making the native mistress invisible so the costumed wife can appear to reign over the civilized house she yearns for. As the maid tells her, "dis house full of shadows.[. . .] Too much shame, miss" (95). The protagonist witnesses contempt and hostility for native peoples, together with exploitation of their work: the mother hoses the mistress; aboriginal gardeners provide "cheap labour" (94); the roads were built by aboriginal prisoners "chained at the neck" (97); and the son calls a shell midden the natives' "garbage heap" (152). A similar racist hostility to Asians segregates Chinese and Malay people in the movie theater and creates a separate "Chinatown" in Broome, as it places a Sinhalese couple at the bottom of the social scale (103, 86, 139). A related abhorrence for the natural world—a preference for all things manufactured, unnatural, stripped of any earthy connection—distinguishes the family that built its fortune from pearls and the exploitation of natural resources.

Unsettling observations

The protagonist pays attention to all that empire excludes and represses. Part of her charm as narrator derives from her habit of sympathetic notice for others who, like herself, are what William Trevor calls "beyond the pale." Even while she is temporarily housed amid the comforts of empire, she observes those outside: the servants at Elsewhere, a toddler tied to the stall of a food hawker in Singapore, the "dark skinned man in faded clothes" who meets the boat in Broome (81). Because her most meaningful relationships are with the group of outsiders, she sees them in vivid, defining detail. A memorable group of aboriginal lepers, doubly outcast by disease and by race, triggers a deep sense of kinship in the protagonist (143). She sees them once as the fiancé meets the "woman of bells," her blonde antithesis whom he will later marry; in this meeting she describes the lepers as "the image of my nightmare easing into reverie" and a "dark silhouette of extremity cradled by water" (142). Unlike the pale woman so attractive to the Australian, the protagonist identifies with the dark, exiled, hopeless lepers, who play "music of longing and rejection" (143). Later the housemaid takes her to the leprosarium to meet her mother, another figure of desperate pain with whom the protagonist identifies. Smiling through distorted flesh, the mother tells her that lepers experience either "numbness or enough pain to drive you mad" (165), an insight that echoes after the child dies and the fiancé betrays his promise: "On their last morning together in the yellow bed, there is just numbness, or maddening pain" (191).

In the end, the young Eurasian woman practices two slim strategies of counter-assertion: object of the disciplinary gaze of empire, particularly through the cameras of her father and the fiancé, she takes photographs of her own that celebrate difference; and in the fractured poetic narrative of her experiences with the Australian fiancé, she makes a marginalized perspective central. Neither strategy takes her home; but between them, they begin to suggest ways the postcolonial subject can unsettle home and homeland.

In a novel where the camera has come to symbolize the technological gaze of empire, expressed in rules for photography that appear as epigraphs for each section, the protagonist claims the right to her own vision when she takes the fiancé's camera back to Singapore.[16] From her earliest days with her fiancé she covets the camera and the knowledge, common to both her father and the fiancé, of how to represent reality on film, but she only asks to borrow the camera in their last days; "I'd like to take photos of people," she tells him, "Starting with my sister" (168). He replies that "People are too hard" and (looking at the Asian child) "some people don't photograph well" (168). Since he uses photos to "take possession" and "to help him remember what is his" (124–25), he prefers to photograph scenery; he labels and dates each photo and preserves his collection in his albums. Portrait photography appears at Elsewhere in an approved form: in the dining room there are "three photographs: his mother, his father, the King. They are focused, properly lit" (175). These photos remind the Australian who he is—a son, a subject, part of the ongoing imperial project, one who must not marry a biracial Eurasian with no known people.

The protagonist seizes the power of the gaze when, uninvited, she chooses the camera as the only souvenir she will take back to Singapore at the end. She changes the operation of the gaze in the way she uses the camera: rather than where she has been and what she owns, she photographs commoners and poor people. Rather than claiming possession and exercising power in the way she orders and enframes the contents of her photos, she uses them to empower their human subjects. Like the Japanese woman who recorded the outcasts of Broome, the protagonist takes pictures "of the people I live among" in Singapore (204). Her way of seeing preserves individuality, and rather than making the images her own or summing up their meaning, she gives them back with appreciation: "No two of my subjects are the same.[...] I give the images back to their owners. 'You are really something,' I tell them. Unable to say exactly what" (204). This anti-imperial approach to photography uses the gaze to celebrate individuals at the margins rather than disciplining them into categories or collecting them for other viewers.

Simone Lazaroo takes a related, anti-imperial approach to the narration of her story. She writes a poetic, empathic prose that notices individuals, records particular details, and attends sympathetically to minor figures who are invisible and indistinguishable in the eyes of empire. While she narrates in standard English, she breaks enough rules to set off grammar-detectors in the Word program: she often uses sentence fragments to catch the quick, partial thought; she records the vernacular speech of dozens of characters whose English is peppered with imports from other languages; and she gives her narrator a charged sensitivity to nature that infuses her metaphors and colors the tragic situation of the protagonist. The narrative uses the present tense to create the sense of time slowed or stilled: "Bees float between the pale yellow blossoms of the shrubs and a craggy honey-dripping hive of wax stalactites hanging from the verandah rafters" (94). Verbs often disappear or translate action into ongoing gerunds, with the same effect: "All around us the milky turquoise water catching light like frosted glass until the onshore breeze blows; the sun casting crescent-shaped prisms onto the sandy floor of the bay" (118). Lazaroo and her narrator celebrate forms of unphotographable beauty, the subtle play of light and wind that cannot be ordered or framed, the generosity of the natural world that eludes the discipline of empire.

The narrative inverts the totalizing imperial gaze and takes its perspective instead from a marginalized, fractured position looking in at the operations of power. It expresses the marginalized position of the Asian-Australian woman writer with respect to the canon, as Shirley Tucker describes it: "Because Asian-Australian women's writing is invariably positioned in a dialectical relationship with canonical Australian literature, the position of these texts in terms of contemporary Australian myth-making and cultural production is often overlooked" (2003: 187). Writing of Lazaroo's first novel, critic Dorothy Wang praises the appropriateness of its fractured surface: "The episodic, fragmented nature of her novel well captures the narrator's attempts to cobble a self from the souvenirs of her life, the various fragments of history's detritus" (49). In *The Australian Fiancé* as well, the narrator does not presume to add up, unify, or harmonize. The very mobility of the perspective, shifting between first and third person and traversing distances in its focus, frees this narrative from the conventions for producing a final version of events.

While the protagonist returns to Singapore, the narrative does not present this return as a home-coming. Her mother and child are now dead, and the section's title deflects any sense of home: "The Empty Emporium." Functioning as a coda, the last ten pages of the novel present glimpses of her life after the return, including a scene 30 years later when the fiancé appears in Singapore with his wife. In all of the glimpses, the protagonist does not appear at home, but rather in the streets or at the harbor; the narrative gives her no marriage, no family, no new home. She sees the Australian on the street, and rather than feeling relief or resentment, she reflects with sorrow that there are no words to "give thirty years of longing its proper place" (206). She ends her narrative at the ocean reflecting on the child's death and a photo sent by the fiancé of herself on the day she departed, "And immense, enduring distance" (211). Far from the closure of the imperial centered circle, returning to the place of origin with a satisfying knowledge, this return effectively estranges the point of departure, finding in it distance, irremediable loss, and the recognition of lifelong homelessness. The protagonist does not think of the Australian, or of Elsewhere, as her "proper place" or home, but rather the condition of longing itself.

Even the handsome Australian, whose culture has made him exotic to her early in the novel, becomes unaccountably strange to her in retrospect. Writing the narrative 30 years after her return, she emphasizes her frequent uncertainty about what he thought or meant or felt. When she tells him her most painful truth, the story of her daughter's origins, she describes him "hiding behind" his eyes (196). When he takes her to the boat on which she will depart for Singapore, he calls to her three times, speaking words she cannot make out (208). "What sort of man is he?" she wonders, and "Was it love?" (193, 209). At the very end, he sends her the photo of herself, departing for the rest of her life; on the back he writes, *"Stray light and movement, but/ I have kept this"* (211). His comment returns to himself, to his critique of the technique in the photo he took and to his choice to continue possessing it. Yet he has kept the photo, despite his marriage and his acquiescence to his parents' demands, rather than renouncing and forgetting the experience. And, like the protagonist, he ends by giving the photo back to its subject, giving her "back to myself" (211). Complex and indeterminate, the fiancé eludes summary or easy judgment.

Like the leper a "dark figure of extremity," the protagonist of Lazaroo's novel marks the distance between the Victorian woman settling her home and the contemporary woman discovering she has inherited homelessness. Lazaroo's protagonist meets the Victorian woman, the fiancé's mother, and sees inside the moral order she bequeaths to her son along with the white linens and the King's photograph. Inside, what looked like moral order collapses into an immoral system whereby hegemonic power reproduces itself and maintains a racist grip on privilege. The mother has taught her son, the fiancé, well enough so that he betrays his pledge and his own brief impulse to tenderness for the Eurasian woman; he agrees to live as "His parents' man" (193). The home Elsewhere has fulfilled its promise, producing the closed ranks of the same. The fiancé chooses the blonde Australian woman, his mother's replica; both could pass for citizens of Britain. The colonial outpost signals its affiliation with the metropolis, and the well ordered home Elsewhere becomes almost Here.

The enduring homelessness of the protagonist comes, in this light, to appear as a moral virtue: homes exclude, oppress, and use, while making invisible the costs of what they propagate. Homes victimize those of other races, underpay those of other classes, and rely on traditional, repressive gender roles to insure continuities of power. Homes act as seats and agents of empire; they take on sinister intentionality in their elegant white orderings. For the protagonist, the crowded, varied, inclusive streets of Singapore provide greater breathing space and a more welcoming set of human contacts. Yet the longing she feels to the end is surely for the home she cannot have. This place exists nowhere, but fills the novel, her mother's stories, her own abiding sadness, and the child's tuneless hum. It is the space of belonging that—in Australia and in the empire beyond it—displays itself like a mirage before the tantalized gaze of those who cannot be taken home.

8
Conclusion: Unsettling Inventions

The six narrated homelands brought together in this project, like the six private homes with their complexly burdened protagonists, can be connected and compared but not homogenized. The similarities among them need to be understood in the context of a multitude of differences: in particular histories of colonial contact and nationalism in the homeland, including its relationship to indigenous peoples and to slaves; in the race, class, and economic status of the represented home and the specific focus of its exclusionary practices; in the forms and styles of patriarchal power, its cultural and personal roots and socially sanctioned expressions; and in the women protagonists themselves—the routine or traumatic events that leave them self-divided, their education in the values and practices of home and temptation by its pleasures, and their response to unique experiences of homelessness and exile. These and a multitude of related differences require caution in the general conclusions we formulate about transnational women writers.

Nonetheless, I would argue that these transnational women writers are strongly political. Their fictions of home do not sit quietly in private spaces and reconfirm the virtues of domestic orderings or the wisdom of worldly configurations of power; nor do they suggest that leaving home will resolve women's problems. The narratives place private homes in the public and political context of homelands in order to reveal complicated, empowering linkages between them. Energy, they show, flows both ways in a self-confirming circuit through the connection, so that inherited assumptions about power in private homes support national priorities, including acts that discipline, conquer, exploit, and oppress what Kaplan calls the foreign, while national policies and values sanction—even require—the reproduction of those enabling assumptions at home. This is to claim, too, that women writers deliberately attend to national histories and global flows of power. They understand oppressions of gender in connection with those of race, class, and sexuality. The women writers studied here give new and expanded meaning to the feminist motto, "the personal is political." In exploring self-replicating networks of patriarchal and imperial power, they find politics in the privacy of home, home implicated as an actor on the public stage of national politics. As I will show in more detail, these writers also choose experimental modes of narration that alter and reinvent form and genre and thus renew the house of fiction.

These transnational women writers reflect in sophisticated ways on their nation's historical encounter with colonialism and its legacies for the rupturing of postcolonial subjectivity. Toni Morrison, for example, traces the ancestry of her contemporary African Americans to their arrival before 1770 as slaves in the American colonies. These origins locate her characters as descendants of the Atlantic slave trade, part of the heyday of European colonialism in which people, natural resources, and manufactured goods were moved around the world. Morrison does this, not to rationalize the inexcusable acts of Ruby's leading citizens, but to historicize them: in historical context, Ruby's fierce, self-protective enclosure makes a different kind of sense. The town's pride in the purity of its blue-black blood emerges from the brutal conditions of slavery, from the Civil War and the broken promises of Reconstruction. If these legacies leave the men oppressive patriarchs, the women silent prisoners acting the role of pampered queens, and the town performing the very model of mute and segregated blackness dreamed of by the most ardent racists in America, Morrison locates these ironic fractures as a part of the postcolonial condition of her African American characters.

For the other writers brought together in this study, colonialism has shaped the homeland, set the terms in which later events can be understood, and left complex, divided subjectivities to characters grappling with the intersections of personal and national histories. In Nigeria, for example, the colonial encounter with Catholic missionaries has split the Achike family, creating a self-contradictory Eugene who rejects African traditions, condemns African flesh, and renounces his animist father, while taking a brave public stance that affirms Nigeria's right to demand honest leaders. In India, a much earlier colonial missionary encounter brought Christianity to the Ipe family, though they retain Hindu caste prejudices. India's more recent British colonization has left them fractured: brown people who prize whiteness, Malayalam speakers who favor English, mundu wearers who adopt Western dress. Educated in England like Eugene, Chacko calls his kin "a *family* of Anglophiles" who are "trapped outside their own history" (51). Like Adichie, Roy places her crisis with the children who inherit these cultural contradictions from the colonial past; but she adds to the mix their mother's signal act of rebellion in having an affair with a Christian Untouchable.

Canada and Australia share histories as white British settler colonies, shaped by their distance from the metropolitan center and producing divided postcolonial subjects. Like Eugene and Chacko, Atwood's and Lazaroo's postcolonial characters study, imitate, and long for approval from a British imperial culture to which they are invisible and insignificant. In Australia, the fiancé's parents found a home they name "Elsewhere," marking its pretensions to replicate *Here*, the seat of empire in England. Such a home privileges white people of class and property and excludes the foreign other; thus it announces on its door the self-dividing lessons it will teach the young Eurasian. In Canada, button-factory magnate Benjamin Chase establishes a grand home, which his wife Adelia names Avilion to signify her sense of exile. Like Lazaroo's Australian home, Avilion bespeaks a nostalgic longing for the metropolitan center and unthinking endorsement of imperialism. Women like Adelia and the fiancé's mother take on self-canceling roles upholding the regulations and importing the relics of a culture not their own. For Iris Chase and the young Eurasian woman, choosing a partner who invites them into the imperial structure leads to direct confrontations with the misogyny, racism, and class and ethnic prejudices that undergird home's oppressions and exclusions.

Puerto Rico has a complex colonial history, layered by two different conquering nations whose sequential colonizations extend back 400 years and continue in the present day. Rosario Ferré develops a fictional family for her home/land on the Caribbean lagoon with a history of bitter divisions over its legacies from Spain and the United States. Crises occur as Puerto Ricans choose between statehood, independence, and continued commonwealth status, a decision Ferré has likened to an ongoing civil war within families. The Mendizabals' personal conflicts extend and complicate the public ones: emerging from Spanish conquistador ancestors, two generations of patriarchs have engaged in violent misogyny and racism. The current targets of this oppression sift through divided loyalties and complicities and eventually rise up in revolt.

In effect, these novels show that the self-disapprovals and longings constructed within postcolonial subjects make them liable to reproduce the conditions of their own colonization. They carry damaging yearnings to emulate and win approval from the always-indifferent metropolitan center. Such an impulse to perform as what Brathwaite calls "mimic men" renders Roy's Indians cringing Anglophiles, Eugene an abusive disciplinarian who bans his own language, Ferré's Puerto Ricans rigid about "clean lines" in marriage, Atwood's Canadians insistent on class distinctions and Victorian repressions, and Lazaroo's Australians passionate about white linens and the white King's photograph in the dining room. Even Ruby's citizens, living in willed isolation from the colonizing society, end up in curious imitation of it with their orderly white houses. As part of these characters' heritage from the colonial past, they remain invested in the power structures of empire and the hierarchies that were used to denigrate and discipline their culture.

These novels are feminist as well as postcolonial, and the women characters have complex subjectivities, doubly split and self-divided with fractures left by colonialism compounded by others constructed with the devaluation of their gender. Postcolonial and patriarchal ruptures combine to shape their self-difference and to estrange them from home, even from any easy inhabitation of their own bodies. For Rahel, dressed in Western clothes and told to speak English, shown that women have no standing in their father's or husband's homes, the lessons are clear: she does not belong anywhere; she is all wrong. Lazaroo's young Eurasian is similarly fragmented by traumatic events brought on partly by her gender: abandoned by an English father, raped and impregnated by Japanese soldiers, taken up and then discarded by the Australian fiancé, she survives by detaching herself from her body and separating her body into a series of objects—the body of war, the body of hunger. While each piece of violent history can thus be repressed and left behind, the segmented subjectivity that results from these detachments cannot inhabit its history.

Morrison's and Adichie's women live with similar ruptures: their race has exposed most of them to bigotry and confirmed the debility of their gender in patriarchal societies. Inhabiting flesh as women of color and spirits that long for affirmation and fulfillment, they find these needs at war with each other and in conflict with social constructions of their roles as women. As Consolata tells the women near the end of the novel, they have been taught to separate the body from the spirit, leaving the fractured subject with insatiable hungers. Consolata's Catholic faith has advocated the renunciation of the flesh and held women of color (the Arapaho girls and multiracial Consolata) at a distance from God's higher orders. Adichie's protagonist is also the target of racism as well as deeply ingrained misogyny within her own family. Kambili struggles to remain loyal to her father and submissive to a Catholic church that rejects African faith and condemns the unconverted. In both of these novels, the old Cartesian duality of mind and body takes on biting force to press women down into pure embodiment, all the while reviling their particular bodies of color, or upward into an abstract spirituality that would renounce the flesh. Seneca's self-mutilations respond to this doubled message, both punishing the body with painful slicings of the skin and creating symbolic openings to set the spirit free.

Isabel Monfort Mendizabal and Iris Chase Griffen assess their divided subjectivities at the end of long, degrading marriages to brutal capitalists. Both husbands, Quintín and Richard, exploit the poor and racial others who work for them, building lavish fortunes out of "sweat shop" labor practices. Both are racist and sexist as well; each ignores, abuses, and betrays his wife. A closet pedophile, Richard seduces Iris's younger sister and then locks her up in a clinic for an abortion; Quintín rapes a young black servant and then denies the biracial son she bears. Iris and Isabel sort through their fractured lives in retrospective narratives. Isabel understands the fragmentation of her subjectivity as she writes the narrative of her life and marriage: living in a house with its own segmented history, she has been both the acquiescent, submissive partner of a racist conquistador and the secret author of a text that indicts him. Iris also sees her life in shards, and while she collects the fragments in a steamer trunk and writes a narrative that gathers memories, she does not order and unify the pieces into a coherent, chronological whole. The shattering discovery of her husband's role in Laura's suicide, followed by the clear-eyed admission of her own guilt, leave Iris like her writing: split, layered, full of seams and pieces. Like Kambili and the young Eurasian, Iris and Isabel struggle with their histories and find rupture and breakage rather than redemptive wholeness.

For this group of transnational women writers, the ongoing patriarchal oppression of women appears more clearly at home than in the public arena, where legal policies in each homeland have given women nominal rights. At home, longstanding traditional hierarchies continue to subordinate women, regulate their behavior, and silence their expression. Given the sophistication of the contemporary writers brought together in this project, their women protagonists are neither simple nor simply victims. Indeed, they are complex subjects, sorting through a dense mix of historical allegiances and personal longings in the effort to know what they have invested in home. As they meditate on the webs of constrained choice that have brought them to the present, they recognize their own complicities with systems of oppression. Each of them has yearned for home: for its safety and ease, for its material security and beauty, and especially for its pledge that she would be cherished and valued for her unique gifts. To fulfill what Lazaroo calls these "heart-shaped hopes," women protagonists choose flawed and inadequate partners and eventually participate in the very system that stifles their own freedom.

The pleasures of home draw them into investments of time and emotion and then sometimes into self-delusion. Iris begins by liking the clothes she can buy and wear as Richard's wife, and later she enjoys the social position his wealth conveys. Isabel is drawn to her wealthy husband by the freedom, the time to think and write, that she will gain as his wife, as well as by his seemingly passionate pledge to love her. For the Eurasian, the fiancé's home heals the rift and restores her to a place in her father's empire, while his fascination looks like the love for which she has longed. For the wives of Ruby, home is a place of unfailing safety and protection from the racist world "Out There," and it links them to a community with a long kinship history. Kambili's home satisfies the wish for kin and belonging, and she is thrilled with occasional signs of her father's approval. Ammu also trusts in the kinship bonds with family, no matter how damaged and self-obsessed she knows her kin to be. Established in their homes, women tend to stay—to work with or around their partners or kin, to care for children, to manage the house, to accept their lot, to avoid worse alternatives, and above all to avert homelessness.

In these transnational fictions, home teaches children the imperial and patriarchal ideology that defines and sustains the homeland. The novels can be understood as domestic *Bildungsromans*, narratives of the education of young people into their roles in the home, home's role in the homeland. When they learn these lessons, they know the world and their place in it. The novels spend considerable time detailing the teaching of young women: while Atwood's protagonist is the oldest in the novel's present, for example, the novel devotes close attention to her education as a young girl. Although she learns some Latin and a smattering of (European) geography, Iris recalls most pointedly what she learns about power from subtexts in the formal teachings of her tutors and from Reenie's maxims. Ferré's protagonist Isabel and Morrison's women who gather at the Convent also reflect retrospectively on the homes that have shaped them. Rahel and Kambili are the youngest protagonists; Kambili goes to a convent school, while Rahel's formal education appears to be suspended for Christmas holidays during the 1969 events. Both, however, receive formative educations from the

regulating practices of home. Both mothers serve as instructive failures, Beatrice for her inability to produce more children and Ammu
for having produced too many "Half-Hindu Hybrids." Both are imper-
fectly submissive: Beatrice plots murder while she polishes the figurines, while Ammu develops an "Unsafe Edge" and openly condemns
"our wonderful male chauvinist society" (56). With devastating results,
brothers Estha and Jaja learn the masculine code that requires them to
speak up and take responsibility, while Rahel and Kambili learn silent
acquiescence. From the Japanese invasion, the young Eurasian learns her
own vulnerability; she learns the power of empire from Elsewhere. Both
experiences teach her the devaluation of women, especially women of
color.

While their daily occupations and domestic routines lull them into
passive collusion, each protagonist becomes aware of how the mundane
operations of private homes reveal oppressive structures of race, class or
caste, and gender. Home shelters its pleasures at a cost to those it exploits
and excludes—the overseas Chinese ladies in Lazaroo who embroider the
linen, the aboriginal servants who provide cheap labor, the underpaid
Irish who flee the famine in Atwood, the underpaid Paravan who keeps
the factory machines running in Roy, the struggling members of the
working class who labor in factories that support lavish lifestyles in
Atwood, Ferré, Adichie, and Roy. Structures of racial oppression go along
with those of class, defining the raced other as a foreigner within the
home/land, or reducing the raced woman to the embodied subject of
erotic fascination, like the "tasty" young Eurasian woman. In Atwood,
Alex's dark skin and unknown heritage make him unwelcome in the
Canadian house. In Ferré, Petra and Brambon are admitted to the house
as servants, but given cells in the basement as living quarters. Raced
others are not permitted to enter the national family, though sexual
conquest is accepted and excused. The starkest and most ironic example
of the exclusion of the raced other appears in Morrison's foundational
event, the Disallowing, in which poor blacks are turned away from an
all-black town because they are *too* black and poor. These others pay the
cost of home: they keep it running with their labor, enable its lavish
wealth with their poverty, and define its exclusivity by their exclusion.

Intermixed with discriminations of race and class, the women
characters in these novels also confront sexist hierarchies, double standards, misogyny, sexual battery, and other forms of violence against
women. Atwood gives this admissible brutality a name: "Placidity and
order and everything in its place, with a decorous and sanctioned violence going on underneath everything" (371). In every one of the six

novels, women are beaten. Iris thinks that her husband writes in bruises on her flesh. Mammachi's husband beats her nightly with a brass vase that leaves scars and ridges, and both her Hindu husband and her Christian brother beat Ammu. Buenaventura beats his wife Rebecca senseless, and Quintín batters Isabel. Eugene beats Beatrice often and brutally, and he damages Kambili so severely that she is given extreme unction in the hospital. The young Eurasian is raped by the Japanese; the aboriginal mistress is hosed by the Australian wife. Mavis is sexually assaulted by her husband, Seneca is raped as a child, Gigi and Arnette are hit by K.D., Pallas is raped by strangers, and then the vigilantes of Ruby shoot the women at the Convent. When they discipline their wives or daughters (or lovers, acquaintances, or strangers), men assert their right to define the order of home and homeland: to put "everything in its place." Violence regulates sexuality, making heterosexuality compulsory and prohibiting gay and lesbian sexualities: Seneca's care for Pallas rouses indignation in Ruby and helps justify the shooting, and Tony Torres's openly gay sexuality makes him expendable in Puerto Rico. Sexual violence teaches women that their bodies belong to others.

Eventually, many of the women characters in transnational fictions renounce home and leave its protection. They do this only in extreme circumstances: Isabel's husband swears he will murder her, and Mavis believes that Frank and her children threaten her life. Ammu's husband orders her to have sex with the plantation overseer, Iris learns that her husband has seduced her younger sister, and Pallas discovers her lover involved with her mother. Under duress, these women abandon mates and homes; some of them end up in rented and transient spaces, like the hotel on the edge of an island where Isabel settles or the seedy hotel where Ammu dies. Whether they leave home permanently or not, their changed relation to it appears in the final placement of the women protagonists on the road, unsettled, not-at-home. The Eurasian walks the road near the harbor in Singapore; Kambili emerges from the prison where Jaja remains. Iris has died, leaving fragments of narrative in a steamer trunk, and Rahel looks toward a future of diasporic drifting. The Convent women have gone to a dimension open, like the novel's concluding paradise, to both saved and damned.

While they lose the comforts and pleasures of home, these women protagonists gain voices. Home has muted them, prohibited the telling of shameful family secrets, silenced questions and opinions, and enjoined respectful listening ; as they leave or lose home, therefore, many of them speak up. For the girls, Kambili and Rahel, the process of parental training involves sharp and hurtful responses to some words, honeyed praise for others. Kambili demonstrates the self-censoring result: she stammers, panics when called upon to speak at school, conceals her father's brutalities, and never says what she feels. After experiencing her aunt's house, where thoughtful expression is encouraged, Kambili finds her voice. She claims her grandfather, admits her love to Father Amadi, and narrates *Purple Hibiscus*. Rahel, in contrast, does not narrate *The God of Small Things*. She fails to say expected words and speaks a few unwelcome ones to her grand-aunt and to others in 1992; mostly, though, as if in memory of the steep price paid for her mother's public confession, Rahel remains silent.

Telling stories empowers women characters in Morrison and Lazaroo. In moments of self-constructing narration, these characters overcome pressured silences that have amounted to lies about what has happened to them. Lazaroo's young Eurasian finally tells the Australian man that the young child who died on the beach was her daughter. In acknowledging her child, she narrates the story she believed she had to repress in order to secure a place in empire's sheltering home. Morrison's women have also evaded and misrepresented their histories to themselves and others. In a self-numbing alcoholic stupor, Consolata permits the silences and distortions to pass unquestioned; but then she wakes and sobers up. In a period of "loud dreaming," she leads the women to narrate the histories of lost and absent loves that have wounded them and thereby to remember the fractures that have made them. After this phase of communal speech and listening, the women become "calmly themselves," "no longer haunted" (266). The act of recollecting the unacceptable past gives Morrison's and Lazaroo's women power: they are more than what has wounded them. They survive in speech.

Other women protagonists claim voices through acts of writing that connect private lives to public histories. Despite pressures that would silence or direct their narratives, Isabel and Iris write memoirs that verge on family chronicles spanning almost a century. Although she is criticized and threatened by her husband, Isabel writes about Buenaventura's criminal arrogance in taking land, women, and wealth in Puerto Rico and Arístides's scandalous collaboration with the United States governor in the murder of unarmed young nationalists. Her husband rages against these interpretations of his family's history, but Isabel completes the manuscript and rejects her husband's demands not to publish. Iris also turns writer in order to survive a marriage that has nearly extinguished her voice—and to avenge its other thefts. Her first book is the inner novel, "*The Blind Assassin*," credited on its publication to Laura Chase. Cloaked beneath Laura's authorship, Iris's words accomplish a stealthy revenge on Richard for his abuse of Laura: his suicide makes Iris the forceful blind assassin. Her second book, the memoir, relates the founding of a house, its linkages with twentieth-century Canadian social and political history, and its complex decline. Like Isabel's book, hers claims the right to speak for a genealogical counter-memory. Resisting nationalism, these narratives criticize its exclusions and oppressions in parallel with their critique of the patriarchal house.

While they question, disturb, and even disrupt with their contents, the six transnational women's fictions brought together in this project also trouble conventional stabilities of genre and form. They unsettle the house of fiction through a series of chosen alterations in some foundational formulas. In genre, for example, Atwood and Ferré invoke the family chronicle, but shorten its historical sweep and suspend its ordered progression. All of the novels place contemporary events in historical contexts—the colonial encounter, the national political situation—without the reassuring view of time as a stable location taken in most historical novels. These fictions invoke the *Bildungsroman*, but in a form focused on the domestic education of young women at home rather than on the preparation of young men for and by experience in the world. They recall the variant described by Spivak as the narrative "of the development of a feminine subjectivity, a female *Bildungsroman*, which is the ideal of liberal feminist literary criticism" (1987: 116). But in these terms, too, the novels ironically resist and recast: they do not construct the feminine subject, liberated by her inhabitation of a stable subject position. While reviewers may seek or recuperate such a female subject in these novels, the novelists do not produce her. Instead, they create education experiences that do not liberate and unify but rather oppress and fragment. As the maturing protagonists sift through their heritages from home and homeland, they discover fractures and self-difference.

The protagonists' unsettled subjectivities are often reflected in narratives that jumble chronological time, disunify narrative perspective, and fragment style. The surface texture of these novels can be rough and broken, and their endings do not bring disruptive energies to rest. Roy's novel, for example, breaks time into multiple repeating pieces, shifts through the perspectives of many different characters, includes fragments of songs, poems, slogans, and noises from several different cultures, and reveals some outcomes at the beginning but ends without resolution. Atwood's novel includes voices from the public world in news clippings and pieces of the novel, *The Blind Assassin*; Ferré's includes Quintín's voice in written judgments and objections. Lazaroo and Adichie follow a single protagonist, but reveal self-divisions that separate and destabilize her consciousness. Lazaroo's Eurasian has been invaded, leaving her fragmented and detached from an objectified body and subjective memories; her breakage and self-difference are reflected in a narrative perspective that alternates between first- and third-person limited. More quietly traumatized by the punishing rejection of Africa inscribed in her father, Kambili narrates from a single perspective; however, the young protagonist reveals her double consciousness as she infuses ironic later awareness into seemingly innocent accounts.

Many other transnational women's novels would reward readings from the postcolonial feminist approach to home and homeland taken in this project. Kiran Desai's *The Inheritance of Loss* (2006), to choose a distinguished example, begins with the invasion of a house built by a Scotsman under colonization and inhabited in its decaying years by the British-educated judge Jemubhai Patel. Late in the novel the judge reflects on his implication "in a world that was still colonial": "He thought of how the English government and its civil servants had sailed away throwing their *topis* overboard, leaving behind only those ridiculous Indians who couldn't rid themselves of what they had broken their souls to learn" (224). The novel creates witty, comic and tragic portraits of such Indians—the retired judge himself, who has chosen the isolated house for "the solace of being a foreigner in his own country" (32); his cook, a widower who has sent his only son to America to make a fortune; and sisters Lola and Noni, who watch the BBC on their small television. Sai, the judge's orphaned granddaughter who has been educated in an English-speaking convent school, comes to realize that "The simplicity of what she'd been taught wouldn't hold. Never again could she think there was but one narrative and that narrative belonged only to herself, that she might create her own mean little happiness and live safely within it" (355). While it is not clear where this insight will lead her, Sai has seen unsettling connections between her personal narrative and communal or national ones and thus the need for fictions like Desai's novel.

In the new global era, women writers from nations around the world—and those representing diasporic crossings, like Desai—have published narratives of home and homeland. Attending to the postcolonial histories that emerge in their imagined home/lands remains unfinished business that invites further critical work. Their connections among women's issues, postcolonial legacies, national and geopolitical concerns, and the compelling space of the imagined home invite further intervention. A list of contemporary transnational women writers whose published fiction considers home and homeland could begin with the following: Doreen Baingana (Uganda, United States), Shauna Singh Baldwin (India, Canada), Andrea Barrett (United States), Karen Connelly (Canada, Burma), Tsitsi Dangarembga (Zimbabwe), Edwidge Danticat (Haiti, United States), Aminatta Forna (Sierra Leone, United Kingdom), Kate Grenville (Australia), Barbara Kingsolver (United States), Jhumpa Lahiri (India, United States), Rishi Reddi (India, England, United States), Deborah Robertson (Australia), and Carrie Tiffany (England, Australia). Critical reading of these and other transnational women writers in political, national, and global contexts will reveal their unsettling invention of new houses of fiction.

Re-inventing home and homeland is a collaborative enterprise, as is exploring the story of home/land in contemporary transnational women's fiction. Additional perspectives and other knowledges, engaging a range of local cultures and fictions, are needed to extend this project. Since fiction most often narrates the particular stories of individuals, grappling with power relations that originate in and churn naturalized pathways through daily lives in homes, attending to home comes naturally to those who interpret fiction. Thinking home in new ways, being aware of the potential for a changed community, envisioning altered configurations of homeland: these are fit work for critics as well as novelists, especially now.

Notes

Chapter 1 Introduction: Unsettling home and homeland

1. Among the important anthologies in this area, see Jameson and Miyoshi, Shohat.
2. The farmer's wife offers a sentimentalized revision: "I should have called it/ Something you somehow haven't to deserve."
3. All of these locations are nations except for Puerto Rico, which is a homeland and culture but has never been an independent nation.
4. For two measured critical responses to Jameson, see Loomba (173) and Larsen (25–27; 37–38).
5. See Slemon on Commonwealth Literature Studies, 184–86.
6. See McClintock (9–14) for valuable troublings of "postcolonialism" as "a singular, monolithic term, used ahistorically and haunted by the nineteenth-century image of linear progress" (13). Grewal and Kaplan similarly argue in *Scattered Hegemonies* that "As a global, hegemonic term in contemporary cultural studies," the term postcolonial "has to be critically accounted for and, certainly, historicized" (15).
7. See George (1998: 8–11) for a critique of Bowlby's essay.
8. Thad Logan's *The Victorian Parlour*, for example, regards the domestic interior as a site where aspects of the culture can be read; Chase and Levenson's *The Spectacle of Intimacy* explores the "eruption of family life into the light of unrelenting public discussion" (12); Susan Johnston's *Women and Domestic Experience in Victorian Political Fiction* argues that "the very notion of separate spheres may be essentially contested even while it is being constructed" (3).
9. While she stood apart from commerce, domestic woman could still serve as a symbol of her husband's material prosperity, Tim Dolin argues. She functions as a marker for property that endures: "In a market economy in which property became increasingly abstract and unstable [...] the woman in the house was held up as a powerful icon of stable property" (7).
10. See Alaimo's introduction for a reading of feminist theory's struggle with the "historically tenacious entanglements of 'woman' and 'nature' " (2).
11. Exploring the same essay in "Deterritorializations," Caren Kaplan observes: "Pratt's autobiographical essay elaborates a dynamic feminist theory of location and positionality. Moving away from 'home' to deconstruct the terms of social privilege and power, such a feminist practice favors the process of the move over the ultimate goal" (193).
12. George reads Martin and Mohanty as "disassembling the notion of 'home' " in *The Politics of Home* (26–27).
13. Pearce observes that many women do not have the luxury of choice in their dwelling place: "I do not personally subscribe to the more utopian discourses of nomadic existence that cause us to forget, or devalue, the perceptions of all those who inhabit homes and communities they might never leave (from choice, or otherwise)" (23). See also Caren Kaplan (1987), George (1996).

14. Bhabha first articulated the "unhomely" in "The World and the Home" (inverting the title of a Tagore novel *The Home and the World*), published in *Social Text* in 1992: "this awkward word [...] captures something of the estranging sense of the relocation of the home and the world in an unhallowed place" where "the intimate recesses of the domestic space become sites for history's most intricate invasions. In that displacement the border between home and world becomes confused; and, uncannily, the private and the public become part of each other, forcing upon us a vision that is as divided as it is disorienting" (141). Slightly revised, this essay forms most of the introduction to *The Location of Culture* (1994).

15. In a related approach, Kristin Jacobson writes that Kingsolver's *The Poisonwood Bible* is an example of "neodomestic fiction." Within an American frame, she argues that "neodomestic" fiction adopts "a foundational instability" and "promotes the radical ideology that we can gain security when we cease to depend on policed boundaries and locked doors" (120, 122).

16. George's second book, *Burning Down the House: Recycling Domesticity* (1998), collects essays that forward the reinvention of domesticity. George argues that "the social and gender inequalities that buttress domesticity" remain unexamined (2). Rather than rescuing domestic pleasures, George advocates a recycling that can "make the domestic a site from which countertheorizations about seemingly 'larger' and unrelated institutions and ideologies can be produced" (3).

17. See also Friedman's poetic essay, "Bodies on the Move."

Chapter 2   Homeless in the American Empire: Toni Morrison's *Paradise*

1. Donald Pease points out this inclusion of the United States "among the anticolonial nations" in Kaplan and Pease (37). As early as 1978, however, Edward Said writes in *Orientalism*: "since World War II America has dominated the Orient, and approaches it as France and Britain once did" (4).

2. Amy Kaplan reads representations of the war as reflecting a complex unease over the presence of black soldiers "in lands defined as inhabited by those unfit for self-government, those who cannot represent themselves, and who are thus in need of the discipline of the American Empire" (2002: 145).

3. The links between Toni Morrison and Said, who have clearly read each other, are significant: as his epigraph for the first chapter in *Culture and Imperialism*, Said quotes from *Playing in the Dark*, and there are echoes between their assessments of the defining issues of our age. Said writes in *Culture and Imperialism*, "surely it is one of the unhappiest characteristics of the age to have produced more refugees, migrants, displaced persons, and exiles than ever before in history" and he notes Paul Virilio's division of these into those "whose current status is the consequence either of decolonization (migrant workers, refugees, *Gastarbeiter*) or of major demographic and political shifts (Blacks, immigrants, urban squatters)" (332, 326). Morrison writes in "Home": "The overweening, defining event of the modern world is the mass movement of raced populations, beginning with the largest forced

transfer of people in the history of the world: slavery. [...] Nationhood [...] is constantly being demarcated and redemarcated in response to exiles, refugees, *Gastarbeiter*, immigrants, migrations, the displaced, the fleeing, and the besieged" (10).

4. In this essay, Morrison shifts from "Afro-American" to "African" to underline the *othering* of black citizens in the imagination of white America.

5. Davidson calls the novel "a provocative allegory of nationhood" (371); see also Storace.

6. In what Morrison identifies as the genesis of the novel, 200 former slaves were turned away from an all-black town because they did not look prosperous enough to contribute; "Come Prepared or Not at All" ran the heading on newspaper columns (McKinney-Whetstone 2–3). Gray reports in *Time* that she saw this document some six years before publishing *Paradise* (64).

7. Roberta Rubenstein argues that intermarriage, "inbreeding, and insularity have resulted in sterile men, infantilized women, and defective babies" (146).

8. Vietnam exerts a compelling, shadowy presence in *Paradise* as a sign of the American imperialism theorized by William Spanos in *America's Shadow*. Among minor characters dead in Vietnam are the two sons of Deacon and Soane Morgan, the two brothers of Mavis Albright, six classmates of Dusty (34), and eleven members of Misner's high school football team (160). The psychologically traumatized include Menus Jury, who returns a depressive alcoholic, and Jeff Fleetwood, who comes back seething and has four sick children, perhaps the result of Agent Orange.

9. In his unfavorable review of *Paradise*, Geoffrey Bent writes that Morrison divides virtue and vice according to gender: "all the women are good, all the men bad" (148).

10. Reviewing *Paradise* for *The New York Times*, Brooke Allen calls Consolata a "symbolic character" who functions as "the embodiment of an abstract longing for home" (7).

11. Other critical readings, especially those by Rubenstein, Krumholz, and Page, recognize the importance of the yearning for home in the novel.

12. Morrison says, "The tradition in writing is that if you don't mention a character's race, he's white. Any deviation from that, you have to say. What I wanted to do was not erase race, but force readers either to care about it or see if it disturbs them that they don't know" (Streitfeld B2).

13. In a similar reading, Fraile-Marcos writes that the women "are rewarded by achieving that state of plenitude, happiness, and serenity which is associated with paradise," though she reads paradise as open and evolving (32).

14. As Gigi lies in the tub on the night of Consolata's feast, she thinks it is "a new year": "Nineteen seventy-five" (256). Since the shootings occur in July 1976, the women have 19 months between the start of Consolata's lessons and their end in the massacre. During this time, virtually nothing occurs in the outer world that is noted by the narrator, while the women "altered" (265). The condensation of narrative time at the end reflects the rapid passing of clock time as the women spend more of their lives in Kristevan "women's time." For a related discussion of how women's communal life takes them outside historical time in Morrison's first five novels, see Rigney 75–76.

15. In the same essay, Morrison notes that "the ancestor is not only wise, he or she values racial connection, racial memory over individual fulfill-

ment" (1981: 43). Her invocation of Piedade as ancestor spurs moral action and racial connection as Consolata teaches the younger women to accept raced and gendered identities. Morrison also comments on the ancestor in "Rootedness."

16. Consolata resembles the blind old woman, living in a house outside of town, who is sought by the young people in Morrison's Nobel Prize Lecture. Like the old woman, Consolata comes to see that "word-work is sublime" as she expands her dreams of paradise and creates its story together with her younger guests (Nobel, 22, 30).

17. My reading of the women's last appearances diverges from Holly Flint's; she believes that all of them are "able to intervene, to communicate their love and support to their families" (606). Instead, I emphasize their independence of the unmet needs, frustrated by the very individuals they re-encounter, that plagued the women in their earlier incarnations. Rather than love and support, the women communicate assured self-reliance.

18. The first edition capitalized the last word, but Morrison asked that it be changed to lower case: "I wanted the book to be an interrogation of the idea of paradise and I wanted it to move it from its pedestal of exclusion and to make it more accessible to everybody. Thus I meant, but forgot, to make the last word begin with a small letter" (Timehost 6).

Chapter 3   The incandescent home: Margaret Atwood's *The Blind Assassin*

1. Biographer Nathalie Cooke describes Atwood's childhood as a happy period with secure family relationships. Atwood's father Carl was an entomologist who spent summer months in the bush tracking insect infestations, and Atwood's earliest homes were temporary: a succession of winter houses in cities (Ottawa, Sault Ste. Marie, and Toronto) and camps, tents, and cabins in the north (Cooke 22). Atwood's sense of home focused on people rather than place: on her mother, who taught her during the northern expeditions, on her brother Harold, who was her constant playmate during those months, on her father, who encouraged his children to think independently, and on her younger sister Ruth, born when Margaret was 12.

2. Throughout Atwood's fiction, homes function as primers of cultural values for girls, who are taught how to make and inhabit homes. In *Cat's Eye*, for example, other girls her age teach Elaine what home involves with the Eaton's Catalog game, where they cut out objects for purchase and paste them into scrapbooks.

3. In Djwa's view, Atwood's nationalism coincides with second-wave feminism, and while "national identity in literature was already rooted in the predominantly masculine world of cultural production" in the United States and England, Atwood represents the Canadian nation in the form of the woman artist (173). In an essay on *The Robber Bride*, Donna Potts observes that "because Canadian women have been regarded as objects not only of the colonizing gaze, but also of the male gaze, Atwood's consideration of the effect of colonization on Canada is inseparable from her assessment of the effect of patriarchy on Canadian women" (281–82).

4. For readings of the politics of Atwood's writing, see Kolodny, Hengen (1993: 11–17), Cooke (1998) and Brownley. For postcolonial readings, see Brydon, Howells (2003), Potts, and Hengen (1995).

5. See also the review at www.dancingbadger.com/bassassin.htm, which notes that the novel "covers roughly a hundred years of Canadian history."

6. Iris's name evokes artistry in various ways: in Greek mythology, Iris is both goddess of the rainbow and messenger of the gods; her name designates both the pigmented membrane of the eye and the group of plants with showy flowers.

7. In her reading of the symbols and imagery of *The Blind Assassin*, Stein misses the radical, liberatory use of fire that I will develop in this essay. She sees fire as only diabolical, arguing that "Imagery of burning and of Hell infiltrates the narrative" (136). The central male characters "are each shown to be sexually demanding and dangerous, and they are repeatedly depicted in imagery of fire and Hell" (140).

8. Dickens 50. See Said's analysis of this passage, (1993: 13–14).

9. Reenie's name may be short for Irene, Greek for peace, rather than a variant of Renee, reborn, like the protagonist of *Bodily Harm*. Reenie adopts the voice and values of the British ruling class, making peace by erasing her own Irish immigrant experience.

10. J. Brooks Bouson observes that "Atwood's description of the circumstances surrounding Richard's proposal to Iris, who has been raised by her father to act the role of the dutiful daughter, is a scathing critique of patriarchal marriage and the historical treatment of women as objects of exchange between men" (2003: 257).

11. Howells, for example, writes that "Iris's 'shabby villain' of a husband and his witch sister [...] are never quite human, imprisoned in the stereotypical roles into which Iris has cast them" (2002: 115–16).

12. Howells argues that Zenia's othering invites not only a feminist reading but also a postcolonial one, "with the focus on Zenia as immigrant, in Atwood's discourse of Canadianness" (2003, 91).

13. Bouson points out "Iris's passive and mute acceptance of Alex's sexist attitudes and callous treatment of her" (2003: 259).

14. Another possibility is that, having read the novel, he can see that Iris wrote it and had the extended affair with Alex, in which case he would also suspect that Aimee is not his daughter. The place of his death, however, suggests that he is grieving over the loss of Laura.

Chapter 4   House of paper: Rosario Ferré's *The House on the Lagoon*

1. Amy Kaplan explores the paradoxical ruling that Puerto Rico was "foreign to the United States in a domestic sense" and the implications for US national identity (2002: 2–12).

2. "Any reader interested in the cultural history of contemporary Puerto Rico," writes Rodríguez Castro, "immediately encounters its most persistent custom: the articulation and defense of national identity" (33, my translation: "Cualquier lector interesado en la historia cultural del Puerto Rico

contemporáneo se encuentra de inmediato ante su hábito más persistente: la articulación y defensa de la identidad nacional").

3. According to Santos-Phillips, Ferré "offended and angered many of Puerto Rico's artistic elite" by publishing *House on the Lagoon* and her next novel, *Eccentric Neighborhoods*, first in English and by writing her piece in the *Times* supporting statehood.

4. Rather than imitating other writers, Ferré makes sophisticated intertextual references to the literary traditions of several countries and continents. See especially Ronald Morrison, Lindsay.

5. Vélez Román agrees in calling the title house "la casa alegórica del espacio nacional," the allegorical house of national space. Lindsay writes that the "dysfunctional family unit" in of one of Ferré's stories is "a metonym for national corruption" (62). Gac-Artigas describes *House* as a novel in which "we slip from the microcosm of the personal and the domestic to the macrocosm of the social and political" (9, my translation: "nos deslizamos del microcosmos de lo personal y lo familiar, al macrocosmos de lo social y politico").

6. In one of the many self-reflexive narrative strategies in the novel, Isabel emphasizes Pavel's original additions and contributions to the Wright design as she describes its first construction, but traces its restoration only to the rediscovery of Wright's plan.

7. While a US military doctor discovered in 1901 that Puerto Ricans contracted hookworm through the soles of the feet, "neither the US corporations nor the federal government had any interest in providing the people with shoes. In addition, the American tariff raised the price of shoes so that only one fourth of the 1930 population had ever worn a pair. Ninety per cent of the rural population continued to be infected to some degree with hookworm. Diseases such as hookworm [...] made the Puerto Rican death rate the western hemisphere's highest" (Christopulos, 138).

8. Claire Lindsay invokes Mary Louise Pratt's notion of the "contact zone" to characterize Puerto Rico as a social space where cultures clash. "With its indigenous Taino ancestry, four hundred years of Spanish colonial rule, the mass introduction of African slaves to the island in the sixteenth century and the North American invasion of 1898, Puerto Rico has been a melting pot of different cultures, languages and peoples throughout its history" (59).

9. See Hintz, especially 1–46.

10. For analysis of the doll in Ferré's short fiction, see Bilbija, Glenn, Murphy.

11. Janice Jaffe points out that Ferré's novella *Maldito Amor*, translated as *Sweet Diamond Dust*, also ends with "the incendiary destruction" of the family plantation, "which indicates that for Ferré the question of Puerto Ricans' identity and the island's future destiny remain far from resolved" (80).

12. Toral Alemañ points out Quintín's "avid reading" of the European masculine canon and adds, "In postcolonial terms, the Eurocentrism of his discourse ineluctably carries with it a repressive ethnocentrism that lasts from generation to generation" (86–87, my translation: "En términos poscoloniales, el euorcentrismo de su discurso conlleva ineludiblemente a un etnocentrismo represivo que se continua de generación en generación").

13. Alejandrina Ortiz suggests that Isabel leaves Manuel another inheritance, "She places her own ideas of personal liberation in the character of her

son as rebel political leader who struggles against the status quo" (132, my translation: "Deposita sus propias ideas de liberación personal en el personaje de su hijo como líder político rebelde que lucha contra el 'statu quo' ").

14. Puleo explores Ferré's creation of a multiple, collective voice in her story, "Cuando las mujeres quieren a los hombres" ("When women love men"). In effect, Quintín's voice and his interrogations of Isabel's authority create a similar effect, undermining the certainty and power of her voice.

15. "La escritura de Isabel da voz a las historias personales y colectivas que la ideología imperante no reconoció."

16. See, for example, Christopulos, 148–49: "On Sunday morning, 80 young Nationalist cadets and 12 girls walked into a police force of 150 well-armed men. When the shooting ended, 17 marchers and 2 policemen were dead, and over 100 people were wounded. [...] The vast majority were shot from behind, and not one civilian could be shown to have had a gun. An American Civil Liberties Union investigation called this police riot a 'gross violation of civil rights and incredible police brutality.' The United States government decided not to investigate the event."

17. "La línea divisoria entre ficción e Historia se desvanece y la ficción assume, pues, el papel de *otra* Historia al cuestionarse la naturalize irrefutable y veridical del discurso imperialista histórico."

Chapter 5   The decolonized home: Chimamanda Ngozi Adichie's *Purple Hibiscus*

1. "The 1991 World Bank Report ranked Nigeria as the thirteenth poorest country in the world, while the United Nations Development Programme concluded from a human deprivation index survey in 1990 that it had one of the worst records for human deprivation of any country in the third world" (Osaghae 204).

2. Adichie published a story about Biafra, titled "Half of a Yellow Sun" (2003). Her second novel narrates the civil war as well: *Half of a Yellow Sun* (2006) won the Orange Prize. She published a story, "Sierra Leone, 1997" in *The New Yorker* (2006), telling of the death of a young man who had served her family as houseboy.

3. Kaplan writes in *The Anarchy of Empire*, "domesticity is a mobile and often unstable discourse that can expand or contract the boundaries of home and nation, and [...] their interdependency relies on racialized conceptions of the foreign" (26).

4. According to one source, Giwa was murdered by the Buhari regime because he had information about the government's murder-in-detention of a woman named Gloria Okon: "No individual in Nigeria had access to what was used to kill Dele Giwa except the military" (Oduyela). Like Giwa, Ade Coker is murdered by a powerful letter bomb. For a discussion of references to Nigerian political events in Adichie's fiction, see Ekwe Ekwe.

5. Adichie says that she merged "events from two periods in Nigerian political history," creating "a collage of two coups" (Spencer).

6. Both Achebe and Adichie grew up in the Christian faith. Achebe's father was one of the first generation converted by the missionaries, and Adichie

describes herself as "a Liberal Catholic" who grew up with an "intense period of God searching. I read the writings of St. Augustine and fat books about Church history. I was always asking questions" (Anya, Garner).

7. Writing in 2004, Clement Okafor says that *Things Fall Apart* "has sold more than eight million copies and has been translated into fifty-five languages." The novel is, he adds, "the most widely read book in Africa except for the Bible" (85). Simon Gikandi calls the publication of this novel "the inaugural moment of modern African literature" and adds, "I want to insist that Achebe was possibly the first African writer to be self-conscious about his role as an African writer, to confront the linguistic and historical problems of African writing in a colonial situation, and to situate writing within a larger body of regional and global knowledge about Africa" (1991: 1, 5–6). Adichie herself calls Achebe "one of the greatest writers the world has ever seen, because he did not only tell us, the writers who would come after him, that our stories were worthy, he also swiped at the disgusting stereotypes of Africa" (Anya).

8. One reviewer wished for a glossary of Igbo terms in the novel, as is often supplied in novels using non-English terms (Bell-Gam).

9. Adichie told another interviewer that "I have been published in Nigeria now, but if it had happened first I probably wouldn't be speaking to you now, because I probably wouldn't have had the book published in other parts of the world" (Spencer).

10. Modeled on Abacha, the dictator is reported by Kambili to have died "atop a prostitute, foaming at the mouth and jerking," and pro-democracy demonstrations follow (297).

Chapter 6   Exiles and orphans: Arundhati Roy's *The God of Small Things*

1. Ghanshyam Shah writes that "The word Dalit is of relatively recent origin— of the 1960s" and "gained currency in public spheres during the SC [Scheduled Caste]–caste Hindu riots in Bombay in the early 1970s" (2001: 22).

2. During the two-week period, Christmas passes, unremarked by the narrator (128). With no nativity, there is no one to keep an eye on the sparrow: "A sparrow lay dead on the backseat. [...] She died on the backseat, with her legs in the air. Like a joke"(280).

3. Roy was sued for obscenity because of her explicit representation of lovemaking between Ammu and Velutha in the last chapter; she was separately sued for slander by the family of Kerala's leading communist, E.M.S. Namboodiripad. The novel was criticized in reviews by Ahmad, Mathai, and Clark, among others. Initial critical reception also included many positive reviews, including Agarwal, Kakutani, and Truax. Roy received an advance of a million dollars for the book, which made her a celebrity and created widespread interest in the novel.

4. See also the Clarity Press Publisher's Note in Rajshekar: "Hindus were in reality a minority population. They might have remained a minority until today, but for the interlude of British conquest of India. Seeking a local instrument to help it dominate the Indian masses, the British found the Hindus appropriate to their needs. They defined the Hindus as the dominant

population, even though huge masses of the population [...] were not Hindu" (6).

5. As French sociologist Louis Dumont describes the system, Indian society is organized by a "hierarchy of the four varnas, 'colours' or estates" led by the "Brahmans or priests, below them the Kshatriyas or warriors, then the Vaishyas, in modern usage mainly merchants, and finally the Shudras, the servants or have-nots. [...] There is in actual fact a fifth category, the Untouchables, who are left outside the classification" (45). Within the four Varnas, there are about four thousand individual castes, B. R. Ambedkar estimates (70).

6. The terms "Scheduled Castes and Scheduled Tribes" come from the Constitution of India, where schedules identified Untouchable groups eligible to receive benefits.

7. As an expression of Hindu cosmology, caste prejudice should not appear among Syrian Christians, but according to Rajshekar, "the Indian Christian Church itself is divided into castes, and Black Untouchable converts are segregated" (49). A. Anthony Dass Gupta agrees that Christianity in India "is nothing but a modified Hinduism, as it still observes the caste system" (qtd. in Rajshekar 72).

8. Rajshekar writes, "India has become a stagnant society. A sick society" (65).

9. Portraits of British citizens in the novel emphasize their decadence: Kari Saipu and Mr. Hollick are sexual abusers who exoticize Indians. Americans do the same in crasser terms: a drunk arrives each night to tell Rahel, "*Hey, you! Black bitch! Suck my dick!*" (179). Roy calls herself "black" twice in interviews with David Barsamian (5, 156).

10. There are serpents in the ruined garden; see Kanaganayakam 145.

11. Untouchables were limited to low dwellings, Indian sociologist G. S. Ghurye writes: "In Dravidian India the disabilities of the lower castes went so far as to prescribe what sort of houses they should build and what material they might employ in the construction thereof. The Shanars and Izhavas, toddy-tappers of the eastern and western coasts, were not allowed to build houses above one storey in height" (37).

12. The Naxalites emerged from the Chinese-communist inspired faction of the Indian Marxist party and were named after an uprising in Naxalbari. For more on this party, see Human Rights Watch, Shah (2001).

13. Paul Brians observes that Ammu is "extremely self-centered. [...] Her fatal flaw as a mother is to make her love for her children conditional on their pleasing her. They are starved for her affection and terrified of losing her" (172).

14. Sophie Mol is herself diasporic and doubled. Going to school in London, she is profoundly aware that she is not quite white: "You're both whole wogs and I'm a half one," she tells the twins (17). She emphasizes her Englishness through her "Made-in-England go-go bag that she loved" and her yellow bell-bottoms (6).

15. Gail Omvedt writes that "Girls are simply not as important to the interests and needs of parents in such societies. As a common western Indian saying has it, 'Girls are not ours; they belong to other people.' [...] Women remain propertyless, powerless, and resourceless" (1997, 41–42). Though Kerala is liberal in education and health care, unusually successful in achieving high

literacy rates and long life-expectancies, Omvedt notes that it is "socially conservative": "feminists have also found it to be so" (1998, 32).

16. Traditionally, members of all castes below the Brahmans were forbidden to cover the upper part of their body; see Ghurye 37.

17. Roy was criticized by, among others, Aijaz Amhad and E. M. S. Namboodiripad for her representation of Pillai and Communism. Paul Brians makes a valid argument: "Her criticisms of Marxism come from a radical perspective rather than a conservative one. It is the failure of Marxists to remain true to their own ideals that she objects to, not the ideals themselves" (167).

18. Cabaret points out, recalling Dumont, that the word "caste" derives "from the Latin *castus* meaning 'chaste'" (81). Velutha's symbolic castration (another offshoot of the same root) punishes him for violating codes enforcing caste segregation and chastity.

19. Sacksick argues that the narrative replaces the chronological line with "an interlacing design" (64).

Chapter 7   The home elsewhere: Simone Lazaroo's *The Australian Fiancé*

1. David Walker's book, subtitled *Australia and the Rise of Asia 1850–1939*, focuses on the proximity of Asia, though its title aptly reflects national anxieties related to Aboriginal people and Britain as well. David Brooks writes, "a kind of ontological anxiety—uncertainty as to the nature/status of one's own being—might well be the long-sought trademark of the Australian line" (20).

2. Nugi Garimara is Pilkington's Aboriginal name. Griffiths writes, "The very wiping out of distinctive collectivities under an undifferentiated term such as 'aboriginal' is an example" of "the deliberate suppression of pre-colonial cultures, and the displacement of their peoples in a policy of assimilation which aimed at the suppression of difference" (1995: 241).

3. This policy restricted immigration to those who could pass a dictation test in a European language, effectively blocking the immigration of non-Europeans. Pacific Islanders and Asians who had worked in the country were deported in the early 1900s, and as late as 1945, Australia's Immigration Minister proposed to deport non-white immigrants who had married Australians. See Australia (2002).

4. Lowe points out that the United States enacted "immigration exclusion acts and laws against naturalization of Asians in 1882, 1924, and 1934" (5).

5. In an essay analyzing the history of Australian literary studies and postcolonialism, Robert Dixon observes a lack of correspondence between them, partly because literary studies emerged from a comparative, nation-based practice and "Colonial discourse theory, on the other hand, has been less concerned with the national and with creative writing and more interested in historical and discursive analysis of the imperial archive" (111).

6. Stephen Slemon takes a different position, writing that "While 'feminist theorists' [...] may generally understand themselves to be working in the interests of feminism [...] few 'post-colonial theorists' will understand

their work as operating specifically in the interests of 'post-colonialism' itself" (183).

7. In her study of Australian women writers titled *Exiles at Home*, Drusilla Modjeska writes, "To be a woman and a writer in Australia during the twenties was an isolated and often desolate existence" (16).

8. This conclusion seems too easily optimistic, though much else in the end of the novel mitigates the simplicity.

9. Lazaroo has published three novels. The first, *The World Waiting to be Made* (1994) won several awards. Based on transformed autobiographical material, it is narrated by a young Eurasian protagonist who emigrates with her family from Singapore to Western Australia. She struggles to integrate her Eurasian heritage with Australia, described as "relentlessly racist" in one review (Temby 148). The isolation and self-fragmentation she experiences are, like those of the protagonist in *The Australian Fiancé*, designed to reflect national issues: "the personal narratives of migrant cultures, like those of Aboriginal cultures, are crucial for rethinking [Australian] national identities. The story of the self's socialization and construction described in Lazaroo's narrative is in a tangible sense the retelling of recent Australian history" (Dougan 7). One critic calls Lazaroo's first novel "a prototype Asian-Australian migrant *bildungsroman*, beginning with the narrator as a young child who experiences and internalizes both anti-Asian racism and Orientalism, particularly after her migration with her family to Australia" (Lo 33). Lazaroo's third novel, *The Travel Writer*, appeared in 2006.

10. Pam Allen observes that the protagonist's "Eurasianness means that she occupies an ambivalent space in her home country too" (28).

11. Tracy Ibrahim suggests, "In remaining unnamed, the narrator is perhaps reflective of a voice for other outsiders, as well as of her own lack of identity" (6). Olivia Khoo makes the valid observation that while her partner is identified "either by his nationality (always posited as white) or by his heterosexual desire and their romance," the young Eurasian woman is "symbolically infantilised and racialised (without nationality, without citizenship)" (77). The repeated reminder of the protagonist's youth also places the novel as a *Bildungsroman* or education narrative and underscores her vulnerability.

12. Through the eyes of outraged Rosa Coldfield, whom Sutpen proposes to use to beget a son in *Absalom, Absalom!*

13. Tucker argues that "The figure of the Asian woman functions in the Australian imaginary as a signifier of the erotic and the exotic," alluring but linked with sexually transmitted disease (2000: 150–51).

14. Henke writes that autobiography can function as "scriptotherapy", allowing a traumatized and fragmented subject to "reassess the past and to reinterpret the intertextual codes inscribed on personal consciousness by society and culture" (xv). Lazaroo's protagonist reveals at the end that she is narrating 30 years later, and her account comprises just such a re-interpretation.

15. See Genoni for a comprehensive look at photographs and maps in contemporary Australian fiction.

16. For an excellent reading of the technological gaze as part of the fiancé's imperialism and a means through which he privileges whiteness, see Morris.

Works Cited

Achebe, Chinua. *Things Fall Apart*. Oxford: Heinemann, 1958.

Adebanwi, Wale. "Nigerian Identity is Burdensome." Interview with Chimamanda Adichie. *Nigerian Village Square*. http://www.nigeriavillagesquare1. com/BOOKS/adichie_interview.html. Retrieved on 6 Jan. 2006.

Adichie, Chimamanda Ngozi. "Half of a Yellow Sun." *Zoetrope: All-Story* 7.2 (Summer 2003). http://www.all-story.com/issues.cgi?action=show_story& story_id+191. Retrieved on 8 Jan. 2006.

——*Half of a Yellow Sun*. New York: Knopf, 2006.

——*Purple Hibiscus*. New York: Anchor, 2003.

——"Sierra Leone, 1997." *The New Yorker* (12 June 2006): 72–73.

Agarwal, Ramlal. Rev. of *The God of Small Things*, by A. Roy. *World Literature Today* 72.1 (1998): 208–09.

Ahmad, Aijaz. "Reading Arundhati Roy *Politically*." *Frontline* (8 Aug. 1997): 103–08.

Aidoo, Ama Ata. *Our Sister Killjoy, or Reflections from a Black-eyed Squint*. 1977. Essex: Longman, 1988.

Alaimo, Stacy. *Undomesticated Ground: Recasting Nature as Feminist Space*. Ithaca: Cornell U P, 2000.

Allen, Brooke. "The Promised Land." Rev. of *Paradise*. *New York Times Book Review* (11 Jan. 1998): 6–7.

Allen, Pam. "The Insuperable Longing to Forget: *Love and Vertigo* and *The Australian Fiancé*." *Island* 92 (Autumn 2003): 25–30.

Ambedkar, B. R. "Caste in India." In *Caste and Democratic Politics in India*. Ed. Ghanshyam Shah. 2002. London: Anthem P, 2004: 59–78.

Anderson, Benedict. *Imagined Communities: Reflections on the Origin and Spread of Nationalism*. London: Verso, 1983.

Anya, Ikechukwu. "In the Footsteps of Achebe: Enter Chimamanda Ngozi Adichie, Nigeria's Newest Literary Voice." *THISDAYonline*. (19 Oct. 2003). http://www.nigeriansinamerica.com/articles/347/1/In-the-Footsteps-of-Achbe-%3A-Enter-Chimamanda-Ngozi-Adichie%2C-Nigeria%92s-Newest-Literary-Vo ice. Retrieved on 9 Jan. 2006.

Armstrong, Nancy. *Desire and Domestic Fiction: A Political History of the Novel*. Oxford: Oxford U P, 1987.

Ashcroft, Bill, Gareth Griffiths, and Helen Tiffin. *The Empire Writes Back*. London: Routledge, 1989.

——(eds) *The Post-Colonial Studies Reader*. New York: Routledge, 1995.

Atta, Sefi, Jeremy Weate, Olaokun Soyinka, and Ike Oguine. "Reviews of Chimamanda." http://farafina.dbweb.ee/?issue=4&category_id=26&article_id=78. Retrieved on 9 Jan. 2006.

Atwood, Margaret. *Alias Grace*. New York: Doubleday, 1996.

——*The Blind Assassin*. New York: Doubleday, 2000.

——*Bodily Harm*. New York: Bantam, 1983.

——*Cat's Eye*. New York: Doubleday, 1989.

——*The Handmaid's Tale*. New York: Ballantine, 1987.

——"Haunted by their Nightmares." Rev. of *Beloved*. *Toni Morrison: Modern Critical Views*. Ed. Harold Bloom. New York: Chelsea, 1990: 143–47. Rpt. *New York Times Book Review* (13 Sep. 1987): 1, 49–50.

——*Morning in the Burned House*. Boston: Houghton Mifflin, 1995.

——*Negotiating with the Dead: A Writer on Writing*. Cambridge: Cambridge U P, 2002.

——*Oryx and Crake*. New York: Doubleday, 2003.

——*The Robber Bride*. New York: Doubleday, 1993.

——*Strange Things: The Malevolent North in Canadian Literature*. Oxford: Clarendon, 1995.

——*Survival: A Thematic Guide to Canadian Literature*. Toronto: Anansi, 1972.

——*Wilderness Tips*. New York: Doubleday, 1991.

"Australia." *Political Handbook of the World: 1998*. eds Arthur S. Banks and Thomas C. Muller. Binghamton, NY: CSA Publications, 1998: 51–58.

Australia. Department of Immigration and Multicultural and Indigenous Affairs. "Abolition of the 'White Australia' Policy." *Information Resources*. Fact Sheet No. 8. (22 Nov. 2001): 6. http://www.immi.gov.au/facts/08abolition.html. Retrieved on 27 June 2002.

"Author Q&A" [with Chimamanda Ngozi Adichie]. *Random House Website*, undated. http://www.randomhouse.com/catalog/display.pperl?isbn=1400076 943&view=qa. Retrieved on 11 Jan. 2006.

Balvannanadhan, Aïda. "Re-Membering Personal History in *The God of Small Things*." *Commonwealth* 25.1 (2002): 97–106.

Barak, Julie. "Navigating the Swamp: Fact and Fiction in Rosario Ferré's *The House on the Lagoon*." *Journal of the Midwest Modern Language Association* 31.2 (1998): 31–38.

Baym, Nina. *Woman's Fiction: A Guide to Novels by and about Women in America, 1820-1870*. Ithaca: Cornell U P, 1978.

Beauvoir, Simone de. *The Second Sex*. 1952. Ed. and Trans. H. M. Parshley. New York: Vintage, 1989.

Behdad, Ali. "On Globalization, Again!" *Postcolonial Studies and Beyond*. Ed. Ania Loomba, Suvir Kaul, Matti Bunzl, Antoinette Burton, and Jed Esty. Durham: Duke U P, 2005: 62–79.

Bell-Gam, Ruby A. *H-Net Reviews*. December 2004. http://www.h-net.msu.edu/ reviews/showpdf.cgi?path=298191105719553. Retrieved on 9 Jan. 2006.

Bent, Geoffrey. "Less than Divine: Toni Morrison's *Paradise*." Rev. of *Paradise*. *Southern Review* 35 (1999): 145–49.

Bhabha, Homi. *The Location of Culture*. New York: Routledge, 1994.

Bilbija, Ksenija. "Rosario Ferré's 'The Youngest Doll': On Women, Dolls, Golems and Cyborgs." *Callaloo* 17.3 (1994): 878–88.

Birns, Nicholas. "Soundings from Down Under." *Antipodes* 19.2 (2005): 232–35.

Blunt, Alison and Gillian Rose. *Writing Women and Space: Colonial and Postcolonial Geographies*. New York: Guilford, 1994.

Bose, Brinda. "In Desire and in Death: Eroticism as Politics in Arundhati Roy's *The God of Small Things*." *ARIEL* 29.2 (1998): 59–72.

Bouson, J. Brooks. "'A Commemoration of Wounds Endured and Resented': Margaret Atwood's *The Blind Assassin* as Feminist Memoir." *Critique* 44 (2003): 251–69.

——*Quiet as it's kept: Shame, Trauma, and Race in the Novels of Toni Morrison.* Albany: SUNY P, 2000.

Bowlby, Rachel. "Domestication." *Feminism Beside Itself.* Ed. Diane Elam and Robyn Wiegman. New York: Routledge, 1995: 71–91.

Brathwaite, Edward Kamau. *The Development of Creole Society in Jamaica 1770–1820.* Oxford: Clarendon P, 1971.

Braziel, Jana Evans and Anita Mannur (eds). *Theorizing Diaspora.* Malden, MA: Blackwell, 2003.

Brians, Paul. *Modern South Asian Literature in English.* Westport, CT: Greenwood, 2003: 165–76.

Brooks, David. "The Australian Line." *Agenda* 41.1–2 (Spring/Summer 2005): 11–21.

Brown, Gillian. *Domestic Individualism: Imagining Self in Nineteenth-Century America.* Berkeley: U of California P, 1990.

Brydon, Diana. "Atwood's Postcolonial Imagination: Rereading *Bodily Harm.*" *Various Atwoods: Essays on the Later Poems, Short Fiction, and Novels.* Ed. Lorraine M. York. Concord, Ontario: Anansi, 1995: 89–116.

Cabaret, Florence. "Classification in *The God of Small Things.*" *Reading Arundhati Roy's The God of Small Things.* Ed. Carole Durix and Jean-Pierre Durix. Dijon: Editions Universitaires de Dijon, 2002: 75–90.

Chase, Karen and Michael Levenson. *The Spectacle of Intimacy: A Public Life for the Victorian Family.* Princeton: Princeton U P, 2000.

Chatterjee, Partha. *The Nation and its Fragments: Colonial and Postcolonial Histories.* Princeton: Princeton U P, 1993.

Christopulos, Diana. "The Politics of Colonialism: Puerto Rico from 1898 to 1972." In Adalberto López, Ed. *The Puerto Ricans: their history, culture, and society.* Rochester, VT: Schenkman Books, 1980: 129–69.

Cingal, Guillaume. "Excess in *The God of Small Things.*" *Reading Arundhati Roy's The God of Small Things.* Ed. Carole Durix and Jean-Pierre Durix. Dijon: Editions Universitaires de Dijon, 2002: 91–100.

Clark, Alex. "Fatal Distractions." Rev. of *The God of Small Things,* by A. Roy. *The Guardian* (19 June 1997): T 16.

Cooke, Nathalie. *Margaret Atwood: A Biography.* Toronto, Ontario: ECW, 1998.

Davidson, Rob. "Racial Stock and 8-Rocks: Communal Historiography in Toni Morrison's *Paradise.*" *Twentieth Century Literature* 47 (2001): 355–73.

Davies, Carole Boyce. *Black Women, Writing and Identity: Migrations of the Subject.* London: Routledge, 1994.

——"Feminist Consciousness and African Literary Criticism." *Ngambika: Studies of Women in African Literature.* Ed. Carole Boyce Davies and Anne Adams Graves. Trenton, NJ: Africa World P, 1986: 1–23.

Davies, Rebecca J. "Dissecting the Narrative." Rev. of *The Blind Assassin. The Lancet* (7 Apr. 2001): 1138.

DeKoven, Marianne. "Postmodernism and Post-Utopian Desire in Toni Morrison and E. L. Doctorow." *Toni Morrison: Critical and Theoretical Approaches.* Ed. Nancy J. Peterson. Baltimore: Johns Hopkins U P, 1997. 111–30. Rpt. *Modern Fiction Studies* 39.3–4 (Fall/Winter 1993).

Denyer, Simon. "India 'Boom' an Environmental Disaster, Arundhati Roy says." *Reuters* (10 June 2005). Common Dreams NewsCenter. http:://www.common-dreams.org/cgi-bin/print.cgi?file=/headlines05/0610-04.htm.

Desai, Kiran. *The Inheritance of Loss*. New York: Grove, 2006.

Dirks, Nicholas B. *Castes of Mind: Colonialism and the Making of Modern India*. Princeton: Princeton U P, 2001.

Dixon, Robert. "Australian Literary Studies and Post-Colonialism." *AUMLA: Journal of the Australasian Universities Language and Literature Association* 100 (2003): 108–21.

Djwa, Sandra. " 'Here I Am': Atwood, Paper Houses, and a Parodic Tradition." *Essays on Canadian Writing* 71 (2000). 169–85.

Dolin, Tim. *Mistress of the House: Women of property in the Victorian Novel*. Aldershot: Ashgate, 1997.

Dougan, Lucy. Rev. of *The World Waiting to be Made*. *Far* 9.1 (Feb./Mar. 1994): 7–8.

Douglas, Mary. "The Idea of a Home: A Kind of Space." *Home: A Place in the World*. Ed. Arien Mack. New York: New York U P, 1993: 261–81.

Du Bois, W. E. B. *The Souls of Black Folk*. 1903. New York: Norton, 1999.

Dumont, Louis. "Hierarchy: The Theory of the 'Varna.' " *Caste and Democratic Politics in India*. Ed. Ghanshyam Shah. 2002. London: Anthem P, 2004: 44–55.

Durix, Carole and Jean-Pierre Durix, Eds. *Reading Arundhati Roy's The God of Small Things*. Dijon: Editions Universitaires de Dijon, 2002.

Dvorak, Marta. "Translating the Foreign into the Familiar: Arundhati Roy's Postmodern Sleight of Hand." *Reading Arundhati Roy's The God of Small Things*. Ed. Carole Durix and Jean-Pierre Durix. Dijon: Editions Universitaires de Dijon, 2002: 41–62.

Ekwe Ekwe, Herbert. "Adichie, Chimamanda Ngozi." *The Literary Encyclopedia*. 9 Jan. 2005. http://www.litdict.com/php/speople.php?rec=true&UID=6014. Retrieved on 6 Jan. 2006.

Elam, Diane and Robyn Wiegman, Eds. *Feminism Beside Itself*. New York: Routledge, 1995.

Falola, Toyin. *The History of Nigeria*. Westport, CT: Greenwood, 1999.

Fanon, Frantz. *Black Skin, White Masks*. Trans. Charles Lam Markmann. 1952. New York: Grove, 1967.

——*The Wretched of the Earth*. Trans. Richard Philcox. 1961. New York: Grove, 2004.

Faulkner, William. *Absalom, Absalom!* New York: Modern Library, 1936.

Ferré, Rosario. *The House on the Lagoon*. New York: Plume, 1995.

——"On Love and Politics." *Review: Latin American Literature and Arts* 37 (January–June 1987): 8–9.

——"Puerto Rico, U.S.A." *New York Times* (19 Mar. 1998): A 23.

Finke, Laurie. *Feminist Theory, Women's Writing*. Ithaca: Cornell U P, 1992.

Flint, Holly. "Toni Morrison's *Paradise*: Black Cultural Citizenship in the American Empire." *American Literature* 78.3 (2006): 585–612.

Fraile-Marcos, Ana María. "Hybridizing the 'City upon a Hill' in Toni Morrison's *Paradise*." *MELUS* 28.4 (2003): 3–33.

Friedan, Betty. *The Feminine Mystique*. New York: Norton, 1963.

Friedman, Ellen G. "*The House on the Lagoon*." *Review of Contemporary Fiction* 16.1 (1996): 168.

Friedman, Susan Stanford. "Bodies on the Move: A Poetics of Home and Diaspora." *Tulsa Studies in Women's Literature* 23.2 (Fall 2004): 189–212.

——"Feminism, State Fictions and Violence: Gender, Geopolitics and Transnationalism." *Communal/Plural* 9.1 (2001): 111–29.

——*Mappings: Feminism and the Cultural Geographies of Encounter.* Princeton: Princeton U P, 1998.

Frost, Robert. "Death of the Hired Man." *Complete Poems of Robert Frost.* New York: Holt, Rinehart and Winston, 1964: 49–55.

Gac-Artigas, Priscilla. "Reflexiones sobre la identidad, el oficio de escritor y sobre el género a partir de *La casa de la laguna* de Rosario Ferré y *Cuando era puertoriqueña* de Esmeralda Santiago." *Visiones alternatives: Los discursos de la cultura hoy.* Ed. Manuel F. Medina, Javier Durán, and Rosaura Hernández Monroy. np: Universidad Autónoma Metropolitana, 2001: 8–13.

Garner, Clare. "An Interview with Chimamanda Ngozi Adichie." *HarperCollins Reading Groups.* http://www.readinggroups.co.uk/Authors/Interview.aspx?id+ 581&aid=6620. Retrieved on 8 Jan. 2006.

Gates, Jr, Henry Louis, Ed. *Reading Black, Reading Feminist: A Critical Anthology.* New York: Meridian/Penguin, 1990.

Genoni, Paul. "The Photographic Eye: the Camera in Recent Australian Fiction." *Antipodes* 16.2 (2002): 137–41.

George, Rosemary Marangoly. *The Politics of Home: Postcolonial Relocations and Twentieth-Century Fiction.* Berkeley: U of California P, 1996.

——Ed. *Burning Down the House: Recycling Domesticity.* Boulder, CO: Westview P, 1998.

Ghosh, Amitav. "The Diaspora in Indian Culture." *Public Culture* 2.1 (1989) 73–78.

Ghurye, G. S. "Features of the Caste System." *Caste and Democratic Politics in India.* Ed. Ghanshyam Shah. 2002. London: Anthem P, 2004. 29–43.

Gikandi, Simon. "African Literature and the Colonial Factor." *The Cambridge History of African and Caribbean Literature.* Ed. F. Abiola Irele and Simon Gikandi. Cambridge: Cambridge U P, 2004, Volume I: 379–97.

——*Maps of Englishness: Writing Identity in the Culture of Colonialism.* New York: Columbia U P, 1996.

——*Reading Chinua Achebe: Language & Ideology in Fiction.* London: James Currey, 1991.

Glenn, Kathleen M. "Text and Countertext in Rosario Ferré's 'Sleeping Beauty.' " *Studies in Short Fiction* 33.2 (1996): 207–19.

Gqola, Pumla Dineo. " 'History was Wrong-Footed, Caught Off Guard': Gendered Caste, Class, and Manipulation in Arundhati Roy's *The God of Small Things*." *Commonwealth* 26.2 (2004): 107–19.

Gray, Paul. "Paradise Found." Rev. of *Paradise. Time* 151.2 (19 Jan. 1998): 62–68.

Grewal, Inderpal. *Home and Harem: Nation, Gender, Empire, and the Cultures of Travel.* Durham: Duke U P, 1996.

Grewal, Inderpal and Caren Kaplan, Eds. *Scattered Hegemonies: Postmodernity and Transnational Feminist Practices.* Minneapolis, MN: U of Minnesota P, 1994.

Griffiths, Gareth. "The Myth of Authenticity." *The Post-Colonial Studies Reader.* Ed. Bill Ashcroft, Gareth Griffiths and Helen Tiffin. New York: Routledge, 1995: 237–41.

——"The Post-colonial Project: Critical Approaches and Problems." *New National and Post-colonial Literatures: An Introduction.* Ed. Bruce King. Oxford: Clarendon, 1996: 164–77.

Grossman, Judith. "*The House on the Lagoon.*" *The Women's Review of Books* 13.5 (1996): 5.

Gussow, Mel. "An Inner Eye That Sheds Light on Life's Mysteries: Margaret Atwood on Vision, Sacrifice and Lyrical Complexities." *New York Times* (10 Oct. 2000): B1, B7.

Gutierrez, Mariela. "Ideology in Literature: Images of Social Relationships within Puerto Rico's Historical Context in 'Isolda's Mirror,' a Short Story by Rosario Ferré." *The Social Studies* 83.1 (Jan. 1992): 12–16.

Hall, Stuart. "Negotiating Caribbean Identities." *New Left Review* 209 (1995): 3–14.

Hardt, Michael and Antonio Negri. *Empire*. Cambridge: Harvard U P, 2000.

Heller, Ben A. "Landscape, Femininity, and Caribbean Discourse." *MLN* 111.2 (1996): 391–416.

Heller, Dana. "Housebreaking History: Feminism's Troubled Romance with the Domestic Sphere." *Feminism Beside Itself*. Ed. Diane Elam and Robyn Wiegman. New York: Routledge, 1995: 217–33.

Hengen, Shannon. *Margaret Atwood's Power: Mirrors, Reflections and Images in Select Fiction and Poetry*. Toronto, Ontario: Second Story, 1993.

——"Zenia's Foreignness." *Various Atwoods: Essays on the Later Poems, Short Fiction, and Novels*. Ed. Lorraine M. York. Concord, Ontario: Anansi, 1995: 271–86.

Henke, Suzette. *Shattered Subjects: Trauma and Testimony in Women's Life-Writing*. New York: St. Martin's, 2000.

Hintz, Suzanne S. *Rosario Ferré, A Search for Identity*. New York: Peter Lang, 1995.

——"The House on the Lagoon." *Publishers Weekly* (3 July 1995): 47.

Hollander, John. "It All Depends." *Home: A Place in the World*. Ed. Arien Mack. New York: New York U P, 1993: 27–45.

Howells, Coral Ann. "Lest We Forget." Rev. of *The Blind Assassin*. *Canadian Literature* (Summer 2002): 114–16.

——"*The Robber Bride*; or, Who Is a True Canadian?" *Textual Assassinations: Recent Poetry and Fiction*. Ed. Sharon Rose Wilson. Columbus, OH: Ohio State U P, 2003: 88–101.

Huggan, Graham. *The Postcolonial Exotic: Marketing the Margins*. London: Routledge, 2001.

Human Rights Watch. *Broken People: Caste Violence Against India's "Untouchables."* New York: Human Rights Watch, 1999.

Hunt, Kristin. "Paradise Lost: The Destructive Forces of Double Consciousness and Boundaries in Toni Morrison's *Paradise*." *Reading under the Sign of Nature: New Essays in Ecocriticism*. Ed. John Tallmadge and Henry Harrington. Salt Lake City: U of Utah P, 2000. 117–27.

Ibrahim, Tracy. "Questions of Identity." Rev. of *The World Waiting to be Made*. *Australian Women's Book Review* 7.1 (March 1995): 6–7.

Isichei, Elizabeth. *A History of Nigeria*. New York: Longman, 1983.

Ismail, Qadri. "Constituting Nation, Contesting Nationalism: The Southern Tamil (Woman) and Separatist Tamil Nationalist in Sri Lanka." *Subaltern Studies XI: Community, Gender and Violence*. Ed. Partha Chatterjee and Pradeep Jeganathan. London: Hurst & Co., 2000: 212–82.

Jacobson, Kristin J. "The Neodomestic American Novel: The Politics of Home in Barbara Kingsolver's *The Poisonwood Bible*." *Tulsa Studies in Women's Literature* 24.1 (2005): 105–27.

Jaffe, Janice A. "Translation and Prostitution: Rosario Ferré's *Maldito Amor* and *Sweet Diamond Dust*." *Latin American Literary Review* 23.46 (1995): 66–82.

Jaffrey, Zia. "Toni Morrison: The Salon Interview." http://www.salon.com/books/int/1998/02/cov_si_02int.html. Retrieved on 11 June 2001.

Jameson, Fredric. "Third-World Literature in the Era of Multinational Capitalism." *Social Text* 15 (Fall, 1986): 65–88.

Jameson, Fredric and Masao Miyoshi, Eds. *The Cultures of Globalization*. Durham, NC: Duke U P, 2003.

Jana, Reena. "Winds, Rivers, & Rain." *Salon* (30 Sep. 1997). http://www.salon.com/sept97/00roy2.html. Retrieved on 1 June 2005.

Johnston, Susan. *Women and Domestic Experience in Victorian Political Fiction*. Westport, CT: Greenwood, 2001.

Kakutani, Michiko. "Melodrama as Structure for Subtlety." Rev. of *GOST*. *New York Times* (3 June 1997): C 15.

——"Wary Town, Worthy Women, Unredeemable Men." Rev. of *Paradise*. *New York Times* (6 Jan. 1998): B 8.

Kanaganayakam, Chelva. "Religious Myth and Subversion in *The God of Small Things*." *Literary Canons and Religious Identity*. Ed. Erik Borgman, Bart Philipsen, and Lea Verstricht. Hampshire, England: Ashgate, 2004: 141–49.

Kaplan, Amy. *The Anarchy of Empire in the Making of U. S. Culture*. Cambridge: Harvard U P, 2002.

———"Homeland Insecurities: Transformations of Language and Space." *September 11 in History: A Watershed Moment?* Ed. Mary L. Dudziak. Durham, NC: Duke U P, 2003: 55–69

——" 'Left Alone with America': The Absence of Empire in the Study of American Culture." *Cultures of United States Imperialism*. Ed. Amy Kaplan and Donald E. Pease. Durham, NC: Duke U P, 1993: 3–21.

Kaplan, Amy and Donald E. Pease, Eds. *Cultures of United States Imperialism*. Durham, NC: Duke U P, 1993.

Kaplan, Caren. "Deterritorializations: The Rewriting of Home and Exile in Western Feminist Discourse." *Cultural Critique* 6 (1987): 187–98.

——*Questions of Travel: Postmodern Discourses of Displacement*. Durham, NC: Duke U P, 1996.

Kaplan, Caren and Inderpal Grewal. "Transnational Feminist Cultural Studies: Beyond the Marxism/Poststructuralism/Feminism Divides." *Between Woman and Nation: Nationalisms, Transnational Feminisms, and the State*. Durham, NC: Duke U P, 1999: 349–63.

Katrak, Ketu. H. "Post-Colonial Women Writers and Feminisms." *New National and Post-Colonial Literatures*. Ed. Bruce King. Oxford: Clarendon P, 1996: 230–44.

Kevane, Bridget and Juanita Heredia. *Latina Self-Portraits: Interviews with Contemporary Women Writers*. Albuquerque, NM: U of New Mexico P, 2000.

Khoo, Olivia. "Whiteness and *The Australian Fiancé*: Framing the Ornamental Text in Australia." *Hecate* 27.2 (2001): 68–85.

King, Bruce, Ed. *New National and Post-Colonial Literatures: An Introduction*. Oxford: Clarendon P, 1996.

Krumholz, Linda J. "Reading and Insight in Toni Morrison's *Paradise*." *African American Review* 36 (2002): 21–34.

Kumar, Amitava. "The god of all things: the West reads India's 50 years." *Race and Class* 39.3 (1998): 83–94.

Larsen, Neil. "Imperialism, Colonialism, Postcolonialism." *A Companion to Postcolonial Studies*. Ed. Henry Schwartz and Sangeeta Ray. Oxford: Blackwell, 2000: 23–52.

Lazaroo, Simone. *The Australian Fiancé*. Sydney: Picador, 2000.
——*The World Waiting to be Made*. Fremantle, Australia: Fremantle Arts Centre P, 1994.
——*The Travel Writer*. Sydney: Picador, 2006.
Lindsay, Claire. *Locating Latin American Women Writers: Cristina Peri Rossi, Rosario Ferré, Albalucía Angel, and Isabel Allende*. New York: Peter Lang, 2003.
Lo, Miriam. "Shopping and Cooking for the Hybrid in *The World Waiting to be Made*." *Interactions: Essays on the Literature and Culture of the Asia-Pacific Region*. Ed. Dennis Haskell and Ron Shapiro. Nedlands, WA: U of Western Australia P, 2000: 31–43.
Logan, Thad. *The Victorian Parlour*. Cambridge: Cambridge U P, 2001.
Loomba, Ania. *Colonialism/Postcolonialism*. 1998. 2nd edn. London: Routledge, 2005.
López, Irma M. "*The House on the Lagoon*: Tensiones de un discurso de (re)composición de la identidad puertoriqueña a través de la historia y la lengua." *Indiana Journal of Hispanic Literatures* 12 (1998): 135–44.
Lowe, Lisa. *Immigrant Acts: On Asian American Cultural Politics*. Durham, NC: Duke U P, 1999.
Lurie, Susan. *Unsettled Subjects: Restoring Feminist Politics to Poststructuralist Critique*. Durham, NC: Duke U P, 1997.
Martin, Biddy and Chandra Talpade Mohanty. "Feminist Politics: What's Home Got to Do with It?" *Feminist Studies/ Critical Studies*. Ed. Theresa de Lauretis. Bloomington, IN: Indiana U P, 1986: 191–212.
Mathai, Manorama. Rev. of *The God of Small Things*, by A. Roy. *IndiaStar Review of Books*. Ed. C. J. S. Wallia. n.d. http://www.indiastar.com/roy.htm. Retrieved on 10 May 2005.
Matus, Jill. *Toni Morrison*. Manchester , NY: Manchester U P, 1998.
McClintock, Anne. *Imperial Leather: Race, Gender and Sexuality in the Colonial Contest*. New York: Routledge, 1995.
McConnochie, Mardi. *Coldwater*. Sydney: Flamingo, 2001.
McKinney-Whetstone, Diane. "A Conversation with Toni Morrison." *B.E.T. Weekend*(Feb. 1998).http://www.betnetworks.com/weekend/current/wk_cover. html. Retrieved on 6 Mar. 2001.
Menand, Louis. "The War Between Men and Women." Rev. of *Paradise. The New Yorker* 73.42 (12 Jan. 1998): 78–82.
Michael, Magali Cornier. "Re-imagining Agency: Toni Morrison's *Paradise*." *African American Review* 36 (2002): 643–61.
Modjeska, Drusilla. *Exiles at Home: Australian Women Writers 1925-1945*. Sydney: Harper Collins, 1981.
——*Stravinsky's Lunch*. Sydney: Picador, 1999.
Morgan, Sally. *My Place*. Boston: Little, Brown, 1987.
Morris, Robyn. "Reading Photographically: Translating Whiteness through the Eye of the Empire." *Hecate* 27.2 (2001): 86–96.
Morrison, Ronald D. "Remembering and Recovering *Goblin Market* in Rosario Ferré's 'Pico Rico, Mandorico.' " *Critique* 41 (2000): 365–79.
Morrison, Toni. *Beloved*. New York: Knopf, 1987.
——"City Limits, Village Values: Concepts of the Neighborhood in Black Fiction" *Literature & the Urban Experience: Essays on the City and Literature*. Ed. Michael C. Jaye and Ann Chalmers Watts. New Brunswick, NJ: Rutgers U P, 1981: 35–49.

——"Home." *The House that Race Built: Black Americans, U. S. Terrain.* Ed. Wahneema Lubiano. New York: Pantheon, 1997: 3–12.

——"Introduction: Friday on the Potomac." *Race-ing Justice, En-gendering Power: Essays on Anita Hill, Clarence Thomas, and the Construction of Social Reality.* Ed. Toni Morrison. New York: Pantheon, 1992: vii–xxx.

——*The Nobel Lecture in Literature, 1993.* New York: Knopf, 1994.

——*Paradise.* New York: Knopf, 1998.

——*Playing in the Dark: Whiteness and the Literary Imagination.* 1992. New York: Vintage/Random, 1993.

——"Rootedness: The Ancestor as Foundation." *Black Women Writers (1950-1980): A Critical Evaluation.* Ed. Mari Evans. Garden City, NY: Anchor Doubleday, 1984. 339–60.

——"Unspeakable Things Unspoken: The Afro-American Presence in American Literature." *The Black Feminist Reader.* Ed. Joy James and T. Denean Sharpley-Whiting. Malden, MA: Blackwell, 2000.

Mudimbe, V. Y. *The Invention of Africa: Gnosis, Philosophy, and the Order of Knowledge.* Bloomington, IN: Indiana U P, 1988.

Mulrine, Anna. "This Side of 'Paradise.' " *U. S. News and World Report* 124.2 (19 Jan. 1998): 71.

Murphy, Marie. "Rosario Ferré en el espejo: Defiance and inversions." *Hispanic Review* 65.2 (1997): 145–58.

Nair, R. Hema. "'Remembrance of Things Past': A Reading of Arundhati Roy's *The God of Small Things.*" *CIEFL Bulletin* 9.2 (1998): 49–56.

Namboodiripad, E. M. S. "Sexual Anarchy Leitmotif of Roy's Novel: EMS" *News India-Times* (5 Dec. 1997): 17.

Ngũgĩ wa Thiong'o. *Decolonising the Mind: The Politics of Language in African Literature.* Oxford: James Currey, 1986.

Obi, Joseph. "Things Do Not Fall Apart." *Emerging Perspectives on Chinua Achebe, Vol. I. OMENKA: The Master Artist.* Ed. Ernest N. Emenyonu. Trenton, NJ: Africa World P, 2004: 77–83.

Oduyela, Seyi. *Nigeria World.* http://nigeriaworld.com/feature/publication/oduyela/090604.html. Retrieved on 2 Apr. 2006.

Okafor, Clement. "Igbo Cosmology and the Parameters of Individual Accomplishment in *Things Fall Apart.*" *Emerging Perspectives on Chinua Achebe, Vol. I. OMENKA: The Master Artist.* Ed. Ernest N. Emenyonu. Trenton, NJ: Africa World P, 2004: 85–96.

Okpewho, Isidore. "Introduction." *Chinua Achebe's Things Fall Apart: A Casebook.* Ed. Isidore Okpewho. New York: Oxford U P, 2003: 3–53.

Omvedt, Gail. "Disturbing Aspects of Kerala Society." Eds. R. Franke, W. Barbara, and H. Chasin. "The Kerala Model of development: a debate (Part 1)." *Bulletin of Concerned Asian Scholars* 30.3 (1998): 31–33.

——"Rural Women and the Family in an Era of Liberalization: India in Comparative Asian Perspective." *Bulletin of Concerned Asian Scholars* 29.4 (1997): 33–44.

Ortiz, Alejandra. "Los reflejos sobre *Una casa sobre la laguna.*" *Horizonges: Revista de la Universidad Católica de Puerto Rico* 40.78 (Apr. 1998): 127–33.

Osaghae, Eghosa E. *Crippled Giant: Nigeria since Independence.* London: Hurst & Co, 1998.

Page, Philip. "Furrowing All the Brows: Interpretation and the Transcendent in Toni Morrison's *Paradise.*" *African American Review* 35 (2001): 637–64.

Pateman, Carole. *The Disorder of Women: Democracy, Feminism and Political Theory.* Cambridge, UK: Polity, 1989.

Pearce, Lynne. "Introduction: Devolution and the Politics of Re/location." *Devolving Identities: Feminist Readings in Home and Belonging.* Ed. Lynne Pearce. Burlington, VT: Ashgate, 2000.

Pearson, David. *The Politics of Ethnicity in Settler Societies: States of Unease.* Hampshire, UK: Palgrave, 2001.

Pease, Donald E. "New Perspectives on U.S. Culture and Imperialism." *Cultures of United States Imperialism.* Ed. Amy Kaplan and Donald E. Pease. Durham, NC: Duke U P, 1993: 22–37.

Philip, M. NourbeSe. *A Genealogy of Resistance and Other Essays.* Toronto, Canada: Mercury P, 1997.

Pilkington, Doris. *Rabbit-Proof Fence.* New York: Hyperion, 1996.

Poovey, Mary. *Uneven Developments: The Ideological Work of Gender in Mid-Victorian England.* Chicago: U of Chicago P, 1988.

Potts, Donna L. "Intertextuality and Identity in Atwood's *The Robber Bride.*" *Tulsa Studies in Women's Literature* 18 (1999): 281–98.

Pratt, Minnie Bruce. "Identity: Skin Blood Heart." *Yours in Struggle: Three Feminist Perspectives on Anti-Semitism and Racism.* Ed. Minnie Bruce Pratt, Elly Bulkin and Barbara Smith. New York: Long Haul P, 1984: 11–63.

Puleo, Augustus C. "The Intersection of Race, Sex, Gender and Class in a Short Story of Rosario Ferré." *Studies in Short Fiction* 32 (1995): 227–36.

Radhakrishnan, R. "Adjudicating Hybridity, Co-ordinating Betweenness." *Jouvert* 5.1 (2000). http://social.chass.ncsu.edu/jouvert/v5il/radha.html. Retrieved on 10 May 2005.

——*Diasporic Mediations: Between Home and Location.* Minneapolis, MN: U of Minnesota P, 1996.

Rajshekar, V. T. *Dalit: The Black Untouchables of India.* 1987. Atlanta, GA: Clarity, 1995.

Rigney, Barbara Hill. *The Voices of Toni Morrison.* Columbus, OH: Ohio State U P, 1991.

Rodríguez Castro, María Elena. "Las casas del porvenir: Nación y narración en el ensayo puertorriqueño." *Revista Iberoamericana* 59.162–63 (1993): 44–53.

Romines, Ann. *The Home Plot: Women, Writing & Domestic Ritual.* Amherst, MA: U of Massachusetts P, 1992.

Roy, Arundhati. *The God of Small Things.* New York: Harper, 1997.

——*An Ordinary Person's Guide to Empire.* Cambridge, MA: South End P, 2004.

——*Public Power in the Age of Empire.* New York: Seven Stories P, 2004.

Roy, Arundhati and David Barsamian. *The Checkbook and the Cruise Missile: Conversations with Arundhati Roy. Interviews by David Barsamian.* Cambridge, MA: South End P, 2004.

Rubenstein, Roberta. *Home Matters: Longing and Belonging, Nostalgia and Mourning in Women's Fiction.* New York: Palgrave, 2001.

Sacksick, Elsa. "The Aesthetics of Interlacing in *The God of Small Things.*" *Reading Arundhati Roy's The God of Small Things.* Ed. Carole Durix and Jean-Pierre Durix. Dijon: Editions Universitaires de Dijon, 2002: 63–74.

Said, Edward W. *Culture and Imperialism.* New York: Vintage, 1993.

——*Orientalism.* New York: Vintage, 1979.

——"Reflections on Exile." In *Reflections on Exile and Other Essays.* Cambridge, MA: Harvard U P, 2000. 173–86.

Santos-Phillips, Eva L. "Abrogation and Appropriation in Rosario Ferré's '*Amalia.*'" *Studies in Short Fiction* 35 (1998): 117–29.

Schwartz, Henry. "Mission Impossible: Introducing Postcolonial Studies in the US Academy." *A Companion to Postcolonial Studies*. Ed. Henry Schwartz and Sangeeta Ray. Oxford: Blackwell, 2000: 1–20.

Shah, Ghanshyam, Ed. *Caste and Democratic Politics in India*. 2002. London: Anthem P, 2004.

——Ed. *Dalit Identity and Politics*. New Delhi, India: Sage, 2001.

Sharpe, Jenny. *Allegories of Empire: The Figure of Woman in the Colonial Text*. Minneapolis, MN: U of Minnesota P, 1993.

Shaw, Donald L. "Three Post-Boom Writers and the Boom." *Latin American Literary Review* 24.47 (1996): 5–22.

Shohat, Ella, Ed. *Talking Visions: Multicultural Feminism in a Transnational Age*. New York: MIT Press, 1998.

Simmons, Jon. "Arundhati Roy." http://website.lineone.net/~jon.simmons/roy/tgost4.html. Retrieved on 10 May 2005.

Slemon, Stephen. "Post-colonial Critical Theories." *New National and Post-Colonial Literatures: An Introduction*. Ed. Bruce King. Oxford: Clarendon P, 1996: 178–97.

Smith, Sidonie. "Performativity, Autobiographical Practice, Resistance." *Women, Autobiography, Theory: A Reader*. Ed. Sidonie Smith and Julia Watson. Madison, WI: U of Wisconsin P, 1998.

Spanos, William V. *America's Shadow: An Anatomy of Empire*. Minneapolis, MN: U of Minnesota P, 2000.

Spencer, Daniel. "Morning Yet on Creation Day." Interview with Chimamanda Adichie. *Semper Floreat Online* 2, 2005. http://www.semper.uq.edu.au/articles/01.htm. Retrieved on 8 Jan. 2006.

Spivak, Gayatri Chakravorty. "A Literary Representation of the Subaltern: Mahasweta Devi's 'Stanadayini.'" *Subaltern Studies V: Writings on South Asian History and Society*. Ed. Ranajit Guha. New Delhi, India: Oxford U P, 1987. 91–134.

——*Outside in the Teaching Machine*. New York: Routledge, 1993.

——*The Post-Colonial Critic: Interviews, Strategies, Dialogues*. Ed. Sarah Harasym. New York: Routledge, 1990.

——"Three Women's Texts and a Critique of Imperialism." *Feminisms: An Anthology of Literary Theory and Criticism*. Ed. Robyn R. Warhol and Diane Price Herndl. New Brunswick, NJ: Rutgers U P, 1991: 798-814.

Stavans, Ilán. "*The House on the Lagoon*." *World Literature Today* 70 (1996): 690–91.

Stein, Karen F. "A Left-Handed Story: *The Blind Assassin*." *Textual Assassinations: Recent Poetry and Fiction*. Ed. Sharon Rose Wilson. Columbus, OH: Ohio State U P, 2003: 135–53.

Storace, Patricia. "The Scripture of Utopia." Rev. of *Paradise*. *The New York Review of Books* (11 June 1998): 64–69.

Streitfeld, David. "The Novelist's Prism: Toni Morrison Holds Race Up to the Light and Reflects on the Meaning of Color." *The Washington Post* (6 Jan. 1998): B1–2.

Tally, Justine. *Paradise Reconsidered: Toni Morrison's (Hi)stories and Truths*. FORE-CAAST. Hamburg: Lit Verlag, 1999.

Tate, Claudia. *Domestic Allegories of Political Desire: The Black Heroine's Text at the Turn of the Century*. New York: Oxford U P, 1992.

212   *Works Cited*

Taylor-Guthrie, Danille, Ed. *Conversations with Toni Morrison.* Jackson, MS: U P of Mississippi, 1994.

Temby, Kate. Untitled rev. of *The World Waiting to be Made. Westerly* 39.4 (Summer 1994): 148–50.

Tiffin, Helen. "Plato's Cave: Educational and Critical Practices." *New National and Post-Colonial Literatures: An Introduction.* Ed. Bruce King. Oxford: Clarendon P, 1996: 143–63.

Timehost. *"Toni Morrison."* Transcript from 21 Jan. 1998. http://www.time.com/ time/community/transcripts/chattr012198.html. Retrieved on 13 Mar. 2001.

Tompkins, Jane. *Sensational Designs: The Cultural Work of American Fiction 1790-1860.* New York: Oxford U P, 1985.

Toral Alemañ, Begoña. "La política de la (auto)biografía en *The House on the Lagoon* de Rosario Ferré." *Horizontes: Revista de la Universidad Católica de Puerto Rico* 43 (2001): 81–99.

Truax, Alice. "A Silver Thimble in Her Fist." Rev. of *GOST*, by A. Roy. *New York Times Book Review* (25 May 1997): 5.

Tucker, Shirley. "The Great Southern Land: Asian-Australian Women Writers Review the Australian Landscape." *Australian Literary Studies* 21.2 (2003): 178–88.

——"Your Worst Nightmare: Hybridised Demonology in Asian-Australian Women's Writing." *Journal of Australian Studies* 65 (2000): 150–57.

Vawter, Norah. "Author Explores Faith and Country in Acclaimed New Novel." Interview with Chimamanda Adichie. *Allafrica.com* 13 Oct 2004. http://allafrica.com/stories/200410130920.html. Retrieved on 12 Jan. 2006.

Vélez Román, Lydia. "Violencia y fronteras móviles en *La casa de la laguna*, de Rosario Ferré." *Alba de América: Revista Literaria* 20.37–38 (July 2001): 167–76.

Walker, Brenda. *The Wing of Night.* Victoria, Australia: Penguin, 2005.

Walker, David. *Anxious Nation: Australia and the Rise of Asia 1850-1939.* St. Lucia, Australia: U of Queensland P, 1999.

Wang, Dorothy. "The Making of an 'Australian' 'Self' in Simone Lazaroo's *The World Waiting to Be Made." Journal of Australian Studies* 65 (2000): 44–49.

Washington, Mary Helen. " 'The Darkened Eye Restored': Notes Toward a Literary History of Black Women." *Reading Black, Reading Feminist: A Critical Anthology.* Ed. Henry Louis Gates, Jr. New York: Meridian/Penguin, 1990: 30–43. Rpt. *Invented Lives: Narratives of Black Women, 1860-1960.* New York: Doubleday, 1987.

Wilson, Sharon Rose, ed. *Textual Assassinations: Recent Poetry and Fiction.* Columbus, OH: Ohio State U P, 2003.

Wood, Michael. "Sensations of Loss." *The Aesthetics of Toni Morrison: Speaking the Unspeakable.* Ed. Marc C. Conner. Jackson, MS: U P of Mississippi, 2000: 113–24.

Yeats, William Butler. "The Second Coming." *The Collected Poems of W. B. Yeats.* New York: Macmillan, 1956: 184–85.

York, Lorraine M., Ed. *Various Atwoods: Essays on the Later Poems, Short Fiction, and Novels.* Concord, Ontario: Anansi, 1995.

Young, Robert J. C. *Postcolonialism: An Historical Introduction.* Oxford, UK: Blackwell, 2001.

Zabus, Chantal. "Language, Orality, and Literature." *New National and Post-colonial Literatures: An Introduction.* Ed. Bruce King. Oxford: Clarendon, 1996: 29–44.

Index

In this index notes are indicated by *n* enclosed in parenthesis. E.g. 192*(n4)* indicates that the reference is to be found on page 192, note 4.